# WIN [illegible]

Tony Parsons [illegible] at the age of ten. Educated at Nick Logan's *New Musical Express,* he left the music business to write his bestseller, *Platinum Logic*. He is a regular contributor to *The Face, Arena, Tempo* and *Elle*. He lives in Highbury, London, with his wife and his son.

*Also by Tony Parsons*
*in Virgin Books*

Platinum Logic
Limelight Blues

# WINNERS AND LOSERS

Tony Parsons

*Published by*
the Paperback Division of
W.H. ALLEN & Co Plc

All characters in this book are fictitious, and any resemblance to actual persons, living or dead, is purely coincidental


First published 1982 by Pan Books Ltd

This edition published 1988
by Virgin Books, a division of
W. H. Allen & Co. Plc
44 Hill Street, London W1X 8LB

Printed and bound in Great Britain by
Anchor Brendon Ltd, Tiptree, Essex

ISBN 0 86369 222 2

# WINNERS AND LOSERS

# Prologue – Mixed singles

The town had already started dying when Johnny Sangster got born. Foreign imports had left the small Massachussetts textile town with nothing but closed mills, unpaid bills and stunned ex-consumers. Like the Sangsters.

Johnny's brothers whined, fought, tossed in the dark. Johnny's mother suffered drudgery in a sighing trance, thoughts of disease ever gentle on her mind. Johnny's father was slowly falling to pieces, his days spent loathing the young stars of soap operas with a six-pack at his feet.

Johnny's contemporaries, who his mother optimistically referred to as his friends, escaped by bludgeoning themselves into a similar state of semi-consciousness with barbiturates, beer and loud rock music. Johnny wasn't like anybody else in that little town. They all wanted to fade away. Johnny Sangster wanted out.

Thorn Sayre was in training before she was in a trainer bra. On a thousand acres of prime Virgina farmland in a house set back among silver maples, the Sayres set about grooming her. She was their only child, their only hope.

Thorn's father was forever at pains to point out that he wasn't a *farmer*. He *owned farms*. If this vital nuance wasn't understood, then what chance did he have of being more than just another social-climbing hayseed smelling of cow pat in THEIR eyes? Farmer Sayre would never be invited to dinner, to play a leisurely eighteen holes, to marry his daughter into the highest strata of Virginia's vicious caste system.

To ten-year-old Thorn her life seemed small-time tame compared to the lives of the young heroines of the small screen and printed page. She invented a private life, in which she was the abandoned offspring of a handsome buccaneer and a beautiful *naif*. The dream Sayres, good honest childless folk, had taken the infant Thorn and raised her as their own.

The fantasy faded as she grew older. Other avenues offered

a more satisfying self-image than this Orphan Annie nonsense. An imaginary mother and father were no match for make-up and a mirror.

Johnny's only possible escape route was clear before he reached his teens. He wasn't dumb and numb enough for a life of crime. He didn't have the crawling conceit needed for show business. Getting an education was too much of a monastic slog with too little too late at the end of the rainbow. On field and track and court Johnny Sangster *shone*, an all-round achiever excelling at everything with power and pace and a dancer's grace.

Sport was the only thing he loved. It was the only thing he was good at. He made it all look effortless and heroic, and in turn it made him feel the same way. Tennis was when he felt it most.

He was only happy out there alone, bouncing around the high school tennis courts and the public parks. His whites were grey and baggy, his racquet taped and scarred. But he was winning – it came easier than breathing. None of his teachers wanted to know – he had spurned their team games. His parents were vaguely suspicious – white shorts, dinky little socks with hoops, *love all*? What was it with this game?

Why couldn't he mix with kids his own age? (Because they're cretins.)

Why couldn't he get a job? (Because they're non-existent.)

Why couldn't Johnny be *normal*, learn his place, be more like us? (Because normal *stinks*, the place is the pits and I left you all behind years ago.)

From dawn to dusk through all seasons he was on court in the public park. All amenities – shade, showers, lockers, water – were missing. He had to run the 1500 metres every time he went to the can. In summer the park filled with local goons looking for prey and entertainment. Johnny's speed increased overnight.

There were never enough balls or partners. Johnny wore them out faster than he could replace them.

By the time she was twelve Thorn had memorized every last demure and decorative stroke in the Southern Belle operations manual.

The submissive coquette at the mercy of male approval – that one was a cinch.

The sultry passive plaything untouched by human hand – she had it down pat.

She was encouraged to practise on her father's friends, yet more farmers in business suits. They leered and drooled, jostling each other to eat out of her pale palm.

She was a throwback, wiping away a century with just a shy smile and one honey-dripping word. The farmers could fool themselves that feminism, free blacks, world recession and suchlike modern world irritations had never happened when Thorn called them uncle.

The Sayres were delighted. They awarded their daughter cash and clothes, a pony and the promise of a car. Thorn accepted her new toys with gracious thanks and eyes that saw right throught them. They were filling her out like a prize cow for stud or slaughter. Her own parents. Disgusting. Greed *and* stupidity. She loved her parents – if an emotional cocktail of habit, duty and genuine, though fading, affection can be called love – but she also thought they were contemptible.

She felt sorry for them. She kept up the charade because it was the easiest option open, only venturing forth from her cotton plantation alter ego when her parents were out of sight and mind.

Thorn was content just to cruise on her beauty. She wasn't interested in making it work for her.

Not yet.

Johnny hitched the thirty miles south to the country club on the edge of Boston. He was the only player in the finals of the junior tournament without support and transport. His opponents were club *members*. They had had lessons from a former pro from the age of five. They threw up in the locker room before walking out to face their families and their own failure.

On court they were educated to a synthetic expertise. They sweated blue blood and had no bite under the hammer.

Johnny, who had never had a formal lesson in his life, Johnny *ruined* them.

Rich parents fell into bitter silence until they got their beaten boys home; then they demanded better returns for their money, for all the world as though their pride and joy had welched on a loan.

Johnny repeated the performance enough times to prove it was no aberration of nature. That's when the Circuit began hearing the name *Johnny Sangster*.

At thirteen Thorn's friends were bland and read Rona Barrett. Thorn was blonde and wanted something *better*.

Every month she waited at a local drugstore for *Vogue* to arrive. She was always joined by a pale brown boy on the same errand. They became acquaintances slowly and friends fast. Then they roamed rich stores and streets looking at and talking about clothes. He said he wanted to go to France, maybe to dance.

Her parents – who she had never heard say a bad word about anyone except the Arabs and the President – found out. A word in the ear fròm a kind-hearted neighbour, no doubt. They raved about diseased niggers and dragged her to a doctor. He did a good thorough job of raping her with assorted stainless steel implements before pronouncing her clean.

Back among the silver maples her parents raved some more. Then they did a remarkable thing. They opened the safe, flourished some papers and rubbed them in Thorn's face. They were her adoption documents.

Thorn stared at them for a long moment. Then she went up to her room, blanched, dry-eyed and silent. Downstairs she could hear the woman getting hysterical. A different doctor came. He gave her some shots and she slept. Thorn heard the man get drunk and cry after the doctor had gone.

The next day the Sayres made a big Born Again show of forgiving and forgetting. Thorn pretended there were cameras. She cried and smiled beautifully for them.

The cameras were shield, chaperone and constant companion to her all through the following five years of sleepwalking. When she was eighteen she went to New York City looking for the real thing. The people who had brought her up offered a monthly allowance for a weekly collect call. That seemed like a pretty good deal.

Thorn left the Sayres with a lump in her throat and a lump sum in her suitcase.

*

Dave Pepper, the former Davis Cup team coach, approached Johnny Sangster after watching the boy make chopped liver of the adolescent nobility of Newport and Forest Hills to win his first National Junior Championship.

The next year, fifteen-year-old Johnny left his home for a private school in Los Angeles where the sun never stopped and the studying never started. He spent his time on court with Dave Pepper, learning. Dave Pepper knew that fifteen years ago tennis couldn't have produced a Johnny Sangster. Until the sport went open in 1968 and released the floodgates for big money, none of the public park brats could have afforded it.

When Johnny had the shots and the speed they spent another year building his strength. With his classic big game of blistering service and sweet stinging volley he would be living at the net.

At seventeen, Johnny Sangster burst on to the Circuit with precocious ferocity. Two years later he was ranked thirteenth on the ATP computer.

Dave Pepper was still with him; Johnny could have made it without him but not this far this fast. They had the usual arguments about late nights, lapsed training and especially the number of exhibitions Johnny was playing.

The Grand Prix tournaments were the backbone of the game and the backbone of Johnny's world ranking. But the exihibitions were the backbone of his bank balance. Exhibitions meant endless hotels and planes, a different city every day and fat fees.

Dave Pepper knew the exhibitions didn't tire Johnny as much as they would a baseline player like Borg – with the big game the points were over quickly, win or lose. With a baseline player the points were long and exhausting. But Pepper still complained that he could see the effects of the exhibitions in Johnny's legs. He asked him to slow down, take it a little easier, rest.

'Dave,' Johnny Sangster said, 'these are not my resting years.'

# one

Johnny Sangster had the limo drop him a block away from the advertising agency. He wanted to savour the city and allow its citizens to savour him. He didn't mind that the streets were full of people with somewhere to go because he knew he was going to get there first.

He moved fast and as faces registered recognition he reflected that you could forget all that cosmopolitan melting-pot crap, there were only two creeds that counted in this town – the competing and the defeated.

The competing boiled with scheming ambition – their eyes gleamed with something to believe in. If it had been carved on a stone tablet and carried down from a mountain the word from the prophet would have been *push*.

The defeated were the most wretched rejects that ever waved a white flag. They were dull eyed and anaesthetized, combing streets paved with crumbs. Whether someone was a contender or a cop out was a bald brutal fact, obvious at a glance.

A towering immaculate black girl whistled for a cab and three – all driven by young blacks – pulled up. Under her arm she carried an accordion-pleated folder bound with a white satin sash. Wherever she roamed with it she was in leather and demand.

A wafer-thin junkie stood in the traffic stuffing huge mushy chunks of chocolate and cream Sara Lee cake into his mouth. His skin was translucent, his sweet tooth torture.

A gaggle of senior executives emerged purring from a restaurant, squinting and smiling as the real world filtered through the euphoria of expense acount oysters, egos stoked with Pisco sours and a deal closed.

An ancient bag lady pushed a pram containing all her worldly junk, her rags and corrugated skin black with grime, threadbare and finished.

The rich, on the run from thieves who would steal the gold from around your neck, had recently started to dress down drastically. Johnny recognized a newsreader with a seven-figure smile stalking boldly to work, a babushka around her head and a coat she could have rolled the bag lady for on her camel's back.

Defeated or competing, every individual on the street looked *caged*. Johnny liked this – he had to cope with the feeling every time he walked on court. It made the rat race even more like coming home.

And so few people in the street seemed to be together. You'll always walk alone. That suited him – Johnny Sangster had known that team spirit was a sham and that team games were sick by the time he was ten.

How much did winning mean when you had to share it around? Very little.

How bad did losing hurt when you spread it around? You hardly felt a thing.

As if it was the taking part that mattered! And if you were having a rough time in a game you could always get cover and stay away from the play.

You could hide.

*Sick*.

The limo kerb-crawled at his side. A child-sized bald man wearing spectacles and a chalk-striped suit watched him from the rear window. He was Harald O. Holden, Johnny's personal representative up at Global Management Enterprises, his corporate agent.

Holden knotted his brow and licked his lips. He had the physique and intellect of a pocket calculator while lacking its human warmth. He was sweating in case Johnny got shot before he had a chance to endorse 'Caesar – The Smell Of Success.'

Johnny always had a few words for his paying public. But that was about it. After a few words – he had worked it out to be around the three minute mark – they started expecting you to be a regular nightclub act. After five minutes it was sheer hell – they told you where you were going wrong, they told you their problems, they told you how come they never turned pro. As if you were wondering.

Citizens back from vacation remembered his face from the last sixteen out at Flushing Meadow, going out in the Louis Armstrong Stadium in his quarter final against the vulpine Pole. Johnny insisted that the Pole didn't beat him – the floodlights and demands of television did. Scraps of paper were thrust at him and he scribbled his name on them. He always signed unless he was eating.

'This is it, Johnny,' Holden called. Johnny stopped and watched him bother the bored driver with already arranged car parking details. A small group of fame addicts had trailed Johnny, and now they gathered.

'Can I come, Johnny?' a kid who looked like a dazed farm boy said. 'Where you going, anyhow?'

'Selling perfume,' Johnny said.

'Promoting cologne,' Holden muttered on reflex, tapping his attache case irritably. 'Enough, Johnny, please.'

'You moving into acting maybe?' said a little silver-haired old lady. 'Like Tarzan Weissmuller?'

'No,' Johnny asured her. 'They just figure a jock will make splashing on a bit of scent look as macho as driving a tank.'

She nodded politely, handing him a pen and note pad. He wrote his name.

'Thank you very much, Mr Connors. Please ask your wife not to print anymore of those pictures.'

Holden studied his Rolex and sighed loudly.

Johnny made his famous name appear for a small boy and a pair of shy silent stenos. A fat tattooed hard hat stepped forward, leering and peering with possessive paternalism, with that familiarity peculiar to those who have watched everyone do everything on the TV screen while leaving their own life a blank. Power by proxy, your adoring public. As a crowd they were bearable sometimes, if he was alone behind a locked door, they were even lovable. But when you could put a face to a unit it became demanding and devouring, hell bent on getting back every drop of attention it ever lavished on lucky you. Few things are so unsettling to the celebrity as the fan who comes to collect.

The hard hat pumped Johnny's hand before pushing a scrap of paper into it. 'Got no pen. Make it out to Doug. What happened with the Polack? You let him run the show exactly how he wanted. I thought your feet was nailed to the baseline. The umpire ran around more than you. You should have hit a few short slices, chop up his rhythm then finish him off with your big game. He had you in the palm of his Polack hand. You was like a mongoose with a snake, a mongoose with a snake.'

'Thanks for the tips. I'll have them written down on cue cards in future.'

Johnny handed him his souvenir of Sangster. Hard Hat snatched at the pen as Johnny pocketed it, then stared blankly at the paper.

'Oh no. This just isn't good enough. I'm not satisfied with

this at all. Do it again.' He was gaining speed and getting louder as he trailed Johnny and Holden to the door. 'Why didn't you write my name? Why not mine? Look at me!'

Johnny turned and faced him. 'I wrote your name, I wrote "To Doug".'

'This says "To Pig",' Hard Hat declared. 'You've dedicated it "To Pig". Who you calling pig, punk!'

'It says "To Doug".'

'I'm taking this so-called autograph, Sangster!' Hard Hat shouted. 'And I'm gonna wipe my ass on it and send it right back to you! Huh?' The noise brought Security running; Hard Hat crossed the road and elaborated on his plan from a distance until his lunch break was up.

'Forget it, Johnny,' urged Holden, his client still silent after being escorted to and ensconced in the elevator that now ascended direct to the door of Dreiser and Dreiser. 'Just a failure creep. Just jealous.' Holden snickered conspiratorially. 'You can't blame the sucker. Why, in just one minute you're going to walk into a room filled with beautiful model girls and just pick the one you'd like to have stroke cologne all over you. *And* some dupe's paying you *money* to do it! I'd pay Metalon-Fabey every dollar they're paying you for the privilege, believe me!'

'No, you wouldn't, Harold. You only married Mrs Holden so you wouldn't have to pay for it anymore.'

Holden chuckled as the elevator doors opened. Johnny was shaping up just great.

Thorn Sayre opened her portfolio and flicked through it with critical narcissism. She took her time. It was going to be a long wait. The reception area of the agency was desperate with girls living on their looks and looking for a job. The working girls dressed down, idly scanning that morning's *Womens Wear Daily* from behind their hiding shades, waiting for a camera eye to come along before they came alive. The novices wore their wardrobe's finest moment. One of them – the platinum blonde who had been told she resembled Jean Harlow on more than one date – was so nervous that she scratched at a hot pink fingernail until it tore in two. Suddenly imperfect, she ran away.

The receptionist didn't bat an individually-applied eyelash. She had seen it all before. Like yesterday. Hell, she had *done* it all before, eight years ago now. Way back when she was young enough to believe that the world owed her a living because of those *looks.* When she was still smart enough to be keeping her first husband at telephone's length, the jerk. When she was dumb enough to think that there was something about *her* to get the edge on the glossy herd.

The platinum blonde cried on the subway all the way home to her suburb. Thorn moved fast and got her seat. It was good to get off her feet, but not as good as it had been to get off the street.

When she first arrived, the city's promise that absolutely anything could happen at any time without prior warning had been exhilarating beyond belief. After too many closed doors the same streets were just debilitating.

Back home she had never felt threatened when she saw a good-looking girl. She knew the girl was heading for a grey job or marital nothingness or both. But here Thorn was just another refugee in search of a reputation and her eyes automatically frisked every pretty girl for possession of a portfolio. Here they were in competition.

Girls talked, their interlocking monologues as foreign to Thorn as all the pyjama party confidences, all the useless girls' talk she had ever been bored by.

'Adel Rootstein wants me for a dummy . . .'

'I had two inches taken off my hair and Eileen went through the *roof* . . .'

'Calvin really, really *communicates* his energy . . .'

'. . . one nostril between her eyes and another level with her lower lip. Well, almost. A bad nose job makes a car crash look like a facial. Work again? Never. Oh yes – she's a cinch for a Coney Island freakshow . . .'

'I fast all day Sunday and drink hot water to flush out my toxics . . .'

'You know when Woody's expected to drop by a party because every girl will be wearing loafers instead of heels.'

'Whenever I find myself thinking of cocaine, caffeine or cholesterol I just jog down to the gym . . .'

Johnny and Holden walked in. Thorn caught her breath when she saw that face looking back at her. Quite objectively, it was stunning. She touched up her lipstick and put the mirror back in her bag. She saw Johnny Sangster staring at her and she sneered straight through him. She was here to get work, not to get picked up by some glorified ad man. It wasn't until he was led away and awed mouths began to wag that she realized who he was.

'I've seen the one that I want,' Johnny said. 'Dark blonde hair and legs all the way up to her cheekbones. She's sitting outside, Patsy.'

Patsy Rhodes sighed patiently. 'Johnny, you've just described ninety-nine per cent of the girls sitting outside.'

'Just go take a look at her. See how right I am.'

Patsy Rhodes, the Dreiser and Dreiser account executive responsible for the Metalon-Fabey campaign, was a convivial man who truly believed in the corporation he bled for. He was genuinely delighted to be working with a fine American boy like Johnny Sangster but he wasn't going to let his feelings get in the way of a licence to print profit margins like the Metalon-Fabey account. Rhodes might have to give his bonhomie bleeding ulcers but Johnny – and the unknown model – was going to have to back off.

'Johnny, Johnny,' he agonized, 'Johnny, we want you, we need you. You're on the team and you don't know how much that means to me. To all of us at Dreiser. But right now it's our ball and we're going to run with it. This is B.U.S., Johnny, B.U.S.'

Johnny looked at Holden.

'Business,' Holden explained.

'None of those girls out there is going to make the team, Johnny,' Rhodes said. 'The trial is off. We've already got a full squad.'

'What got her the part?' asked Holden. 'Q-rating or sitting on your Chairman's face?'

'Q-rating. Some estimates say she earned her first million of this fiscal year before Independence Day.'

Johnny looked at Holden.

'Your Q-rating is how much the public loves you,' Holden explained, 'in hard cash.'

'Actually, it's a gauge of the public's *familiarity* with a specific personality. As an IQ test measures intelligence, so Q-rating measures mass intimacy.'

'Exactly what I said. It counts how well you sell. Open the envelope and announce the winner, Patsy.'

'Sherry Ward.'

Holden's small eyes gleamed behind the thick lenses. 'Love it,' he hissed. He swallowed hard.

'Sherry Ward,' Johnny said. 'I've heard that name.'

'It should be branded on your brain,' said Holden. 'Sherry Ward is the highest-paid model in town, which is to say *the world*. Unlike every other top model, the only work she accepts is TV commercials.' Holden laughed apologetically. 'Johnny doesn't get to see too much TV, what with all that tennis.'

'To me,' Rhodes said reverently, 'what Sherry Ward does is not even modelling. It's beyond the realms of modelling. If Garbo was a fine American girl of the Eighties she too would aspire to be what Sherry is.'

'*Garbo*!' Johnny exclaimed. '*That's* who she looks like!'

'What?' said Holden irritably.

'The girl outside, the one I told you about.'

'Don't be stupid, Johnny. Miss Garbo is a senior citizen.' Holden turned back to Rhodes. 'Why does she want to do the commercial?'

'Because of Johnny.'

'She said that? You spoke to her?' Holden quizzed.

'To her agent.'

'Of course, of course.' Holden looked at his client with swollen respect.

Johnny said nothing. He was thinking about Sherry Ward's money and the girl outside's face. He wasn't going to push it. He was flattered and he wasn't big enough. He told Rhodes and Holden he had a practise session and left them gloating in perfect harmony.

The receptionist had broken up the cattle call. Down in the street the car was collecting tickets waiting for him while that acute object of desire was standing on the sidewalk, looking like a lapsed competitor and unable to get a cab.

He walked up to her. 'I've seen enough of this place to know that the ugliest New York girl could have stopped ten cabs in the time I've been talking to you. Where you from?'

'Guess.' She turned away; she turned the word into four syllables of sarcastic mollasses.

'Well, hush ma mouwth!' Johnny's guffaw was a Yankee reflex.

'Do you people know quite how pathetic and predictable you are?' She turned and looked at him; she was so beautiful he took a step backward, attacked.

'Hear an English voice and you tell it to have a nice day. Hear a Southern voice and you have a nice bray. I hear we're the new Polacks up here – the slob in the street's one chance to feel superior.' She tried to make it a great exit, stepping off the sidewalk with a hand in the air, only to be left pining after the yellow blur of another cold shoulder.

'All sweetness and light in them old cottonfields back home, is it?' Johnny said as she stepped back from the traffic. 'Tell it to anybody on the wrong side of beige.' He had recently scratched from a tournament in Johannesburg, declaring that he looked forward to playing in South Africa the day after apartheid ended. This wasn't strictly true – he dropped out because Harald O. Holden predicted that the bad European press he was getting might infect America and affect future endorsements adversely – but a lippy Southerner now made him feel like Abraham Lincoln. 'From what I hear, what you people call Niggertown makes Harlem look like Zimbabwe.'

She thought about the boy who had waited with her for *Vogue*. 'What do you want?' she said wearily. 'A written apology? I *left*, didn't I?' Suddenly she was exhausted. There was a taxi in the traffic but it wasn't for her. Her body ached, her eyes were sore and worst of all she was sure her make-up was a mess. She'd never been turned away without being *looked* at before. Things were just getting *worse*. The cab shot past and Thorn rubbed her forehead, tired of trying.

He looked at her curiously. 'You can't crack here. The natives will eat you on rye.'

She smiled at him. Her smile was a disappointment after the power and intimacy of that first sneer. It was practised and of no value, a smile that had tried too hard to be a commodity, a smile more familiar with lipstick than laughter. 'Do you have a car?'

He nodded at the double-parked limousine. 'And a driver who'll take you anywhere you want to be.'

'Well, the only place I want to be right now is in your car fixing my make-up, ok?'

'Sure.' He opened the door. The driver, survivor of many self-important self-made semi-successes, sat bored and silent as they settled themselves inside the car. 'Where to?'

Thorn looked up from her mirror. 'It's more difficult if we're moving.'

'Not in a limo it ain't.' The driver looked to be settling down to yet another siesta; Johnny didn't like his attitude. 'Give the man direction.'

Serve the bum right if she lived in Flatbush.

She leaned forward. 'Algonquin Hotel, West 44th Street.'

'You live there?'

'No, of course not. It's a famous landmark. It's near my agency.'

'That's the people who find you work?'

'No, that's the people who don't find me work.' She selected several silver and black tubes from her purse. 'Just one minute, please.'

He watched, amused, as she made serious faces at the mirror. He watched her try in vain to improve eyelashes that were longer and blacker than eyelashes had ever been. He watched her powder skin that could never be paler or cooler than it was already. When she stroked gloss over her lips he shivered and turned to stare at the shabbiness beyond the window until she said, 'Now I feel real.'

'Why don't your agency find you work?'

'My face is all wrong. I'm beautiful instead of cute.'

'I was just going to tell them about you up at Dreiser when Sherry Ward called up *pleading* for the part. Otherwise it was all yours. The rest of those girls were washed out dogs but you're too beautiful to be a reject.'

Thorn looked at him. 'What about Sherry Ward? She beautiful too?'

Johnny smiled and shrugged. 'Number One is always beautiful.'

'Why do so many big shots talk like groupies?' She gazed at her face reflected in the bulletproof glass as the car swung off Eighth on to West 44th Street. It pulled up outside the mouldering elegance of the Algonquin.

Thorn opened the door. 'Thanks.'

'What's your number?'

'I'm in the book.' she said, stepping out.

'But I don't know your name.'

She closed the car door and put her face close to the window. He rolled it down frantically.

'Pretty soon I'll be asking you *your* name.'

'I'm from out of town myself.'

'Then how come we didn't run into each other coming through Ellis Island? Oh, I remember you! The rest of us were kissing the ground but you were kissing the Statue Of Liberty's ass.'

He laughed tolerantly. 'We should stick together.' He scrawled something down in his pocket book, tore out the page and gave it to her. 'My number.' He looked straight ahead. 'Okay,' he told the driver.

As the car pulled away he wondered how many times she would have called his answering service before he got home. Only once or twice, he suspected – a real ice maiden, this one.

Thorn Sayre stood on the sidewalk smiling for herself, dropping the unlisted number into the gutter with the rest of the garbage and watching Johnny Sangster's tail-lights fade from her horizon.

# two

Just one look and I knew, Thorn thought bitterly.

One look at the competition up at Dreiser and it was boringly obvious what she had walked into. The other girls were this year's model – well-scrubbed vinyl blonde with intimidating teeth, baby blue eyes with nobody home. The look hinted – reassuringly – that they had never had a man or a thought in their lives. They would never look hurt, they would always look inviolate and interchangeable. They all looked like Sherry Ward, the bland bitch.

*She* won't use Curly's number for litter, Thorn mused, she'll have it stuffed and mounted. Thorn loathed Sherry baby. If not for her – and every man who wanted every woman to be like that – all the better to tattoo WELCOME on your forehead and use you as a doormat, my dear – Thorn wouldn't be where she was today, which was climbing the shabby staircase that led to the Barbra Martin Agency.

'Thorn Sayre. Miss Crow is expecting me.'

The girl on the desk was sullen because she didn't have the energy to be belligerent. She looked at Thorn disbelievingly before relaying the information in slow motion. The walls were plastered with studies of the girls who had made the Barbra Martin Agency proud and money. They looked eager to please and hard as nails. Thorn stared at them with disgusted fascination.

'Thorn! Come in, take a seat, tell me how you went down!'

'Like a cement overcoat.'

Miss Crow pulled the plug on her warm friendly smile. 'Who got it? Who's she with?' Miss Crow was always looking to swell the books of Barbra Martin. She had the title of Chief Personnel Executive and the job of pimp.

'Sherry Ward got it.'

'Oh well, what can you expect?'

'At this rate I expect to be a bag lady before I'm out of my teens.'

'You can either cut the defeatist crap or close the door quietly on your way out.'

Though past forty Miss Crow still had the cool dark beauty that had once made people mistake her at first glance for Camelot's Frst Lady. When they looked twice they noticed the very bad hare lip. She was born to turn heads and disappoint; the joke was on her and she didn't find it funny. 'Face up or fuck off, do you understand what I'm saying, Thorn?'

'Sure. But don't expect me to be your pound of flesh.'

Miss Crow didn't flinch. 'I don't know what you're talking about, Thorn. Don't you *want* to work?'

'I want *legitimate* work, Miss Crow.'

'And what do you think we find you?'

'Do you really want me to tell you?'

'Go right ahead, I'd love to hear it.'

'You find me work where every customer—'

'– Client! –'

'— who checks out the quality of the garment I'm wearing sees fit to feel me up. You get me jobs where the client makes sexual advances, usually involving a camera crew. One time you sent me to a fried chicken convention where the clients got violent when I tried to leave their hotel room after the subject of blow jobs for the boys had been skirted.'

Miss Crow smiled saucily, then became sincere. 'Let me ask you this, Thorn – what do you see as the role of the model?'

'To model.'

'That's just where you're wrong. The function of the model is to *transfix*. If you're doing your job properly then the buyers or whoever are inevitably going to admire you.'

'Miss Crow, when I came here first I was assured that the

Barbra Martin Agency would find me work. That was six months ago. I have given money to the photographer who made up my portfolio – and who broke the zip on my Calvin Klein. I have also, on your advice, donated money to a dietician, a hairdresser, a make-up artist and a deportment trainer – *none* of which I needed – not to mention the mysterious Barbra Martin herself. What do I get? Apart from another year older and deeper in debt, I mean. I already know about that.'

'You get a start in the fashion business. Who told you it was going to be easy?'

'The *fashion* business? All I've got is pushed from pillar to post and the chance to get a start in the porn and prostitution business.'

'Naturally the big agencies get their girls the big jobs.'

'And the little agencies get their girls the blow jobs.'

'A portfolio that's not being pushed by an agency like Ford or Wilhelmina is just a beggar's cup in this town. For every Eileen Ford there are fifty agencies like Barbra Martin and we have to get our girls what we can. We're a small agency operating on a small budget and if you find us so unsatisfactory I suggest you try *Eileen* right now.' Miss Crow pushed the phone across the desk, smiling. 'Call her up right now.'

'You know I tried Ford and Wilhelmina before I came here.'

'Well, it's not Barbra Martin's fault that they didn't think you were good enough for their books, Thorn.'

'Not enough like Sherry Ward for their books, not enough like a Barbie Doll for their books. They wouldn't even allow me in the office at Ford's because of how their girls would look next to me . . .'

'Whoever told you that was just hitting on you, dear, they're probably *laughing* about it right now! *Laughing*, Thorn!'

'I know my worth.'

'You've yet to prove it to me.'

'You've yet to give me a chance.'

Miss Crow flicked through her bookings tray. The service required by the client was reflected in the colour of the booking slip. Thorn watched her select a pink one and knew what was coming.

'Here it is. Eight at the Pierre.' Miss Crow glanced at Thorn and then studied the slip. 'Modelling for a party of business gentlemen. They want to buy lots of lingerie for their wives –

you know how strict they are with their women in the Middle East. The suite number is at the top—' She held the pink slip out to an empty chair just as Thorn closed the door. She gawped and felt foolish, slamming the booking back into the tray.

Madam would come round eventually, Miss Crow thought. A smart-assed bitch like that, when she breaks she snaps in two. Tears, tranquillizers, the works. Ready to do anything. Miss Crow stared at the door. She could hardly wait.

Back outside night had broken in a diamante blaze. Thorn could never love anyone the way she loved those carbon arc lights. Not many people would understand – but Maxine did. As a rule Thorn had no need for friends. She thought that having fun was boring – having a career was so much *more* – and she didn't care what people thought of her; those were the reasons Joe Pleb had friends, they were the reasons she didn't. But when she stumbled across someone who appreciated the importance of being there when they turned on the arc lights when the sun went down in this town, then she was ready to commit herself, totally and gladly. She hurried home.

In the shadows some Oliver Twist taking time off from his methadone treatment hefted a wallet and a lead pipe in his hand, asking some dangerously alone insurance clerk for more. Thorn skipped ahead, glad it wasn't her, heading for the hole where steam poured out like the ghosts of commuters past.

When she let herself in Maxine Capra was in the kitchen turning trash into casserole.

'Hi, honey, I'm home.'

Maxine stood at the stove, smiling at the *Dick Van Dyke Show* joke. They were both nineteen and their cultural references were the same, though little else about them was. 'How d'you do today?'

'Lousy. They didn't even look at me. *That* never happened before. Sherry Ward got it.' She sipped from the wooden spoon that Maxine held to her lips. 'Too much salt.'

'You'll just pick at it, anyhow.'

'How about you? Do Sugar Coated Wheatiechomps want you for their breakfast table?'

'They said I was the best-looking girl there.'

'You got it!'

'They also said I looked like the kind of girl who'd be sneaking out the back door as the happy family sat down to their delicious Sugar Coated Wheatiechomps.'

'They said *that*? Jesus, Maxine, that's *slander*. They can't be allowed to get away with that. You should file a suit.'

'Oh, it's nothing. I think it's pretty funny.'

'What about your agent? Can't she do something? What's the matter with her?'

'Ah, come on, Thorn. It's better than looking like Sandra Dee. I wouldn't have *told* you if I'd known you'd call in the National Guard.'

'You must see they can't be allowed to get away with it – it's *racist*.'

'Listen to you.' Maxine laughed. 'You were burning crosses over at Grand Central when I found y'all. This looks about ready to me. Let's go.'

'You're too casual about your career, Maxine. It's all wrong.'

She shrugged; they ate. Maxine left the table and settled down to roll a joint in front of Barbara Walters.

Thorn was infuriated. 'Now you're going to get stoned. Typical.'

'I've been retiring to the smoking room after dinner every night since I was twelve. I *enjoy* it. Don't worry, it's just the one – I'm not going to get out of my tree.' Maxine lit up and took a long, leisurely suck. 'You want some?'

'You know I don't smoke.'

'You smoke cigarettes.'

'That's different. Cigarettes are a fashion accessory. Never heard of Lauren Bacall? Don't you know *nothing*?'

'You should have some of this. Relax you.'

'If you relaxed any more you'd keel over.'

'I'm not going to fight, Thorn, I don't like to fight.'

'That's your trouble.'

Maxine sighed and arranged herself all along the couch. Her looks – light brown velvet where other people had skin, been-to-bed eyes and the body of a Vargas girl – implied that she knew every hotel room in Manhattan better than she knew the back of her hand. She wasn't really worried about correcting the impression; she wasn't really worried about anything. 'I've explained all this to you before, chile. You and me are different. Being a model means everything to you and being an actress means nothing to me.'

'That's not true and you know it.'

'Well alright – being an actress means never having to work for a living.'

'You went to the High School of Performing Arts for four years. A drifter doesn't do that.'

'Yes, she *does* . . . if she's fourteen, allergic to honest toil and a cocktail of Cuban, PR and Italian genes. The school had to fill those ethnic minority quotas somehow.'

'But you're from Hell's Kitchen! – how can you act so much like a Californian?'

'I knew I shouldn't have let you wait up for that old Cagney movie last night. Like I said, being an oppressed spic from the Projects really paid dividends.'

'It's not funny. Six months we've been rooming together—'

'Derby and Joan who used to be Jack and Jill.'

'—you must have noticed some improvement in your acting in that time.'

'My acting is *adequate.*'

'Adequate for what?'

'For paying the rent.'

'That's not *enough.*'

Maxine finally flared. 'There's been plenty of times when I wished your modelling was that adequate.' She jumped up and glared at Thorn. For most of the summer past the part in the off-off Broadway production *Hey White Boy, What You Doing Uptown*? had been what they relied on for life's little luxuries like the roof over their heads. If they had counted on Thorn bringing home the Baco-Bits their problems would have been all over, starved or frozen on some park bench.

Thorn's superior cheekbones burned with shame.

Maxine's temperature cooled as quickly as it boiled over. 'For off-off that was a pretty long run we had there.' She grinned. 'You think that was a laugh a minute sitting in that peanut butter jacuzzi singing "God Bless America"?'

'The audience seemed to enjoy it.'

'If you can combine tits and harangues then off-off Broadway belongs to you.'

'Don't think I don't appreciate what you did. If it wasn't for you I'd have had to go back. What can I say?'

'Don't say thank you or I'll kick you out. It could easily have been the other way around. Go to bed now – you're twice as gorgeous as the rest of them, got to get twice as much beauty sleep to keep it that way.'

Thorn slept long before midnight – she wanted to be up early next morning to hunt for work among the designers and sweat shops located around the garment centre of Seventh Avenue. Work, not pin money from ponces. She could. She *had to*.

Maxine sat smoking in the window seat, staring at Thorn's arc lights all aglow. She shouldn't miss this, Maxine thought, I'd better go and wake her up. But she forgot about it – suddenly ravenous, she called the little Italian place down on the corner and had them send up pizza and Pepsi for her supper. She feasted in front of the Late Late Show and smoked a couple more expensive cigarettes.

Surprisingly this polished off the rest of the deal she had made at the weekend.

All gone already? It *was* a small deal – her dealer had said that if it wasn't for *her* he wouldn't waste time with a deal that size, *he* got nothing out of it – but she had thought it would last a little longer than *this*.

All I could afford, she thought wistfully, wondering sleepily whether it was the TV or her that was out of focus.

Thorn slept head to toe in night cream; Maxine slept in her earrings.

# three

The crowd stopped breathing and watched Johnny Sangster. He wiped the sweat from his eyes and stared down his opponent with a kind of hypnotized hostility. The giant on the other side of the net touched his headband nervously. He crouched low, grim and wary, ready to receive serve. Johnny pawed at the baseline with his foot, bounced the ball twice, flung his racquet arm far back, winding up for his serve. He tossed the ball above his head, squinting up at it until the moment before it was about to fall, the moment when it seemed to hang suspended in the air, waiting to be hit.

Johnny struck it with a clean resounding crack. It was good, whipping over the net hard, fast and deep. Johnny sprinted to the net in a blur of speed. The giant needed all of his considerable reach to scramble back a short return. Johnny snapped it up just before the ball reached the top of its bounce and began to move the giant all over court with strong supple strokes.

Grunting, the giant tried a desperate last ditch lob. Johnny anticipated the shot with arrogant ease, as if he had heard about it before the giant, dancing backwards to put away the winning shot, a blistering merciless smash that left the giant sprawling on the ground and the crowd on their feet going wild.

*'Game, set and match to Sangster.'*

The joyous homage to Johnny Sangster still filled the air when he walked into the locker room. Johnny smiled at camera one and took off his shirt. He was glad for the chance to air his lean hard torso – he felt ridiculous wearing his tennis whites in a crowded studio under all these lights, like a grown man playing a child's game of make believe.

'When I come off court after a hard match I need to freshen up.' He stepped into the shower, shouting over the steaming hiss of hot water. 'But I don't see why I should leave the feeling of being a winner back in the locker room.'

Grinning confidently, he was towelled down and dressed in a designer copy of something any self-respecting black teenager would have thrown down the incinerator last season, all in a split second.

He combed his hair gazing at his best friend, the mirror, reached for an ornate bottle of bright green liquid and looked the camera in the eye. 'I rely on the cologne I choose to keep the smell of success around me long after the match is over.'

Outside an orderly mob of loyal subjects waited with heads bowed in respect as Johnny signed his name in their clean convenient autograph books with the shiny new pens they thoughtfully provided.

'Johnny! Johnny, you were *sensational*!' Sherry Ward flung herself at him, yellow hair flying and blinding teeth flashing. She was thirty and dressed in clothes that a forty-year-old designer imagined a chic fifteen year old should wear.

'Yum, and you *smell* sensational, too!' she enthused, wide-eyed. 'Like a real *winner*!'

'That's *Caesar* – The Smell Of Success, Sherry. I wear *Caesar* because it reflects what I am. I wear *Caesar* because it feels *good* when you're a winner.'

The happy couple climbed into an English sports car, Johnny at the wheel making eyes at the camera, Sherry melting with adoration at his side. 'I will always use *Caesar,*' he vowed. He glanced at the household blonde around his neck and looked back at the camera with a conspiratorial smirk. 'Because although tennis may be all about winning, winning isn't just about tennis.'

They tore off into the sunset while the disembodied growl of an All American caveman drove home the point. '*Caesar*! The Smell Of Success! For the man who wins everything!'

'Cut and print. Thank you very much, Sherry. Thanks, Johnny. Thanks everybody.'

The rumble of conversation swelled as the set stood easy. Stage hands, technicians and electricians started to stroll about their business. Many of them muttered oaths about the biggest star on the lot. But none of them risked looking in her direction.

They climbed out of the car. Sherry Ward bared her teeth uncertainly at Johnny. She seemed to find putting one foot in front of the other an impossibility without a script. A host of zealous serfs gathered around her protectively, draping a white robe over her shoulders. Johnny managed a strained smile. They gently led her away, like an invalid or royalty. She looked back, revealing her impressive bridge work even more feebly. Johnny nodded encouragement and she disappeared into her dressing room. Only a few of the flunkies were considered worthy of admission and the rest sashayed away loudly.

Johnny shook his head and started for the door.

Harald O. Holden's little legs pumped furiously to catch up with him. 'Where are you going? Where are you going?'

'With your permission, Harald, home.'

'You can't just walk out on her. Why do you think she's doing this job? You think she needs the money? You can't walk out without—'

'Let go of my fucken arm.'

'Sorry.'

'I don't care why she did the commercial. I care about being kept waiting for over *three hours* today. I've met kings and queens, I've met rock stars and fighters. Nobody was such a big shot they kept me waiting three minutes, let alone three hours.' Johnny kept walking.

Holden fell into step beside him, gazing up at him desperately. 'It was nothing *personal*, Johnny. She kept everyone waiting for three hours. It was unfortunate but I did explain the situation to you, if you recall.'

Sherry Ward had arrived on set an hour late shielded by a small army of flunkies, specialists in everything from small firearms to Swedish massage. Her agent gave the director a curt no comment and she spent another hour with her drama coach, 'preparing for the role'. After that she locked herself inside her dressing room with her make-up artist. When the studio's make-up man offered his services to her agent, the agent looked at him as if he had proposed that he and Sherry spend a long weekend licking out drains.

Everyone on the set seethed but swallowed it. Johnny confronted Holden.

'Isn't she ready yet? You sure she's just putting on a bit of lip gloss in there? You sure it's nothing more elaborate like open heart surgery? Can't you get this thing moving, Harald?'

Holden had looked shocked. 'Certainly not. Ms Ward may take another hour. The well-scrubbed super-fresh look is her trademark. Do you think it just *happens*? Because it doesn't. The natural look takes a lot of work.'

Now Johnny sneered at Holden. 'This is the first time you failed to come through for me, Harald. I won't forgive or forget it.'

'Forgive *her*, then, Johnny. Not me – but *her*, poor insecure thing. You think it's easy having all that dough? And no friends, just leeches and roaches disguised in designer jeans. Trust me. Just come back and say a few words to her. She'd appreciate it.'

'She should appreciate it if I don't spit in her eye.'

'Okay, Johnny, forget it. Walk out, go home. After what her agent told me I'll be sorry and so will she. But in the long term none of us will be more sorry than you.'

'What did her agent say?'

'He said – tastefully – that you and Sherry are a distinct possibility. He let it be known that she has hours of you on video – she watches in slow motion! You and Sherry Ward – don't you see how good it would be?' Holden bounced on the balls of his feet, smiling and breathless, his hands pushed deep inside his pockets as he absent-mindedly yet vigorously played with himself. Johnny stared at him incredulously. Holden controlled himself.

Johnny laughed with revulsion. 'I never knew mere flesh and blood could get you so hot, Harald. I think I prefer you the way you were. What exactly is it about Sherry Ward that steams up your spectacles? Go into the men's room and draw me a diagram.'

'It's not *her*,' Holden confessed sheepishly.

'What then?'

Holden's eyes grew misty. 'I was – I was just thinking about all the publicity, Johnny, thinking about all the offers that would be sure to follow. Think about it, Johnny.'

Johnny thought about it. 'But I don't *like* her.'

'Since when does a boy have to *like* a girl? Not even *your* generation's that unhealthy. Close your eyes and think of your sponsors. You'll like *it* just fine.'

Holden looked at Johnny for a moment and then turned away, starting over to the dressing room with the armed guard outside. The set was abandoned now except for the carpenters tearing down their hard work and the old black who swept up.

He helped himself to some of all this cologne that nobody seemed to want anymore. He sniffed his arm appreciatively and began to load his overall pockets with bottles of *Caesar* – The Smell Of Success.

Holden had not gone very far when he heard his client's familiar footsteps following close behind him.

'It's only a small world if you can afford it,' Sherry said. 'Nobody knows what a small world it can be until they've lived here for five years.'

'This building?'

'This tax bracket.'

She's certainly got her home life well scripted, Johnny thought.

'You can't imagine how drastically my horizons have shrunk in the last decade. Let me show you around my lush little world, Johnny.' She took his arm and they gave each other their winning smiles.

Her penthouse duplex was protected by photo-electric cells and men who would catch cold if they went out without their shoulder holsters. All over the city lawyers, accountants and brokers were building careers protecting her fortune.

She showed him rooms full of *haute couture*.

'Which one are you wearing tonight?'

'Oh, I would never wear any of these in public. I only wear these at controlled social gatherings.'

'What does that mean? Weddings and bar mitzvahs?'

'It means private parties where stewards prosecute trespassers with extreme prejudice.'

'Oh, I read about those parties.'

'Are you making fun of me? Is this just a set up so you can humiliate me?'

'Nothing could be further from the truth, Sherry.' He placed his fourth glass of white wine on top of the baby grand. Better take it a little easier; he had wanted to be relaxed but not *this* relaxed. He nodded at the two framed photographs on the piano. 'Who are those old guys?'

'That old guy is my boyfriend, who is a small-time photographer living in Los Angeles. The other old guy is my husband, who is a small-time photographer living in New York.' She touched their frames like an actress. 'I love them both very, very much.'

'Do you see much of them?'

'Every chance I get, which isn't often what with all the television work and the concept album I'm recording down in Nashville. And when I *do* see them someone always ends up crying on the way to the airport.'

'Yeah, it's real hard on the social life when you're someone.'

'I'd see more of Bernard if I could. I really would. But my work keeps me away from him.'

'Which one is Bernard?'

'Neither. Bernard is my analyst. I'm booked with him every Monday and Friday – weekends are hell, hardly anyone works – but I very rarely manage it. Still, he gets his money. I could never bring myself to cancel Bernard. I just know he'd suffer a rejection trauma.' She took Johnny's arm. 'Let me show you my diamonds. I love my diamonds. Corny but true. I think when a woman has a baby it's just a diamond substitute.' She opened a wall safe hidden behind a Norman Rockwell and showed him her diamonds. 'I'm going to wear this little beauty tonight, Johnny. Will that make you feel like Richard Burton in his prime?'

He shook his head. 'It'll make me feel like Richard Burton on the rocks.'

'But why?'

'Because I'd say what you've got in that wall safe are just

clever copies of what you've got stashed away in some bank vault, never to see the light of day.'

Sherry Ward laughed. 'You worked it out, Johnny!'

And that's not all I've worked out, he thought. He had her number – and not just the unlisted one. Sherry Ward had more than her fair share of health, wealth and happiness, yet the zombie élite among who she moved considered an uncomplicated private life a sign of peasant stock. It didn't matter how many millions she amassed in darkened vaults – without her holdings in a conspicuous neurosis she would have felt like an imposter. Johnny couldn't tell what was a fashion accessory and what was a distinguishing feature. He was sure Sherry Ward had the same trouble.

In the car she laid her head on his shoulder and sighed with pampered melancholy. 'Oh, why do we work so hard, Johnny?'

'Because this is our time, Sherry.'

'But what are we missing out on?'

'Search me.'

'I guess it doesn't matter. Because whatever I miss out on now I can buy back later.'

Every moment has its price tag, he thought. He wanted to get it over with. He was certainly going to earn every dollar he made as the boy about town with the great Sherry Ward. He idly wondered what endorsements would come out of this love match of convenience. Analysts' couches? Rhinestones?

'Why are you so quiet, Johnny? Why are you smiling?'

'I don't feel we need to talk. I'm happy just to be with you.'

She snuggled close. 'I feel exactly the same way, darling.'

Johnny saw her driver watching them curiously in his rear view mirror. The man quickly looked away and Johnny had a twinge of unrest. He dismissed it. No one could possibly suspect they were mixing business with pleasure – business for him and pleasure for her. They arived at the restaurant and the driver held the car door for them. Johnny stared into the man's face. He wouldn't meet his gaze and kept his eyes on the sidewalk. That's much more like it, he thought. Sherry took his arm and looked at him with her commercial worship.

The meal was marvellous. The food wasn't too good – Johnny's stomach turned somersaults when confronted with the French cuisine custom of serving everything floating in blood – but the position of the table couldn't have been better. At Table One you dined on display.

Waiting behind the rope on the whim of the *maitre d'* the public gawped at them. On the right side of the rope those who aspired to the *bon ton* table hopped over to pay their respects. Gossip columnists, sports writers and other aesthetes clamoured for a few words and had to be restrained by waiters.

'How do you feel about that advance, Sherry?' one young blade called.

'Was it more than you expected? Very much more?' a young woman demanded, note-pad and shorthand at the ready, her elbows stuck out to ward off evil waiters.

'Do the publishers expect to recover the advance?'

'Just a word or two!'

'Obviously they expect to get it back or they wouldn't have loaned it me,' Sherry Ward bristled angrily. 'I'm hardly a registered charity.' She turned to Johnny. 'I'm so sorry about this. It's about my book.'

'I heard about it. Congratulations.'

She smiled wearily and faced the press. 'One question each and one at a time.'

'How many of the publishers actually offered a seven figure sum at the auction?'

'You'll have to consult my people if you need a blow by blow account. Next.'

'How did you feel getting all that money before one word of your autobiography had been written, Sherry?'

'It was just a minor detail. I don't recall feeling a thing. Next.'

'Some publishers consider it immoral that over a million dollars should be paid for the rights to one book when that money could be used to publish a whole library of titles by promising new authors, especially those not commercial.'

'That's not a question. What's so moral about publishing books no one wants to read?'

'How do you feel about that view?'

'I know nothing about the writing game and if there's anything wrong with it those in the game are going to have to put their own publishing house in order. But I know we didn't hold a shotgun to anybody's head. I know that if you want a box office certainty you have to pay for it. I know that if you've got a million bucks you can spend it on whatever you want.'

'And what do you think of an advance that size, Sherry?'

She shrugged. 'That's the trouble with writing. There's not much money in it.'

The press dissolved into laughter, pens and microphones shaking in their hands as they recorded for posterity what was destined to be her most famous quote. They left still chuckling at that dry deadpan wit. Only Johnny realized she meant it.

They went dancing, which they both despised, and were besieged by photographers, which they both adored.

# four

'Guess who called?' said Maxine.

'I give up.' Thorn pulled off a stiletto to examine a fresh hole.

'Come *on,* Thorn! Guess who called! Who came round?'

Thorn saw the glasses and empty bottles. 'Alcoholics Anonymous.'

Maxine laughed. 'Peg! My agent!'

'No wonder you're happy. I got a call from my agency once, I remember it well.'

'She brought Dave Brown with her.'

'Who? I mean, forgive my not fainting.'

'The producer of *A Virtuous Woman.*'

'That soap? That soap about the cripple?'

Maxine nodded enthusiastically. '*A Virtuous Woman*. You know, Dr Steve Maddock and his wife Eve, ex-nurse, mother of Steve Jr, Buddy and Cassandra. *A Virtuous Woman* where Steve Maddock MD is driving home drunk from Thanksgiving dinner at his partner's house and gets in a car crash that confines his wife to a wheelchair for life! He's tortured with guilt and remorse and all that but she sticks with him through thick and thin!'

'Yeah, that soap about the cripple.'

'Guess what's going to happen in the new series.'

'I don't know. The quack gets pumped full of lead and everyone wonders who done it. Mrs Quack elopes with Ironside. Oh, how should I know?'

'Dr Steve Maddock commits *adultery* with this, um, floosie type called Jolene Gentry. Guess who Dave Brown wants to test for the part? Me!'

'You?'

'That's right.'

'But – I don't understand.'

'The last time Dave – Dave Brown – was over from the coast a friend of his who lives right here in town took him around all the hip tourist attractions. One of the sights he saw was an off-off Broadway production called *Hey White Boy, What You Doing Uptown*?'

'Your show.'

'He loved me.'

'But that part was a joke. You always said that part was just a joke that paid the rent.'

'Dave Brown said it was a joy to watch an actress who realized that acting is not an art form.'

'Ah, the sensitive type.'

'He's been auditioning here and on the coast for a Jolene Gentry and he says it's been driving him screwy. People don't understand that soap requires a cast that is essentially *decorative*. Getting inside the character, discovering motivation and psychological make-up, that's all a waste of time. It's all in the script.'

'Who has copyright on this little theory? You or Dave Brown?'

'Both of us.'

'No wonder he wants to test you. You've got so much in common.'

'I never thought you'd be like this, Thorn. He wants to test me because he thought my performance was *refreshing* and *natural*, like a child's. Because he's sick and tired of auditioning people who mistake mannered ham for artistic integrity. What's the matter? Aren't you happy for me?'

'Of course I am,' Thorn said. 'Of course I am, pal.'

'Many of my friends are marrying men ten or so years younger than themselves,' Sherry Ward said. 'Personally I don't think it can work unless he's prepared to give up his career.'

'That's very interesting,' Johnny said. They stared at the ceiling, the silence hanging heavy as Sherry Ward's black velvet drapes. This is madness, he thought. Screw Harald, screw the endorsements – when a bed starts feeling like a doctor's waiting room you know it's time to quit. 'It's no good, Sherry, we can't go on fucking like this.'

'What are you saying?'

'Why kid ourselves? Passion is a chore with us. Every orgasm is like a sigh of relief.'

'What do you mean?'

'Maybe I'm just an old fashioned boy, but I think sex is no good unless you feel it in the heart or the crotch. When you feel it in both, I guess that's what they call love. But when it comes straight from where you keep your wallet it just doesn't work.'

'Then you know. I'm so sorry, Johnny. I hope you can find it in your heart to forgive me. How silly of me to think I could fool you.'

Johnny was speechless.

'I didn't mean to hurt you, Johnny. You must believe that. It was just . . . well, when I taped the synopsis of my memoirs, two directors up at the publishers had a nervous breakdown. Are you ok? You look white.'

'Go on.'

'Well, they seemed to think my synopsis didn't have too much for my ghost writer to go on. One of them got very emotional and said it was ten years of making commercials, one failed marriage to a nobody and a succession of affairs with characters so sketchy they had to be skeletons. Of course they *weren't* – but that's why I was so mad to meet you. To flesh it out, as it were. You sure you're ok?'

'I'm staggered.'

'I hope you don't think I've used you.'

'That was the last thing on my mind.'

'Would it be ok if I tell my ghost writer that we had a long and meaningful relationship?'

'Feel free.'

'You *are* sweet.' She kissed him chastely on the lips and snuggled under designer sheets.

Good publicity, Johnny thought. Good publicity for somebody. He wondered what the girl who was passed over in favour of Sherry Ward was doing now. Stupid girl, he thought, stupid girl to go and lose my number. He looked down at Sherry Ward pretending to be asleep, and wished she was someone else.

Maxine Capra flew back from a week on the coast, a contract in her flying suit and a mouth like an insider. 'Dave's great, but the rest of the brass – forget it. If you sleep with the studio head or the producer nobody takes any notice, but do it with the gofer and they think you're just plain *kinky*, some kind of streetwalker, and everyone goes into shock. It drives the brass insane when you say thanks but no thanks when they know you'd take a busboy to bed if you liked him enough.'

'I knew I should have kept up that subscription to Rona's *Hollywood*,' said Thorn. 'I thought the casting couch went out with the Keystone Cops.'

'Well, these days all the heads of casting are women. But the brass still expect you to bring them their cocoa last thing at night. They look on it as one of the perks of the job.'

'Like getting a car dirt cheap if you work at General Motors.'

'You don't like me very much any more, do you, Thorn?'

'Whatever gave you that idea?'

'Why is it?'

'Maybe it's because you've changed since you became someone.'

'*I* haven't changed.'

'You've become a real career bore.'

'It's your attitude towards me that's changed, Thorn. The degree of sympathy you can feel for me has diminished.'

'What are you getting so sore about? *You're* the one who's leaving.'

'So I'll be working on the coast. I'll commute. I'll still be living in New York.'

'But not here.'

'No, somewhere *better*. I can afford it, so why not? It's not as though you'll be evicted into the snow, Thorn. I already told you you can move into the new place with me.'

'Your heart is bigger than a Salvation Army soup kitchen. Stop feeling sorry for me, Maxine, it turns my stomach.'

'It's hardly charity. Don't you think I'll feel better when I'm on the coast to know that my place is being looked after?'

'Oh, like a guard dog. I'll have to get me some barking lessons.'

'I'm not going to beat my brains out, Thorn. The offer is there and you know you can't afford this place alone. You're going to have to decide what you want.'

They heard the sounds of laughter and bottles chinking in cases coming from outside.

'Your hail and farewell party has arrived,' Thorn said as the revellers rang the bell. 'You better get it.'

Dave Pepper found him when he was fourteen and lost him when there was nothing more he could do for him. Johnny still wanted him around – there was nothing left to learn but there was a level to maintain.

'You're not at the net to *rally*!' Dave Pepper shouted. 'You're like a novice nun swatting flies! Show me a *winner*, John!'

Dave Pepper called him John. Nobody else had ever called him John – his mother had called him son, his father had called him Dipshit, everyone else called him Johnny or Sir. Only Dave Pepper ever called him John.

The empty stands around the showcase court echoed with the sound of Johnny putting away whatever the ball machine shot at him.

'Don't volley *over the net*, volley *into the court*.'

'I'm a match player, Dave, not a practise player. It'll all come right at the Australian Open.'

'If you play like this in Melbourne, John, you'll be on your way back home before your luggage has cleared customs.'

Dave Pepper gave him a chance to make his fortune and eventually Johnny gave him a chance to make a living – from mentor to employee in a few years. Some days they were just like father and son. Other days they got on fine.

Thorn picked her way round the thrill debris of bottles and bodies to the trilling telephone. For Maxine the party had been a triumphant baptism of Chianti on the eve of a fantasy life in *A Virtuous Woman*. For Thorn the perpetual diet and off-off Broadway thespians attempting to prove their heterosexuality to each other meant just another evening of hunger pangs and pawing lechers. The longer she lived in this city the less like home it felt.

'Hello?'

'Oh, hi! Is Thorn Sayre home?'

'This is she.'

'Oh, hi! This is Nancy Kent from *18* magazine. Thorn, we're writing a piece on young hopefuls and we'd like to do something on you.'

Dump on me, maybe, she thought. But her pounding heart

was nowhere near as sceptical; *18* was bought by half a million germ free adolescents monthly.

'Promising newcomers?' she asked hopefully.

'Not exactly – more of a young veterans spread. Kids that came to town awhile ago and are still under twenty. You know. The teenies lap that stuff up, the little bloodsuckers. We'll be covering a singer, a dancer, an actress and a model – you're up for the model. Hello?'

'Yes! I mean, sure, I'll do it – yeah, why not? And Maxine could be the actress.'

'Maxine Capra, your room-mate? Didn't she just get that part in *A Virtuous Woman*?'

'That's right.'

'We'll be covering Maxine in her own spread a couple of issues from now. When can we talk? Is this evening ok?'

'Let me check, if you please.' Thorn held her breath, staring at the receiver. 'Yes, I can make it this evening.'

'Know the Collonades on Lafayette Street? Next to Lady Astor's? Meet you there at nine.'

Thorn hung up, laughing, and burst into Maxine's bedroom. 'Me too, kid!' she exalted.

Maxine was sitting up in bed sharing a bowl of lasagne with some high yellow Adonis. She regarded Thorn disdainfully. 'Don't you knock before entering down there in the Southlands? What do you think this is – the coloured quarters?'

'*18* want me for an article!'

'How nice for them. Shut the door on your way out, will you? Something is giving me a pain in the neck. Maybe I'll see you outside Graumann's.'

'It's a date. You can shine my shoes.' Thorn closed the door on their friendship just before the bowl of lasagne hit it.

I should have known better than to try to patch it up, she thought. Should have known it was too late. It wasn't important now – she had lost a friend and gained a career. That seemed like an excellent trade.

She scoured the resale shops on Madison Avenue where the once-worn, twice-discarded *haute couture* cast offs of women on the best dressed lists were on offer for a fraction of their original price. She found just what she was looking for just before she gave up the fight – something black as night and tight as a tourniquet.

She used the Collonades as a catwalk at ten to nine and

Nancy Kent had arrived before her Perrier did.

Kent was a big girl who avoided eye to eye contact, making feeble efforts to look stylish by dressing in the kind of leathers that went out with Jim Morrison's last bath water. She asked Thorn about growing up in the South, realizing she was going to be a model, her 'adventures' in New York. She quizzed Thorn about clothes, make-up and men. After forty-five minutes she picked up the tab.

'Finally, Thorn – you wouldn't advise just *any* girl to come to New York with dreams of being a model, would you?'

'No, no – obviously you've got to have something going for you, and even then it's possible to get chopped up into little pieces. Fortunately I've been lucky.'

Nancy Kent clicked off the cassette recorder. 'Thanks, Thorn. Let's hope this dissuades a few thousand cupcakes from dropping out of school and leaving home to take on the Big A.'

Thorn thought about it constantly, but she didn't understand how Nancy Kent saw her until she saw the next issue of *18*.

Johnny was at home waiting for a call.

'Beauty's an asset anywhere, but in Virginia you need it to get a driving licence,' Thelma Ritter wisecracked to Clark Gable.

*The Misfits* couldn't hold him and he switched channels to the news, banality in the face of catastrophe.

'Well, Bob, that was a pretty bad twister they had down there in Corpus Christi.'

'Sure was, Doug. We've lost our pictures of the devastation but we hope to have them for you soon.'

Johnny thought he could struggle by without them. He couldn't settle, he'd been waiting for this call for days.

Jean Harlow was bluffing in *Red Dust*. 'My family just wanted me to stay home and marry the son of another FFV.' Johnny assumed this was Virginian dialect for something dirty.

The telephone came to life and he picked it up on its second ring. But it was only Harald, bitching about his separation from Sherry Ward. He hung up and watched Jolene Gentry come between *A Virtuous Woman* and her husband. When it was over there was live coverage of the match currently under floodlights between Tom Dougherty and Ray Velez.

Johnny couldn't watch televised tennis – he found his legs

wanting to push him to the net, his left arm wanting to jerk up ready to hit a winning volley, as though that was why God had made it. It made him especially edgy when Dougherty or Velez were on court. They were all the same age and even before turning pro they'd been his closest rivals on the national junior circuit. Now they were directly behind him on the ATP computer rankings, forever waiting for him to sneeze or slide.

He switched channels, tense. He needed matchplay, he needed to keep his edge. That was the good thing about flying to Melbourne tomorrow noon, the *only* good thing. He didn't want to leave her before he'd even found her.

The telephone squatted on its stand like a mute, malevolent toad. Johnny changed channels to *Winners And Losers*, where members of the public pitted their wits against those of fading personalities who had somehow slipped. Why did they do it? *They needed the money.* Or rather, they wanted *big* money. When a celebrity on the skids got the answer wrong they were obliged to make a nationally networked spectacle of themselves.

Johnny watched the quarterback who broke his back eat a bucket of hard boiled eggs without using hands. The studio audience roared. Ritualized humiliation for all the family ruled the ratings war. Johnny remembered that his parents never missed a show.

He must have fallen asleep because the next thing he knew the television was crackling blank and the sky had turned grey. They had turned off the arc lights. He realized what had woken him and bolted for the phone.

It was the call.

'Sorry to call you so late, Johnny, but you said you never close.' The friendly Global secretary stifled a yawn in his ear.

'Did you do it?'

'You wouldn't *believe* how many modelling agencies there are over by the Algonquin. And you wouldn't believe how many of them claim to represent a young Garbo with legs up to her cheekbones and an accent that whistles Dixie. My!'

His heart sank to his loafers. 'You didn't do it?'

'I broke them down. When they realized I was *not* looking for a girl who could tawk lark thay-at for some cotton commercial. I said if *that's* all the man wanted he'd be dating me. It was the hair that did it. My, I'm damn glad her hair is *dark* blonde, not standard.'

'What's her name?'

'Thorn Sayre.'

'Spell it out.'

'T-H-O-R-N-S-A-Y-R-E.'

'Thorn. Thorn Sayre.'

'That's the girl, honey. Get a pen and I'll give you her address.'

When he got there the dawn was breaking and the doorman was sleeping, seventy years on his face and the *Daily News* on his knee. 'Go hang. What are you – crazy? I'll call the cops. Beat it.'

'Come on, wake up, Pops, it's *important.*'

'Why should I? What is it? A fire?'

Johnny peeled off three bills. 'No, a fifty.'

The old man blinked. When he saw the young man's face he blinked harder, grinning with delighted disbelief. 'Damn. Johnny Sangster, as I live and breed! *Are* you Johnny Sangster? You are, ain't you?'

'That's me.'

'Boy, wait till I tell my granddaughter I see you. She's crazy for you. Got her room covered with you. You and Fleming. Drives her mother mad. What you doing here?'

'I have to see a friend of mine. Urgently. Thorn Sayre, Apartment 19.'

'She'll be in bed. Boy, it *is* you.'

'*Please.* She'll be getting up soon anyway. Probably brushing her teeth right now. It's very important.' Johnny proffered the money.

'Put it away.' The old man got up. 'I'll take you up, as it's you. The buzzer ain't working. Nothing works in this building except me. Put it away if you want to see your friend.'

Johnny did as he was told. 'Want my autograph or something? For your daughter?'

'Granddaughter. She's already got it. And Fleming's.'

They waited for the elevator.

'What's she like?' Johnny said.

'My granddaughter?'

'No, Thorn Sayre. Apartment 19.'

'How should I know?' The old man eyed him. 'I thought you said she was your *friend.*'

'What I mean is, how do you like her? She's a great girl, isn't she?'

'You know her better than I do, Johnny. 19, 19 – that's those two – what are they? Dancers?'

'She's a model.'

'Something like that. In my day it was dancers.'

The elevator came and they rode up at a strained snail's pace.

'Say, I see you at the Open against that Pole. What's his name – Sandwich?'

'Yeah, old Sandwich.'

'Why'd you play under floodlights? That's no damn good for a big game player like you. You need fast points under floodlights like a hole in your head. Why don't you boys get together in a union and tell the television boys to go hang?'

'We've already got a union.'

'Ain't it strong?'

'Not as strong as the networks.'

The old man laughed. 'You mean it ain't got as much *money* as the networks!'

'That's it. I never seen an elevator as slow as this one.'

'It's getting old, Johnny, like me. *Borg* always says it's the floodlights that whip his ass at the Open. I read it in the paper. But I don't see it's as bad for a baseline boy like him as it is for a big game boy such as yourself, Johnny.'

'Me neither.'

'Know him? Know Borg do you, Johnny?'

'We've shaken hands once or twice.'

'What's he really like?'

'The life and soul of the party.'

'Well, they say there's one Bjorn every minute! Get it? Think that's funny? Use it next time you see him. Cheer him up a bit. Seriously, Johnny – you think his game will go downhill now he's married to that Communist broad, that Maria Simenon?'

'I certainly hope so.'

The elevator stopped. 'We're here,' the old man said.

They walked down the hall to Apartment 19. When there was no reply Johnny persuaded the old man to open the door.

'This is against all regulations,' the old man said, pulling out a huge bunch of keys. 'How's Superbrat these days, Johnny?'

Johnny wandered, lonely as he was proud, through the rooms she had lived in and left. They were all empty now.

There was a half-burned copy of *18* magazine by a wine bottle that had been converted into a candle-holder, but Johnny had no reason to look at it. She was gone.

'Like that damned boat,' said the old man. 'The *Marie Cholesterol*. Your dancing friend has danced away, Johnny. Nobody tells me a damn thing, I swear.'

When Johnny got home there were gifts, cards and telegrams piled up against his door. He picked up a card and read it. The stuff had been forwarded by his fan club. Best wishes, have a happy day – lots of love, yours ever! He had forgotten all about it. Today was his birthday. He was twenty.

From the December 1982 issue of *18*

*Foxy Failures*
Nancy Kent reporting on the girls who came to make it – only to die a death before they got old.

Kay Buchanan, 18 – singer: 'They're dehumanizing music here. The only way for me to succeed would be to come on like a burlesque queen, having sex with the microphone and what have you.'
Justine Corelli, 19 – dancer: 'Dance is an art form, but men think it's just a cover for something dirty. I can't even dance in a disco for fun anymore. It just depresses me.'
Michaela Weinglass, 18 – actress: 'I'm certain that if Olivier was starting out today he wouldn't get any further than the chorus line of an *Oklahoma*! revival. Here they penalize quality and make it live on pasta.'
Thorn Sayre, 19 – model: 'I wouldn't advise *any* girl to come to New York. Even if you've got something special going for you they'll chop you up into little pieces.'

This city has ten thousand foxy failure stories. Here are just four of them.

# five

The room at the top of the rue de Babylone hotel was a prison of ambitions. Hard evidence of dreams kept in quarantine was everywhere. Make-up spilled over from mechanic's tool boxes on to bare floorboards and camp beds. The walls were lousy with mirrors from the flea market, dresses preserved in plastic and faces from *Elle*. On a card table sat a Primus stove, a portfolio and an American passport. The bare lightbulb was draped with a flame red silk scarf, giving the room a rose-coloured glow.

'Take that rag out of my light, will you?' Thorn Sayre said, jabbing her tweezers up at the scarf.

Mary Gunn looked hurt. 'It's not a rag, Thorn, it's a Pierre Cardin.'

'I don't care if it's Old Glory. It could be your grandmother's wedding dress for all I care, Mary. I'm trying to pluck my eyebrows here and I might as well be blindfold.'

Mary retrieved her Cardin. 'It made the room more friendly. Like when you have a real fire.'

'Oh? And when did *you* ever warm your toes in front of a real fire?'

'Back home.'

'In Miami? Honey, you were had – it was probably just the Cuban huddled masses burning down an embassy or two.'

'My brother and I holidayed in Aspen every year. My father and his wife took us. What do you figure they had in those log cabins, Thorn?'

'Termites?'

'Oh, forget it.'

'Woodworm? Dry rot? I give up.'

'Do *try* to get out of bed the right side tomorrow, Thorn.'

'Bed? Is that what this is? I thought it was a sack of *pommes de* stinking *terres*.'

'Every day you're the same. Why is it?'

Thorn yanked an eyebrow, intent on her hand mirror.

'You weren't like this when I met you,' Mary said. 'You were *happy* to be in Paris. Why can't you be like that again, Thorn? What happened?'

'Thorn Sayre: What Happened.'

'What?'

'Nothing, Mary. We can't all be like you, thank God.'

'What does *that* mean?'

Thorn put down the mirror and looked at her room-mate. 'Once upon a time an American in Paris got the red carpet and the locals got stockings and gum. But *you*, you're so *grateful* to be here! You're not in *Paris*, Mary, you're in the *Promised Land*!'

Mary tried her flame Cardin in different ways in different mirrors to avoid having to come up with an answer. Thorn went back to her hand mirror, smiling sparsely.

Mary Gunn had the extravagant healthy good looks of an ad man's girl next door, easy to admire and easier to forget. She had been born with hair the like of which Rita Hayworth had dyed for. Her eyes were pale green – faraway, like those of a saint or a simpleton. Mary Gunn was neither, merely someone who had arrived where she wanted to be.

It seemed like she had felt this way about Paris for ever. She couldn't remember how it started. She recalled a Gene Kelly hoof routine, a French mistress she had loved lonesomely from a distance, her father standing on the stairs being sick over his golf clubs in front of both her friends. She graduated the year after her parents were divorced, and her father gave her enough money for a year in Paris, just to spite her mother.

Her heart singing, she found this room in the *Quartier Latin* and hawked her portfolio around every *haute couture* house on the rue de Faubourg-Saint-Honore and avenue Montaigne. Back home Mary Gunn was considered too beautiful to handle. She never had any doubt that she would be a mannequin.

But she never got past the gophers.

They never made any attempt to be polite. They didn't pretend they would call her if they had something. She just wasn't anything they were interested in. They turned her down flat and sniggered at her French.

Mary Gunn had believed she was not far from fluent. Apparently not. She discovered that the native tongue travelled too fast for even a straight A student such as herself to follow with a degree of accuracy. The French didn't help much – Mary Gunn learnt that their language was almost impenetrable and that they liked it that way. Sometimes it seemed that they despised straight A students even more than the English tourists who refused to learn a word of any language bar their own, believing that if English is good enough for God then it should be good enough for everybody else.

She had come to Paris thinking she had the looks and the language. She was very wrong. *Je n'ai rien à declarer*, she thought. But it could not change the way she felt. She kept the faith. It would all come good in the end. It would all come good in this city. She hoped it was soon.

She hung up the Cardin with the others and noticed Thorn reading her face.

'May I ask you the question that has haunted mankind since the dawn of time?'

'Sure.'

'What happens after the money's gone?'

'I don't know. Obviously, I shall have to get a job. In a cafe or a chorus line, I guess.'

'*Jesus*. Going home or getting bitter never crossed the great divide you keep between your ears, did it?'

'I can never go back, Thorn. How could I go back?'

'I bet you still make your weekly pilgrimage, right? Even after the fall.'

'If you mean do I still place one red rose outside 4 avenue Foch every Sunday, yes, of course I do. It was the birthplace of Diana Vreeland.'

'Yeah, so you said.'

'There's nothing wrong with having respect for genius, is there? They have that in Virginia and New York City, don't they, Thorn?'

'Respect? For you it's a religious experience. The only difference between you and the daytrippers crawling all over Lourdes is that you have your hair done by Alexandre. As for genius – I know there's inflation, Mary, but that's ridiculous.'

'Vreeland did as much as anyone to build our business – the *fashion* business, Thorn – as much as anyone. Those forty years on *Harper's Bazaar* and *Vogue* . . . can't you appreciate Vreeland as a *pioneer*, one of the handful of people who helped make fashion into a *business*? She helped make fashion what it is today.'

Thorn laughed.

'What's so funny? Don't you think a journalist can have genius, *real* genius?'

'If the journalist can get it on expenses, sure.'

'I don't understand you,' Mary said. 'The press are our best friends, it's always been that way. The clothes have to be promoted, the people have to be told how good they are. And it's not just the clothes and their designers who benefit. It's the models, too. To listen to you talk anyone would think you don't *want* people to read about Thorn Sayre. And I know that's just not true,' said Mary Gunn.

Like a child who still believed in Christmas, Thorn went to bed early that night and lay there for hours, sleepless with anticipation. Nervous exhaustion overtook her shortly before dawn and when she awoke the first of the traffic was cawing and the Manhattan skyline was traced against huge rolling clouds.

After her usual discipline she showered, put on her clothes and make up, ate her customary breakfast of half a grapefruit and lots of black coffee. Then she looked into her favourite mirror for a long time. She rode down to the street with her nerve ends singing.

The nest of newsstands on the south side of West 42nd Street all had the latest *18* on display. Thorn bought a copy and flicked quickly through it until she saw Nancy Kent's centre-spread report.

Standing under unlit neon signs advertising canned sex, Thorn Sayre read the article and she didn't understand. She looked at her name there on the page and it shocked her. Everything she had said to Nancy Kent in the Collonades had been given drastic cosmetic surgery. Thorn's tongue had been twisted. Words had been put in her mouth – *things she never said*. She didn't *think* like that, she wouldn't *say* those things, that was *not the way she talked*. Nancy Kent's questions in *18* replaced Nancy Kent's questions in the Collonades. The prose was flatter than a pancake under a steam hammer but the author's message was loud, clear and brutal– this ain't no hatchet job, this is a burial. Thorn read it through a second time and then she began walking, wanting to kill.

She cherished the idea of Nancy Kent opening a letter bomb. Maybe it would take a few more of those lying *18* hacks along with good ole Nancy – ah, what was the use? It was absurd, she would never send a letter bomb to *18*. Even if she knew how to make one she would never have the nerve to go through with it. How could she? *She might get caught.*

It was all useless, everything was ruined. She walked on, her knuckles white with rage and her cheekbones red with shame.

Frustration and misery swelled and filled her chest as a huge sob. She gritted her teeth, blinked her eyes and swallowed hard.

She would kill herself. It was all over now anyway. She would fill the bath with hot water and instead of bath salts she would drop in shards of broken glass. She would strip in seconds and throw herself into the water.

Thorn shuddered, feeling sick.

She knew she could never do it. She could never betray her beautiful, special face and her fabulous, flawless body. It would be profane.

She stared dry-eyed at the rolled up copy of *18* she was carrying. Why was this so terrible? She had suffered criticism before, from physically repellent sows very similar to Nancy Kent. She had anticipated the big break before and been bitterly disappointed. What was so terrible about being DOA in *18*?

Because until now all the flak I got floated off into thin air. It was different from Nancy Kent, journalist; her abuse was right there in black and white, writing off the career of Thorn Sayre 19, model, for posterity and public consumption. When the lies appeared in print they seemed somehow legitimized. It's the truth, I read it in a magazine.

For one insane moment she almost believed it herself. Then she smiled bitterly. That's what they call life imitating yellow journalism, she thought.

Thorn knew what she must do.

If she couldn't get even she had to get out. She wasn't going to take a life and she could never face anyone who had seen those lies. She was going to go somewhere they didn't know about the article, someplace they couldn't laugh at her. She was more hurt and humiliated than she could stand. She was proud that she could keep a grip on herself and not fall to pieces.

She went to the bank and drew out all her money. The Sayres of Virginia had just transferred her monthly allowance into her account, which made Thorn feel that her luck was changing. She wondered if she should tell the Sayres she was leaving but decided against it. She would call them when she got there. They would have to know where she was. They had to know where to send the money to.

Walking back to the apartment to pack with a large sum of

money to spend on her person Thorn started to feel good. Maxine had gone and now she was moving. When her suitcases were fit to burst she draped the five plastic covered dresses she would be carrying as hand luggage over her shoulder and gave the taxi driver orders as he struggled into the elevator.

Thorn turned in the doorway to look at the used apartment. *18* was burning. She closed the door with a delicious laugh. She knew she was either very happy or hysterical.

She settled herself in the back of the cab and was suddenly very tired. She held her Air France tickets on her lap and watched Manhattan's streets slip by.

She broke when they crossed the East River because she had lost her city. The taxi driver looked at her in his rear view mirror. 'Don't worry, doll face, you ain't alone. Queens has that effect on a lot of people.'

Thorn laughed. By the time they reached Kennedy her make-up was immaculate.

The American model hit Paris looking for work and had very soon suffered severe *couture* shock.

She had to go right back to the start. The American and French modelling worlds were as alike as cocaine and Camembert.

Thorn covered the *master couturier* beat on avenue Montaigne and rue du Faubourg-Saint-Honore and avenue George-V and she learned fast. The lessons were so graphic that she tossed her phrase book into the Seine.

Back in the States models had bodies again. Thorn Sayre and Sherry Ward were five feet ten inches and weighed one hundred and eighteen pounds each. This was considered perfection. America wanted its sweethearts to look healthy – or, more precisely, to look just like this year's blonde, Sherry Ward.

But in Paris the mannequins were positively skeletal, stick insects smothered in eyeliner and lip gloss. They weren't on a health kick here – the mannequins had to look glossy, gaunt and diseased. They look like a fag's revenge on women, thought Thorn.

When she arrived in Paris the fittings for the spring collections were months away, but already the competition to stalk the catwalk was fierce. At Claude Montana, Twist and Kenzo, Thorn never got past the receptionists, who seemed more

Alsatian than Parisienne. At Emanuelle Khanh, Ungaro and Feraud she got through to the domain of some sort of senior clerks who all told her she was not quite what they wanted and would she care to have dinner some time and later *really* see Paris? At Saint Laurent and Chloe she was admitted to the semi-sacred atelier – 'I think I was expected to remove my shoes,' Thorn later reported to a wide-eyed Mary Gunn – only to be told by apologetic general managers that they already had all the mannequins they would need. At Thierry Mugler, Chantal Thomass and Daniel Hechter she made it to chaotic offices adjacent to the workshop and was informed by impressed personal assistants who made no attempt to pick her up that she was very beautiful but *malheureusment* they had nothing to offer her.

It was the old story. Her face was beautiful – her face didn't fit. She looked too sophisticated for the synthetically wholesome taste of American advertising and not emaciated enough for the anorexic chic that dominated French fashion.

You either had to look sick or you had to look foreign – be Eurasian, Oriental or black. Like Cuba.

Cuba looked like an African princess who had recently come off hunger strike. She came from a Chicago tenement where there were more children than days in the week and where her mother's pay-cheque never quite matched up to the bills in the cookie jar.

Cuba's brothers went into heroin or the US Army, sometimes both. One of them died in a jail during a riot, one of them died in a paddy field during a search and destroy mission. Cuba's sisters made marriages that went bad when another month's mortgage payment could not be met. One of them worked her way through university, getting a reasonable degree that couldn't help her get a reasonable job back in the real world. Cuba was the youngest of the brood and avoided the footsteps of her brothers and sisters as if they were mined.

She was always different, even before she was Cuba. While they were lost in TV, Cuba was looking at the cracked bathroom mirror. Cuba had secret plans, she wished and waited her childhood away, wanting to be old enough to try, old enough to convert dreams into action. She was impatient, painfully impatient, for she believed in her own infallibility the way only the dangerously young can. At fifteen she went to New York on a Greyhound. Cuba found there wasn't too much modelling work waiting in Manhattan for a six-feet-one-inch fifteen-year-old black girl from the south side of Chi. The precious few occasions when a catwalk or photographic job came on the market, the word went round the agencies like dirt dished in Washington. A forest fire seemed like a snail on Seconal in comparison. And most of the agencies had a model on their books who was was too stunning to waste but too black to earn rent regularly. So many black models would show up for the job that Cuba thought it looked like a Civil Rights rally in its party clothes. She made a habit of asking what time Andy Young was coming by. That always got a laugh.

For the first few months she found it interesting to see the changing faces at these all-black cattle calls, the familiar faces that were still there, the battle weary who suddenly didn't show up anymore, the new kids in town, eager and bubbling over, who all thought they were on the verge of having a household face. After a few months the novelty wore off and the changing faces meant nothing to her. All black models look the same to me, ha ha. She was a veteran of the cattle call and fake sentiment was just excess baggage. Her sixteenth birthday came and went without a word to anyone. It was no big deal, it was *zero.*

If fashion and photographic modelling were hard to come by for a black, then work in the lucrative world of television commercials was as good as impossible.

Not that commercials or their adoring public had anything against ethnic minorities as one hard-seller of a producer graciously explained to Cuba.

'But most of the work is for minority mother types and minority child types.'

'I see.'

'Would you like to come back to my duplex and see my collection of handguns?' the producer offered as a consolation prize.

'Maybe I'll give you a call after I've given birth a few times. Then maybe me and my minority child type will stand a chance.'

She was seventeen when she left America for Paris, France. She was sick of a diet of crumbs, but she would probably never have got on the plane if she hadn't heard about a cousin down South who had recently been castrated by the regenerated, rampantly unchecked Klan.

The talent scouts of Paris *couture* took Cuba to their collective concave bosom right away. But she was never under any illusion about her assets.

In the City of Light there were girls more beautiful than her, girls with better bodies, girls more photogenic and girls who were better at that art of seductive deception called modelling. There were literally hundreds of all these girls.

Paris could not convincingly project secret plots of strange sex on to these girls' willing blanks of face and body, that was the answer to her success. These girls could not make Paris believe that its most *recherché* dreams were about to be realized. These girls were not every exotic, erotic fantasy that Paris ever concocted in its jaded old crotch come – apparently – true. These girls could not give the queens and the workers and the drones of *haute couture* a multiple cerebral orgasm.

Which was why they were between parts and Cuba worked constantly.

One of these girls was, of course, Thorn Sayre.

Cuba could not go out without knowing what the camera knew.

Every night she had someone take her picture with a camera that developed the shot in sixty seconds exactly. Her first consumer gadget – Cuba loved her perfectly candid camera. It was the only place she could get a totally objective opinion. Mirrors and word of mouth both flattered to deceive.

Cuba could not trust them.

She believed that only photography is believing.

Whenever she went out from the rue de Babylone hotel where she rented a slick glossy white studio suite on the first floor (she could have rented bigger and better with the money she was making, but that would have meant her mother back in Chicago renting smaller and smellier), Cuba would carry her camera up four flights of stairs to the room at the top. But now that fittings for the spring collections had begun she had been staying at the *couturier*'s later and later, and on the rare occasions when she hadn't been so exhausted that all she could do was return to the rue de Babylone and collapse, she had a little midinette at the workshop take her photograph and then left for the night straight from the atelier.

It had been several weeks since Cuba had seen the two cute white stiffs at the top of the stairs. She had forgotten what a long hard climb it was to the cheapest room in the house. She stood on the shabby landing for a while catching her breath and then rapped sharply on the door with her silver cane.

'You look sensational, Cuba,' Mary Gunn gushed as she stood back to let *the model* enter.

'We'll let the camera be the judge of that, shall we?' Cuba said, handing her the Instamatic. 'How can you live up here? Without oxygen masks, that is.'

'It's not so bad,' said Thorn Sayre. 'Three times a day we sit under the skylight with our mouths open and a short-sighted sparrow slips us some worms.'

She sat on her camp bed, long painful flamingo legs stretched out straight in front of her, wearing a blouson mini dress she had bought that day on rue du Faubourg-Saint-Honore. It was barely there and had cost almost everything – all of next month's allowance, anyway. *Everybody* knew about French girls – their elegance, their effortless chic. Thorn Sayre could disappear here. Clothes had become the bare necessity of her Paris life; other considerations, other *convention*, like food and rent, were secondary to being Ambassadress of the American Dream, and they would have to wait.

Cuba looked for Thorn Sayre's cheeks, breasts and hips and couldn't find them. She was shocked at the weight loss – *she*, who'd never carried more than one hundred-ten, was shocked. 'Come to a party,' she rasped casually. 'Twist, he's throwing a party for all his people.'

Mary Gunn gasped at the celebrated syllable. 'Twist? A party? A party by *Twist*?'

'That's right, yeah. That's why there's no fittings tonight. We all got the night off – well, it was either that or a collective breakdown. The old fag is trying to restore morale before the last lap to the collections.'

'We're *invited*?' Mary breathed.

'Of course not.' Cuba caught Thorn's eye. 'But gatecrashing is the prerogative of the decorative.'

Thorn picked up a hand mirror and began listlessly to redden her white lips. 'We'll come to get looked at, thank you very much, Cuba,' she said.

'Come to get fed. Ghandi used to make a fuss about fasting for forty-eight hours. You must have those old toxics well on the run by now.'

She's not fasting.' Mary picked up the tails of Cuba's

diaphanous jacket and rubbed the material respectfully between her thumb and forefinger. 'She's just not eating.'

'Cease soiling my schmatter with your sweaty pinkies, Mary. Thank you. Now do your thing. No – just a minute.'

'I do so dislike this foreign food,' said Thorn to her reflection. 'Don't you?'

'Ok, Mary.'

Mary Gunn took a photograph.

'*Un jour je quitterai tout*,' Twist boasted to the crowd of employees and other admirers surounding him. They had cocaine eyes and voices raised in shrill exaggeration, the fashion industry's Esperanto.

They shrilled.

'Twist's clothes have mystery and imagination like other clothes have seams and stitches.'

'One of Twist's desires is for everyone in the world to resemble a beautiful skeleton. Flesh fudges the purity of the line.'

'Have you seen the sketches? Twist calls it Cadaver Couture.'

'*Oh!*'

A reverential sigh of delight did the rounds of the courtiers. Twist tapped his ashes – Gauloise Blue Way, bought solely for the package – on to the freshly raked beige shag pile carpet and sighed with impossible boredom. He was forty and prone to fainting, he was long and limp with skin the colour of cold *café au lait*. For nearly twenty years he had been the *enfant terrible* of Paris fashion and for most of them parties such as this one had bored him senseless.

He wished he was up at the atelier on avenue Marceau fussing over his forthcoming collection. He sighed again. The *grand* ennui had him in its grip.

Then he saw her.

She was an emaciated Venus, a fleshless fantasia, starved to perfection. She was standing over at the buffet table stuffing canapes, chanterelle and chateau potatoes into her clutch bag. She took his breath away. Twist shrieked at her, pointing with his Gauloise.

Thorn had made up her mind to save the food for later. She couldn't face anything right now – the very thought of it made her entrails contort. But blacking out on the Metro was a *non-non* – it had frightened her badly and it had made Cuba angry and Mary shocked. It was ridiculous to try to *argue* with Cuba. She had to eat or she was going to *die*. Party food pilfered from Twist's buffet would feed her until next month's allowance arrived. She was dropping handfuls of hot hors d'ouevres into her clutch bag when she heard the screaming.

'Look at her! Look at her!' a strange – *really* strange – man was screaming. 'Look at what she's doing!' He clapped his hands to his mouth and shook his head with horrified disbelief. 'Stop her!' He was becoming ever more shrill. 'Stop her immediately! Oh, you wretched *fools*! Can't you see what she's doing?'

Everyone was staring at her for the wrong reasons. Thorn stared back, a creature caught in headlights. Then security were on her, snatching her clutch bag, happily pinning her arms to her sides. They cursed her in French – '*Salope*!' '*Conasse*!' – as they dragged her to the door.

Twist was apoplectic. 'What are you *doing*? Do you want to take her from me? Do you hate me that much?'

French muscle is much the same as any other kind; numb from the neck up. The security guards exchanged confused looks. One of them pinched Thorn's arm. They stared at their boss with sheepish bewilderment.

'She was stealing the food, Mr Twist.'

'We thought you wanted her out, Mr Twist.'

'You said—'

'She's not—'

'Oh, you apes!' Twist spat, waving them away with impatient contempt. He smiled at Thorn like a ravenous shark. 'Come here, my dearest,' he said in English, holding out his hands. 'Come here and tell me everything.'

Thorn approached him warily. 'Look, I'm sorry about the food. I'll pay for it. I'll borrow money and pay for it.'

He laughed easily. 'It is I who apologize, for the brutish behaviour of my staff.' Her clutch bag was retrieved and handed to him. 'Take it away,' he frowned.

Thorn watched a flunky carry her clutch bag away.

Twist smiled. 'You misunderstand, concerning the food. I do not wish to stop you from *stealing*. I wish to prevent you from *eating*. Tell me – you are a Caesarean?'

'No, I'm a Virginian.'

Twist screamed happily. He translated unto the constant in-crowd that had formed and they chuckled, jostling each other to look at her bones and shoes. Thorn glared at them uncomprehendingly.

'I mean you were *born* by Caesarean section,' Twist shuddered delicately. 'Operation, yes?' He smiled winningly. 'Your eye sockets, your bones – too perfect for an ordinary birth. Birth does something bad to the bone structure. Birth spoils perfection. Bones can be *good* after an ordinary birth – but they can never be perfection. You understand?'

'I don't know.'

'Surely you know – did your mother not tell you? Try to think – do you remember if your mother had a scar – just here?'

'I don't remember.'

'Oh.' He waved memory away. 'It doesn't matter. I am sure of this – you *are* a Caesarean.'

Caesarean, mused Thorn, Caesarean, the smell of success, ha ha.

'It doesn't matter,' Twist repeated. 'You will be magnificent, like a marble angel in a churchyard, wearing my new designs. I call the collection "Variations On A Shroud" – it is my finest work, inspired by a trip to Turin. But you must stay *exactly* as you are. Do you understand?'

Thorn took back her bag from a flunky. He tittered and bowed. The bag was empty. The food was gone. 'I understand,' she said.

Twist clapped his hands. 'Your name, my new *vedette*?'

'Thorn. Thorn Sayre.'

'Thorn! So sharp, so stark, drawing blood!' Twist turned and capered across the room to skank with Cuba.

She leaned against the wall, fighting tears of hysterical joy and hunger. She was hired, *she was a model.* One small step for mankind, but a giant step for the mannequin.

# six

The crowd packed into the Foro Italico smelt the blood of an American.

*'Attàco! Attàco! Attàco!'*

*'Il bel Claudio! Artista della rachetta!'*
*'Il Americano è morto, Claudio!'*
*'Attàco, Claudio, attàco!'*

Johnny Sangster disliked Italy.

The shirt-sleeved crowds were rabidly partisan and the red clay courts were slow and treacherous. Players of the big game were cornered into demonstrations of the finer arts of the game, and players with US citizenship were howled at from knock up to match point inclusive. The stomping, shouting Romans turned the Foro Italico into a cauldron boiling with a national fervour that transformed every Italian into Adriano Panatta and every American into General Patton.

Johnny disliked Italy.

He glared across at Claudio Falconi hoping that this look would kill and then raised his eyes to the sky as if in prayer, serving to save the match. Johnny hit the ball sweet and hard, yelping with effort as it shot from his racquet with the sharp ringing momentum of a cracked whip. Johnny sprinted to the net holding his racquet as though it was a nightstick and he was policing a prison riot. The service was fast, fierce and long, but a bad bounce took out its sting and gently tossed it up in front of the chest of Claudio Falconi, sticky beneath his Ellesse shirt. What could have been an ace had all the pace and bite of a snowflake falling from the sky, thanks to this damn clay court.

Jeez, thought Johnny. Like shooting gift-wrapped ducks in a barrel.

Falconi chipped a delicate backhand down the line, catching Johnny wrong-footed and bringing the Foro Italico on to fever pitch. Johnny made them choke on it. He sprinted across court with the sleek power of a greyhound, and at full stretch desperately scooped the ball out of the abyss of defeat, getting back a wristy return charged with lethal topspin.

He saw the shot clear the net low with Falconi in nimble pursuit, pulling back his racquet fist ready to strike. Johnny's run was still carrying him out of court; he slammed on the brakes and tried to turn. Suddenly he felt like he was hurtling down a fairground ride. Except it hurt. It hurt like hell. His shoes were skidding across the court's loose and shifting red shingle surface and the last thing he saw before he went over was the Roman, gliding across the same red surface with a refined athleticism, bringing up his racquet to meet the ball the way a surgeon's scalpel meets a prized patient.

Then the cloudless blue Roman spring sky and the massed thousands of enemies and the red clay of the Foro Italico were careering madly and rushing towards him like the end of a bad dream as his vision blurred with the red-tinted film of an abrupt and brutal pain as he slid across the ground and the red shingle sank its sharp little razor teeth into his leg. It burned off several layers of skin before he came to a halt with a frightened, prostrate Roman ballboy under his feet.

He opened his eyes. He was so close to the front row of Italians that he could see their shoddy fillings. He screwed up his eyes and a solitary tear oozed out. He opened them again to see why the entire Foro Italico was cawing bitterly.

Johnny gripped his racquet elbow – he was surprised to see that it *wasn't* on fire – and looked up to see Claudio Falconi with his head buried theatrically in his hands and the ball bobbing cheerily around his feet.

He had dumped it into the net.

Johnny watched him sink to his knees, the Dying Swan in short shorts, and laughed with vicious relief. Then his leg registered. It was agony, an awful penetrating agony that made him feel nauseous. He swallowed hard and looked at the metre of golden brown skin missing from his left thigh. The blood welled rich and red from the wound and ran down into his groin, staining his gleaming match whites. He shivered.

'*Quaranta pari*!' The umpire's voice crackled around the stadium and there were hoots of contemptuous resentment.

Deuce, he thought, deuce at five games all in the final set. You can do it. He tried to get up, swaying crazily. Someone put an arm around his shoulder. It was a tournament doctor saying something Johnny couldn't understand. He shook his head and breathed deeply. Vision cleared, sickness faded, he began to understand.

'You must scratch from the tournament. You need stitches. The wound is dirty.'

Johnny hobbled a few steps, testing his weight on the treacherous leg. It wasn't as bad as it looked. It was stiff and it stung but it would do. He might look like a red rag after a bull had finished with it, but get it cleaned and stitched up on the trainer's table in the treatment room and it would look good as new.

A television camera zoomed in for a close-up.

Johnny watched a paper cup whistle past Falconi's contorted face. All around the Foro Italico fists were being shaken by their owners, oaths were being shouted, advice was being given.

*'Idiota, Falconi!'*

*'Stupido bastardo, Falconi!'*

*'Pazìenza, Claudio, pazìenza!'*

The rats were already deserting the sinking idol. Johnny narrowed his eyes, savouring the sight of the Roman talking to himself and wiping his eyes with his sweat band, bothered and bewildered and all but beat. He still had the lion's share of the crowd's affection but as he mooched moodily around the back of the court it was only the accusations of being Italia's answer to Judas that he was taking to heart.

'Come to the treatment room, we will mend you.' The doctor tried to lead Johnny away.

Johnny shrugged him off. 'I don't want to scratch. I want a shot – painkiller, yes?'

When the match resumed Claudio Falconi's guilt and shame did as much for his game as advanced rigor mortis. Johnny Sangster took him to pieces, and after stitches, a shower, clothes and a press conference – sullen questions about money and promotions, smarmy enquiries about injuries – he returned to his hotel room and turned on the television to find out who he would be meeting in the final of the Italian Open.

Twist asked her to stay behind. Everyone else had gone, even his personal assistants, all five of them, and his lone general manager. Thorn had been standing around in various stages of undress at the avenue Marceau atelier for two weeks and she had never seen Twist so alone. She knew that the pretty Mauritian chauffeur and the ugly French bruiser were downstairs waiting for the master's voice, but up here in the office behind the studio it was just the two of them. He smiled and took her hand.

His office had red Chinese lacquer walls featuring black beading and a ceiling made of glass as high as a house. Bunches of dried – *dead*, really – flowers and blow-ups of mannequins stalking catwalks like haughty poltergeists hunting their supper were everywhere. A massive polished pine desk was buried under sketches and swatches of fabric. Large address books – one engraved with the legend 'Lovers & Losers', another boasting 'Blondes–Brunettes–Redheads' – advertised themselves. In the midst of it all a small crystal ball sat serenely. Twist giggled and covered it with a red silk cloth sample. 'From Liberty's in London, you know? Just for fun.' He made distracted attempts to discipline his belongings while Thorn sat down.

'*Café noir* or Perrier with ice and lemon?'

'Perrier. Thanks.'

'Here's looking at you,' sighed Twist.

'*Salut.*'

'Excuse me one moment.' Twist jumped up and locked the door.

Thorn sipped her fancy water, wondering whether Twist was planning to fuck her, fire her or both. None of it made much sense but her heart was pumping fast as he sat down across from her and rubbed his chin speculatively.

'So, Thorn – you like working for me?'

'I like it a lot, Twist.'

'And you do not intend to keep your side of the bargain? Do you hate me so much?'

'I – what? What are you talking about? Bargain?'

'You promised not to change. You promised to stay as sweet as you were the first time I set eyes on your bones.'

'You sound like a graverobber, Twist.'

'Look in this mirror, Thorn, and tell me what you see.'

Thorn flashed her eyes and bared her teeth, feeling her throat contract with love. 'I look pretty good, Twist. Yeah, I look pretty good.'

'That's the trouble, dear. *Pretty* good is *no* good to the house of Twist!' 'Ok, then – I think I look *great*. Won't that be useful to the house of Twist?'

He shook his head, pensive. 'You don't understand. The world's richest – and most *desirable* – women come to the house of Twist twice a year. Arabian princesses! Wives of Greek ships! Shipowners, I mean. And all dear friends of mine. I know their minds. They don't come here to see a *girly* show, Thorn, to see a big bosomy bottomy *broad* bouncing like a beach ball down the catwalk. They come here to be offered the chance of a unique and unrepeatable experience – they come here to compete for my creations. To view my *art* – not the ample *derrieres* of greedy American girls.'

'Oh, I get it. So why hire girls if we offend you so?' Thorn blushed with bruised ego. 'Why not sew your dresses on to a shoal of showroom dummies and save all this migraine and money?'

'Because clothes are *events*, *alive*, Thorn, they must move and breath. I'm not the tablecloth maker. I'm not an unreasonable man. If we were in the 1920s and I was Balmain I wouldn't *look* at you with a view to letting you air my creations. In those days the masters purposely chose the plainest, most forgettable girls in the world, girls straight out of the *bibliotheque*! Because these girls were content to be walking clothes hangers. They had no ego. They submerged their identity for the sake of the creation. These days models want to be bigshots. I don't mind. I picked you for your startling looks. But I also picked you for your exquisite non-physique. Sure you look good still. *But there's twice as much of you.*'

'Five pounds, Twist, five pounds is all. I was a *scarecrow.*'

'And now you are a burlesque. What are you trying to do? Bury your bones alive?'

'Look, Twist—'

'Oh, your beautiful Caesarean bones! They're being *smothered.*'

'Listen to me, Twist. I'll explain, you've got it all wrong. That first time you saw me I was sick, *really* sick, ok? I hadn't eaten a *thing* for ten days. I've never been a compulsive cud-chewer but this time I was *starving*, see?'

'So? Fasting is essential to purge the poisons. It sounds an excellent health and beauty regime. What's the fuss and bother?'

'I'll tell you – a funny thing happened on the way to the party. I keeled over in the Metro. You ask *Cuba,* she was mad as hell, she said I was killing myself and she was right. I looked as if I'd been dead since – since before the President was born again.'

'I want you as you were then.'

'If I hadn't started eating I'd have stopped breathing. I'm still a long way from one hundred-eighteen. That's my natural weight, and that's considered *perfection* in America.'

'*Natural*! *America*!'

'I'm only taking in eight hundred calories a day, for God's sake! What do you *want*?'

'*Less* of you, Thorn.'

'I can't let myself get any thinner. I can't force myself to starve. I should be having a good time. This is Paris and I'm a model—' Thorn put her hands over her ears. 'I can't do it.'

'Then allow me to do it for you, my dear.'

She watched him unlock a desk drawer – funny, he wasn't a locks and secrets kind of person. Glass clinked as he pushed something across the crowded desk top.

'What's this?'

'The road to perfection. We'll soon have you back to, ah, normal. Here are iron pills for your blood; Vitamin B for your eyes and skin. Vitamin C looks after your teeth and gums. And here is Vitamin E.' Twist twinkled wickedly. 'For your libido, if ever you should want one.' He slid the remaining container, a slim plastic phial, into her hand. 'And this.'

'It all seems pretty painless. Vitamins, sure, I've taken vitamins before.'

'Yes, of course you have, they're *very* American.'

'If it will make you happy, sure, I'll take them.'

'It would make me *so* happy. I would dance and sing over my work.'

'You didn't tell me what these are for, Twist.'

'That's right, I didn't, did I?' He chuckled with sweet delight. 'That is your Vitamin A.'

'Yes, but what's it do?'

'It conquers ugly hunger, it spurns tiresome fatigue. Of course it is not real, useless, *natural* Vitamin A.'

'Then—'

'Amphetamine – for the young, a wonder drug.'

'Pep pills?' Thorn rolled the phial urgently back to him. 'Sorry, Twist, I don't take drugs. I can't risk my looks.'

'But it will give you your looks back! It will kill your appetite and increase your enthusiasm! It will fuel ambition and obliterate self-doubt! It will make you forget! Every mannequin should be fed on Vitamin A, so she walks with the arrogance of blood royal and rids her body of *baggage*.'

'*I don't take drugs*.'

'Oh, the cry of the bourgeoise! Or else it is 'I take all drugs, I'm a mess!' You will take my Vitamin A, dear, if you wish to work. You will take my advice and my A if you do not wish to be returned to your life of vagabond scavenging. Oh, Vitamin A is not a freaky *drug* – it is the key to success for the young at heart.'

'Do *you* take it?'

'It would make no difference to me.' Twist drooped dramatically. 'When one reaches a certain age it is impossible to leave terra firma. Thrills are practically nil. It takes *youth* to tap and spark off the effects of amphetamine. But I do second best, I give it to all my models – except Cuba, who is a Negro and has seen too much of the chaos that chemicals can create when used foolishly. She hit me when I offered, so I made an exception of her – she is naturally skeletal, anyway. But all other mannequins take it from me – I am like a mother with her milk.'

'I was bottle fed.' Thorn took back the phial. 'All right, Twist, you win. I'll get thin.' She stood up to leave. She would throw the muck into the Seine from the Pont Notre-Dame on her way back to the Latin Quarter. The crazed old fruit-bat would never know. 'Thanks for the Perrier and the pills, Twist. I'll see you tomorrow.'

'Wait,' he smiled, 'we're not finished yet. Lift that pretty little dress you are wearing up to your middle.'

'Listen, Twist, you're a great—'

'Do as I say! Don't you want my present? Do you loathe me so much?'

'No, but I don't—'

'Oh, stop worrying about the virginity of your big American butt! If I was attracted to little girls do you honestly believe I would have devoted my life to covering their bodies? Now do as I say, stop this nonsense.'

Thorn hoisted her dress up grimly. Twist took something from his desk and held it up, smiling. It was a thin chain of spun gold. 'Pretty, no?' He advanced on her, holding it like a precious garrotte.

'I couldn't, Twist, it must have cost—'

He slipped the slender chain around her waist and fastened it. He turned a tiny gold key and put it in his pocket. 'How do you like your better judgement?'

'It's very elegant. Something so understated must have been over-priced.'

'It was, nosey. But you are more than worth it.'

'Thank you. One thing . . .'

'Yes?'

'It's very *tight*. It's almost cutting into my skin, Twist. Can't I have it adjusted?'

'I'm sorry, that is impossible. What we will have to adjust is *you.* Good luck with your course of vitamins. Let me know when you need more. You may pull down your dress now, *mechante bébé.* I feel very fatigued. Go home now and let your life begin.' Twist whistled and collapsed on to his leather chaise. Thorn passed the pretty chauffeur on the stairs.

Somewhere along the lonely, lovely journey that the night had become, Thorn stood at the window of the room at the top of the rue de Babylone hotel and vowed, *swore* to herself that she would never forget what Twist had done to her, and that she would always love him a little for it.

The amphetamine was everything he'd promised it would be, and more. She didn't eat and she couldn't sleep and she had never felt better. She had never *felt* before. What a self-centred, narrow-minded brat she had always been! After the pills life's dust-covers fell away and everything was clear and clean.

She had ridiculously exaggerated the importance of the *18* debacle, she could see that now. It had been a sour grapes set-up setback in what was destined to be the world's most glorious career. Poor Nancy Kent, to have to carry so much useless ham. You couldn't really blame her for lashing out at the blessed ones. Actually, the kid had done Thorn a favour; brought her to Paris, turned her into a real model, brought her to the brink of being the thinnest, most beautiful girl the world had ever deified. *18* would beg and plead and weep over the telephone for just one precious picture to put on their poor cover one day soon. She was sure of it. She was a world beater. Nothing could touch her, nothing could stop her. She felt full of youth and blood and destiny. She felt like the only beauty in the world and she felt ready to fight anyone to defend the title. She looked down over Paris and she knew that every brick, every brain belonged to her.

She went to the mirror. Already she was changing. A pale, primitive, hollow otherness was annexing her familiar face. She stared at the future legend till dawn and beyond.

Mary Gunn stirred as the street came alive with noise pollution. The unemployed redhead turned on to her back and began to snore softly. Thorn's head snapped disbelievingly in her direction. She knew a moment of pure territorial hatred. She walked over to the bed and poked Mary Gunn sharply in the stomach with the hair brush she held.

'Stop it!' she hissed. Trust a mortal to make life just that little bit more mediocre. Thorn felt dirty and depressed. Time for breakfast. She reached for the phial.

The stewardess brought them drinks on a tray and a smile from a can. Johnny bolted his strawberry daiquiri and stared down at the huge white clouds scudding across the Alps.

'Go easy, John,' Dave Pepper said. 'Those concoctions won't change anything.'

'You ain't kidding – not more than thirty per cent hooch.'

'It's no good for your game.'

'McEnroe drinks them. It don't do *his* game no harm.'

'And it probably doesn't do his ulcer much *good*.

Johnny ordered another. 'Medicinal purposes,' he told his coach. 'Soothe the pain.'

'If you want to kill the pain just take a look at that cheque you've got in your inside pocket.'

'Very droll. But you know I don't give a fuck about the money. It's nothing compared to what I could pick up playing an exhibition in Dubai or Sào Paolo or some place. Exhibitions pay more for just walking on to the court than Grand Prix tournaments pay for winning the title. I wanted that title,' he said bitterly.

'You'll get it another time, John. You'll get them all. But . . . just think of the next one. Try not to be so afraid of failure.'

'I'm not *afraid* of losing. I'm more . . . *disgusted* by the thought of it.'

'You looked tired in that final set. Maybe we should have stuck to that carbohydrate diet. Plenty of pasta, lots of nervous energy to burn off.'

'Dave, I love Italian food but I could no more *live* on the pap than fly. If I looked rough it was because my leg lost a side of ham on the Foro Italico.'

'You eat too much junk.'

'I'm a poor boy, Dave. I've got a fast food tooth. Look at my stomach, go on, feel it – flat as a flapjack and hard as a rock. The day you catch me running to fat you can enrol me in Weightwatchers and put me on a warm water fast. Until then I'll cut up my own food, ok?'

They watched Ray Velez walk down the aisle with his silver trophy and his silent girlfriend. She looked like one of his harem of sisters, small and dark, and she read bodice-rippers constantly. Johnny didn't notice her. He was staring at the trophy he should have won.

'Hey, Dave.' Velez smiled shyly.

'Hello, Raymond. Hello, Lupe.'

Lupe nodded.

'How's the leg now, Johnny?' said Velez.

'Oh, still hanging on by a thread but the gangrene's clearing up nicely thank you.'

'Great,' Velez smiled uncertainly. 'Well, see you guys after we land.'

'Bravissimo, fuck face,' Johnny muttered to his pink drink. He had always been a sloppy drinker and being locked up with Velez and *that trophy* at thirty thousand feet didn't help to make him merry. There was no escaping. Pros on The Circuit lived in each other's laps. They brushed past each other in hotel lobbies and escort lounges, they changed in the same locker rooms and played each other and practised next to each other, they rubbed suntanned shoulders at every restaurant, bar and party that came within the Circuit's vicinity. For Johnny Sangster there would be no peace around Ray Velez until he had his scalp.

The shock of shrill braying from the rear of the plane shuddered through the subdued passengers. Maria Salewicz, top of the women's world rankings and dedicated defector, was hell bent on packing in all the FUN! – alcohol, risque stories, talking loud, laughing, spending, spending, spending – she had ever gone without during those twenty-one years in Poland. She had a rangy body and a grinning carnivorous face that would look old at twenty-five. Her make up was endorsed by Sherry Ward and her voice could make eardrums bleed.

'You'd think they'd know better than to bring their livestock on to the plane, wouldn't you?'

'The life and soul of the Communist Party,' Johnny mumbled sullenly.

'She's a better American than *you* are, you pinky integrationist. Who wouldn't go to South Africa?'

'I wish I fucking had, now. What a waste of money.' The braying broke out afresh, even louder and Johnny half stood and turned in his seat, grimacing. '*Jeeez* . . .'

'Put your headphones on if it gets to you.' Dave Pepper opened a pristine John le Carré novel with relish.

'It's opera. It'd take a couple dozen Iron Curtains to blot that hee-haw out, anyhow.'

'She's excited. She's never been here before. She told me she's got a neutron bomb's ransom to spend, and that she won't leave town till it's gone.'

'Tennis is just a side-line with her. Consuming is her serious career.'

'Well, she certainly wants to consume *you.*'

'You are what you eat. She looks at me and she sees all-American junk grub. I swear, she's only the second person I've ever seen trying to eat a burger and smoke a cigarette at *exactly* the same time.'

'Who was the first?' Dave Pepper looked at him, amused.

'Old father slime. Sangster Senior.'

'Spoken to him lately?'

'I rung my mother up after I had the stitches. She seemed a little worried – *he* was in the background, laughing and shouting curse words at the phone. He gets weirder and weirder – he's a fucken *liability*, you know, Dave, one big meatheaded millstone. I wish he'd just—'

'Stop feeling sorry for yourself, John. I'll fetch Maria up here to tell you a Polish joke. Been thinking any about Harald's helpful Dating Do's and Don'ts?'

'No, no, Dave, I thought we understood each other. The days of public relations romances are over. I don't care if she's number one, I don't care if she just so happens to be America's Commie-crushing heroine at this particular moment. She revolts me.'

'Fair enough, John, personal chemistry can't count pictures of George Washington. Harald just mentioned that you've never been a great favourite with the crowd, and that every American man, woman and child admires Maria—'

'—for ditching her old crone of a penniless mother and hopping over the wall? Some saint.'

'—for throwing her lot in with freedom. That's just what Harald said. Every product from sewing machines to orange juice is just lining up waiting to be touted by her brave, broken pidgin American. An appealing public image is essential when promotions are in the air. The *Caesar* money won't keep you in pink muck for a month. I'm thinking about *you*, John. Standing in front of a TV camera isn't half as taxing as capering around on endless exhibition courts. Save yourself. Show Maria around.'

'Dave, do you really think those last two orders are compatible?'

'Good God, sure I do. She's a plain girl in a strange strata all of a sudden. She's enjoying her *freedom*; she wants a traumatic triste with a bellyaching brat the way she wants a tax bill. She *likes* you, that's all. Take her out then take her back to her hotel. Then take a raincheck.' Dave Pepper beckoned to Johnny and lowered his quiet voice. 'You know what she said to me about you? She said you were curly like a lamb.'

'Oh, Jesus!' Johnny Sangster buried his face in his headrest. 'Get me a sick bag, quick! Get me *out* of this zoo.'

The stewardess came by, not with first aid but dispensing fond farewells and duty free goods. 'We hope you have enjoyed flying Air France and will fly with us again soon. We will be arriving at Charles De Gaulle airport in a few minutes. The weather is warm and bright with occasional showers.'

The plane banked steeply to the right and suddenly the lights of Paris rushed up at fantastic speed to Johnny Sangster's window, giving him the first real thrill he'd had that year.

# seven

Thorn arrived at the atelier for the final fittings, Twist's gold chain slipping down over her hips.

The endless hours of tension and tedium on avenue Marceau could not grind her down. Amphetamine turned what might have been a gruelling slog into a piece of cakewalk. Let the other mannequins and the midinettes and the fitters and the cutters and the *vendeuses* and the master couturier himself crack up and take crap and cry – Thorn Sayre was beyond, *above* all the petty emotional tripwires that left those who were somehow lacking shattered by the wayside. Thorn Sayre was above all that now.

And she knew this – when Twist's spring collection finally opened under that giant awning on place des Victoires in just five days time, then *she* would be there, prowling the catwalk like some strange magnificent predator gone a-hunting for

God knows what under the blind benevolent gaze of the giant Louis Quatorze.

She would be there and she would be sensational.

Amongst the bedlam of the *cabine* Thorn stood dead still in front of a mirrored wall wearing nothing but her shoes and her chain. She was waiting for a muscular midinette to quit bickering with a flamboyant sketch artist about how many stitches Twist wanted in the shroud she was being fitted for today. In the *cabine* the noise – French, English and Italian oaths – was loud, the lights – bright white, like those of faith healers (Twist would be flattered by the comparison, she must remember to tell him) – were hot and the walls were mirrors. It was easy to get lost in there. She studied her reflection like it was a crucial map.

All around her huge scissors chomped deftly through giant rolls of white Japanese silk like barracudas going through crispbread. Comrade mannequins stood in various stages of undress, glistening with sweat and Chanel, ignoring everyone, hands on hips waiting for their swaddling couture to be unrolled, measured, cut, pinned, fitted, stitched, adjusted *endlessly.*

Thorn didn't notice the boredom and short tempers that were all around her. She didn't notice the frayed nerves and the tears in the silk and the tears on the cheeks of the young seamstress sobbing in the corner. Because it was so easy to get lost in the *cabine* and she was bewitched by her own evolution. Garbo was gone. Thorn Sayre was now notoriously thin, dangerously white. Her mouth was a glossy red manhole and her kohled eyes stared a challenge to some cold combat. Her body was on a voyage to boyhood. She was either less or more than human.

Cuba slunk up behind her. Her black shroud had a veiled hood which hid her face and an oval porthole snipped in the rear, framing the wearer's buttocks. She displayed herself mockingly to Thorn. 'Who does he plan to sell *this* little number to? A passive bee-keeper or two?'

Thorn shot a look of irritation at the interloper. 'I've no idea.'

'Neither has Twist. Jeez – can they wonder that *haute couture* is dying two little deaths every year? Who could possibly *want* this monstrosity? Some old fool with more money than taste or time left. I tell you, Thorn, only the old and the out of touch and the new know-nothing rich – *Americans*, if you will – come calling at the French collections these days.'

'The house of Twist made a massive profit last year,' data'd Thorn coldly.

Cuba laughed. 'Sure it did – by selling *pret-à-porter* and perfumes. If Twist had to rely on the fruit of his brain to bring home the *baguettes* we'd have all been begging on the streets long ago. And it's the same for all the poor old legends in Paris – they sell their name on a lipstick and make their fortune. Or make the house's fortune – only Cardin is a major shareholder in his household name, for Pete's sake. The rest – forget it.'

'No, no, no!' A distracted Cockney whine waylaid them. 'Jap – you know Jap, right? – he's a shareholder in himself, he told me so.'

Cuba gurgled with glee. 'I never listen to pillow talk, little girl.' She reached out a hand and lazily caressed the shoulder of the willowy young giantess who had wandered up to them.

Thorn stared, fascinated. A midinette had followed the model on hands and knees and now knelt pinning oceans of grey chiffon around a handspan waist. The newcomer ran her hands absentmindedly over her sallow, sunken torso. Then she stared up into Thorn's eyes and smiled.

Thorn gasped.

Cuba roared. 'Meeting Nicola is like riding a very classy ghost train. Don't worry, baby, she doesn't bite . . . not in daylight.'

Nicola smiled absently at Cuba. Her eyes were entirely scarlet, as though brimming over with blood, courtesy of creative contact lenses. But her crowning horror was her hair – it was thick, lustrous, Marcelled, waist-length and gun-metal grey. It jarred distressingly with her heart-shaped, pale-skinned, childlike face. The effect was shattering.

Pre Thorn, Nicola had been Twist's pride and toy ('Your toes are like ten tiny tombstones.') Her relegation meant nothing to her – so what? she had been thinking since she could talk. Now she pretended to be concerned. 'Yeah, yeah, this is all trash now, this Paris thing. It's an old age pensioner, you know? I brought my little sister – she's fourteen and *gorgeous* – over here as a birthday present last season. Honest, she couldn't have been boreder. She said 'I was wearing that tat last summer! I gave a kilt like that to Mum for dusters, she's still using them!' And it's true in't it? First that punk junk, then that Mod black and white rubbish, then the pirate tat – kids in London do it at least a year in advance.' She gazed down at her midinette's fumbling hands. 'That's why *he's* gone all ghoulish. He's cleverer than the rest, he knows what the papers say, he's sick of poncing a living off teenage truants' old hats.' She touched the grey drapery. 'I'm meant to represent Decay, ain't I?'

'Look,' Thorn snapped, 'thousands and thousands of people from all over the world flock to the French collections every year. What's that? Mass hypnosis?'

'Sure they come here, for the ride and an eye-full of the Eiffel.' In her mind's eye Thorn helped Cuba up on to a box marked SOAP. 'But how many of them ever put their hands in their pockets, Thorn? Very few – only three thousand women in the world regularly buy Paris *haute couture* in the Eighties. In the Fifties it was . . . oh, thirty thousand plus.'

'Thirty thousand lobotomies.' Nicola shrieked with laughter, then relaxed back into her silent smile.

You weirdo, Thorn sneered silently. She smiled tolerantly at Cuba. 'But Paris will always be a *myth*, a legend, Cuba. No number of dry statistics can take that away from Twist and Co.'

'You're suffering from an extreme case of Mary Gunnitis, Thorn; I thought you was immune, too. I'm sorry, but it's a plain fact that fashion *used* to be dictated from the top – *now* it's dictated from the bottom, the street, and that's the way it'll always be. Twist'd be better off copying the English kids like everyone else. For Pete's sake, it's because he's trying to turn the clock back, be an *innovator,* that I'm standing here dressed like a vicar on a meat-rack. And just how many variations on your shroud do you think he'll sell?'

'I think Twist's sales will go up this season, certainly.'

'You *like* these rags?'

'Who said anything about the *clothes*? I'm not very interested in clothes, Cuba, I don't think they matter a damn. Bones maketh the mannequin. It's not *clothes* I'm selling.'

'The rue Morgue will always be willing to take the collection off his hands if he don't flog any,' Nicola whispered.

Thorn turned on her, angry. 'Why do you do this, if it's so pathetically square?'

'Me?' Nicola tossed her terrifying hair and sneered malevolently into Thorn's face, her head thrown back. 'Well, I'm only here for the absinthe. Reminds me, I must go and drink my lunch.' She smiled at Cuba and wandered dreamily away, the midinette crawling at heel behind her.

'Absinthe?' Thorn frowned at Cuba. 'I thought it was extinct, like the unicorn.'

'They make it in Spain and smuggle it over. It's been illegal for sixty years, that's why you don't find it on tap in every bar. They say it drives you nuts.'

'Then why—'

'Oh, she's just a nice little girl who's terrified of not being interesting. She just wants to be an addict. She's tried being addicted to every kind of chemical you can think of – but absinthe's harder to get, it's harder to handle. She's happy now. Don't sneer – she's actually a very sweet little girl.'

'I think she's a walking nightmare.'

'Actually, *I* think she's a walking personification of this cute little three ring circus we call *haute couture*.' Cuba lifted her veil and smiled sweetly at Thorn.

'Actually, I think you're wasted on the catwalk, Cuba. Your heart is in the pulpit.'

'Well! And your head is up your royal white ass.' Cuba turned and walked away.

Thorn caught her arm. 'Cuba, Cuba, please, please! Tell me something, I'm a bit mixed up. Why do . . . why do all the mannequins look like you and me and Nicola?'

'Wellll . . . people can look at us and fantasize about . . . huh, sex and death, I guess. *Ai No Corrida* – I know what white men like. Modelling is about sex, I'm sure you'll agree, and in bad times you don't get happy sex. I see myself as a pall-bearer, actually.'

'Oh?' Thorn leaned against the mirror. 'And what's in the coffin?'

'Pleasure. Pleasure's dead. But don't you fret. I've got a feeling in my bones that you'll be the first post-pleasure pin-up.'

'That's just what I always wanted, Cuba! Pleasure's just a placebo, it spoils the purity of the line. Really, there's nothing more anachronistic than a smile, these days, is there?'

Cuba veiled her face, Cuba smiled.

*

On avenue George-V, Johnny Sangster nursed his thigh and a cognac while Maria Salewicz razed the champagne and gazed at Les Girls.

'Oh my Gard! It's like the Weimer Republic all over again!'

Maria Salewicz was the fifth girl Johnny had known who equated any mildly risque revelry with that complex libertarian Communist doomed Utopia. He'd looked it up; he loved hard fact, he had no time for anything else, and in America hard fact was so hard to get hold of. *Cabaret* had a lot of cliches to answer for, he thought, as Maria nodded her head wisely and repeated her shopsoiled analysis once more with awe.

'Yeah, just like the Weimar Republic. Oh, wow! Doesn't that chick have a great body?' She spoke boldly yet tentatively; you could tell bisexuality wasn't par for the cool course behind the Curtain. Maria pointed rudely at the object of her admiration. 'That one there, the black haired one.' Johnny simulated interest, peering at the dozen or so females sashaying around a stage the size of a bath mat. They were all bathed in lights of red stripes, they all wore black thigh-length boots and black elbow gloves, they were all made up to look chunky, cutesy and thirty and they all wore black bobbed wigs.

'Oh, yeah, she really stands out from the rest,' Johnny said sarcastically. Little delicacies like sarcasm were lost and harmless when volleyed at a pidgin Pole.

'You know I read in my guide book that it took the old guy they call Le Boss over *thirty years* to perfect this show. Wow, Johnny!'

'So these broads are all in their fifties? Ah, that changes things; as grandmothers go, they're glamorous.'

'Oh Johnee!' Maria leaned close to him, pantomiming the act of being doubled up with laughter. 'These aren't the original Crazy Horse ladies, man!' She caught his eye and switched to simmer. 'Don't you find their work a turn on?'

Johnny had been dreading this move, this moment. He had tried to dissuade Maria from visiting the Crazy Horse Saloon – no sex, *please*. He had suggested the ever-popular eyesore the Eiffel Tower (all those tourists to hide in) and he had suggested Notre Dame (she wouldn't start anything in church, being a Roman Candle.) She had done them and more earlier that day, though, at a gallop in harness with her coach.

She hadn't exiled herself in order to linger over views and

religion, that was the point. She wanted glamour, amour, ammunition to fill the void of being an alien plain millionaire. She wanted dimly-lit luxurious rooms like wombs, clothes that no one else in the State owned a copy of, rich and golden American bodies on top of her between designer sheets. She wanted everything that had ever been advertised; she believed in the American Dream one hundred and one per cent because she had never been less than a millionaire while resident there.

Now Johnny answered carefully. 'I'm wild about the lighting. I'd like to see what that lighting guy could do for a real good rock band.'

'Oh, I love real dirty rock and roll! Just straight down the line rock and roll!' Maria's face turned sour. 'Nothing like Nugent in Poland, just bubble gum. Nothing like *this* in Poland. Gee, I'd like to magic this place away to Lublin for a weekend. Show people what a great time we have here. Show up the Soviets for the squares they are.'

Johnny shrugged. 'This ain't such a great kind of place. There's no point in bringing this kind of thing into a country that can get along fine without it. New York is lousy with places like this; after a while it gets as boring as a row of identical park benches.' He laughed. 'No, you get more action on a park bench.'

'Yeah?' murmured Maria.

Oh, *fuck*. He'd sweet-talked his way full circle back to the point of proposition. 'Yeah, action . . . you'll get rolled at least.' Pretty quick thinking.

'Let's leave,' said Maria. 'I want to catch the floorshow at the Alcazor. They've got *transvestites.*'

Johnny shook his head. 'I'll take a raincheck, Maria. My leg's throbbing and to tell you the truth I don't really go for that kind of freak show.'

Maria Salewicz nodded seriously. 'Yeah, it's the pits, really. Those guys must be sick in the head. Hey – you ever seen Mistinguett's mirrored bedroom?'

'No.'

'Take me back to my hotel. I sleep there.'

'Hey – listen – Maria – *what* was the name of that joint? Alcazor? Yeah, I've heard good things about it. The audience is completely straight, I heard. We might have a few laughs there – yeah, let's do what *you* want.' As he helped Maria into her horrible satin jacket he stroked her lacklustre hair sympathetically. She wasn't ever going to do what she wanted with *him*, poor little rich refugee.

A couple of professional cameras clicked as they left the Crazy Horse. Big deals from little rumours grow. He smiled at Maria with real affection, thinking about the endorsements, thinking about money – the climax of the cheque in its chaste envelope. He would always be a poor boy in his soul and the thrill of money never faded.

Winning, *earning*, had stoked his ego so big and so easy that he'd put sex to one side awhile ago out of sheer satiety. He didn't want to sleep with a girl who excited him less than winning or earning always did; it would have been a sad comment on the both of them. So he smiled at Maria for the photographers and he waited for the girl who'd make winning seem like a reflex action, the girl who'd make the latest five-figure cheque seem like junk mail.

Cuba stretched and swallowed a grape and grinned at Thorn Sayre who sat on the bed seriously filing Cuba's naked toenails. 'I could get to like this. You do *mine* next.'

'No, you paint mine next – base, three layers of colour and a top coat. Then hardener. Then I'll do you.'

'I'm not sitting here all night putting five layers of varnish on your toes, Cuba, I don't care *what* an exotic tableau this is. There are no photographers here, anyhow. I use one-coat varnish. I'll lend you some of that.'

'It doesn't do the job. You're green.'

'We can't all be black.'

'A joke! I put my varnish on once a week and it *lasts*. One-coat crap chips on the hour every hour.'

'I change my nail varnish twice a day.'

'It's that drug. I've noticed that you never leave yourself alone. Say, why don't you get some fag at Twist's to make you a little mirror on a chain to wear round your neck, like some people have spectacles? You could start a craze.' Cuba cackled. 'Be the first fashion to originate here since the cloche.'

'Oh, very—'

The door burst open.

'I've had it up to *here*!' Mary Gunn declared, indicating the pale orange freckles that dappled the bridge of her nose. For once her body had lost its languor, and she paced the small room obsessively, opening closets and drawers. 'It's *enough*! I don't need this scuzzy little dump *no more*!'

'Oh, don't sweat it, Mary.' Cuba made a faint *moue* of impatience. 'So. You're going to another hotel? Or you've found an apartment.'

'I'm not talking about this lousy hotel! I'm talking about this lousy *town*!'

Thorn gaped at Cuba in disbelief, then looked at Mary, who was glaring at her.

'Where are my fucking bags?'

'Under your fucking eyes,' said Thorn playfully, perplexed.

'Oh, very funny, you cracker cow!' Mary spotted her vast collection of Vuitton luggage and began to pack everything she owned.

'Why, you trashy—'

'Stop it, you boring bitches,' Cuba spat. She sat up straight. 'Mary. What's happened to you? You *love* Paris. You worship Paris.'

'We had it annulled!' Mary snapped.

'Well, bile has certainly made you quite a wit. I'm starting to like you at last. But I'm confused – I thought things were starting to move for you. You just got the job at the Crazy. You've only been there a week.'

'Flashing your fanny and miming to smutty songs for the benefit of sweaty fat tourists is hardly the *big* time. There's more Americans there on a fast night than there are in *Miami*. Wouldn't it be just great if my father's friends came in and started shouting "Hinky dinky parlez vous!" at me?' Mary frowned, thinking hard. 'Hold on – it's even worse, they wouldn't *recognize* me, the disguise you've got to wear! I look like every other *sow* in that place. Have you *seen* them? I've seen sacks of potatoes that have been hit by trucks looking foxier!'

'I think those girls look pretty good.' Cuba shrugged.

'Oh, spare me the Peace Corps!' Mary's face crumpled. 'It's all right for *you* to be kind to the competition. You're a m – a m-model.' She began to sob. 'Me, I came all this w-way for a – to be a *stripper*. They give you a dumb name and a stupid rug and march you about under some tenth-rate light show on a stage the size of a postage stamp! I was Mary-Lou fucking Bang-Bang, if you can believe that!'

'Everyone has to start somewhere. Think of Gypsy Rose

Lee.' Thorn revelled serenely in her own success.

'You cow!' Mary's tears were dry black streaks now and her anger was foremost once more. 'Why *should* I have to strip? You're a model and you look like a – like a stick insect. You look *weird*. Where I come from *you* wouldn't get a wolf whistle in a cabana crammed full of *Cubans*.' Mary shook her head. 'This isn't the city I came looking for. My father's wife said Paris reminded her of a cute museum, but this place is a mausoleum, lousy with weirdos like you.' Her lip curled. 'The French ain't half as hot as they're painted. They don't even have barbecues in their backyards, for God's sake!'

'I guess that's the secret of the bluebird of happiness,' Cuba murmured. 'A barbecue in the backyard and as many cow-burgers as you can cram.'

'Oh, stow it, Cuba!' Mary gathered her packed bags together. 'America may be too tame for you, but it's good enough for *me* and *I'm* the kind of American who *matters*. Paris is past it – I'm going to New York City right now and Lauren and Klein are going to *lap me up*! Have a happy decay! Here!' Mary Gunn tossed something furry into Thorn's lap. 'Keep it safe for me. Give it a saucer of milk and put it out every night! I won't *need* it.' The door slammed and Mary Gunn flounced furiously out of the charming hotel – she now thought of it as a crappy *hovel* – for the last time.

Cuba stared thoughtfully at Mary-Lou Bang-Bang's unwanted hair.

'Maybe we can teach it a few tricks.' Thorn laughed nervously.

Cuba pulled on her stockings. 'We can at least give it a decent burial.'

They put on their gloves and dark glasses and stepped out into the Latin Quarter's night full of shabby romance.

They let the two great romanesque towers of Notre Dame be their guide down to the river. The *Quartier Latin* featured streets that were straight and narrow and shops that were foreign and cramped. The aroma of Tunisian pastry floated past bookshops that sold only Zen and cinemas that showed Italian films to a capacity crowd of fifty. The fast food and serious art of many countries jostled for air and your custom.

Overgrown children from Arkansas or Andover or Alberta or anyplace hoisted grubby backpacks and wandered in a daze, looking for a youth hostel, distracted by the colours. Thin pale boys hunched, tormented, over coffee cups, watching *les Americaines* coming . . . thin pale boys gave *les Americaines* the eye and tried to give them the impression they were something big at the Sorbonne. *Les Americaines* made them feel invisible. The thin pale boys pouted with emasculated pique and waited for something easier to come along, like an *Americaine* with a camera.

'I understand that once upon a time it was possible to *feel* the unrest here,' Cuba said. 'But now it just feels restless. I guess it's standard pre-collection nerves.'

'Don't lose any sleep over it. What's it matter to us whether they're throwing petrol bombs at the American Embassy or trying to pick up strays from a Schnectady tourist party? They hate us anyway.'

'Us?' Cuba smiled slinkily. 'Speak for yourself, white girl. *L'Afrique, c'est chic.*' She did a few dance steps, the upper half of her body completely immobile. 'Do you dance?'

'No.'

'I'll teach you. I never saw a paleface that didn't go to pieces on the dancefloor. Waving their *arms*, if you can believe it.'

'Maybe we can go to discotheques together when the collections are over.' Thorn thought about what she had just said, slightly stunned. She had never thought about what would happen after the collections before. It scared her a little.

'Oh, sure. Grace and Jerry were here together at our age, not too successful, and they made great accessories out of each other around the dives. They'd dance till they dropped and then French wags would pour champagne over them, to revive them.'

Thorn thought about Jerry Hall. She felt better. Far be it from Thorn to *bitch*, but she could detect an uncanny resemblance between the Texan tigress and last year's quadruped winner of the Kentucky Derby. If *she* could get famous and feted and a millionairess (Jerry could keep her menopausal old pop singer), well, then Thorn could . . . her looks could *kill* Jerry Hall.

At the banks of the Seine Thorn and Cuba stopped.

Cuba dug into her trenchcoat's voluminous pocket and cast Mary Gunn's wig to the tide.

'There she goes,' Cuba said. 'Our poor little redhead.'

'She doesn't stand a *chance* of showing clothes in New York,' Thorn said. 'Hell, she'll be hard pressed to find a job taking *off* clothes.'

'Oh, I somehow don't think she'll be heading for pastures new.' Cuba looked down into the river but she couldn't see the dead hair. 'I think she just wants to go back to Miami and forget she ever tried and failed. I'd guess that a beautician's diploma awaits her somewhere. I'll tell you something – she did the right thing getting out *now*. To be a failed model living through the Paris collections – you'd want to toss yourself in the Seine, let alone your wig.'

'I suppose one would,' Thorn mused. 'But *Miami* . . . Miami, for God's sake.'

The rain poured down over Porte d'Auteil in the lush west suburbs of Paris and made the sycamores, acacias and chestnut trees on the southern tip of the Bois de Boulogne glisten like new bank notes.

In the locker room of the nearby Roland Garros stadium the finalists of the French Open sweated and waited for the rain to clear. They did not speak. They had too much time on their hands for that.

Out in the arena the crowd waited for them with growing impatience and their bright umbrellas up. Players who had failed to get that far amused themselves with exchanged insults and five card stud up in their private lounge. Other players went shopping with prize money and a loved one. Still others were already on the plane to the next stop on the Circuit. Some of them had wounds to lick.

In the Roland Garros treatment room beaten quarter finalist Johnny Sangster lay on his back while a physiotherapist from the French Tennis Federation gave him heat treatment.

'You should have scratched from this tournament,' the physiotherapist told him as he turned off the lamp. 'The femur bone in your leg was too badly bruised for matchplay. It was dangerous, you could have come to harm.'

'But I didn't,' Johnny said. 'And getting through to the last eight here will do my world ranking no harm at all.'

'Just because you're young and heal fast don't think you're immortal,' the physiotherapist said. 'And just because a local anaesthetic kills the pain don't think it has cured the injury.

Novocaine is a cosmetic, it is a remedy for nothing.'

He wished Johnny good luck at Wimbledon and left.

Johnny sprung down off the treament table and pulled on his pants. 'What was that he gave me?' he grinned at Dave Pepper. 'The Desiderata?'

'You can't stay home knitting just because of a bruised femur,' Dave said. 'Not during the French Open you can't. If you need to shake off an injury then you should cut back on the exhibitions. You play too many exhibitions as it is, I can see it in your legs.'

'But don't drop out of a Grand Prix tournament until they're reading you the last rites, eh, coach?' Johnny laughed.

'You can't afford to,' Dave said seriously. 'The tournaments make you a reputation, the exhibitions only make you money. When you've got a reputation you can go anywhere, the limits are off. Look at Maria Salewicz.'

'Must I?'

As Johnny finished dressing the stadium started to rumble. It was the crowd.

'The rain must have stopped,' Dave Pepper said. 'They're coming on court.'

The Frenchman and the Czech had finished knocking up and were taking off their tracksuits. Ball boys scampered. The best seats in the house were up in the players lounge. Compared to them the views reserved for heads of state were cheap tickets.

The players gathered at the glass to watch the match, their coaches one step behind them, the wives and girlfriends of the players one step behind the coaches. The players felt most alive when they were most alone – out *there* – and their loved ones were used to being treated as excess luggage.

Tom Dougherty walked into the lounge, the latest Miss Universe attached to him. He saw Johnny Sangster and approached him, grinning. 'Congratulations, Sangster, you old creep!'

'Thanks, Tom,' Johnny said. 'What exactly have I done?'

'Don't give me that! You did it, at last!'

'What are you talking about, Tom?' Dave Pepper said tensely.

'You haven't heard? You haven't seen the ATP ratings?' He could see from their faces that they hadn't. 'You've moved up from thirteen to number nine, Johnny. You made it into the ten.' Dougherty fumbled in the pocket of his leather jacket, pulling out a folded photostat. 'I got it right here, you want to see it?'

Johnny snatched the list, his eyes hungry.

Dave Pepper gripped his arm tightly. 'Only eight players in the world above you, John. Only eight more of the geeks to go.'

# eight

Twist's collection had a soundtrack that was cold and black as oil with a robotic big beat.

Backstage, *cabine* fever reigned. Midinettes and mannequins bet their livelihoods on split seconds. Thorn retched, wretched with catwalk-fright. Cuba strode languidly back to base, clothed in costly yellow cobwebs.

She was flanked by twin sisters from Tokyo, wearing the same creation twice in black. The midinettes pounced and peeled them. Thorn felt a hand in the small of her back and with a slight twinge in her central nervous system she moved off towards the music beyond the curtain.

The drapes parted and she stalked out into captivity. The long and winding stage snaked out into the Grand Salon, just above the heads of the audience. *Clients*, Twist had stressed. But no, they were an audience, gathered here just for her. She caught the big beat's rhythm by its colossal bassline and let it carry her along the catwalk, slinking in her white silk shroud, a lynx captured and choreographed by clockwork. The audience were so many cogs in her world.

The lights above her were hot and bright, the faces below her were blank and white. Pale with anticipation, buyers, fashion writers and aimlessly rich women sat in search of youth in the shape of a life-saving ensemble. Not so much a fashion show, more a saline drip.

Thorn spun on her stiletto heel, ecstatic, and scowled down at her precious public with contemptuous boredom.

Bored too late. To her surprise the Grand Salon stared back at her shroud with exactly the same expression on its collective face.

*

Maria Salewicz stood the French Open women's singles trophy on her hotel room TV and then she forgot about it.

Maria mobilized her driver by snapping her fingers and recruited her escort by begging. She had always longed to attend the Paris collections. It was a dream come true and one she could easily afford.

Johnny put down the phone and scowled at Dave Pepper, who reclined on Johnny's hotel bed. 'I get to take her shopping for clothes again. I get *collected* as usual.'

Dave laughed. 'How are they gonna keep her down on the collective farm now that she's seen Paree?'

'What?' Johnny shrugged himself into his leather jacket. 'She lives on Zuma Beach.'

'An old song.'

'Yeah. I gotta clear out now, Dave, sorry. You want to dump those old songs and memories. Sentimental people got a dusty old attic where their brain should be. Better to have a headful of cotton candy like Salewicz or a pocket calculator in your cranium like Harald O.' They walked down the cool corridor to the elevator. 'I've had it with souvenirs. If I can't touch it then it don't exist. Parents, hometown, girls – you name it, I don't need it.'

In the lobby Maria lunged, and she didn't let go till she had him settled next to her at the latest freak show, their noses pressed right against the stage. He'd lost count of the number of parades she'd dragged him to so far but he remembered that each time she'd been sufficiently impressed – 'Oh my *Gard*, Johnny! Isn't that too much?' – to order at least two thirds of the tat.

One of the couturiers had had to sit down.

'I got cash,' Maria gloated.

Johnny was mute with boredom by the time they got to the place des Victoires. Then he saw Thorn Sayre's ghost and he couldn't believe it.

She had changed so much. He thought the shots in his leg were playing tricks on him. She was thinner and harsher and she walked like she needed nothing. But it was her all right. Thorn Sayre, Johnny thought, looking up at her, at last a captive audience. A couple of minutes later she retraced her steps – wearing something different, he guessed – and this time she saw him. She glared down intimately for a long moment and then she turned. He watched her till she disappeared behind a curtain and then he watched the curtain.

'Jeez, but these clothes are so typically Twist,' Maria gurgled as Nicola, blood-eyed and smiling, sleepwalked towards her wearing a black net nun's habit. 'So decadent, such unhealthy fun – it's Weimar all over again! Don't you think I should have this one, Johnny?'

His empty seat signalled assent; Maria scratched another tick on to her catalogue.

He headed backstage with old love and new confidence. His face was his pass; he was immediately homed in on by a Twist assistant, a pretty boy's pin-up truck-driver wearing Levis and singlet as exotic fancy dress, living only to crawl all over the famous. He nodded seriously at Johnny's disjointed desires – 'Model . . . Miss Sayre . . . good friend . . . must see her' – and spirited him away to see Twist's business manager. He was a bald, broad Corsican who had earned a place in Paris folklore by kicking a photographer in the face (it was the Sixties and Twist was forgivable).

But he was gentle with Johnny. In fact he took Johnny's hands and would not let them go. 'You are a beautiful and I welcome you. It iss fantastic you are here. Twist will be heavenly. Once many beautifuls come to the shows – the Czar and the Shah would bring their wives. Evita and Bianca would bring their husbands. But now it iss all gone. Lenin and the Ayatollah, death and divorce . . . ah, it happens to all of us.'

The Corsican led him into a large chaotic room. Beautiful black girls and odd white girls scrambled in and out of terrible cloths. A thin, tired man ran towards them.

Johnny could not see her. But a row of clothes rails all bore a large colour photograph of a girl. Johnny recognized several in the flesh. He cast his twenty-twenty vision down the line till he found the one he wanted. *So special*, he thought, and he felt it in his head and in his groin. He remembered something he had once said in bed to Sherry Ward, and the memory made him smile.

Twist thought Johnny was just pleased to see him.

'My God! It's really you!' Twist grabbed and shook Johnny's hand as though it was a drowning man's straw. 'You! You were magnificent at Stade Roland Garros.'

'Thanks.'

'Tell me . . . are there any more of you out there?'

'Tennis players?'

'Tennis players, pop stars – celebrities!'

'Well, I came here with Maria Salewicz . . .'

Twist and his business manager gazed raptly at each other. Obviously Maria's reputation had preceded her.

'Has she seen anything she desires?' Twist's business manager queried.

'Well, her catalogue has more ticks on it than a Monmartre tom cat.'

Twist and his business manager gazed blankly at each other.

Twist said something in fast French to the Corsican, with Bloomingdale's in it and a question mark at the end.

'*Ils partent.*' The Corsican looked at Twist coldly, shook Johnny's hand warmly and left the room.

Twist tutted distraughtly and began to mutter under his breath.

'Excuse me, Mr Twist? I can see you're busy here. I just came back to see a friend of mine. Thorn Sayre. She's a model of yours. If you could just tell me where I could wait . . .'

Twist snapped out of his morbid reverie, sensing the only celebrity in his captivity about to get away. He took Johnny's arm. 'A friend of Thorn's! Thorn is my muse! How lucky you are! Of course you don't want to wait in here amongst these . . . these *cows*. Come with me. We'll sit it out. It will soon be over.'

They stood sidestage, critically eyeing the mannequins; Johnny because they weren't Thorn, Twist because they weren't magicians. The models couldn't stop the fashion reporters – identifiable by their bitter, make-up-free scowls and their notepads – from hating the designer for not giving them a new rule for the people, a new reason for existing. The models couldn't stop the photographers from letting their Leicas lie largely idle.

A beautiful Negress threw her head back, bared her teeth in a satirical savage snarl and danced dazzlingly down the catwalk, her vitality for a moment making wilting cameras click and bored ballpoints scribble.

'Yes, Cuba . . . dance,' Twist murmured urgently. He glanced at Johnny. 'Next year all black girls, *all* black girls.

White women are about as interpretive as the wooden mannikins we used before the Twenties. Except *Thorn*, of course. Whose beauty is more still-life, statuesque, anyway.'

'Yes.' Johnny considered it an insult to drape such an athletic girl in such a moribund rag.

'Once models were an inspiration to a designer – Dior had Alla, Balmain had Bronwen – but I have to create around silly girls who think of nothing beyond melting pop stars and having careers. Being a *muse* is foreign to them.'

Thorn materialized in black – mourning became her. She walked moodily down past the gyrating black girl, casing her coolly. Twin Orientals trotted on to the stage, tossing their hair and holding hands.

'The press sit there – look! – with that Impress Me look. It makes me so angry. Awhile ago it was so different – tears, bravos, trampling each other underfoot. Paris was a *tyrant* way back when – A line, this line, that line, change its mind every few months like a beautiful fickle girl, and all the world rush to do its bidding. 1966 . . . space age clothes – we did tennis clothes then, you know! – and Donyale Luna started the dancing. It seemed as though Paris would go forward and onward for ever. It's hard to realize, when you see designer jeans now. Designer jeans, the final white flag. I'll never do it. Better to retreat into perfume. If YSL and Courreges can surrender, all but the fragrance . . . ah, Montana had a bad year. I'm allowed one, too.' Twist shrugged a smile at Johnny. 'Ignore me. It's not so bad. See my finale. See your Thorn.'

The full score of mannequins had marauded the stage, the ethnic minorities doing their best to rev up a party mood. Thorn and a grey-haired ghoul stood stock still, looking on. The catwalk looked like a crypt, and so did the mezzanine. A couple of kind corpses clapped.

'Come on. Back to the *cabine* for condolences.'

In the huge dresing-room Twist immediately disappeared into the concerned throng of his models and his staff. A couple of girls stood alone against walls, drinking and fixing their hair. Infrequent champagne corks popped like ejaculations in a coma.

She sat on a chair, her hands on her knees, her head bowed, her blonde hair waterfalling. Cuba stood behind her rubbing her shoulders seriously. Many men would have found it a titillating tableau. Johnny found it touching. She got tired and tense. She was touchable. He was going to touch her till she trembled.

Cuba read his stare and his stride and shook Thorn. 'Wake up, white girl. You got a groupie.'

'Hi, Thorn.'

'Hello.' She kept her head down. 'What are you doing here?'

'The Circuit's in town. How are you?'

'Never been thinner, thanks.'

'It's ok, she just stopped believing in Paris Power. Now there's only the Tooth Fairy.' Cuba laughed, pulling Twist's folly up over her head as she ambled away.

'Well, how did you enjoy our French farce? What did you think of the clothes?'

'I wouldn't be seen dead in them.'

They laughed and she looked at him for the first time. He was good-looking and American. They were a lot alike.

Johnny saw the cool evaluating look in her eye. He wanted more than that. But it was a start. 'I'm in the top ten. I heard yesterday.'

'Fantastic. Twist's your man. He dotes on famous feet.'

'I've talked to Twist. I came here to see you.'

'Like what you see?'

'Sure. There's less of you, but you still look great.'

'I look ghastly, like a gravedigger's dream date.'

'Have you had dinner?'

'Not for weeks.'

'Aren't you hungry?'

'Yes. Yes, all of a suden I feel very hungry.'

'Ok.'

'Let me get some real clothes on. Wait outside.'

'Sure.'

Stepping out of the *cabine* an hour later, her smile rose from the dead beneath a veiled black hat. 'Why, a stage door Johnny!'

'I looked for you.'

'And now you've found me.' She took his arm.

Johnny smiled shyly and they went out into the place des Victoires, looking for a taxi.

Johnny looked at her standing outside his hotel room and he took out his key.

The door swung open and she went inside, staring solemnly

at the suitcases and unstrung racquets and tennis whites and flame red track-suits scattered all over the floor of the rich room that for a while Johnny Sangster called home. He had gone out without turning off the television.

Thorn glanced at the screen and turned to face the full-length mirror set in one wall.

Johnny swallowed, his nerve ends raw and his heartbeat racing. He had never felt like this with a girl before – never since the first, forgotten girl. Not a girl in a bar who followed the Circuit, not a stewardess on the flight to Stockholm or Ceylon or Sao Paulo, not a girl in the front row with a number to call, not a black girl, not an older woman, not a Sherry Ward. No girl had made him feel like this. This was more like the way he felt before a match.

Johnny looked at her by the mirror. The lean, Copa legs. The tight round behind. The brave broad-shouldered back. The dark blonde hair curtaining the face from a photograph. The blood had rushed to his cock, making it hard as a bone. It strained against his pants, feeling like it was lashed to his leg. Johnny shifted awkwardly.

He sat on the edge of his bed and dialled room service. 'Can I get you a drink, Thorn?' He looked up at her. He froze, sucking air.

Thorn was still lost in the mirror. But she had lifted the skirt of her black dress up around her hips and the fingertips of her right hand were relishing what she kept between the top of her legs. 'I don't know, Johnny. What have they got?'

She let her dress fall and smoothed it straight, moving towards him. He sat on the bed, still cradling the telephone receiver between his ear and his shoulder, and he slid his hands up her dress until they were caressing the firm circles of her behind. Room service came on the line. Thorn grabbed Johnny's cock, squeezing it hard. Johnny cried out with pain, the telephone crashing to the floor, room service babbling, bewildered, in five languages. Johnny sprang to his feet, swearing at her and shoving her backwards. They sprawled across the bed. She reached for him and he knocked her hands away, cursing. He began to tear off his clothes. Thorn propped herself up and started to unzip her dress.

'Not you,' Johnny said. 'You keep your clothes on.'

Red shoes, white legs, black dress. He licked his lips and got on to the bed beside her. Thorn arched her back and he pulled her underpants over her hips and down her long slim thighs and legs. Thorn kicked them off and Johnny climbed between her knees, spreading her legs wide. He hauled her dress up around her neck and pushed her breasts together so he could suck on both her nipples simultaneously. He held the full pink points with his lips, suckled on them with his tongue. He couldn't resist it, he bit her.

She dragged his face away by a fistful of hair. 'If you ever do anything to mark my body I'll kill you. Understand?'

Johnny nodded, moving his mouth up to her face.

Thorn yanked his hair, keeping him back. 'Do you *understand*?'

'Yes, for Pete's sake!'

He tried to kiss her on the mouth. Thorn turned her head away. He tried again. The same thing.

'What's the matter *now*, for Chrissakes?'

'I don't want you to.'

'Why the hell *not*?'

'My lip gloss.'

Johnny cursed and grabbed the gold chain around her waist, dragging her down the bed on to the three straight fingers he jammed up between her legs. He gave her the short sharp shock treatment until she was wet and noisy. Then he pulled out his fingers with the sound of cork parting company from claret bottle. He gave her his sticky fingers to suck on as he guided the point of his inflamed cock to the lips of her cunt.

He pushed it in carefully for a few inches and then hooked it up savagely, trying to ram in the rest. It was tight, very tight. Thorn had a small cunt and Johnny had a big cock. It hurt both of them. Johnny loved it.

Thorn squirmed on the end of it, crying for him to take it out. He kept it in and put a pillow under her behind. Then he swung his cock up inside her with a pelvic uppercut that slid it in to the hilt. He pulled it back a way for pumping length and started to feed it to her with smooth long rhythmic thrusts.

Thorn began to scratch and scream, fighting to get away. Johnny stared at her, uncertain whether this was rape or pillow play. Thorn clawed his face. Johnny's nails raked her back.

Then as if on cue she gave up all thoughts of escape and relented, writhing languidly beneath him, her eyes closed and her fingers wrapping round the hair at the nape of his neck, letting herself be used.

Thorn began to smile as Johnny began to moan.

The hardness broke and diluted into almost unbearably pleasurable spasms pumping warm jets of semen deep inside her. Johnny had wanted to hold it back, he had wanted it to last longer, and now he cried out. Thorn comforted him, murmuring encouragement as her cunt gripped him, squeezing out every last drop.

Johnny just lay there on top of her, sweating and spent, his soft cock inside her, his face in the sheets, panting like a happy idiot. He hugged her tight, looked at her and smiled.

Thorn smiled like a stranger. 'Do you think they could send up some Perrier?'

'What?'

'Perrier? Room service? You were just talking to them, remember?' Her face had become animated. 'I'd love some Perrier. Ice and lemon, too, if it's not too much trouble.'

Johnny rang room service.

Thorn got out her tool box.

'Is there something wrong with me?' he said when he hung up.

Thorn didn't come out of the mirror. 'Not that I know of, Johnny.'

'Style? Content? Size?'

'Oh, come on now! How should I know? It's not my field.'

'I must be doing something wrong. You're not very . . .'

'Enthusiastic?'

'Yeah, that'll do. Enthusiastic. You act like nothing happened. How do you think that makes me feel?'

'Inadequate?'

'In one.

'Next thing you'll be telling me you never had any complaints in the past.'

'Well, now you come to mention it—'

'Skip it, Johnny. If you want hearts and flowers then go screw a string quartet in a florist.'

'All I want—'

'And all *I* want,' said Thorn, staring at him, 'is to be left to do my make-up in peace. Do you have any idea how hard it is to apply kohl properly when you're surrounded by a debating society?'

Johnny made some phone calls while Thorn painted away. He spoke to his mother in Lowell, Harald O. in Manhattan and then he dialled the number of the room next door. Then he put the phone down. He didn't want to talk to Dave Pepper just yet.

He sat facing the television but watching Thorn make the mirror do her bidding. She took out a grey phial and shook two canary yellow pills into her hand.

'I'll get you that Perrier water,' he said, dialling the servants.

'Vitamin C,' she explained.

'Very good for your bones,' Johnny nodded approvingly.

Room service in the shape of a dark pretty French girl – Thorn snooted her – slipped Perrier water and strawberry daiquiri silently into the room.

Thorn swallowed the pills. She flashed her eyes from the mirror to Johnny Sangster and back again. 'There. I'm ready.'

He saw that she was asking his opinion even though well aware of how good she looked. He was touched. 'Sensational,' he said, crosing the room to her and taking her out of the black dress.

Johnny pushed her down on all fours and greased her with Vaseline. He thought maybe it had hurt her too much, maybe that was the trouble. He got behind her and hooked it up, slamming his groin against her ass until he shuddered and came with his arms wrapped tightly around her waist and his cheek pressed against her spine. 'I've never known a girl like you, Thorn. I'm crazy about you. Can't you see—'

Thorn turned and looked at him, quizzically, and Johnny shut up.

Later he fucked her in the shower with the hot water turned on full blast and the steam rising up all around them, face to face, one on one, Thorn pressed up against the wet marble and Johnny pressed up against Thorn. The gushing water, thank God, almost blotted out the sound of her voice bitching about her ruined make-up.

He turned off the water and tried to kiss her on the mouth. She turned away.

He was ready to cry.

'Sssh, don't do that, Johnny. Come on, let's you and me dry each other off and drink our drinks and do our make-up and go to bed.'

They slipped between the crisp sheets, her toting her tool box. She looked at herself and he looked at her.

Johnny was sore and exhausted and more down than he'd

been when he lost to Velez in the Italian Open. In fact he was more down, now he came to think of it, than he had been since last year on his twentieth birthday. The last time she evaded him.

Thorn held out her arms and he went to her gratefully. He lay there in her arms feeling like an ecstatic wretch. Why was everything so weird all of a sudden?

'It's not your fault,' she said.

'What do you mean?'

'It's me, Johnny.'

'I don't believe you. You're just saying that.'

'To boost your ego? What am I, a *bimbo*?'

'What is it then?'

'What do you think?'

'Well, I mean, I don't *know*. Are you a – no, no . . .'

'Think real hard, Johnny.'

'Don't you *like* sex?'

'I will when I'm famous.'

'Oh.' He snuggled deeper into her arms. Johnny Sangster could understand that. He smiled at her, touching her face. It was certainly an improvement on the Sherry Ward method acting close-your-eyes-and-think-of-your-career-opportunities school. He was relieved, most of all, that it wasn't *him* who was out of synch. 'What will you do now? Stay in Paris and model for someone a little more successful than old Twist?'

She shook her head, knowledgeable. 'Fashion is finished here, all washed up – I reckon any model that bases herself here is finished, too. Oh, you can make a packet if you're one of the chosen few – chosen *two*. Marie Helvin, Jerry Hall, fame by association, you know. But they only come here for a couple of weeks – literally – every year, to cash in. And boy do they cash in! But if you're unknown, all you can hope for is pin money and maybe a husband, if you're a sexual gymnast.'

'And you're not interested in any of that.'

'Oh, no, Johnny, that's my ambition – make my pile of pin money, buy a copy of the Karma Sutra and waltz down the aisle with Mr Right!'

'Then where will you go? Back to the States?'

'Eventually,' Thorn said. 'There's some unfinished business I have to attend to in Manhattan. It will have to be seen to sooner or later.'

'Modelling?' Johnny asked. 'Modelling business, Thorn?'

'That's it, Johnny.' Jeez, he's a sweet kid, she thought. Too bad he's so stuck on me. We could have got along fine. 'But right now I want to work in London. I hear they're mad about American models over there. We're supposed to be hard-working, efficient, punctual – we're meant to be regular Girl Guides, in fact.'

He laughed, thinking of her in a blue uniform.

'And of course, the streets of London usurped the catwalks of Paris a long time ago. Late seventies. Whatever clothes those London kids are wearing – punk, Mod, Two Tone, swashbuckling, whatever – it will invariably show up in some swishy Paris salon about eighteen months later. All the Paris designers are old men living on young men's crumbs. Who needs it?' She had surprised herself; she had convinced herself.

'I'm going to London.'

'When?'

'Tomorrow. Why don't you come with me?'

'What? Well! I can't just . . I mean, I have to—'

'Of *course* you can come! I'll be there for six weeks.'

'Isn't that a long time for you to stay in one place?' It was beginning to seem feasible.

'I've got three tournaments there – Queen's, the Metalon-Fabey Challenge and Wimbledon—'

'Oh, the big one. Must be, it's the only one I know of.'

'Come with me, Thorn. We'll have six weeks together and then I'll see you back in the States when you're ready. Who knows? Maybe you'll be ready to leave after six weeks!' Johnny smiled broadly, his eyes shining at the thought of it all, all the days and nights.

'Ease up, Johnny. I didn't say *yes* yet.'

His face fell. 'You should think about it, at least.'

She didn't speak.

'Thorn?'

'Ok, I'll think about it.'

'Sleep on it. Let me know what you want in the morning.'

'I'll do that, Johnny.'

He curled up like a contented embryo and soon drifted off into a deep, dreamless sleep.

Thorn finished her face and her Perrier water. By that time

she was sure he was asleep. She got out of bed, dressed herself and closed Johnny Sangster's hotel room door very quietly on her way out.

The taxi dropped her off outside the rue de Babylone hotel. The birds were singing and the pills were working. She paid the driver and looked up at Cuba's window. Her lights were on. Thorn's heart soared and she felt like serenading her. Instead she went up and knocked.

Cuba opened the door quickly. She was bright eyed and flushed in places you wouldn't put blusher. Thorn could've sworn she was on speed if Cuba hadn't been so square.

'I've been expecting you, kid,' said Cuba, but she didn't step aside.

'Couldn't you sleep?'

'Not tonight.'

'That's not like you.'

'I'm not feeling myself tonight.'

Thorn saw that Cuba was not alone. On the bed sat a big black man in a business suit. He was dressed too sharp to be anything in the fashion industry. *He* must be the stimulant, thought Thorn. A slight indentation on the eiderdown beside him told her he and Cuba had been holding hands, or worse.

She looked at Cuba. 'I'm sorry, I thought you were alone.'

'Oh, this is business,' gestured Cuba. The black man smiled. 'I'm glad to see you, Thorn. Thorn Sayre – Oscar Washington.'

The black man smiled coldly at the Southern belle.

'Hi there,' she said.

'I'm glad to see you, Thorn, because I've got to say goodbye.' Oscar Washington smiled; he was obviously pleased with the way Cuba had learned her lesson. 'I'm leaving for New York City as soon as it gets light. I've got to sign a contract.'

'I don't – what? You're going to be a contract girl for some cosmetic house?' But you're *black*. Thorn felt an angry pang of envy; Johnny Sangster's sperm trickled down her thigh and made her want to retch, to cap it all.

'No, no, a recording contract. Three tailor-made singles by Mr Washington here – if I get two *Billboard* Top Fifty hits I get a seven year contract. Singles, albums, *Soul Train*, the works.'

'But you can't sing!'

Cuba coughed. She stretched her neck. Then she sang *'Oh say, can you see, by the dawn's early light—'* Her voice was stunning, sweet and true.

Oscar Washington laughed uproariously, and he applauded.

'I see.' Thorn shook her head. 'Now I see.'

Cuba grabbed her and kissed her, cool and passionate, and closed the door.

Cuba sang. Oscar laughed. Thorn packed.

When she awoke it was morning and she had the bed to herself. She could hear the *tennis player* in the bathroom as she reached for the phial.

It wasn't there.

She rummaged frantically through her clutch bag but they weren't there. She padded desperately to the bathroom door.

Johnny Sangster gave her a sly smile. 'Vitamin C. Really, Thorn.' He had the phial in his hand.

'You stole that.'

He gave her the phial. It was empty.

'You lousy creep! What have you done with—'

He was peering down the toilet bowl. Thorn joined him and her worst suspicions were confimed. There they were, her canary yellow treasures, surrounded by soggy, shreddy toilet roll and floating on top of the water.

Johnny flushed the toilet. The package disappeared for a moment under the torrent of water and then surfaced. 'Damn this French plumbing,' he murmured.

'What are you *doing*?' Thorn yelled. 'Who the hell gave you—'

'You're not carrying illegal drugs through customs at Heathrow,' Johnny said. 'They got guys trained to spot users a mile away. They'll take one look at you and *queue* to strip search you.' He smiled shyly. 'I know *I* would.'

'Well, Johnny Sangster, you can just stick your compliments up your ass and your hand down that john. *Give me those pills*!'

His face was serious. 'I'm sorry, Thorn, but we just can't risk it.'

'*I'll* take the fucking risk, *pal*.'

'No.'

'What—'

Johnny flushed the toilet once more. This time the pills vanished. Thorn couldn't believe the nerve of the bastard. She swung a fist vaguely in the direction of the Sangster solar plexus. 'You weird bastard! What are you – on some sick fucking *health kick*? Who the hell do you think you are to pull this crap with me?'

'My, my, Miz Sayre, youse talking jes' like some white trash.' Johnny laughed at her, then smiled tenderly. 'Relax. You don't need this stuff if you're with me.'

'Oh?' She sneered at him. 'How's that? Are we going to be high as kites on life itself? Is that it? Huh?'

'No. I get this stuff on prescription.'

The telephone rang and Dave Pepper told his boy that the car was waiting.

# nine

From the June 1983 issue of *Tennis Circuit*

SANGSTER – SON OF SUPERBRAT

***Adam Harrison reporting on the young American who won Queens but lost a lot of friends in the process.***

The curly-haired young man in the red track suit sits spinning a steel tennis racquet in one of the large leather armchairs the Queens Club reserves for its members.

A few hours ago he won the tournament the Circuit sees as the traditional warm-up for Wimbledon. A few hours ago he also won himself the dubious honour of shooting up the tennis world's rankings of rotters to become Public Enemy Number One. With clinical savagery this young man destroyed his fellow countryman Raymundo Velez in straight sets. With frequent eruptions of his violent temper, he had the normally sedate Queens crowd calling for the return of capital punishment.

It hardly seems possible that the white tiger on court and the pleasant boy in the armchair are one and the same person.

*Are you a Jekyll and Hyde character, Johnny?*
'I think I'm more of a Superman and Clark Kent character,' Johnny Sangster grins.

*You seemed terribly angry in the final against Velez.*

'That's because a lot of the calls I was getting were pretty terrible themselves.'

*In the press box I heard several journalists comparing you to Ilie Nastase. Do you think that's a valid comparison?*
His boyish good looks grow serious. 'That's garbage,' he says tersely. 'Towards the later part of his career, Nastase made the tantrums more important to his game than his groundstrokes were. He became a comic turn, not so much a tennis player, more Bobo the Clown. I think he got that way because he never fulfilled his potential, he never won the big tournaments he was expected to win. Sad, sad.'

*But surely you can see the similarities between the way you behaved today and what made Nastase famous?*
Johnny Sangster sighs, shakes his head, sips his strawberry daiquiri. 'Maybe you've got to be a pro to appreciate the difference. Maybe you just got to open your eyes. But the way I behaved out there today was simply because somebody else's incompetence was costing me points. Valuable points. I'm a professional. This is what I *do*, this is my *job*. It's like John McEnroe. Exactly the same. Bad line calls make you mad and you react normally and the crowd gets on your case like you're Attila the lousy *Hun* or something.'

*Is winning the only thing that matters to you?*
'I do what I do for pleasure and profit. The more I win, the more I get of both. But don't confuse reacting normally to bad line calls with the desire to win. Reacting to dumb calls is not about winning and losing. It's about *right* and *wrong*, it's about the pursuit of justice.'

*So you and McEnroe earned your notoriety in the pursuit of justice?*
'That's right,' he smiles. 'Maybe I chase it a little faster than McEnroe – I'm a lot younger than he is, you know.'

*How's the leg injury you sustained at the Italian open?*
'Oh, that's fine now, thanks.'

*What treatment did you have on it?*
'Ice treatment and cream massage and the shots, you know.'

*There's a lot of players on the Circuit with injuries these days. Why do you think that is?*
'The promoters keep putting up the prize money.'
A beautiful blonde girl enters the room, turning every head, looking for someone special. She is Fawn Sayre, a Southern Belle who works as a famous Paris model. She is travelling with Johnny.

*So how does the temperamental number nine feel about wedding bells?*
'Sorry,' the Son of Superbrat chuckles with humour straight from the locker room, 'but you're not my type.'

The interview is over. It is time for me to leave. Johnny Sangster is distracted, he only has eyes for his stunning girlfriend. The svelte Fawn tells me she has to take the controversial young pro to a practise session.

*Finally, then, Johnny, how do you think your Wimbledon will be this year?*

'Oh, my Wimbledon will be much the same as usual, I guess,' he grins. And when Johnny Sangster talks about his *usual* Wimbledon you know you can expect strawberries and cream.

And plenty of fireworks.

'Oh, *fuck* it,' spat Johnny Sangster. 'The jerk spelt her name wrong!'

'What?' Dave Pepper looked at him through narrowed eyes. 'What are you? Her agent or something?'

Johnny tossed the disgraced copy of *Tennis Circuit* on to his hotel double bed. He looked at his coach. 'You don't like her, do you?'

'Whether I like or dislike *her* doesn't really come into it. This has nil to do with personalities. I'm just considering her effect on you, John.'

'Her effect on me? Or on my game?'

'Oh, don't give me that crap, not *you*. You know as well – *better* than I do that the two are inseparable.' Dave Pepper picked up the magazine and shook his head wonderingly. 'This is supposed to be a piece of writing about *you*, for Chrissakes! What's all this Southern Belle lovebirds bullshit? This rag is supposed to be a *tennis* paper! What's all this moonlight and roses rubbish doing in it?'

'It's half a dozen lines, Dave. You're being ridiculous. It's human interest and it *sells*. Besides which I'm proud if people know I go with Thorn.'

'They're trying to make the Circuit into a damn soap opera.'

'It's been happening for years, Dave, and it was the players themselves who mixed it up. Evert and Connors. Borg and Simonesceau. And the rest. Think of all the famous faces you've seen going up and down in Circuit hotel elevators lately. The Circuit is stranger than soap and more gripping than bland old Hollywood – the press just let the public have a little taste now and then to keep them panting and paying out. If they knew the truth, they wouldn't believe it.'

'Ok, skip it. I can see how the circulation figures climb at the scent of a little *romance*. You kids get paid too much to get away with not being *personalities*.' Dave Pepper smiled, for the first time he almost *sneered* at Johnny Sangster. 'But, oh *John*, you can do better than *her*.'

'Watch what you say about Thorn Sayre,' Johnny said quietly, 'I'm serious.'

'I've got nothing against the girl *personally*—'

'What? I've never heard you attempt a civil conversation with her. You just grunt and turn white, you just make your excuses and leave.'

'If I can't conduct a civil conversation with someone, for whatever reason, then I'd rather say nothing.' Dave Pepper looked pious and put upon.

'But you don't mind talking about her behind her back.'

'It's for your own *good*, John. She—'

'Her name is *Thorn*, Dave.'

'*Thorn* is all wrong for you, John. She's not stupid, she's not a bimbo, far from it. Don't misunderstand me. But she's a bright young girl on the make. Extremely beautiful and extremely unsuccessful.'

'In Paris—'

'Screw Paris. Success is at least national and success starts at home, like charity. She's an American girl and no one back home ever heard of her. And that's where she – Thorn – wants to make her mark and her money. And you're her coast to coast ticket. America. If you can make it there, you can make it anywhere.'

'It's not like that anymore, Dave. The rest of the world caught us up. Some countries have gone right past us. I been around. The Arabs are richer and the Russians are stronger—'

'Bullshit.'

'I been around. Why, even over here some of the banks won't accept US beads and bits of broken mirror anymore.'

'The girl you want is not some gorgeous hustler,' Dave Pepper insisted.

'Careful what you say.'

'What do you think a girl like that will *do* to you? Even if you try to help her become an actress—'

'You know that's a *model*, you bastard.'

'—then you'll have to give up more of your valuable time than you can afford. Just to give her the leg up she's expecting – that's *expecting* – from you, John.'

'Sure. Now listen. I've never known *less* of a hustler than Thorn Sayre. She turned me down and left the country last year. Now, that really sounds like she wanted to use me. She never *speaks* to any of the guys, she *never* tries to get on the right side of *anyone*. That's a very odd way for a *hustler* to act.'

'She's biding her time.'

'Now, Sherry Ward, Dave, *there's* a hustler for you. Rich and hell bent on getting richer. One big pig of a girl, a real glutton. She slept with me so her lousy bio wouldn't be a turkey, for God's sake. And I thought I was doing the using! I'd know if Thorn was a hustler, Dave, I'd recognize the moves. I got them all down pat myself.'

'John, John.' Dave was solicitous. 'You're twenty now. A nice age for a mechanic but not especially hot for a professional athlete. It goes so fast, John. Believe me. Ten years time it'll be all over for you. For life. Finished. No more winning.'

'Laver and Rosewell were world beaters past thirty,' Johnny said sullenly.

'Laver and Rosewell were not playing the Circuit in the Eighties. The career expectancy of the tennis pro is considerably shorter these days. Hell, by thirty you're all too rich and too tired to lift a racquet.'

'So what you want me to do? Stay celibate? That was last year's thing, Dave.'

'John. You're normal and healthy and I wouldn't have it any other way. I'm advising you to find a girl that will be *good* for you – and you can wipe that dirty smirk off your mug for a start.'

'I can't believe you're acting like this, Dave. You're a cross between a moral tutor and a jailer. You're not my fucking keeper – *I* keep *you*, in fact. So just forget it, huh?'

'Somebody's got to do your thinking for you, John, until your brain comes back from lunch. Look at Raul Ramirez – he's engaged to that beautiful ex-Miss Universe, Maritza Sayalero. Tom, Tom Dougherty, he's got the *reigning* Miss Universe, Francesca what's her name. They all seem happy.'

'So? What am *I* supposed to do? Wait for next year's Miss Universe parade and bag the winner?'

'Look at Jimmy Connors – married to Patti Macguire, she

was a *Playmate Of The Year*! A beautiful simple girl. They got a kid now. A boy.'

'You sound like my mother, Dave.'

'I sound like sense and you don't like that. The point is that all those boys got girls who've arrived at where they're going. They've had some small bit of glory and they can give it up with a good heart. Not like your Thorn. She'll sap your energy and your ambition, she'll eat up your time and thoughts and *push*. She'll slow you down, John. *She's got dreams of her own.* You've got *eight more* geeks to beat before you're *number one in the entire world*. How bad do you want that, John?'

'I want her, too,' Johnny said quietly. 'I want it all. And I'll get it. You'll soon see.'

'Or get yourself a nice contented little girl who never wanted to go anywhere in the first place. Like Ray Velez' little Lupe. *She'll* never get in his way . . .'

'Yeah, she's a great little girl. She's on my payroll, you know. She's busy boring Velez to death.'

'Lupe is *restful*. Just right for a pro to come home to. Back to the hotel to. Couldn't you try a girl like that for a while, a girl from your hometown maybe? All I want is the best for you, John. That's all.'

'Thorn's the best for me. She's the best there is.' He looked at his coach shyly, determined to show him how wrong he was. 'I think I definitely feel something . . . *special* towards her. You know what I mean, Dave?'

Dave Pepper nodded. 'Where is the lucky girl right now? Out shoplifting?'

Johnny's eyes grew cold. 'Plotting the downfall of the house of Sangster, I bet. Working out weird ways to wreck my brilliant career. Like Samson and Delilah, the bitch.'

'John. I can see how much you like her. But—'

'Ok, enough. When I need a nanny I'll hang out a white flag. Be a coach or be someone else's wet nurse. Someone who needs you.'

Dave Pepper looked old and drawn. 'You can get to the top all by yourself, John. It's a fact. I'm only trying to give you some good advice. Like you was my own . . .'

Johnny put his hand on a hunched shoulder. 'I ain't a kid anymore, Dave.'

'No, no. You never were.'

'And I ain't your own. Or anybody else's. So shut your mouth and let's go endure Harald. I got to earn your wages, old man!'

Dave Pepper smiled wanly.

They drove to the London offices of Global Management Enterprises, a baronial Georgian house bordering Regent's Park. Johnny checked that London still looked the same, bright and calm, a nice place to lie low in. If you ever had to lie low. Like Lucky Lindbergh.

The aura of elegant grandeur was shattered the moment they entered the building. The house's interior had been completely gutted and converted into a riot of stripped pine, shag pile, elevators, English secretaries, fluorescent lighting and false ceilings. Johnny gazed around and snickered at Dave Pepper. Dave Pepper was admiring the depth of the carpet pile.

They found Harald O. Holden up in the penthouse suite wheedling into a white telephone to Geneva and screaming into a black telephone to Manhattan while trying to fluster the cool English secretaries with an ill-tempered stream of contradictory instructions.

He saw them and looked fleetingly ashamed of himself. Then he smiled bravely, like a mighty mogul at bay, and slammed the telephones down. He came out from behind his massive oak desk, his hands raised importantly and his teeth gleaming wetly through a shark's smile.

He gripped John's hand and pumped it frenziedly. 'Johnny, Johnny. It's damn good to see you, son!'

'Hello, Harald.'

'I take it you've seen the new rankings?' boasted Dave.

'You betcha, baby!' leered Holden. 'Isn't it swell? Isn't it great, Johnny? Boy, I bet your mother's proud of you. And Dad too! How you feeling, son? Tip top? One hundred per cent? Ready to whip their asses at Wimbledon? The championship of the world, for Pete's sake! How you feeling, huh?'

'Sweaty, Harald.'

'Huh?'

'Your hand is mangy with sweat, Harald.'

'Gee, Johnny, let me wipe that for you.' Holden fussed over Johnny with a handkerchief the size of a tablecloth. It bore the proud boast HOH in gold flake and it looked none too clean. Johnny pushed him away and took a seat. Holden barked demands for refreshment for his guests. A siren from the

Shires filled their glasses with their orders with the air of a Hon. giving alms to the poor. She favoured Johnny with a smile.

'Attaboy!' wheezed Holden. It mattered not that Johnny was in a world of his own and that the secretary was closing the door on her way out. His mind was intent upon its dirty dream. Mechanically he reeled off a list of the cities in which he had sealed deals since leaving Manhattan a week ago. 'Hamburg – boy oh boy! – Tokyo – them geishes – Sydney – big blondes – a quiet weekend in Vegas then the Big Orange, Paris and London.' He twinkled behind his thick-lensed spectacles. 'International representation, protecting our clients' interests and making them thrive. We pay your taxes and feed your pets, we negotiate your contracts and navigate your career to balmy waters. We all profit, we all get a – heh heh – blow job from capitalism. They said it wouldn't last!'

'My boy is number nine now, Harald.'

'Don't I know it better than anyone? I've been out there fighting for you, Johnny. I've been on the defensive – income conservation and management – turning prize money into smart money, investing wisely and wiping away unwanted tax liabilities. And I've been on the offensive too, Johnny – exploiting your new status to the full – letting the reams of giant size offers roll in. That's income generation. That's the way the money grows.'

'How much am I worth now? Now I'm in the top ten?'

Holden smiled beatificially. 'Double everything. Blessed are those with product to endorse.'

The console on his desk buzzed and he flicked a switch. 'They're all here, Mr Holden.'

'Send them in.'

Five men filed into the office. Harald O. Holden made the introductions and the drinks. All five were the fiscal type and treated Johnny Sangster with the reverential greed that he had watched intensify every time his star ascended. The five men shook hands with Dave Pepper as if he was a valuable statue that belonged to the guest of honour.

Holden set up what looked like an artist's easel made of stainless steel, puffing and panting enthusiastically. Then he flourished a huge portfolio and pulled out a sheave of graphs. Holden coughed importantly. The five took their eyes off their prey, Johnny Sangster.

'Gentlemen. It is twelve months since we met. My client's current commercial commitments to your companies' products will soon terminate and new terms have to be negotiated. Before I give you Global Management's yearly report on our client I would ask you to identify yourselves.'

'But we were already introduced,' objected one of the five.

'He doesn't mean your *name*,' another hissed impatiently. 'He means the company you represent and the product that, um, Johnny endorses for you.'

'Just to refresh my client's mind,' Holden said. He stared at Johnny, his small myopic eyes shining with sly pride. 'Of course, my client always *experiences* the product he endorses, *personally* and *thoroughly*, before allowing his name to be borrowed.' He looked at the five men boldly, as if expecting some madman to dispute this lie. 'Just refresh his memory. From the left, if you please.'

A smooth-featured Englishman, dapper in black mohair and his late thirties smiled at Johnny coldly. 'Remember me? Last year at Wimbledon? Oh, you must meet so many – I'm Lawrence Gilkes of Havington, Johnny. The product that you endorse for us is – let me see – I'm as vague about it as you are.'

Holden shot him a filthy look. Lawrence Gilkes blithely fished in his briefcase.

'Ah, here we are – Havington shirts, shorts, shoes, wristbands and a Havington arm patch. And we're all very pleased—'

'Next,' Harald barked.

A heavy-set German with cropped white hair licked his lips and seemed uncertain as to whether he should address himself to Harald O. Holden or Johnny Sangster. Holden smiled encouragement. Johnny looked up from his strawberry daiquiri and stared at the man with mild interest.

'I am Martin Schwarz,' he finally said, and closed his eyes in thought. 'For us, for us at Eisen-Kinder Leisure Facilities, your client endorses stereo, video, track suit, running shoes, weights, sweatbands, Ace tennis balls, Wunderkind tennis racquet, Johnny Sangster jocks and socks sets and, of course, the Johnny Sangster doll.'

'Of course,' Johnny nodded.

'Don't knock it,' said Harald, and laughed too loud for it to pass as an amiable witticism.

Martin Schwarz stared blandly from Johnny to Holden.

'Actually, the doll sells badly. We will drop it.'

'What?' Johnny sat up straight in his chair. 'Harald, can they do that?'

'Sure. Don't worry, Johnny, I'll rescue a dolly for you!' Harald looked at him bitterly.

Johnny slouched back down. He cursed himself for trying to be smart. He cursed the Johnny Sangster dolly for selling badly. He cursed Dave Pepper for being out of his depth, for being no protection against these plebians. Money not only talks, it *gags* the listener.

'Hi, there, Johnny boy,' boomed a fat man with a red face and a Stetson that perched on his ugly head like a defiant gesture. A sticker declaring I AM A REDNECK couldn't have communicated the wearer's wishes better. 'Jim Coe Junior. Personal representative these past eleven years at Bandolero-Matchplay of Houston. You give your seal of approval to our Bandolero-Matchplay steel racquet. And it's a mother, let me tell you.'

'I hope the little racquets are doing well,' Dave Pepper murmured. Johnny looked at him, humourless. A bit late *now*.

A youngish blond looked at Johnny with the synthetic bonhomie that thrives better than a bunch of grapes in Southern California. He was dressed in noncommital beige and a shirt that screamed. London in the springtime gave him goose pimples. His yellow thatch was thinning fast but what he lacked in hair he made up for in cornflake-coloured scalp. 'I'm Francis Salinger of Metalon-Fabey. Hi, Johnny. *Loved* the commercial you did for us to *death*. Let's see – I've got it right here in my head – for us you endorse cologne, shampoo, after-shave, talcum powder, suntan lotion and the Metalon-Fabey face pack for the outdoor man.'

'Does that stuff sell?' Johnny had to ask. 'That – last one.'

'Mostly in San Francisco.'

'Oh.'

Holden nodded at the last of the five.

He was an immaculate Japanese man of fifty or so with smooth skin and rimless glasses, gold rings on his fingers and a watch bearing the proud image of Mickey Mouse on his wrist.

'Charlie Hang, Mr Sangster. Personal representative for Tora Sports and Games. You have been gracious enough to give your good name to the promotion of the Tora Matchplay tennis racquet, the Tora hamburger chain, the Tora Space

Invaders game and five flavours of Tora bubblegum.'

Johnny shrugged and smiled at the polite little guy. 'Fine. Sounds colourful.'

'Thank you,' Holden intoned. He pointed at the graphs charting the profits that the five companies had mostly enjoyed during the past year as Johnny Sangster climbed through the rankings, and people all over the world acknowledged his notoriety by blessing most of the product that carried his famous name with millions of dollars. 'You will note, gentlemen, that the player's progress is at an all time high. At number nine on the ATP computer world rankings. I should think with the fast court here at Wimbledon that we can expect to go even higher by the end of the summer. Johnny?'

'Fingers crossed,' said Johnny gamely.

'The green line on this final graph charts Johnny's meteoric rise through the world rankings. The climbing black line indicates your profit margins from product endorsed by my client.'

'How did you get those figures?' asked Salinger.

'The point where the green and black lines meet is what we at Global call our client's lifeline. Johnny's lifeline has never been healthier. You gentlemen are being honoured with the chance to share in Mr Sangster's rude health.'

The five men stared at the serene Holden.

'If your companies choose to take a raincheck, don't worry about leaving us on the shelf.' Holden grinned smugly. 'There's plenty more of you waiting nervously in the wings. We're not going to be wallflowers. Please don't worry about our welfare.'

'How much extra will it cost us?' Martin Schwarz asked.

'Treble it,' Holden breathed.

Gilkes groaned. Jim Junior buried his hat in his hands. Salinger's eye began to twitch uncontrollably.

'You shit, Harald Holden,' spat Charlie Hang. 'Oh, you evil little shit. What are you going to do now? You've got us by the balls, you little shit. What are you going to do now?'

'Squeeze,' Holden said, touching Johnny on the back of the neck the way his mother used to do.

Johnny smiled uncertainly. No matter how much money he was making, he never really felt comfortable off court.

Never take money from a man you're not married to. When you've hooked him, though, *bleed* him.

That was one of Mama Sayre's commandments. Thorn had mannequin money in her pocket, so when Johnny Sangster tried to force a fistful of American Express travellers cheques on her she pulled away protesting. He insisted.

Do traveller's cheques count, Mama?

American Express? That's different, my darling daughter.

'Listen, you were nineteen when we met and you're twenty now. I missed your birthday. I regret that. The twentieth birthday is the only one that hurts. So take this stuff, go on. Buy yourself another black dress. I'll see you later. I've got to do some business and I've got to get a couple of hours on grass.'

'On what?'

'Grass, that's the surface at Wimbledon. I've got to get the feel of it.'

'I see.'

'So take this . . . happy birthday, Thorn.' He stared at her uncertainly, not sure if she'd let him kiss her on the lips in the lobby of the Grosvenor. Thorn brushed her mouth against his, enough to make his heart skip one stung beat but not enough to blot her lip colour.

Then she went shopping.

Tom Dougherty also had business and practice to attend to. It was just like some insurance office dinner dance, Thorn thought. Segregated by gender, all the little women expected to chitter chatter and get along like new found friends at summer camp. It beats hanging around a tennis court anyhow, she reflected, rubbing the roll of pounds sterling safe in her raincoat pocket. She followed Miss Universe into the back of a black London cab. She wanted to jump back out and rub her face all over the glossy paint – it was a beauty, like a hearse going somewhere exciting. She smiled and folded her hands in her lap.

As the cab cut up Arabs and tore down Park Lane, Francesca gave Thorn a delighted, dazzling smile. She was a black-haired beauty who had left her Naples slum two years ago at the age of fifteen, that day when a fat rich man saw her, wept and whisked her right the way round the world. Her mother didn't mind – she had eight more children, all of them beautiful, all of them useless.

Somehow Francesca found herself in South Korea at seventeen wearing a rhinestone crown. The satellite beamed her beatific smile all over the world, right into Tom Dougherty's

Tokyo Holiday Inn solitude. He was reaching for the telephone before the first tear streaked her eye-black.

Francesca shivered deliciously. She was simply ecstatic to be out of the slums and the clutches and wearing designer jeans. Everything else – the title, the tennis player, the money in her pocket and the city at her feet – was a bonus.

This girl will never be unhappy, Thorn decided. Her career has been settled out of court.

'Eye-spreez, pleaze,' Francesca murmured at the cab driver. 'West One.' West One; lazy uptown. Manhattan with manners. Asprey's; a wanton 'open sesame'. Five floors full of millions of millions of dollar's worth of Faberge bibelots, white gold, silver baby rattles, lapis lazuli snuff boxes, gold toothbrushes, Victorian walking sticks, rubies, Limoges eggs, a jewelled Hungarian sabre all the way from 1848, mahogany, Baccarat crystal. Thorn narrowed her eyes and Francesca squealed.

The Neapolitan bought lots of red coral for her neck, a magnetic travelling backgammon board in a leather case for her mind and a silk umbrella for show. A svelte silent girl wrapped Francesca's thrills in purple paper; Thorn was transfixed, yearning through glass at a supreme *sautoir*, pearls and diamonds set in platinum.

'Excuse me . . . how much does the *sautoir* cost?'

'Eight thousand nine hundred and fifty pounds. It's 1920s.'

'Ah. I see. Thank you.' Thorn turned her face away to hide her florid fury.

Gucci. *Grisly.*

Everything in the shop bore a green-red-green stripe and the initials GG. Towels, perfume, pret-à-porter, fountain pens, all *branded* with the wrong name. You'd have to have a bad case of disappearing ego to wear any of these *commercials*, thought Thorn.

Francesca snapped up some Gucci loafers – Thorn thought they looked tacky Taiwan counterfeit – and a camel hair sweater for Dougherty. Francesca spent four times as much money on the sweater as she did on her shoes!

True Love (Thorn wanted to puke.)

'You don't want to buy, Forrrn?'

'Not my style.'

Francesca shook her head and smiled.

Janet Reger . . . lingerie to linger in, not so much a shop, more a sin bin. Francesca bought miles of oyster satin – underwired brassieres, French knickers, suspender belts, cami-knickers and negligees. Thorn hesitated, then ordered the same in black lace. She couldn't resist it. She would never wear a *bra* beneath her *clothes* – but she could imagine many magnificent hours spent admiring the deathly glamour of black lace against her white skin in front of some mirror.

Francesca giggled in her ear. 'That will bring out the best in Johnny! Or do I mean the *beast*?'

Thorn wanted to vomit. You coy cow, she sneered, smiling at Francesca. Francesca was statuesque and sweet and she bored Thorn senseless. Sweet as a sugar cube and twice as square.

Out on the sidewalk the Virginian slipped into the slick teeming hordes as though they were a warm bath. Ciao, bambino.

Thorn stared about her hungrily. Miss Pizza was gone and the show was on. Big red buses, more buses than people practically. Grass all over the place, enough grass to keep Johnny Sangster busy forever. Primary colours and plain folk.

Thorn fell in love with London the first time she asked for directions. 'Excuse me, madam? I want to go to Chelsea.'

The Londoners looked so steeped in nostalgic isolation as they got around their sprawling citadel, as if each one of them carried the weight of the world recession of their shoulders. But when some lost polite stranger approached them for directions they immediately came alive, men and women, young and old, black and white alike, smiling with reserved glee at this chance encounter, only too delighted to take the waif under their protection as fair exchange for a little human contact. They pointed Thorn in the right direction and didn't even tell her to have a nice day.

They looked cold in their eternal queues, but the people of London were blushing jelly beneath the ice that somebody else had to break. Thorn could at last understand why so many Europeans stared at camera-clicking American archetypes – and America was definitely a country under a plague of archetypes, God help it – with silent contempt.

On cue a sub-human voice screamed, 'Lemmee take a pick-chure!'

Thorn hurried on.

Uncle Sam's sightseeing, snowblind masses poured over Europe in their millions each year – this pretty little city had to suffer ten million tourists per annum! – *positive* that the continent was just one huge alfresco historical mausoleum, a quaint fancy dress sideshow existing solely for *their* benefit and photo album.

*As though nobody lives there.*

Everything that was horrible about Americans came out fighting in their abroad voices. Just so LOUD – a hysterical, destructive loudness that had no roots and nothing to say and hated being that way yet was too pigheaded to change.

Thank Dixie for your honeypot of a Virginia drawl, she pampered herself. Why, I just bet you talk *so* soft, *so* un-American that you could pass for a European anywhere. The thought made her feel slick and superior. She stalked down the King's Road, and even there, sober in a trenchcoat, she made jaded tongues flick out over dry lips. She felt the street *swing*, and she strutted with it, enjoying this wide and watchable catwalk.

Music blasted out momentarily from boutiques and drugstores and then changed tempo with just one giant step of hers, like an impatient hand driving a radio from station to station.

Finally she found Anthony Price's arrogant plain glass front. Inside the bare mirrored temple she thought she had literally died and gone to heaven. She gazed at the almost grotesque glamour that screeched back shocking pink and electric blue, slick and sleek, and she knew she had to buy everything. A brown boy fetched and carried and flirted stylishly with her. Thorn looked around. She had hoped to see Anthony Price – no, to let Anthony Price see *her* – but when she'd poured herself into a shiny, slender Schiaperelli pink rumba dress and dared to look in the mirror, she knew that her eyes needed to look on nothing else. She was so beautiful, she could . . . no, I can't cry here, she scolded herself, blinking the water away. Thorn didn't trust herself to look in the mirror again; she scrambled out of the swanky mode and shrugged on her raincoat. It broke her heart to look at her perfection, because she knew that glamour would never be the norm again, that glamour would always be a gimmick, that onlookers would think she was on some wacky Hollywood kitsch kick when they saw her in these clothes, these beautiful clothes that summed up so starkly just how tough and sharp and transient she, Thorn Sayre, was.

She wanted to be buried in these clothes. Instead she paid for them all and led them away, not looking back at the mirage.

She caught a cab to Covent Garden; sterile and arty and self-regarding, Greenwich Village purged. She slunk into The Dance Centre. Their leotards were so tight that they made the naked body seem overdressed and fussy in comparison. She chose from the twenty-two colours; one Gunmetal, two Fondue Pink, three Black, all French-cut high on the thigh. She bought a black towelling tracksuit; she'd wear it when running for the phone.

Round the corner she cased Clive Shilton's place. She ordered a portfolio, to be appliqued with the letters T and S. A new showcase in a new town. The portfolio would cost more than Monopoly gave you for passing GO, but so what? She caught a cab back to SW1. Cuba had prepared her for Cosmetics à la Carte. 'I know an English model who won't wear anyone else's paint. She tosses me a tube of lipstick now and then. Honest, I'll do anything for a lick of that paint. Their lip gloss, Thorn – I swear, you could eat a hundred enchilados and suck a thousand cocks and that lip gloss stays put! Never before!'

She found a lethally slick red gloss. She selected a shader – Nutmeg – that was an actual true shadow, that tempted out the cheekbones without leaving any tell-tale colour on the cheeks. She found creamy eyeshadow powders in smoke and gold and bold brave black. She invested in a cream tint foundation concocted especially with photographic modelling work in mind. She paid her money and looked around the store. Four girls stood around in old jeans and plaits, dabbling with the make-up palettes and talking in high soft voices. She recognized two of the faces from magazine adverts – she never forgot a photographed face. She guessed the others were things to look at for a living too. Their talk was not of work and health and vitamins and work, but of pets and pop music and parties. They were like lazy pretty high school girls. They acted as if they had all the time in the world. No wonder British photographers preferred professional *Americaines* . . . she took her change, picked up her parcels and skidded out into the street, laughing.

It was glorious to be on the loose on this elaborate stage of a city, this city whose history and beauty contrasted so shatteringly with her own youth and loveliness. New York had cramped her style somewhat, all those skyscrapers . . . nowhere near as good in the flesh – in the brick? – as that skyline was in photographs. The Statue Of Liberty was *green*, too, if the truth be told. French trash.

She bought a *New Standard* just to savour the pleasure of buying a newspaper without using sign language. She read the signs outside of cinemas and was shocked and the destinations on buses and was charmed. Being a model in London would be one long cruise. She would find a good agency, she would start right away.

Well, *almost* right away.

Tonight there was a party.

On the eve of Wimbledon Dave Pepper drove his boy and his boy's practise partner out of the radiant metropolis, down a motorway and into impossibly green countryside until they came to Stockwell Lawn Tennis Club.

Stockwell is the cozy Hertfordshire club of grim weekend players who are something in the City. They take their tennis deadly serious at Stockwell. They have all the equipment credit cards can buy but few of the shots that Mother Nature hands out *gratis*. They suffer from fallen arches, expense acount ulcers and ridiculous headbands.

Once a year they move over – gladly – and moon over the greatest tennis players in the world, who with the practice facilities available to them at the All England Club forever limited and grudging are frantic for work-outs on fast grass courts.

The players show their gratitude to the Stockwell hearties by drinking one drink with them, offering advice on improved services and rejecting the coy whinnying advances of horsey offspring.

The Wimbledon staff could never bring themselves to think of the boys on the Circuit as anything other than hub-cap stealers with hearts of gold, High School punks out on a spree who might get up to all kinds of mischief if not watched carefully. But the Stockwell Lawn Tennis Club treated them as if they'd got off the flight from Olympus.

Which was a little more like it. All the boys *really* wanted was to be left alone to practise in furious peace. There wasn't much room for improvement at this heady strata of the game, but standards had to be maintained.

The players trooped out on to the showcase grass court that lay waiting for them. Johnny ambled on to what his coach liked to call *the rack*, the most punishing test of skill, stamina and character that a pro would ever have to endure. The player on the rack played a one-handed doubles game against a mob-handed duo, the best out of five sets.

Johnny looked across the net at Tom Dougherty and Dave Pepper and then he started winding up his serve.

He couldn't hope to win. That wasn't the point. The goal was to gauge just exactly how hard you could fight back when you were down. They knocked him all over court, they ran him ragged and brought him to his knees. He was bent double and retching up nothing, sweat and bitter tears glistening on his grubby skin. He had had enough. He was exhausted. Sleep, Johnny . . .

'Get up,' Dave Pepper called.

Johnny shook his head numbly.

'Fuck you, John! Get up and fight!'

Johnny got up and it started all over again, only twice as bad. He chased everything down but his arms and legs felt swollen to twice their size. When he got to the ball he slashed it back at those – those *pigs* with a pure screaming hate and devastating accuracy. These sweet shots of revenge gave him the shatterproof bite he needed to push himself right past his level of endurance. This was the purpose of the rack. But as a bonus he was getting red and black dots doing an orbit around his head. The precious moments of raging retribution didn't last long and soon they became rarer and weaker. Sometime before they dried up altogether, Johnny had lost his faculty for coherent thought.

He reeled across the court like a flickering silent comic, nothing left, his eyes crossing crazily. He knew that he was wearing diving boots and he kept trying to get a look at them, but when he looked down everything went black.

'You're not even *trying*!' Dave Pepper bitched. 'Come to the net more! Where's your volley? Leave it in your locker?'

Johnny lifted his steel racquet like a tomahawk and then he collapsed.

Tom Dougherty cleared the net and knelt by his side calmly. 'Johnny? You ok, Johnny?'

'There's nothing wrong with him.' Dave Pepper banged a couple of balls into the net. 'He's just after an Oscar nomination.'

'Fuck . . .' Johnny breathed.

'Get up, John, you jerk! Come on! What would your actress say if she could see you now?'

Johnny hauled himself painfully to his feet. He walked groggily towards his coach and when he reached the net he lunged for Pepper's jugular and felt his fingers sink in. Almost immediately he could feel hands crawling all over him trying to pull him off, someone shouting at him to stop. Tom Dougherty, no doubt. Other players ran over from the practice courts and soon there were enough of them to drag him off Dave Pepper.

Johnny cursed and struggled. They held him tight. It felt good and he relaxed thankfully. He didn't want to kill. He wanted to sleep.

'Let him go, boys,' Dave Pepper bluffed. 'It's all right now.' He smiled at his boy. 'You see, John? You *did* have something left. That's what I was trying to get out of you. That's what the rack's there for. If you want to sock me, go right ahead. But I'd prefer it if you saved it all for tomorrow.'

'You honestly think I'm going to be in any fit shape to play tomorrow after—' Johnny swallowed hard and gestured emotionally.

'I could never doubt it. I'd bet my life on you. Now you go get yourself a shower. I promised Tom here I'd work on his return of serve with him after he was good enough to help me put you on the rack. Don't look at me like that, John. You'll want to thank me when Wimbledon's done.'

Johnny looked at him blankly for a moment before staggering off in the direction of the dressing room. The hot shower washed ten years off him and the cold shower toned ten pounds off him – it felt that way. He climbed sleepily on to the treatment table and closed his eyes. Nearby he heard locker room gossip about the Ladies Doubles and in the distance he listened to that pleasing whipcord whack of perfection. Only a pro could make music like that.

The sounds soothed him. They were more familiar to Johnny Sangster than the sound of his own breathing. The sound of the Circuit. He yawned, rubbed his eyes and slept like a safe baby.

When he awoke Dave Pepper was leaning over him, massaging his legs. They felt better already. Dave smiled down at him with reassuring tenderness. He made Johnny feel like the only winner in the world.

'Don't you worry 'bout a thing, John.'

Johnny closed his eyes happily and listened to the voices of two men, one young, one old, talking, hid away on the other side of the locker room.

He recognized the defeated voice; it was Fish Brady, the old Australian hot shot who had peaked over a decade ago and who still clung to the Circuit like it was a life support machine. Old Fish Brady, yeah, he'd been better than the mess that was the mass. By the time Johnny Sangster was old enough to win, though, old Fish was well past his prime. Thirty-five against unimpeachable seventeen! – but Johnny didn't let the loaded racquet spoil his fun. Beating big Fish by so much when so young was a joy forever, as tangible as any trophy.

'Any tips you can give me at all, Mr Brady,' a young American voice said. 'Anything at all . . .'

'Well, you got to know how to go out there and hit a few or you wouldn't be here, would you, mate?' Fish pointed out, all swaggerman public bar benevolence.

'I don't need any help with my *shots*. I've had them drilled into me since I was five years old.'

I'd know that accent anywhere, Johnny jolted. That's a *Boston* boy. A *country club* cub, for sure. Daddy's probably a lawyer . . .

'Dad's a banker. He would have loved to be a tennis player but banking got in the way so . . .'

Banker, lawyer, wanker, gloated Johnny. Wrong job, right tax bracket. Jeez, are they *still* knocking these kids out back in Massachusetts? I thought I killed their sons years ago . . .

'I'll tell you about Wimbledon,' said Fish Brady. 'It's like Christmas for the English. They love it because they're only allowed it once a year. The whole swining country goes tennis crazy for a fortnight and then for the next eleven and a half months they walk about denying it ever happened, like a bloke trying to live down a dirty weekend. Then before you know it it's June again and they're running around screaming in shorts.'

'But can you tell me anything about the real Wimbledon, Mr Brady? How do I handle it? Why is it so special? I think I'm going to throw up . . .'

'You're ok, mate. There you go. All right, let me see . . . well, trying to get practise time there is like trying to get lager out of a llama . . . they give you a bloody *tea* voucher and a bloody little *luncheon* voucher for each day of the circus, as though it's a hairdresser's convention instead of a *tournament.* The best courts are a big game wet dream and the worst courts are like vandalized window boxes. It always rains . . . and it's the championship of the world, mate. If you don't win it you don't die happy. That's all there is to it.'

'That's all? It doesn't tell me too much.'

'Don't worry about using the wrong fork, mate. Sod the traditions. It's the players that make a tournament. Always has been, always will be. Worry about the bloke you're playing, not the little finger you're crooking. Who you drawn, anyway?'

'Johnny Sangster.'

'You poor little bastard.'

Johnny opened his eyes. Dave Pepper was looking at him. They barely smiled, but they stared at each other for a long time with that secret savage intensity that people keep reserved for loved one and worst enemies.

# ten

On the first day of Wimbledon rain stopped play before it had begun and the players tearoom quickly filled to capacity. Johnny Sangster, childish in his red track suit, ate a fish while he waited out the weather. Thorn didn't order. She felt awkward in here; this was *their* room and if you weren't one of them you would always feel as though you were sitting on a drawing pin.

Even committed loners – like Johnny – were unspoken members of the Circuit's exclusive fraternity. For a while Thorn had been irritated by the bond, but now she thought she understood. Which was most unusual for Thorn Sayre; ordinarily, the very thought of seeing the other guy's point of view made her insides squirm. But the Circuit, a young and wildly glamorous meritocracy blazing a path through a world of terminal mediocrity – Thorn got the picture.

The Circuit spent years of its prime in endless airplanes, it made fast fortunes in the only game in the world that doesn't know the meaning of a close season. To Thorn, pro tennis was show business and big business masquerading as a sport. The country, the city, the hotel, the courts, the climate and the crowds were forever changing. But the same faces were always there, waiting to nail you across the net. The Circuit was often a grind and you could grow old out there if all the travelling, all the overlapping injuries, all the tensions, all the tennis and all the other excesses caught up with you. You roamed five continents like a jet set gypsy gladiator, but you had to make it and make it fast and make it stick. You're a long time dead and resting. Anything could happen.

Yes, Thorn felt an instinctive empathy with these impatient young men who sat hating the rain. It made her sad to think that her beauty was as finite as their golden years. If her make-up wasn't such an immaculate conception today then it might have made her shed a tear.

Johnny smacked his lips appreciatively, pushing his plate away. He felt her leg under the table, his smile shy and obsessed. She squeezed his hand and gave it back to him.

'Another whole *month* in this town,' he sighed happily. 'I haven't stayed out of the sky for that long since I started shaving.'

'I thought you enjoyed travelling.'

He shook his head. 'I enjoy having a destination. Can't stand travelling. But we're on the move so much that after a year or so you just feel like you're sitting still. You get to see so many different places, so many politicians and rock stars that you get to feel like you're sitting in your room watching TV. It's the same stuff moving at the same speed but it's in the flesh. That's no big deal. I never met a household face who didn't look prettier from a distance. It's ok, you know. I don't go stir crazy. Travelling sucks but I like watching television.'

At the next table a gaggle of players swapped racial and political taunts.

'Hey, Pole,' said the Russian, 'I hear that if you people don't shape up the Pope is going to send the tanks in.'

'I don't believe it,' the Italian said. 'I thought there were no jokes left in Russia. I heard that the Cheka had them all shot.'

The American laughed.

The Yugoslav sneered. 'Hey, Yankee. Is it true that in your glorious democracy every child has the chance to grow up and become the man who shot the President?'

A sleek young French black joined them. This gave the Rumanian and the American real scope to shine.

Thorn grimaced at the gales of laughter. 'Why do so many players make jokes all the time about other players' colour and country and religion, Johnny?'

'Because that's the only gimmick that sticks out far enough for them to grasp.' Johnny looked at his comrades with bored indulgence. 'Don't sweat it. There's no animosity or manifestos behind the insults.'

'Well, when I heard some of the things they call each other I was *shocked*. And I'm from the *South*.'

Johnny smiled reassuringly. 'It means nothing, honest.' He held her hand.

'I guess you're right.' She took back her hand gently, making the retreat feel like a caress. Too corny, by God, like one of Mama Sayre's old Beatles records.

A reporter crouched at Johnny's feet with a pen and a notepad poised to pounce on a few quotes. 'Two minutes, Johnny?'

'Sure. I finished eating.'

Thorn listened to the questions and answers for a minute or so; then she realized that the nasty little fag wasn't going to feature *her* in his hackwork. He completely ignored her. As if *she* wasn't a key figure in the Johnny Sangster story! Little *he* knew! *Ask* Curly, for Chrissakes! Ah, forget it . . .

She looked out of the window on to the Centre Court. The rain had stopped and the sun was trying to look out from behind the spent storm clouds. The protective covers were still shrouding the precious lawns. Old men squinted up at the sky, young men waited to be given orders with enthusiastic patience. All over the players tearoom they could feel it, it was getting nearer and they were growing restless and quiet, shutting everything out as the nerves and anticipation gripped them like cramp. Johnny could feel it and the reporter could sense this. He got to his feet and wished Johnny good luck. Johnny nodded, his mind elsewhere. You were either going *out there alone* or you were an outsider who could never know how it felt.

Thorn sighed and crossed her legs, looking around her. She could find only one player who wasn't dead to the world and there was something strange about him. It wasn't his tender years, around the seventeen mark – Johnny said some of the tennis brats scrambling for a place on the Circuit still had the cradle marks on their behinds – and it wasn't the horrific powder blue track suit with the white epaulettes or his stack of shiny black racquets trimmed with steel. The strange thing about the boy wasn't even the way he was neglecting to psyche himself up for the First Round of the championships of the world.

The strange thing about him was the way he stared at Johnny Sangster. With absolute terror in his eyes.

'Johnny? Who's that kid over there?'

Johnny glanced up. 'Kid called Billy Lennox.'

'Why is he looking at you like that?'

'Because he's got to play me real soon.'

Dave Pepper appeared. Thorn was invisible to him. 'Covers are off. Let's get you down to the locker room.'

Thorn brushed each of Johnny's cheeks with her lips.

'Wow, I've been French kissed,' he laughed, scooping up his battery of racquets. '*A bientôt*, angel.'

Dave Pepper let Johnny lead the way. The coach glanced at Thorn with total indifference. Thorn didn't dignify his petty pique with even a sneer. Her sneers were precious.

Instead she looked at Billy Lennox.

He waited until his opponent was a safe way away before he rose. Thorn watched the forlorn powder blue figure bob out of the tearoom with the cowed resignation of one about to meet his master.

Thorn couldn't imagine anyone being so scared of Johnny Sangster. But then, she had never seen him play.

The number nine seed had a corner locker in Wimbledon's Locker Room A. It was household names only in here. Thank God for the British class system. When you've worked for years to get within spitting distance of the top the last thing you need is bug-eyed tyros throwing tantrums and throwing up in the locker next door.

He did a few exercises to get his blood pumping and some more to get his central nervous system motor running. Then he looked at his locker and smiled. The lockers at Wimbledon were always good for a laugh. Every other stop on the Circuit boasted huge stainless steel lockers big enough, as Johnny had once remarked to Ray Velez, to house an average-sized Mexican family.

Velez didn't crack a smile. 'I'm an American.'

'I know you are,' Johnny had assured him.

But there were no walk-in vaults at Wimbledon. Here there

were lockers of sweet-smelling old wood that had probably seen passive service on the Ark. Here they were so small that Johnny had to hang up his suit on a metal peg above a grim wooden bench. He looked at the men around him, the only feared and loved tennis players in the *world*, all doing the same. Johnny loved it.

Either the English thought the colonials were getting above themselves and saw Wimbledon as their rude awakener, or they were whacko. Some of the top seeds simmered with annoyance and bouts of superstition. They were having to alter the toilettes of a lifetime because what they were using as a *locker* would have been better suited as a coffin for cold Munchkins.

The usher came for him and told him it was time to go.

Johnny thanked him, collected his racquets and walked out into the tunnel. He gasped with the sweet shock, and he came alive.

Billy Lennox found Locker Room B, located the lavatory and neatly vomited up a light lunch. His cheeks were burning, his back was wet and sticky. As he undressed he saw his hands shaking like food mixers with low batteries. And now there was something wrong with his locker. Nothing would fit. He must have been given the booby prize. He piled his street clothes and track suit pants on the bench in an untidy heap. He rushed back to the can. If he didn't urinate immediately his bladder would pop like a bubble, Billy was sure of it.

When he got back to his locker there was no time left. The usher was waiting for him, looking at his watch with snide exaggerated patience.

Billy couldn't move.

'Ready yet, Lennox?'

In the States they call me *Mr* Lennox! 'Let's go.' He picked up his impressive array of custom made racquets. They seemed to mock him now – *are we meant to do it all by ourselves*?

Billy Lennox followed the usher into a tunnel at the end of which a figure in red waited for him. He had his back to Billy and on that back was written SANGSTER – USA in large black capital letters. Johnny didn't look at him. Billy Lennox fell into step and they walked on court to cheers, applause and jeers which Billy knew weren't meant for him. He felt a desperate yearning for his mother and the toilet in Locker Room

B. But what Billy Lennox missed most of all was his irretrievable golden past at the Boston country club.

Billy was afraid he would freeze, he was *certain* he would freeze. *Losing* wasn't really what mattered – what mattered was the humiliation of looking like a stuffed turkey in front of all those cool camera and crowd eyes. He couldn't stand the prospect of looking like a fool. It had never happened to Billy before.

Then in the first game of the first set Billy Lennox broke Johnny Sangster's serve and he had the world on a gutstring!

He was laughing with incredulous delight as he passed Johnny at the changeover. Johnny shot him a wicked look. Billy Lennox didn't give a flying *fuck*! He was living in a dream come true and loving it to death! His heart pumped with the brittle certainty of youth. He really *was* as good as they said back home! He could *not* be beat! Could *never* be made to look like a fool! Sangster was an *old man* compared to Billy the Kid! He wasn't in his *teens*! He had had his day and now it was time to move over for the youngblood! Sangster couldn't even hold that legendary *serve* of his any more! Ha! I kicked the white tiger and he cried *uncle*.

Sangster was changing his racquet. He bounced three racquet heads off the palm of his hand until he found what he wanted. He walked back on court swinging it round in huge arcs.

Billy Lennox smiled grimly at his antics. He went to the other end of the court and the crowd applauded. Applauded *him*! At Wimbledon! Billy had no doubts, he had no fears, he wound up his service feeling that his life had just begun.

Billy Lennox didn't win another game. J. Sangster won 6–1, 6–0, 6–0 in less than an hour. As they shook hands at the net Johnny Sangster was glowing and his breathing was steady and relaxed. Billy Lennox had sweated himself to the point of dehydration and now he was crying his eyes red.

'Hey, don't be so upset, Billy,' Johnny said, appalled. You didn't behave like this on the Circuit. He was shocked. 'You just tried to move up into the big playground too soon. Go back to Boston and give it another year or two.' Johnny put his arm around the kid's shoulder. 'Hey, hey, don't cry now.'

The comforting, triumphant arm only made Billy Lennox weep harder. This was ridiculous. The photographers were having multiple orgasms. The crowd were bewildered, confused by nasty Johnny Sangster's show of sympathy, embarrassed by Billy Lennox' blubbering upper lip.

The umpire coughed. 'Do you feel well, Lennox?'

Billy nodded, raising his racquet head in assent the way the pros do. He dried his eyes and subsided into sniffles as he collected his racquets, track suit and lucky mascots. The photographers glared at him, deprived, and drifted away to talk about him scornfully. Johnny watched the kid seriously.

They pulled on their track suits and left court to hesitant applause. They left Court Number Three – Johnny looked forward to the Centre Court with its big crowds and good bounces and TV cameras. Oh yeah, and the Royal Box. His mother thought those magic moments when he bowed to whatever duchess or other in-law of Her Majesty was up there when her son played was the major achievement of his career. She said he looked like a knight when he bowed to the Royal Box.

The players parted company at the locker rooms that segregated them into their respective castes. Johnny watched the boy disappear behind the door marked B. Lennox had all the shots but none of the spirit. He would never make a winner but the way he was carrying on he had a very good chance of making himself a nervous wreck. Johnny thought about it in the shower and decided he would talk to the kid before he flew home. He would tell him not to worry, he played well, Rome wasn't built in a day and all the rest of that lying garbage. It just might stop the kid becoming another All American mess.

Johnny got dressed and went looking for Lennox. When he found him he dropped the idea. Let the neurotic little rich geek look after himself.

Billy Lennox was in a telephone booth talking to Boston. He was telling his proud parents how unlucky he'd been to lose to Johnny Sangster in the fifth set. He could have clinched it if not for his injured arm. The Wimbledon crowd had loved him. Lying through his expensively straightened teeth. He wasn't alone. Every pay phone free was occupied by a young American lying to his rich parents. Incredible. Exactly the same routine each time. *I lost, but I lost good.*

Sick, thought Johnny. Billy Lennox blurred into the line of American Dreams pretending it really happened. Johnny couldn't tell Lennox apart from the rest. They were all the same.

Johnny turned away. Country club, he thought with old, fresh contempt. What do you expect from country club clowns?

She was waiting for him in the back seat.

'So that's what you do,' said Thorn. 'Very nice.'

Johnny got into the car. 'How d'you enjoy the match?'

She could tell this had been his ace card with girls for ever. 'I like the way you move,' she said. 'But I think I'll prefer it when I see you picking on someone your own size.'

'Don't worry, that part comes round soon enough,' he semi-snapped. 'You have to beat up on all shapes and sizes in this game, you know.'

'It's the same for all of us, Johnny.'

Who the hell does she think she is? he thought. Number *eight*, for Pete's sake?

All the other girls he'd known would have felt privileged laying out the red carpet for him. But not her, she still acted like she was doing him a favour. What made *her* so special?

He looked at her resentfully. Thorn almost smiled. He melted and moved towards her on the back seat and told the driver to move it a little faster.

Johnny sat up in bed and reached for the grey phial. 'Vitamin C,' he said as he handed it to Thorn, and they laughed like children having a good time getting up to no good. She touched his hair and opened the phial. She shook six tablets the colour of Schulz' Woodstock on to the palm of her hand. Johnny took three and Thorn held the phial upside down to demonstrate its emptiness.

'That's the last, Johnny.'

'I can easy get some more.'

'On prescription?'

'That's what fame is for.'

They washed down the amphetamine with Chablis. It hit their cerebral motors almost immediately, making them want to talk about themselves. Thorn talked about the profit and loss for an American girl after a modelling career in London. The chemical stimulated their central nervous systems and they stared at each other with a kind of euphoric intensity. Thorn said she thought her chances were pretty damn good.

'Here they don't want models to be a huge regiment of

homogenized vinyl blondes. It's not like the States where any model who wants to pay her rent regular has to look like she was hatched by Old Mother Hen Sherry Ward.'

'Yeah, but you told me that Paris wasn't like the States either,' Johnny said, anxious to keep Sherry Ward's name clear of the idyll.

'Yeah, but Paris is desperate. Paris is fine if you're an ethnic minority member or a wafer thin freak who doesn't mind going down the drain with the entire miserable redundant *haute couture* mess.'

'What's the money like here?'

'Even at the very top London rates you could only get about half of what you'd be paid for the top jobs in the States. There's a real weird magazine here, true class, called *Ritz*, and for that the models work free, just for the kudos. Imagine that on Madison Ave! They're still having some kind of party here, I swear, left over from the Swinging Sixties, Cuba says. But I have got sort of an instant *in*; the London fashion industry tends to think that if a girl's worked in another country she must be good – something to do with the easy come, easy go *manãna* mentality of their own models, I guess. Tell them you just flew in from Paris or New York and they'll practically hire you on the spot.'

'I find that hard to believe.'

'It's true, Johnny. Cuba said. In America modelling is a business, an ulcer-giving one. In England it's more of a hobby, a jog. Here the girls – and most of them are *beautiful*, twice as beautiful as those American blanks, Cuba showed me photographs of Kari Ann Moller and Polly Eltes and Clemmie Simon – are happy to earn enough to keep them in bare essential luxuries. Back in the States the girls never stop hustling. Because it's so tough keeping your head above water back there, all the American models who come to London have a reputation for toughness and time-keeping that smooths the way for them.'

'Well, I'm sure they'll love the way you look here. Anywhere'.

'What's wrong with *you*?'

'Nothing.'

'Come on now, Johnny.'

'I was hoping you'd come back to America with me. Where you belong.'

'Where I *belong*? Are you *crazy*? All I got as a model in the States was kicked in the teeth by the status quo. I deserve better than that. Don't I?'

'Yes.'

'And even if I *did* go marching home, how long would you be sticking around before you had to hit the Circuit again, Johnny?'

'A few days.'

'Great.'

'Maybe longer!'

'Thanks but no thanks.'

'You can have the apartment. My apartment.'

'I want one of my own. A bigger one.'

'I see.'

He got out of bed and began to dress. She asked him if he was going to see his doctor. He nodded, not looking at her. She watched him while he dialled the driver's number and asked for the car to be brought round to the front of the Grosvenor.

'Johnny?'

'What?'

'It wouldn't work out, Johnny.'

'You're wrong. I'm going to show you how wrong. You've never been so wrong in your life, Thorn.'

He stomped out grimly. Thorn grimaced with irritation and began to perfect herself for the night. He would be ok when he got back from Harley Street. A fresh prescription always gave Johnny Sangster a pep talk.

The prescription had started five years ago at fifteen, when Johnny's puppy fat had not been shaken off by constant practice and rigorous training. His prole roots had cursed him with a taste for food that verged on being greasy trash. He complained that Dave Pepper's diets left him starving and took to sneaking off to a nearby Burger King whenever the opportunity presented itself. Dave had seen it many times before. Plenty of the public park brats had junk food habits – even now, Jimmy Connors stopped at every changeover to guzzle a river of Coca Cola. Johnny Sangster was eating Dave's diet, but his real meal of the day was still two triple cheeseburgers with a side order of fries.

Steps had to be taken. Dave tried reason – every hour Johnny spent in Burger King made him a second slower on court. Johnny scoffed; he had just won the Orange Bowl, the major junior championship, he had evidence of his invincibility. Dave tried disciplinary measures; giving Johnny extra work and restricting his free time. Johnny sulked and refused orders and used every chance he got to rebel against his coach. His game began to suffer. He lost a tournament he should have won. This was the last thing Dave Pepper wanted. He sent Johnny to a doctor who put him on black capsules that killed his appetite.

The puppy fat fell away but the pills stayed on. He liked the way they made him feel – they gave him more pace, more strength, more stamina and faster reactions – and found them an invaluable ally. Dave Pepper gave him grave warnings, good advice and a note for the doctor. Johnny always got the prescriptions filled without any trouble.

But since Paris the pills were going twice as fast. He had never shared his wonder drug until now. Of course, Johnny thought of Thorn as an exception.

His coach didn't.

He returned to his hotel room white with anger.

'What's wrong?'

He didn't look at Thorn as he snatched up the receiver and punched out a number.

'Johnny!'

'It's me,' he said into the telephone. 'Get down here now. *Just do it*!' He slammed down the telephone.

'Johnny! I'm fucking *talking* to you!'

'It's Dave Pepper.' He stared at her thoughtfully.

'What about him? Something to do with the prescription?'

He nodded. 'I need his authorization. Just a piece of paper. But the doctor told me Pepper had given him a note telling him *not* to let me have any pills. The bastard.'

'But didn't he always . . .?'

'Not any more, the bastard.'

There was a knock on the door. Thorn went into the bathroom, locking the door behind her. Let the pair of them hammer it out, *she* wasn't about to become involved in a petty squabble of which she had no chance of affecting the outcome. She pressed an ear to the door.

'So what's the big idea?' she heard Johnny demand. 'The same as usual?'

'What's that mean, John?'

'What have you got against her? What's she ever done to *you*? What's wrong with you?'

'*Listen* to me! According to your doctor's records you should be wasting away by now. Either that or you're playing Johnny Applespeed.' Dave looked sarcastically at the bathroom door.

'Ah, so what?'

'John, those pills were prescribed for *you*.'

'So? I can do what I like with them.'

'You *know* that's not true. You're putting yourself in danger of arousing suspicion, of drawing attention to what must be kept private.'

'Doctors don't talk. It's their oath.'

'They're not *stupid*, John. They're not going to risk their necks and practices, not even for number *nine*. Which they would be doing if they knew that their powerful amphetamine pills were being passed around like after dinner mints. They'd black you, stop giving you so much as an iron pill. Then people start talking. If the tennis authorities find out you've been guzzling those things for five years – that's some diet, John – then everything we've spent so many years working for could be trashed by one dope test.'

'You've got no right . . .'

'I had to. No more doctor's orders until you start thinking straight.'

'What do you call straight?'

'Don't lose your tunnel vision, John. It's your greatest gift.'

Johnny sat down on the bed and stared daggers at his coach. Dave walked to the door. 'I'm presenting the trophy at Stockwell's junior tournament this afternoon. I'll meet you up there for practice tonight. Two hours on their showcase scheduled to start at eight. I'll see you then, ok?'

'Why should I take orders from you, Dave? *I'm* the only one who has to go out there and do it. I'm at the top and I'm going to be there for *years*. I'd be just as effective without you around, maybe even better. So why should I take your orders?'

'Because I'm your coach.'

'Maybe I don't need no more coaching.'

'Maybe. But I never knew any player who could afford to take a raincheck on some good advice. Of course, I've also known careers to be ruined by bad coaching. You have to decide, John. I'll be expecting you around eight. See you.'

Johnny was silent as the coach let himself out.

Thorn came out of the bathroom and saw the expression on Johnny's face. She put her arms around him. 'Don't sweat it. There must be a million places where you can find another man like that.'

'No,' Johnny said, 'Dave Pepper's the best coach in the game.'

Thorn looked surprised. 'Oh, I wasn't talking about him. I was talking about the doctor.'

Down in the bar the girls who waited in bars all over The Circuit – they always knew where to wait, they were probably fitted with antennae – sat nursing their drinks and looking for a seed.

When Johnny went to call his driver they stared at Thorn with nonchalant loathing. There was a gorgeous mirror beyond the bar so Thorn was oblivious to their attentions. The driver drove them over to Alexander's on the King's Road. Every table in the little Italian restaurant swarmed with tennis pros, world famous faces and forehands; a pasta-based diet had become popular with the players after the mid-Seventies success of Adriano Panatta was fuelled by endless spaghetti, proving that countless carbohydrates give players the capacity for furious bursts of extra energy.

The pills had worn off, vanquished by the sight of platefuls of steaming tagliatelli and silver dishes full of Neapolitan ices. Still the tennis pros and their companions were arriving as Johnny called for the bill. There were not too many people on The Circuit who could resist the combination of Italian food and English tradition. Alexander's was part of Wimbledon mythology by now.

They drove to the Berkeley Square club for *chemin de fer*. They won thirty thousand pounds in twenty minutes and lost it in two. They got bored before they got lucky again and left for Simone's where there was noise and cameras and people prepared to be impressed. Nobody could pose properly for too long around a green baize table, no radiance of face could compete with the pull of all those translucent chips.

After midnight, leaving Simone's, they were ambushed by a posse of stray photogs. They'd been waiting outside in the light rain, non-people without a pass who could only poach glamour as it walked from Simone's canopy to a purring car. Thorn tugged Johnny's arm, slowing him down so that the pariahs of the *paparazzi* could capture some class.

'Put your arm around her waist, Johnny!'

'Squeeze the girl and scowl this way, Johnny!'

'How about a nice kiss, you two?'

'What's your name, dear?'

'Thorn Sayre,' she enunciated carefully.

Johnny turned his collar against the cold and damp. 'Come on, Thorn, unless you want pneumonia for a nightcap.'

'Ok,' she said reluctantly, but as the car pulled away she kissed Johnny full on the mouth with something like passion, trying to choke him with her tongue and ruining her lipstick. When she pulled away and began to repair the damage Johnny stared at her with stunned bliss and lipstick on his teeth.

'What was that about?'

'Does there *have* to be a reason?'

'No. Of course there doesn't have to be a reason.' He smiled.

But of course there was – the reflected glory. It wasn't mercenary, it was the real thing. Since arriving in London Thorn had seen her name in William Hickey, her face in Dempster's *Diary* and her legs in the *Sunday Express*. She didn't see it as secondhand fame – she was there in black and white, her name was beginning to become *known*. Countless beautiful escorts of the Sixties and Seventies could have told her a sadder reality – that her face was evacuated from memory when yesterday's papers were thrown out – but she would have dismissed it as grandma's sour grapes.

Johnny leaned forward to give the driver the address of the next party, somewhere else in W1 at the still centre of the West End's turning world, a wide street of lush bland seclusion less than a mile from the teeming, seamy felons of Soho and Arabesque whoring-procuring outside the hotels opposite Hyde Park. Less than a mile but in another world where God was an Englishman and London had never stopped swinging.

The host was something on the fringe where fashion met media. It was all rather vague, like the decor and the music – nothing you could pin down or put your finger on or be offended by. He was said to have a title and a large overdraft, though he never talked about either. He greeted Johnny Sangster with real warmth and smiled graciously at Thorn, hovering beautifully over her hand. The party was progressing well – it had long ago passed out of the host's hands and taken on a life of its own. The alcohol flowed like money. The host filled their glasses himself and made courteous noises as the doorbell rang for Tom Dougherty and Francesca Universe.

Out of the darkness glazed faces became clearer and excited voices louder. The revellers were edging closer to Johnny Sangster, they had smelled his famous sweat and wanted some. But Thorn's glass was empty – that's the trouble with drink, she thought, it goes so quickly – before they could pounce, and Johnny went for reinforcements over on the far side of the festivities. The faces focussed instead on Francesca Universe, who was heading straight for Thorn wearing new clothes and the smile of an old friend.

Thorn smiled swiftly and slipped into the hordes, bent on avoiding terminal tedium. She found herself pressed against a familiar and anonymous stranger, a face that she had seen around but never looked into. He was tall, blond and plain, his manner eager but knowing, his clothes conservative but sharp. He seemed to be a fixture of the fast set; Thorn recalled him smiling at soirees all over W1. She apologized for emptying the contents of his glass all over the carpet.

'That's ok,' he shrugged. 'It was tonic water, and I didn't really want it. Just something to do with my hands. Do you drink, Miss Sayre?'

She was a little surprised; not that he knew her name, that somehow seemed so *right*, but that he was so formal. Anyhow, it was all delicious. She laughed a laugh she hoped wasn't too hearty to cover her shock. 'Only as a last resort!'

'It's strictly for the tourists. Alcohol is the tourist resort of the stimulant world. You'll never go tourist class, Thorn.'

'Thank you.' She was impressed. A compliment that wasn't laced with a leer caught her off guard. 'I'm very sorry, but I don't know your name. Tell me your name.'

'Roche,' he said. 'R-O-C-H-E.' He dug into his pockets and came out with two clenched fists. He extended them and smiled with polite playfulness. 'Take your pick.'

Thorn stared at him and then made her choice. Roche revealed a cache of party-coloured pills. 'For you,' he said.

Thorn hesitated for a moment before grabbing them. 'How did you know? I mean, they *are* speed?'

'Well, I wouldn't give Valium to cheekbones like yours. If Mother Nature ever handed out such cheekbones then I never saw them.' He gave her the contents of his other hand. 'For your friend. I've been monitoring Wimbledon courtesy of the BBC. I notice that Mr Sangster has exceptional cheekbones too.'

Roche smiled at her. Thorn smiled back, surprised that she could be so floored by a human being. There were not too many men who could give Thorn Sayre something without wanting that certain same old boring *something else* back. It took a special type of man. One who had security, success and a standing invitation to all the right parties. At least.

Thorn knew what type of man he was, why he was always in demand, always socializing. Roche was a dealer, a drugs dealer. By appointment to the *demi-monde*.

'I think you've got an admirer.' Roche nodded over her shoulder. Thorn turned and saw a man from the picture books of her childhood – *Vogue* and *Cosmo* – staring at her. He was tall, dark and heavy with a large clear drink – 'Government gin', whispered Roche – in each hand and a great deal of six o'clock shadow on each chin.

The years since all those bright party pictures had been taken and printed had not been kind, but it was still unmistakably the face of Jap Goddard – sometime in the mid Sixties his fame had become so great that everyone and their starry-eyed little sister had stopped tagging the descriptive alibi *photographer* on to it – and it was staring at Thorn Sayre, model, with morbid adoration. He barely raised the ghost of a smile for her as he hit hard on one of his gins, scratched one of his chins and turned his attention to Roche. Jap Goddard looked at the quiet dealer with undiluted hostility.

'Mr Roche, what did you do to upset him?'

Roche laughed. 'I can't imagine. Maybe we'll find out. He's coming over.'

The household name walked heavily towards her. The man who photographed the Face of the Sixties, Thorn thought. Whatever happened to that girl? Jap Goddard bowed stiffly. 'How do you do?' He was old and broke, though still very rich, now, drunk from too much Beefeater, hungover from his golden years. But he was still Jap Goddard. He glared at Roche and smiled at Thorn.

'I'm Jap Goddard and you are quite . . . orchidaceous.'

Thorn liked that. It made her smile for herself. Jap Goddard misappropriated the smile.

'How are you enjoying London?' he quizzed, not wanting or waiting for an answer. 'Allow me to offer my condolences for the so-called *photographs* taken of you by the guttersnipes of Grub Street. They didn't do you justice. They made you look like yet another beautiful girl.' He took a bitter pull on his drink. 'Just what the world doesn't need now.'

'They weren't such bad photographs,' said Thorn. 'They weren't taken at a session or anything.'

'They should have been,' Goddard snapped. 'If I ruled the world, every photograph would be taken at a session. And those so-called *photographers* that crawl on their bellies up and down Fleet Street, I'd have them taken from their dark rooms and put into more suitable employment. In a butcher's shop, for example.' He swilled his drink again, and stared at Roche. 'You really should take more care when picking the company you keep, Thorn.'

Roche touched Thorn's arm sweetly. 'Bye bye.'

'No, *stay*,' she urged him. A nice guy, and a dealer too! – why should she ever want to lose him? She turned back to Goddard. 'You may be a big shot photographer, but you're really little league when it comes to corny old-fashioned courtesy.'

Goddard shrugged, a wan smile creeping across his pudgy features.

'You're very rude, Mr Goddard,' Thorn reiterated.

'And you, *Miz* Sayre, are very young. Excruciatingly young, in fact.'

Thorn looked around to check her bearings with Roche but he was gone, melted back into the party, always popular.

'Why do you dislike him so much?'

'I don't dislike him. I despise him. And all his kind. Pedlars of poison, my dear, pedlars of poison.'

'That's a very nice gin and tonic you have in each hand.'

'This? Chalk and poisoned cheese, my dear.'

'Do you *know* how many rapes, how many *murders* are committed under the influence of cheap booze? You obviously don't.'

'All hearsay, little girl.'

'Anyway,' Thorn controlled her increasingly shrill Southern drawl; who was she to preach against hooch, anyhow, some temperance type? 'Roche is my friend.'

'He's no friend of yours, Thorn. A hole in the head would be more of a chum to you than *that* . . . vermin.'

'You don't take drugs.'

'I don't take drugs. I don't *touch* any human who takes drugs.' Goddard drained one of his glasses and dropped it on the floor. A pretty Asian girl tripped on it, looked up angrily, saw his influential face and faded away. 'I lived through the Sixties. I saw a lot of people become good-looking corpses and ugly old wrecks due to all the bloody uppers and downers and *acids* and smack and what have you. All of them, taking all of them. Except Elle. So I despise them, the Roches of this world. Such an appropriate name for the polluting little ratbag, don't you think? And I never, but *never*, work with their clients.' He smiled. 'I know that beautiful American girls like yourself would never dream of indulging these days. It would harm your looks, it would harm your career. Both very un-American.'

Johnny found her. He looked from Thorn to Jap Goddard with green-eyed hostility.

'You're Johnny Sangster!' Goddard exclaimed.

'You're right.'

'This is Jap Goddard, Johnny.'

Johnny looked blank.

'The photographer.' Thorn was irritated and embarrassed by his lack of real knowledge. 'The famous photographer. He photographed the Face of the Sixties. Elle.'

'Oh yeah,' Johnny said politely. 'Where is she? She here?'

Goddard flinched. What had ever happened to that girl? That girl called Elle? That symbol of the Sixties? Whatever happened to them? 'No. I was just about to tell Thorn here that she really should model.'

Thorn laughed. 'I modelled in Paris. Now I eat.'

Goddard reached into his inside pocket – Thorn noted that he wore a really appalling safari suit – and pressed something into her hand. 'Just in case.'

Thorn sipped her drink, saying nothing. She looked at and pocketed Jap Goddard's silver and black card. Just in case.

Johnny Sangster stared at her, jealous and proud.

You give them the best years of your life and what do you get? A kick in the teeth as they leave you for someone else. That's all you get for all those years. All the work and the worry and the time and the effort and none of it means a damn. As soon as they can scrape by without you you're on the scrap heap, buster, and they're gone, gone, gone. So what were you expecting? Maybe a thank you note?

*Whack.*

Dave Pepper bashed hell out of everything the ball machine threw at him for an hour and then he got tired.

He crouched on the showcase court up at Stockwell, catching his breath. He wasn't as young as he'd been, he was more alone than he'd ever been. He glanced at his Rolex. Just after nine. There was still an hour of court time scheduled but there was no point in waiting.

Johnny wasn't coming. He really wasn't coming.

Dave Pepper drove back to London. Up in his hotel room at the Grosvenor he turned on the TV, found BBC2 and got into bed to watch the edited highlights of the day's play at Wimbledon.

# eleven

Malcolm Ball was the best male player the host country had produced in three decades, and he wasn't much at all.

Malcolm Ball was big and brawny with a bright yellow short back and sides above the face of a petulant stoat. In short sharp straight sets in front of the polite patriotism of a crammed Centre Court, Malcolm Ball was poleaxed.

Johnny Sangster did not attend the mandatory post-match press conference. Thorn wanted to show him what she had bought at Swanky Modes and there was a party tonight. And besides, *he* didn't *feel* like a press conference. The post-match conference, Johnny thought, was just a crock of cow crap. Yes, a crock of cow crap. It was too controlled. When the press corps went after individual scoops it was much more fun and worthwhile. At press conferences players were just expected to trot out trite answers to trite questions in monosyllabic, monotone monotony. Oh yeah – the tennis authorities fined you if you didn't show up. But when you were number *nine* their *fines* gave you no pain – just a belly laugh. Most players attended the press conferences not through fear of fines, but because the bad press might affect the rude health of their endorsement income.

Johnny didn't feel like a press conference. And for once there was no one around to bully him into attending. He overslept, hideously.

It was much too late for the scheduled practise session against Tom Dougherty, very nearly too late to get to the All England Club for his third round match against Claudio Falconi, scheduled to start at 2 p.m. *sharp*. The driver sped like a Bentley out of hell and earned himself a great big fifty pound bill. And when Johnny bowled into Locker Room A Falconi was changed and ready to go, the fiercely partisan Anglo-Italo crowd braying impatiently – half the restaurants in London must have shut up shop for the afternoon, Johnny thought – but the rain had started up again so they all just had to wait until Sangster and the sun were good and ready.

Johnny changed leisurely, the danger of default past, and then he sat on the bench staring unblinking and unsmiling across the locker room at the white-faced Falconi until the usher came to ask if they were ready.

The grass was fast and the crowd was hostile – the partisans at the ringside made sure that the recent humiliation inflicted by *il Americano* on the *campo centrale* at the Foro Italico was daisy fresh in Falconi's mind. The Italian came off the ropes with his big guns blazing. Johnny was ready for him.

On service games Johnny played like Roscoe Tanner with telescopic sight – all the speed and power of the notorious Tanner serve, delivered with twice the accuracy and eliminating the frequent double faults that blighted Roscoe's game. When Falconi managed to scramble back a return of serve Johnny charged the net and executed a sparkling volley. There was no respite for the Italian on his own serve. Johnny spiked his heavy artillery by chopping up the rhythm of the game with heavy topspin lobs and dinky DOA drop shots.

Falconi got tired and the crowd got quiet and Johnny Sangster moved quickly to a lead of two sets to love. Then the crowd got the crank bug and things got ugly.

Johnny had three match points in the third set. The crowd fell silent as he wound up his serve, about to put Falconi out of the tournament and his misery. Johnny tossed the ball above his head, whipping his racquet arm up and round like a windmill with a mission. The second before he struck the ball, one voice from a cast of thousands shattered the silence and Johnny Sangster's concentration.

'Come on,. Claudio!' the voice piped stupidly.

Johnny drove the ball hard into the net, stumbling forward one stunned pace.

'Fault!' the linesman called with hearty confidence.

Johnny stared at him in disbelief. 'Are the batteries in your hearing aid runing down or something?' he called, advancing towards him.

The linesman looked at him with wary vacancy. The crowd began to whistle.

'Sangster,' the umpire warned sternly.

Johnny turned to the man in the chair. 'Did you hear that guy?'

'It was a fault,' the umpire said blankly. 'You have one more serve.'

'He shouted just as I was *about* to serve, for fuck's sake!'

'I didn't hear anything. It was a fault. Play,' said the umpire. 'Play, Sangster.'

'Ok, asshole.' Johnny stalked back to the baseline. 'I'll fucking play.'

'Sangster, I am giving you an official warning. For ungentlemanly conduct. One warning to Sangster.'

The crowd cheered. Johnny gritted his teeth, biting his lip until his tongue tasted his warm and salty blood. He stared over at Falconi, who looked back like a cornered rat with the crowd behind him. Johnny closed his eyes, breathing deep.

'Come on, Claudio!' the moronic male voice cried yet again.

'Quiet, please, ladies and gentlemen,' the umpire called. 'Please be quiet – save your applause until the end of the rallies!'

A trickle of sweat ran down Johnny Sangster's brow. He wiped it away with a red, white and blue wristband and opened his eyes. The crowd was subsiding. Falconi was still there. Johnny still had three match points. He nodded to a ball boy – the boy bounced him a couple of balls. The crowd became silent. Johnny Sangster stood perfectly still, staring across at Claudio Falconi with smouldering malevolence. He began to wind up his serve.

'Come on, Claudio! *Come on, Claudio!*'

Johnny threw the balls away and went for where the voice

was coming from with mad roving eyes. Faces swam. Old ladies, pretty girls, business men who had taken the afternoon off from the City, young bucks from World's End, children with huge bright eyes. A short dark man muscular inside a white Fred Perry. He was in an aisle seat about a dozen rows back from the front. On his face was a satisfied smile.

Half sneering, half leering at Johnny Sangster the man began to slowly clap his hands. 'Come on, Claudio!' he shouted, staring at Johnny. 'You can do it!'

'Enjoying the match, creep?' Johnny shouted above the rumbling murmur of the crowd.

'I'll be enjoying it a lot more when I see you beat, Sangster!'

Johnny nodded to a ball boy. The boy automatically bounced him a ball. Johnny stepped up on to the barrier and smiled at the man in the aisle seat. The smile in the aisle began to fade around the edges. Johnny threw the ball into the air and drove it at the offending head. The ball struck the nose. The noise of the crowd's collective shock drowned the sound of the man's cry as he sprawled backwards, his eyes streaming with tears. Johnny jumped off the barrier and walked back to the baseline as the crowd began to boo and slow handclap. Individual bursts of abuse came hurtfully at him. He didn't blame them, the fools. They thought he had hit the ball into the crowd at random, a display of the spoilt brat tantrums they had heard so much about.

And maybe even those who knew he had been aiming for the crank, that only the crank was going to get hurt – and *that* had hardly been fatal, there would be no blood or hospital for the crank, the crank had nothing to complain about – maybe those people didn't understand, couldn't forgive. What did they think this *was* – a game or something?

'Come to the chair, will you, Sangster,' the umpire droned ominously into the microphone. It wasn't a question but a command. The crowd erupted with vengeful delight and Johnny wondered where all his English support had gone. Johnny went over to the construction that the umpire perched upon like an ugly baby in a giant-sized high-chair. Johnny looked up at him. He had glasses and a handle-bar moustache and he swelled inside a grey flannel suit from the insurance office. He covered the microphone with his hands and leaned over to look down at Johnny. The crowd whistled encouragement to the umpire.

'This is your last chance, Sangster,' he hissed at Johnny. 'If you persist in your disgraceful conduct I will be forced to give you another official warning. You know as well as I do what that would mean.'

'I'll forfeit the point. My match point.'

The umpire nodded. 'A third offence will be similarly punished. A fourth will cause you to forfeit the game in progress. Further misbehaviour and you will be disqualified and the match awarded to Falconi.'

'I'm aware of the Grand Prix rules of conduct,' Johnny said.

'I'll give you one more chance to show me, Sangster. And then I'm afraid you're on the slippery slide.'

Johnny looked around the court. A policeman was talking to the assaulted asshole, who was shaking his stupid head – no he didn't want to press charges. Dave Pepper wasn't in his usual seat. God knew where Thorn was. Falconi crouched down on his haunches, waiting. The troubles had suckered him into believing he wasn't finished. 'One more chance is all I need,' Johnny told the umpire.

'Then you're very lucky.' The umpire took his hands away from the microphone.

'Quiet, please!' The crowd rumbled on. '*Quiet*, please, ladies and gentlemen!'

The noise subsided as Johnny Sangster walked back to the baseline and served out the match with an ace. Falconi lunged helplessly but it was like trying to catch an arrow with his wisdom teeth. Johnny waited at the net for the Italian to pick himself up and dust himself off. Grudging applause filled his ears. The Italian trotted up to him with a sad smile and an outstretched hand. They shook.

'Well played, Claudio.'

'Too good for me again, Johnee.'

Johnny pulled on his tracksuit, picked up his pile of racquets and left the court without waiting for Claudio Falconi. The crowd catcalled but it didn't matter. They had hated him anyway.

The press were waiting when he left the locker room. They no longer waited at the official post-match press conference. An usher was attempting to ush them away, but they crowded in on Johnny exploding flashlights and questions. He pushed his way through the pack without even deigning to give them the benefit of his no comment.

They'll only make it come out as something else, he comforted himself grimly.

He found Thorn in the car. 'That was quite a show back there.

'You saw it?' Johnny leaned forward and spoke to the driver. 'Move it.'

'Me and Miss Universe were watching from the gallery. The good old boys tea room. Do you do that often?'

'You should see my scrapbooks.'

'No thanks. What do you do for an encore? Bludgeon a ball boy with your bat?'

'I have the right to expect silence,' Johnny said primly.

Thorn sighed. 'You're public property, Johnny, not a public library. If I treated my public – or my press, come to that – like you do, I'd be out on my exquisite ear before you can say Schiaperelli. It's like cutting off a major artery to spite a scratch. Real dumb, Johnny.'

Johnny was shocked and bitter. 'It ain't just walking up and down a *catwalk* with your *snout* in the air. There is a little more *to* it than that.' He stared ahead. 'Dave Pepper knew that. He was there to keep all the *crap* away from me so I could concentrate on the only thing that matters, my *game*. Dave understood.'

'That's as may be, but Dave's not around anymore, is he?' Thorn turned to stare out of the window angrily. 'And just watch your tongue when you talk to me. I'm not some nothing umpire. You're an embarrassment.'

At the Grosvenor the desk clerk told Johnny that a Mr Harald O. Holden of Manhattan, New York, USA wanted Mr Sangster to call him at his office *immediately*. Johnny could guess what it was about. They must have reported the latest hot Sangster thrill on the news back there and that was more than enough to throw Harald into paroxysms of moral outrage about Johnny's responsibility to his public, the corruption of innocents who modelled their lives on his every move, the example he should be setting etcetera. What Harald was really mad about, natch, was that the corporation who touted Johnny's name on their junk might get a mite worried if their hero started lashing out at consumers. They might even look elsewhere for a human gimmick. That would not do at all, Harald believed. And so did Johnny.

'Hold all my calls,' Johnny told the desk clerk.

'I'll see you in the bar,' Thorn told Johnny.

He looked at her for a moment and then he rode up to the room Dave Pepper had occupied. He was struck dumb with happiness when the coach opened the door. He had been afraid that Dave might have flown home.

'Hello, John. Come in.'

'I'm a little worried about my second serve. I thought . . . maybe we could work on it over at Stockwell tomorrow.'

'Your second serve. I've been meaning to talk to you about that.'

'Harald has been calling,' Johnny said.

'Don't worry about Harald,' said Dave Pepper. 'I'll take care of Harald.'

Thorn Sayre stared into the funky abyss of the party but she couldn't see Johnny anywhere. She clicked her tongue against her teeth impatiently and then stopped. Careful with that Starlet Red gloss, honey, it took *eons* to apply perfectly. He'd gone for drinks, but where *was* he? She had grown accustomed to people wanting a moment of Johnny Sangster's precious time for a word, an autograph, sex, an insult or a combination of the elements. She had grown accustomed to it but that didn't mean she accepted it. At first she'd been happy here in London, availing herself of the unsurpassable clothes shops and watching him win at Wimbledon every day, celebrating the fast set sacrament of Swinging London every night. But where was he now? Faces swirled in and out of the clamorous blackness. Someone touched Thorn lightly on the arm and she turned, expecting to see Johnny smiling at her with apologetic adoration. But it was only the host, a bald obese piranha smirking inside a corny white suit. She had never seen an Englishman so atrociously dressed. He had been introduced to Thorn when she and Johnny arrived here, but apparently he had forgotten. He had evidently seen an awful lot of Scotch and pretty girls since then. She realized he had forgotten that she had arrived with Johnny Sangster when he slapped her ass like she was livestock.

'How about a lickle dance, beautiful?' he slurred, putting a porky little arm around her waist.

She pushed him away with imperious distaste. 'How about you go fry your gleaming head, porker?'

He stumbled backwards as though he had been jabbed in the snout. 'You – you think you can talk to me like that?'

'Oh, there's not the slightest doubt in my mind.'

'What do you think you're *here* for?' the host laughed incredulously, pushing his bloated face and bad breath up close. 'Why do you think I *invite* you and your friends?'

'Listen, short stuff, you've got the wrong girl. I—'

'To *put out*. Not for your scintillating conversation or to make up the numbers or even to make the place look nice. I got interior decorators for that. I get you here to *put out*. Now stop playing hard to get.'

He pulled her towards him and tried to stick his tongue in her mouth. She clawed at his hands until he yelped and let her go. He looked at her with bitter lust.

'Ok,' he said. 'If that's how you want it.' He snapped his fingers and an ape impersonator came running. He had no neck and hands like hams. The host nodded at Thorn. 'Show this whore the door. She's no use.'

The ape took her tightly by the arm. 'You can go quietly or the other way,' he said, making it perfectly clear that he hoped she chose the latter option. He began to lead her towards the door. Thorn walked quietly, too proud to say the magic words 'Johnny Sangster'. Why should she make excuses? She walked stiffly with strained dignity.

Johnny came out of the blackness, carrying two drinks and smiling. A pack of carnivorous debutantes were trying to keep up with him, trying to keep him within drooling distance. Thorn was too proud to shout. I can look after myself, she thought, as the ape opened the door.

'Hey, Thorn! *Thorn*!' Johnny ran up to her, droping the drinks. He pushed the ape impersonator away, angry and confused. 'What's your game, you? What's happening, Thorn! Talk to me!'

'Keep your voice down!' she hissed. Johnny followed her eyes to the host. He no longer looked rebuffed and bent on revenge. Now he looked worried, he was wracking his pea-brain for a way to apologize, make amends. He smiled at Johnny with sickening bonhomie. 'Johnny, Johnny, I made a mistake—'

'You bet,' said Johnny, driving his fist into his host's ample gut. The breath left the host's stubby body with a whoosh and he bent double just as Johnny brought up his knee to connect with the host's dirty mouth. Skin and teeth and splashes of blood scattered across the white pile of the carpet. Apes pounced, after blood.

'No!' the host on the floor said. 'Don't touch him! Just get them out of here! Nicely! Both of them!'

Johnny waved the apes away. 'The party's over, anyhow. Let's get out of the old guy's old dump, Thorn.'

The driver was waiting. 'Good party, sir?'

'One of the best I ever got thrown out of,' Johnny said. They got in and took off.

'Where are we heading for, sir?'

Johnny looked at Thorn.

'Back to earth,' she murmured, taking out her compact and lipstick. Johnny stared at her for a moment and then he told the driver to take them to the Grosvenor. Back on the bed he put his arms around her.

'I can see you're upset,' he said. 'I understand.'

'Do you, Johnny? I wonder.'

'*Sure* I do. But listen – that could *never* have happened if the prickhead had realized you were with me.'

'Oh, my God. You conceited creep.' She stood up and walked over to the mirror. 'That's the problem. That's it exactly. When I'm on your arm I'm something special, hall-marked. When I stand on my own I'm just like all the other girls, even here, even in England. Just some stupid bimbo with no visible means of support and nothing between my earrings. And the only market asset I've got is between my legs.'

'Don't talk about yourself like that. Stop it.'

'Why should I? It's the truth, it's what the bastards all think. The only value I've got is second hand.'

'Boy, second hand Thorn! We are feeling sorry for ourselves tonight, aren't we?'

'*You're* not. Johnny's on top of the world. And so he should be.'

'Oh, come on.' He crossed the room and put his arms around her. They stared at her in the mirror. 'You mean to say no old prickhead never came on to you before?'

'Of course they have. But I was never so unprepared for it. Don't sweat it though, Johnny. I'm real glad it happened. It taught me a lesson.'

'What lesson?'

'The most important one in the world. It's time to stop relaxing. I've got to get back to work.'

'I know,' he soothed her, 'when we get back to the States . .'

'I'm not going back to the States.'

'What?'

'I'm going to model here in London. I already told you.'

'Yeah, but—'

'I'm not going to be the girlfriend of number nine, Johnny. I'm not even going to be the girlfriend of number one. I'm going to be number one myself.'

Johnny let go of her and stalked around the room. 'Who asked you to give up your career? When was the last time I locked you up in a broom closet to darn my socks?'

'It all works out that way in the end.'

'All I want you to do is *stay with me.*'

'Why? Because the sex has gotten a little better? For a couple of stray orgasms I'm supposed to follow you to the ends of the earth till the end of my days? *What* do you want me to do, Johnny? Tag along from city to Circuit city, carrying the pots you've won, following behind you?'

'You talk like I'd keep you in purdah! You'd still be able to *model*!'

'No, Johnny, our careers can't co-exist. I'm up against Sherry Ward and her sisters – why should I lengthen the odds by taking you on, too?'

'I'm not asking you to *marry* me or anything.'

'You'd be offering me a better deal if you *were*.'

His face lit up.

'But don't bother with any of that, either, Johnny.'

His face fell.

'You want me to stick around, stay single . . . but *liberation* from marriage leaves a girl in a *more* dependant position, not less of one. Neither of us is a resident of California. So I get my career put in abeyance and I don't even get half your worldly goods at the end of it. Not that I want anything from *you*. I just want . . . a chance. Don't look at me like that. I told you it would never work. I told you that at the beginning. It was you who wanted to start all this.'

'I didn't believe you. I still don't.'

'You know, that's really insulting. You really believe I don't know my own mind. You don't believe I've got a mind, just a sort of cipher between my ears that you can feed plans and ambitions into, or syphon them out of. Well, listen to this; *I don't need you and I'm going to be number one.* Believe.'

One of the room's huge twin white wardrobes belonged to her. She went over to it and claimed it by throwing open the doors.

Thorn grabbed her suitcase and started to fuel it with plastic-covered dresses. There were three times as many as she'd taken from New York. Never mind, she could carry all the clothes in the world.

Johnny Sangster grabbed her wrist and whirled her round. She shook him off easily, her eyes blaring bile. 'Don't you *ever* touch me like that, you! You're not on a tennis court when you talk to *me* and don't you *ever* forget it!'

'Where are you going? Where will you stay?' he blubbered.

'I'll stay by my*self*. I'm just going, ok?'

'That's all right, baby, you don't have to tell me. I already know.'

'Yeah, *baby*? You must have the room bugged with crystal balls. I don't know, myself.'

'You're going to someone who can help your *career*.' He leered it as though it was the most evil word in the world, jabbing an accusing finger at her. Thorn crossed her fingers theatrically, and smiled sarcastically. 'Well, here's hoping!'

'You're going to that old lush! You can't sucker me.'

'I don't know who you're talking about,' she said truthfully.

'That old lush photographer. What's his name?'

'David Bailey?'

'Ha-fucken-ha. You know who I mean. What's the old bastard's name? *Jap Goddard*!'

'Oh, yes.' Thorn smiled seriously. 'I remember. Jap Goddard had slipped my mind completely, Johnny. Thanks for reminding me. Thanks to you, that's *exactly* where I'm heading!'

'You fucking pig! What's the old bastard got that I don't?' Johnny Sangster demanded, 'Apart from a camera, that is?'

'I'm sorry, Johnny. You can't embroil me in one of your famous brawls.' Thorn snapped shut her suitcases and flung a few spare plastic-covered party dresses over her raincoated shoulder. She smiled. 'I might be seeing you again soon, kid.'

He followed her desperately to the door. 'But *when*? *Where* will I see you again?'

'At the top.'

'At least – at least stay the night.'

'Why?' She shook her head and opened the door. She stood silhouetted against the light in the Grosvenor corridor for one sweet brief moment, then quietly closed the door.

'Thorn?' Johnny said plaintively.

It was very nearly dawn. Nothing was stirring but the cleaning ladies and the girls coming off the Arab beat. Thorn shared a lift with an Arab's girl. Nearing the ground the girl pulled off a blonde wig to reveal a headful of rich auburn hair. She laughed at Thorn's startled glance.

'Pretty convincing, what? If you don't have a boy's ass then get yourself one of these.' She touched Thorn's hair with delicate approval. 'You're lucky.'

Down in the street a caravan of sleek black cabs waited impatiently for her. Number one cab dropped her on the corner of the silver and black calling card where Jap Goddard lived.

She cased his place. The serene mews house was in darkness and she didn't knock. She didn't even knock when the curtains were drawn around eleven. She just kept walking, up and down the street where he lived. She didn't even knock when she saw Jap Goddard up at the window, pudgy and stubbly and grudging in his kimono, sipping something and watching her.

He emerged around noon. 'Well, what do you know!' He laughed.

'I was looking for a clothes shop.' She set down her suitcases.

'Which one?'

'World's End, I think it's called.'

'Why don't you come inside? I'll give you directions. Honest, it's no trouble. Here, let me carry those.'

She smiled, with just a soupçon of carefully applied surprise. Then she followed him inside. 'You're very kind,' she murmured, pulling off her gloves.

Jap Goddard was charmed. In his time he had had models on the make bang on his door, scream till the whole mews awoke, fix his bell with half a matchstick and be dragged away yelling by the Metropolitan Police. It was horrible. After a girl had cracked he could never want to photograph her again. It had been a long time since a beautiful girl had been naive or wise enough to arrange an accidental meeting . . .

He smiled at Thorn with genuine warmth and told her to take a seat while he made fresh coffee. She didn't offer to help – good, she knew how to be a guest. Models had been pushy enough in *his* day, in the *Sixties*, but such forebearance *now*! He'd been right about this girl, this Thorn Sayre. He'd waited a long time for her.

Jap Goddard sighed with fulfillment and brought the coffee on a silver tray.

Thorn Sayre stayed.

Concorde pointed its nose at the electric blue sky and Johnny Sangster sipped his strawberry daiquiri. Looking down at the lights of London he savoured his tournament. It had been a very good year. In the early rounds Lennox, Ball and Falconi had all been trounced without him dropping a set. In the fourth round Tom Dougherty's strengths had earned him a set but his weaknesses, which Johnny knew so well from the countless hours of practice they had put in together, had cost him the match. Ray Velez came out for the quarter final already exhausted after a punishing doubles match only three hours earlier and found Johnny Sangster in an unforgiving mood.

He had made it to the last four players left alive in the championships of the world and he had done it *without her*. That was what mattered. He had to know he could thrive without her, he had to know his game was intact.

In the semi-final Johnny took the hot black French kid to five sets and then lost him, overwhelmed by the boy's kinetic power. With the evening throwing long shadows over the packed centre court, Johnny Sangster was eliminated from Wimbledon.

On Dave Pepper's prompting he attended the post-match press conference where he was charming, gracious, even humourous in defeat. Johnny promised he would be back next year.

The English press decided that he had grown up this spring, had become a fine young man that any mother would be proud of and that he had developed into a brilliant tennis player destined to be one of the game's all-time greats. The press assured the public – who had perversely warmed to Johnny Sangster – that their boy would be back next year.

Next year, they all agreed, would be the year of Johnny Sangster.

Now he looked down at the city he had lost her in and tears came to his eyes. He wiped them away and said aloud, 'I'll never see her again, will I?'

Next to him his coach smiled. 'Don't sweat it. Think of your career! The best is yet to come.'

They both smiled. They were both about as wrong as they could be.

Concorde flew into black clouds and below them the lights of London town were gone.

# twelve

Jap Goddard had arrived in the Sixties, and he never moved out.

His clothes looked like they came from Carnaby Street before the novelty shops moved in.

His house was a Warhol lithograph.

The room at the top was a studio, skinny and L-shaped. The four skylights let the sun in to highlight the tripods and contact paper and light meters waiting patiently to be put to work.

On the first floor there were bedrooms and darkrooms. Jap Goddard's bedroom boasted a water bed, and smelled of developer and masturbation.

On the ground floor the living room's low slung white wood, white radiators, deep white Wilton carpet and glossy white walls played stooge to Jap Goddard's Pop Art collection, Warhol – the beauty of Elizabeth Taylor, the blankness of Andy's flowers and the menace of the electric chair – and sun-kissed, heroically proportioned hunks of Lichtenstein. There was a TV in every room, even the pine Habitat fantasy kitchen where Jap Goddard prepared endless melon and avocado vinaigrette, and he liked to have them all on at once. He liked to sit on the white plush G-plan couch and fiddle joylessly for hours with the panel of knobs in the arm which controlled the living room TV – Jap Goddard still thought of it in the Sixties vernacular, *colour TV*. There was a games room, where from film posters Marlon Brando and James Dean stared down with morose male camaraderie on to a touching array of lush lonely toys. Jap Goddard spent many hours beating himself at pinball, snooker, Space Invaders ('The only good thing to come out of the Seventies, Space Invaders,' he was fond of saying.) A

Wurlitzer blasted out Kinks, Yardbirds and Rolling Stones. In the games room you could almost believe that the Beatles still dominated the Top Ten and that Harold Wilson still dominated Number 10.

And on the walls of the lavatory were the faces of a girl – *the* girl, Elle. Her face was there in maybe a thousand Jap Goddard photographs, as cold as the Neapolitan ice cream at Alexander's but ten times as sweet. Her huge pale eyes stared straight at the camera and the man behind it with an all-knowing, all-forgiving wisdom that many men had mistaken for vacancy. They looked out from behind the golden brown curtain of her fringe, those huge melting Sixties pin-up eyes, and the light in them shouted that the act of *being photographed* was the reason why she, Elle, had been created.

Thorn Sayre found Jap Goddard wallowing in the white of his living room. 'Beautiful pictures of Elle,' she said.

'I know.' He had been bullying his daily cleaning lady – he was prissy and meticulous about his precious *blanc* blankness of a home – and he felt full of himself.

'How did you find her?' Thorn asked. What she really wanted to know was, why did she finally ditch you?

'I found Elle at Leonard's,' Goddard said proudly and sadly. 'Leonard was a hairdresser that everyone used. I was picking up a girl there – I don't know who, some nonentity or other, I don't remember – and I saw her standing there. With a dryer in her hand and hairpins in her mouth. *Jill.*'

'Jill?'

'Her name was Jill when she was a junior at Leonard's.' He patted the couch and Thorn sat down beside him. He leaned back with the air of a man about to embark on a long and wondrous saga. 'She was fifteen and came from Holloway. Her dad was a taxi driver and her mum done a runner . . . left home,' he translated.

Thorn nodded encouragingly.

'Well, I looked at her face, then I looked at her face through a Nikon and the rest is mythology. Everything was just starting to happen then, everybody wanted to be young – even the stuffed shirts in Paris were designing these vile *youthful* clothes, all faggy black leather, Dior did, a real scream. Saint Laurent got chucked out on his ear for that one, it was the most unpopular Dior collection ever. But the point is, they wanted *it*, they wanted what we had, *youth* and spirits, really brave high spirits. You've got to remember this was before *drugs* got a grip on people, before *young* was synonymous with *doped*. Quant was coming up, Hulanicki – on Saturdays Biba would be so crowded that they had to let people in one by one as customers left. In '65 Mary Quant had thirty outfits and in '66 she had an OBE and a business worth a million. Can you believe that, Thorn?'

'Barely. I think of Quant as a cosmetic house, I guess.'

'Well, that's just the point. Face paint and bed linen, that's what she does these days. Only sixteen people work for Mary Quant limited! Her husband Graham, he said, 'It was pretty obvious to us in the early Seventies that it was difficult to make money in the garment trade.' Biba closes and re-opens under a different name in a different street every year. But in *those* days, we were so young and strong, everyone was dancing the Twist at the Saddle Room and every deb wanted a Cockney in her Christmas sock and the Beatles conquered America and Sassoon perfected The Cut . . . everyone wanted to be us. In New York they called it the London Look and in France they called it *Le Style Anglais*, and no one did it better than Elle.'

'Tell me about how Elle took off.' Thorn put her hand on Jap's knee. He smiled nervously and cleared his throat importantly.

'Well, I guess the big difference between Elle and the models who'd come and gone before her was that she was the first high fashion model to be a common man's heart-throb, too. She had fourteen *Vogue* covers and the heart of every guy on the shop-floor and every mum in the supermarket. The blokes wanted to –' he winced '– *fuck* her and the women wanted to feed her. There was just . . . something about her that people loved. Her sweetness. She was the first model to have a fan club, here *and* in the States. Girls all over the world, blondes even, were dying their hair golden brown, just to look like her. She had offers to make records, literally *thousands* of film offers from Hollywood and Italy and Paris, to go and make movies. But she wasn't interested. She wasn't interested in anything except looking straight into a camera and having it look right back, in love with her. And then one day she wasn't even interested in that.'

Thorn made her voice suitably grave. 'What happened?'

'She started doing the pet shop routine. You know, like a little shopgirl would get gooey about engagement rings in a jewellers. She'd stop me when we passed a pet shop and go into all that how much is that doggy in the window? routine. I said no, he'll muck on the Wilton. She threatened to leave. She said she needed something to look after. To help something. I told her to go and give five bob to Oxfam.

One day she put her hairdryer and her parents' wedding picture in a Union Jack carrier bag and just walked out that door, just dressed in her jeans and her pink ribbed sweater – she loved ribbed sweaters – and her sneakers. Next thing I know she's transferred her bank account down to some godforsaken ghost town in Sussex and shacked up with some Wop-looking male model, younger than her and all, on a *farm*. I got her number off her dad. I called her. She said, "I love Jimmy and Jimmy loves me." You bet he loved her! She'd made a million out of me by '68!'

'Surely . . .' said Thorn, and stopped. Surely *you* made a million out of *her*.

'What?'

'Surely she couldn't love a gigolo.'

'Oh, he wasn't a poncing little nobody for long. Their shacking up got him a bit of publicity and he does a lot of TV work these days, swigging vermouth and looking moody and whatnot, when they're not rolling in the *hay* or milking the *cows*. He put some kind of hex on her, for sure. She didn't even want her clothes. She loved her clothes so much when she lived here. She didn't even want her Ginger Group gear or her Fredrica black dress or the diamante mesh I bought her in New York City. She said, 'It'll be a lot of use to me down here, won't it, up to my neck in cow crap.' She talked like that. I said, 'Exactly, Elle. Up to your beautiful neck in manure. Is that what you want?" "Yes," she said, "that's what I want. Exactly. And call me *Jill*. Better still, don't call me at all." '

'My!' exclaimed Thorn softly. 'What brought all that on? It can't just have been for lack of a puppy dog.'

'Get me a drink, would you, please? Gin and tonic. With the accent on gin. Thanks. Well, as the Sixties ended it was kind of a culture shock to Elle. She never spoke to me about it – we didn't talk all that much – but she'd been going around saying that nothing dates faster than the face of the decade. Her friends said that she'd been scared of the Seventies, frightened of the kind of freaks that were moving into modelling. She felt she couldn't keep up with them, couldn't compete with them.

She called it the Bad Acid look; Antonio's body painting, Gernreich's topless dresses, Paco Rabanne's kite coat, all those space age fright wigs in pink and green and purple Dynel, all that plastic chain mail and silver leather. All that plastic and chrome jewellery. I bought her pearls all the time, really corny, but they looked beautiful on her, they were the same colour as her skin. I couldn't smear that silver and white greasepaint on her face, it would have been like smearing shit on a stained glass window.' He set down his empty glass.

'So what did she do?' Thorn asked quietly, picking up the Waterford crystal. 'Would you like another?'

'Yeah. She had *quads*. Let alone a dog. She had them in 1974.'

'There you go. Did the marriage last?'

'Yeah.'

'Oh.'

Jap Goddard broke a brittle smile at Thorn. 'End of story. Ancient history. All before your time. Must bore you to tears.'

'Oh, no. I'm a great believer in learning from other's mistakes.'

'You've got nothing to learn.' He drained the glass. 'The only lesson Elle could teach you is that she *always stayed clean*. She always stayed off the dope. Vital.'

He shifted round and smiled at her. 'But let's not talk about Elle anymore. She's about as relevant to *now* as white lipstick. Let's talk about Thorn Sayre.'

'Let's talk in your studio. I'll feel more comfortable there.'

'Sure.'

They climbed the white carpeted stairs. 'What you did with Elle,' Thorn mused. 'What you did with her . . .'

'*Created* her,' Goddard prompted. 'Everyone said that. All the magazines said that. I *created* Elle.'

*Created*, that's a laugh, Thorn thought. 'Created, that's it,' she said. 'Very similar to what David Bailey did with Jean Shrimpton.'

'Yes. *But – aprés la belle* Shrimp David made the mistake of trying to *repeat* the process. Sue Murray, Angela Howard, Jane Holzer, Penelope Tree, Marie Helvin and Kim Harris. Oh, they may be *cute* but they're just substitutes, Shrimp's the permanent one.'

'Marie Helvin's very lovely.'

Jap Goddard nodded. 'But Marie Helvin's not the Shrimp.'

'And – after *la belle* Elle – you were never tempted to repeat the process, Jap?' said Thorn as they reached the studio.

'No,' Goddard said, 'not until now.'

He opened the door.

*Caesar's Things* was a thick, glossy, overpriced fashion magazine that had strained to be chic for the best part of fifty years. As it entered middle age everything had begun to sag. 'The fashion revolution is over,' *Vogue* choked in 1969. 'A new quiet reigns.' Yet instead of shutting up shop and sparing everyone further embarrassment, *Vogue* and its poorer relations *Caesar's Things* and *Harpers & Queen* limped gamely on like wheezing great aunts grinding through a familiar party piece. They didn't appreciate that now there was no fashion – even the rags themselves preferred the word *style* – fashion papers were only good for one thing. To gossip.

*Ritz* did it and thrived. The others didn't, sticking with the millstone of stolid, stationary, exotically and expensively located photographs instead of the scandalous quicksilver shock value of stirring insinuations, and were doomed to bore for ever, eternally grooming their Napoleon complex – pretending to themselves that they could lead all on to a glorious new dawn when it was painfully obvious that the campaign was over and the game was up and the only option open was to retreat in the ragged tatters of defeat.

But unconditional surrender never crossed the stylishly senile minds of the fashion magazines, even though every issue was just like the one before. If you bought one it would last you a lifetime.

In her office, among the Lalique-trimmed mirrors and framed covers of *Caesar's Things* past and the smell of rose water, the editor tried to pretend, day after day, that it wasn't so. She was a sleek blonde woman of indeterminate age, still trim after all these years. Now she studied the portfolio of photographs that Jap Goddard had placed on her desk.

'Beautiful pics, Jap darling,' she drooled. 'Will they end up gracing your elegant lavatory, I wonder?'

'Diana. Are you asking me if I love Thorn Sayre, you inquisitive old bag?'

'I suppose I am, darling.'

'Well, I suppose I do, darling. In a voyeuristic, proxy sort of style.'

'Ah, a cosy little *menage à trois* . . .'

'Goddard, Sayre and Nikon. That's right!'

'You *are* quick today.'

'Why shouldn't I be? The photographs are perfection and the pubs aren't open.'

The editor turned the page, nodding her head in sage awe. 'She certainly is a find. Awfully good of you to let *us* have first peek.'

'The pleasure's all mine, Diana. *You* were the cretin who told me – oh, it must be all of twenty years ago now – that I was wasting my film on Elle. Do you remember just what you said? I certainly do. *"Jap, darling, we can't fill our magazine with this waif just because you're sleeping with her."* '

'Ah, yes, I remember it well. I felt like Dick Rowe at Decca when Elle finally broke. You remember Dick Rowe, darling.'

'Sure. The man who gave those four lovable moptops from Liverpool their one and only rejection slip. The man who turned down The Beatles. I'm extremely glad you feel like that, Diana. I hope that you'll carry the memory of saying Elle was nothing to your deathbed with you.'

'Why are you giving me a bite at your second cherry? If you'll pardon the expression.'

'Because I'm not myself today.'

'You mean you're feeling benevolent,darling.'

'I mean I'm feeling sober, darling. And I know you'll be more careful this time.'

'I have to be.'

'That's right.'

'We want these pictures, darling. We want them very badly.'

'I thought you might.'

'Jap Goddard paints his second masterpiece! Of course, *she's* absolutely delicious. A real polished beauty. There aren't many American blondes worth looking at these days. In fact I can't think of one apart from *her*.'

'All those bland gamines in tracksuits,' Jap Goddard snorted contemptuously. 'I approve of the lifestyle they purport to promote but I loathe the look. Seeing Sherry Ward and her ilk makes me want to stab out my eyes with red hot knitting needles.'

'Then Thorn Sayre found you just in time.' The editor closed the portfolio and smiled smugly at him. 'What about a title for the spread? How does *The Last Beauty Of The Twentieth Century* grab you?'

Goddard nodded and smiled. 'Hard.'

'How big will she be, darling? How long will she last?'

'Bigger than Elle. Longer than Sherry Ward. Better than all of them.'

'What touching faith. I can forsee just one problem . . .'

'What?'

'She's unforgettable. These days they'll forgive a model anything but that.'

The editor began thumbing through the portfolio once more, muttering unrequited superlatives.

In Hyde Park on the last day of summer lovers glided slowly across the Serpentine, children on horseback bobbed along beneath the cool green branches, stenographers stretched out on the grass spooning yoghurt and soaking up the last of the sun and Thorn Sayre, shimmering in a black towelling track-suit, jogged along the path by the lake, heading for the distant roar of the Marble Arch traffic.

The *Caesar's Things* photospread had sold and sold and almost stopped her heart when she first set eyes on it. Thorn Sayre, treacherous and upright as Garbo as Mata Hari, in black slashed to the waist and clasped with a gold square, dark blonde hair a stern straight bob. Thorn Sayre tragic in tulle and white satin, her hair in gleaming ringlets – Garbo couched in Camille. Bare shoulders and blatant rhinestones and endless beauty – Anna Karenina. Doublet and hose and a swagger hat – Thorn Sayre as Garbo as Queen Christina, the most beautiful drag artiste since Dietrich. With a sashay and a suitcase for Anna Christie. And Thorn Sayre as Thorn Sayre – in mirrors, on staircases, stark against black, soft against white, playing opposite London cabs. A panoramic tribute to a perfect pulchritude. Lost in first impressions, Thorn had wanted to do something special for Jap Goddard, she felt such overwhelming *gratitude* towards him. She wasn't going to do *it* – why spoil a good thing, he didn't even dare enter her room without knocking on the door – but she was quite willing to jog for her mentor. She knew how wild Jap was about all that health kick schtick. Not that the lazy tub ever got any exercise himself beyond pouring a stiff gin and tonic, but he thought that health faddism was the greatest spectator sport of all time.

Besides, going for a run around the park was an excellent excuse to get out of Jap Goddard's house when she had a lonesome business deal to attend to. Thorn jogged out of Hyde Park at a rangy pace and hailed a taxi on Speakers Corner. She gave the address of a south of the River Thames slimming clinic to the driver and settled down in the back seat for the ride to Battersea.

When Thorn saw the words *slimming clinic* in the Classified section of a back copy of *Caesar's Things* she knew – as Johnny Sangster would have known – that she was looking at semaphore for 'Open, sesame!' to a treasure trove of mild, legal speed. She'd been availing herself of the find for over a month now, once a week obtaining a prescription in less time than it took her to put on her daily make-up. The first time, a tatty lady doctor made her sit through an unbelievably laborious lecture full of dieting dos and don'ts, but after this tedious formality the pills came thick and fast.

There were clinics like this all over London – the further out the clinic, the cheaper and easier the prescription. In Battersea there wasn't much chance of running into any of Jap Goddard's cronies, and on the other hand it wasn't so far out that she would have to take along a pack mule. When she arrived bright eyed and elated back at the mews, Goddard was always delighted that his girl got so high on jogging itself.

Thorn cared passionately about her health and weight – she just didn't care for physical jerks. It was so pointless – why sw*eat* to lose weight when you could swallow a pill, a pill that felt so *good*. She always told Goddard how beautiful the park had looked. She always thought that she'd seen enough grass when she was growing up to last the entire goat population of the world a lifetime.

Thorn paid the taxi driver and went into the clinic. The receptionist asked her to take a seat, her consultant would be with her in a few minutes. She didn't usually have to wait. The sweet old thing must be soft soaping a new client. The door to the doctor's office opened and an elegant young redhead came out smiling softly, dropping something into her shoulder bag as she strode confidently for the exit with the quick cool pace of the happy customer.

Thorn's false name was called – Mary Gunn, what a joke! – and she went to collect her prescription. It didn't take long this time. The doctor had a small glass bottle and its contents ready to go and Thorn had the right money held together with a platinum money pin in her track suit pocket. She came out rattling her goal and scanning the reception area for any signs of life that could concievably be known to Jap Goddard Esq. You couldn't be too careful. If the old lush knew that the last beauty of the twentieth century was hooking down speed pills like Smarties he was liable to go through the roof of his studio!

Only one customer waited for service, a huge young woman huddled deep inside a fake sable – it *had* to be fake on a young woman, in London, in the Eighties, not through lack of funds but through *feeling* – even though the temperature outside was well into the seventies. Her eyes were hidden behind thick black wraparound shades and she was flanked by two bald brawny giants in smart dark neatly pressed business suits. The receptionist was pretending not to look at the young woman. The young woman looked as though she wished to disappear.

Thorn looked at her twice. She was vaguely familiar, maybe a little like Maxine Capra twice the size, Maxine Capra gone to seed. Thorn looked again, advancing towards the young woman, who visibly cringed. One of the dapper bald giants got to his feet.

'I don't believe it,' breathed Thorn Sayre. 'Excuse me . . . it *is* you, isn't it?'

The standing giant looked at the young dark woman for instructions. Almost imperceptably she nodded, slightly raising her hand. 'Hello, Thorn,' said Maxine Capra. 'How do you like my new look?'

'My God, Maxine! What are you *hiding* from?'

'Hate.'

'*What*?'

Maxine nodded at her broken-nosed companions. 'Meet the muscle. This is Sal, a sort of distant cousin of mine from NY. This one here, the lazy one, he's Henry. He's English. Reinforcements. Believe it, they're not related to each other. Incredible.'

Sal smiled tensely, Henry nodded politely.

'Why do you need two?' Thorn asked shrilly, illogically. She noticed the receptionist gawping openly at the tableau and lowered her voice. 'Maxine, kid, I don't understand. What are you doing here, in London? I can see what you're doing *here*. Where did the weight come from? What happened to *A Virtuous Woman*?'

'Oh, nothing happened to *her*.' Maxine Capra laughed bitterly. 'But *my* loving public became a lynch mob and I became a wreck. Pull up a chair and I'll give you a laugh.'

Thorn sat.

'Let's start at the very beginning, a very good place to start. I'll tell you about the death threats later.'

Thorn frowned.

'Remember way back when I auditioned for the Sugar Coated Wheatichomps ad, Thorn?'

Thorn nodded. 'Sure. You . . . didn't look the part, that's the one. They said you looked like the kind of girl who'd be sneaking out the back door as the happy family sat down to their delicious breakfast of . . . of Sugar Coated Wheatiecrap. I remember, I wanted you to file a law suit. It was *slander*.'

Maxine shook her head. 'No, Thorn, that wasn't name-calling, that was my life story.'

'So you looked hot. So what? Looking like that got you the tub song Off Broadway, looking like that got you Jolene Gentry.'

'Yeah, looking like that got me plenty. Looking like that got me my big break, got me typecast. Got me threats on my fucking life, Thorn! Looking like that got me *fans* who wanted to torture me to death! I could show you the *letters*, if that's what you could call 'em – no, I turned them all over to the police in LA. Christ, Thorn, you should have seen 'em!'

'But why?'

'Oh, God, why do people get twisted? Maybe they're born like it. Did you ever see *A Virtuous Woman*?'

'No. After you left the apartment I left the country. I was a mannequin for Twist in Paris before I came to London.'

'Then you never saw Jolene Gentry. You wouldn't know about her.'

'I know about the character, sure I do! I know what you told me. She liked to have a good time, nothing *nasty* or anything. Not a *murderess* or anything.'

'Worse. Jolene Gentry was out rolling in the Holiday Inn hay with Doctor Steve Maddock while his poor ex-nurse wife Eve – crippled in an auto accident one Thanksgiving, thanks to her drunken hubby, you will recall – was stuck back at home with her three kids and her wheelchair.'

'But – my God, Maxine – it's just a story! What's *wrong* with these people?' Thorn gasped. The receptionist looked up with interest. The brace of beefcake stared back at her impassively and the receptionist looked down again.

'*Just* a story? Go tell it to the huddled by the TV masses. Real soap fanatics just can't tell fact from fiction, and now faction's made them even more convinced they're right. Did you know that, in the faint possibility that a fanatic misses a fun-packed episode of his or her favourite prime time melodrama, he or she can buy any one of two dozen magazines devoted entirely to updating the life and loves of all us glamorous soap opera characters? They think it's publications like the Washington Post and the Daily News that are just make believe – after that Pulitzer Prize incident last year, it looks like they could be right. *But they just can't grasp the fact that their precious soap is just let's pretend.* It must be real, it's right there on the screen.'

'OK. So a couple of nuts write to you, jealous, and make totally empty threats . . .'

'A couple of hundred. A couple of hundred every episode.'

'But you don't really believe that they'd actually go through with it, do you?'

'Sure I do. But don't take my word for it. Go ask Mark Chapman and John Hinckley and any other freak who did.'

'My God, I see what you mean.' Thorn gnawed a shimmering fingernail, stopped herself. 'Couldn't you have compared notes, talked it out with anyone in the cast? What about the actor who plays the cheating quack? Surely he attracted kink mail too.'

'Nah,' said Maxine contemptuously. 'Ross – Steve Maddock, MD to you – he never got *one* threat. Those cretins out there will let a doctor get away with anything!'

'So you've come to London to get away from it all for a while, huh? When are you due back?'

'I've left the States for good, Thorn.' Maxine stared down at her chubby brown hands. They were shaking and wet. 'I couldn't take it any more. They *meant* it, Thorn! They're *mad*! That ain't no melting pot, it's an abbatoir. My agent arranged with Dave Brown to have Jolene Gentry get what was coming to her in a domestic plane crash. Maybe that will satisfy the crazy bastards.' She crossed her clammy fingers and let out a shaky laugh. 'Here's hoping.'

'You threw it all away,' Thorn said incredulously, 'just for some illiterate goons . . .'

'You don't know what it's *like*!' Maxine hissed furiously. "You don't know the *pressure* I've been under! Look at me! Look at the way I am! Remember me, the way I used to be?'

Thorn did. She remembered the cosmopolitan cocktail of a girl with light brown velvet where other people had skin, the girl with the been-to-bed eyes, the terminal Vargas girl. Thorn couldn't think where that girl had gone. 'What happened to you, Maxine? How d'you get this way, honey?'

Maxine blinked, hard. She wiped her nose with the back of her hand. 'My problems made me fat. That's no cop out, they really did. I drink to forget, I eat to comfort myself, I don't get no exercise because I'm scared to see people. They might be looking for me. Don't fucking smile, Thorn, it's not fucking *funny*.'

'I'm sorry, Maxine.' She took her hands and was shocked at their slipperiness. 'Take it easy now, honey.'

Maxine squeezed Thorn's hands tight. 'Drink too much,' she repeated. 'Take too many tranks. One of 'em's too many and two ain't enough. Overeat to comfort myself and . . .' She patted her ample stomach.

'You're going to have a baby!' Thorn was stunned.

Maxine laughed horribly. 'Some hope! What I got in here, what I eat to comfort, is *ulcers. Twins*. Room service – I'm staying at the Dorchester, they're secure and boy, do they respect your privacy – room service would have me as big as the Albert Hall if not for the script they give me here.'

'I'm surprised they're keeping you waiting so long. I never have any trouble. Did you see my pictures in *Caesar's Things*?'

'No. What time is it, Sal?'

'Just after two.'

'What time's my appointment?'

'Three.'

'Jeez, I got *years* to wait!'

'Told ya that before we left the hotel,' said Sal with inexhaustable gentle patience. 'Ya remember?'

'Yeah, oh yeah,' Maxine snapped. She looked at Thorn with her tragic puffball eyes. 'These threats made me old, fat and drunk. Any idea how much decent security costs these days? Old, fat and drunk.'

'And an exile,' Thorn said sympathetically. 'Oh, Maxine, I'm so sorry . . .'

'*Exile*? Who's a fucking exile?' She pulled away her hands belligerently.

'I thought you came to London with, you know, paranoia running wild. Like Lucky Lindbergh.'

'I'm here to *work*,' Maxine declared. 'I got a part in an English weekly sit com – on the *BBC*, baby! – about a bunch of kids who graduate from RADA – that's like the High School of Performing Arts with stiff upper lips and no knives. It's called *Resting*.'

'That's great.'

'Pretty good title, right? Pretty juicy part. I play the kooky brown American girlfriend of an *unmarried* black English actor. Not too much ammunition *there* for the British audience to kill me with, right?'

'Have you started filming yet?'

'We go into production in two weeks time. I've got to get rid of half this weight by then. One of *Resting*'s writers, his typewriter never runs on nothing but uppers. He gave me the address of this place.'

'Don't worry about that weight. The stuff they give you here is great. Just one bad thing about it.'

'What's that?'

'It wears off.'

Maxine laughed.

'And don't worry about those death threats either. You have to be pretty big to get them. I reckon it'll be a good six months before I get any. I wish I had a copy of my *Caesar's Things* spread to give you. The Last Beauty Of The Twentieth Century, they called me.'

'I'm happy for you, kid.'

'Mrs Brown?' the receptionist called. 'You're rather early, but the doctor will see you now.'

'Thank you,' called Maxine. She leaned close to Thorn and dropped her voice to a whisper. 'Never trade under your real name, Thorn. It makes it easy for them to find you.'

'I know.'

'Stick around, anyway, kid, we'll give you a lift back to town. Is Park Lane ok for you?'

'Fine. I can jog back to the mews through Hyde Park.'

Maxine smiled slyly. For a moment Thorn recognized her. 'Ah, get serious! You're putting me on!' She turned up her collar and adjusted her shades. 'I won't be long.' In a minute she returned, and Thorn and the muscle got up and escorted her to the exit.

Maxine suddenly stood perfectly still, staring, petrified. She looked at Henry. 'I can't go out there. *I'm not going out there*!'

'You don't have to,' said Sal.

'Sit down until you feel better,' Henry advised.

'You go out there when you're good and ready,' Sal assured.

Thorn watched them help Maxine back to her seat. 'Maxine, honey, what is it? What's happened? What's wrong?'

'They're out there.'

'Come *on*, Maxine! You grew up in New York and this is *London*. Here, take my hand. It can't be more than five steps to your car.'

Maxine curled up in her chair, shaking her head softly, shivering violently. 'No, no.'

'She'll be ok in a while, miss. Don't worry,' murmured Sal.

'It doesn't last long.' muttered Henry.

'I'll wait for you,' said Thorn. 'I'll wait for you and – when you're ready, Maxine – we'll go out together. I've got all the time in the world, honest.' She made to sit down.

'No.' Maxine put her hand on the chair. 'You go on ahead. Sorry about the ride. But you go ahead now, child. I can find my own way out.' Maxine Capra almost smiled. 'It's part of my charm.'

Thorn saw Maxine cowering, taking root in the chair. Remind me never to take you to McDonalds, she joked bitterly to herself. She left Maxine with her shot nerves and her bodyguards.

On the stairs she stopped short. She felt edgy. Psycho-paranoia must be contagious, Thorn thought. I better inoculate myself. She took out the small bottle, unscrewed the top and shook a black capsule into the palm of her hand. She swallowed it. Appetite depressant, it said on the bottle . . . terror depressant, too. If these sweeties couldn't help Maxine, nothing could. She felt better already. In fact she felt *great*! If you've got a couple of these – she slipped the bottle back into her track suit tenderly – you don't only not need exercise, you don't need bodyguards. Because you are not afraid of ANYTHING.

She grabbed a cab. The ride to Marble Arch seemed to take a millimetre of a moment. Then she was running with long, strides along the pathway by the Serpentine, thinking poor Maxine, there but for the grace of Goddard go I. She smiled. It was a good line. It was also a lie. She had done it all herself.

She recalled the first time he took a photograph of her, that first session in his studio. He was giving her the verbal foreplay while loading his camera, trying to build up an atmosphere thick with hot sex once removed.

'A photographer,' Goddard had said, 'has to get a state of trust with his model and then he has to betray that trust to get what he wants.'

Garbage, Thorn had thought. The camera doesn't have that much power, it's a very *passive* thing, a blank wall. Photographers are much the same. Blank walls – draw on them what you will, young girl!

But she'd smiled sweetly and nodded in assent.

Now she turned into the mews and made for the door. She found Jap Goddard at the bar in his lithograph living room, bolting down gin and drooling over his latest photographs of Thorn Sayre. He looked up at her, red gilled and guilty.

'Don't look at me like that,' she laughed, 'I feel like the harbinger of coitus interruptus.'

'I thought you were a prowler.'

'No, I always wear this stocking over my face.'

'Ha . . . very funny.'

Boy, but he's slow when he's loaded. In fact he's not exactly a cerebral Seb Coe when he's sober.

'What's your poison?'

'I want to be alone. For a while.'

Goddard shrugged elaborately and began muttering to himself. 'Be like that.' Thorn, incredibly, heard him say as she climbed the stairs three at a time. 'I'll have *yours* too!' She presumed he meant her drink. 'Why bother?' she heard him reflect, like a tenth rate philosopher who had had ten too many. The glossy photographs swished.

Thorn felt as though she knew what it was like to have one's grave robbed. She took a leisurely shower and wrapped a towel around her body and a turban around her head. She certainly wasn't going to put that corny tracksuit back on – no more jogging until the pills ran out. She padded back to her room – *Elle's* room – checked that the door was locked and opened the closet.

The room was just as Elle had left it. Her father, in a half-hearted attempt to keep his Jill on the straight and narrow, had let her move in with the pansy boy photographer on the condition that she was given a room of her own with a lock and a key. Not that there was much danger of the paisley-troused ponce being interested in a girl, but anyway . . .

In later years Jill came to silently, constantly thank her father for his feeble gesture towards gentility. The room was a haven from Jap drunk, Jap jealous, Jap hell bent on taking photographs every waking moment and just plain Jap boring. The walls were covered with Biba posters and Brigitte Bardot and The Beatles, the dressing table groaned under the weight of hair pieces, false eyelashes and white Yardley Lipslicker, archetype haven heaven of a narcissistic Sixties teenager. Thorn hadn't changed a thing. She loved to sit there and think about herself. It was a soothing room, a swinging museum.

Thorn thumbed casually through the closet. Ruffles, ribbons and frills from Mexicana, a clove wool Dior dresing gown, Ossie Clark's 1967 satin status symbols, a whole Jazz Collection from Liberty's, a Clark Forties fawn jersey suit with square shoulders, lots of sweet Tuffin and Foale shifts. At the bottom of the wardrobe was a jumbled jungle of Marks and Spencer's briefs, Rudi Gernreich No Bra bras and Warners bodystockings. She stretched out her hand towards one . . . There was a sharp rap on the door.

'Yes?'

'Guess who.'

'Yes, Jap? What do you want?'

'Open up. You got a phone call.'

She opened the door and wished she hadn't. He was an eyesore. He had a glass in each hand and a dull leering light in each eye. He had never leered at her before. He's losing his respect, just like Mama Sayre said men would. But he hasn't even waited to fuck me – long wait – before he lost it, she thought. It's because he's got all those photographs. He can't believe that Thorn Sayre could be anything more than what he's got in the viewfinder – just another stain on the contact sheet. Boy, does he have a rude awakening waiting for him somewhere.

He walked past her into the room and stared at the closet. 'Trying on *la belle* Elle's party clothes?'

'No. They're too little girly for me. And the things that are halfway decent are either too pale or too ornate.'

'Hard to please.' He gulped his gin.

'That's right.'

'Why don't you try a bodystocking on? Or those boots? Elle always rouged her knees when she wore boots.'

'Short sight is a terrible thing.'

'Ha ruddy ha. Go on, put the boots on. I'd love to have you in them—'

She pierced him with an icily imperious glare. 'Who's calling?'

Goddard lost his dirty twinkle. It was replaced with surly sulkiness. 'Don't know. He wouldn't give his name. Some Yank. I know that much.'

'Johnny . . .' He must have seen her in *Caesar's Things*. The pictures must have been driving him crazy, he wanted her back, her *and* her career. Sweet boy!

'*Not* John-John,' Goddard sneered nastily. '*Not* the so-called Son of Superbrat. *Not* the so-called White Tiger. *Not* Johnny fucking Sangster, so-called flash little asshole bastard. Some other Yank. Wants you for *business*, not *pleasure*.'

'What's that? A violation of your copyright?'

'Ha bloody ha.'

'You were the one who didn't want me to get on the books of an agency. I wanted to go to Models One.'

'They take twenty five per cent of your money!'

'You'd take one hundred per cent of my life if I let you. But I won't. Excuse me.' She brushed past him and hurdled down the stairs. She could hear Goddard mumbling on the landing, lumbering after her like Caliban. 'Bloody cow Diana must have given the Yank bastard my number . . . just to spite me . . .'

Thorn picked up the telephone. 'Hello?'

'Thorn Sayre?'

'Speaking.'

'Thorn! Good to talk to you, Thorn! *Great* to talk to you, Thorn! Saw your photographs! Great! More than that, *very* great!'

'You're too kind. Who are you?'

'This is Sherwood Klan. K.L.A.N.' The name was a shame but the voice was dark brown with humour and high energy. 'As in Ku Klux! Calling long distance from the Big Orange. El Lay, heh heh!'

It was a rich voice and it was aiming everything at her. Mash calls, like stars got. Her heart pumped overtime with the excitement of attention plus pills.

'The Big Orange . . . Los Angeles? Hello?'

'I'm well aware that the Big Orange is not a fruit and vegetable store in the Fulham Road, Mr Klan.'

'What? Hey, that's pretty good! I like that! You know, old Sherwood Klan is calling you all the way from LA and it's costing him plenty. But what the heck! It's worth it!'

'What can I do for you, Mr Klan?'

'It's what I can do for you, Miss Sayre. You're just the person I need.'

'Just the . . .'

'Yep. Greta Garbo.'

'I am not Greta Garbo.' She approximated a yawn, loudly.

'Close enough. You look like an intelligent girl – you know your way around a mirror, right? You know that on a good day you're the best Greta Garbo facsimile the world has ever known. Providing the hair and the paint and the lighting is right, of course.'

'Of course. But close enough for what? To give old Garbo fans a thrill? Rather useless.'

'Close enough for Hollywood,' Sherwood Klan declared. 'I'm calling from a Bel Air number, Thorn. I can see the Hollywood Sign from my window. I've made a fortune in celluloid. I know what I'm talking about.'

'Oh, I see . . .'

'Ah, now you're interested. The *movies*, Thorn. That's right! Now you know I'm not playing with myself at this end!'

'Of course I'm interested.' She thought of returning triumphant to dullard America, her home, warming her hands at the Hollywood Sign like it was an honest Statue Of Liberty. 'What's the project, Mr Klan? I guess it's a Garbo bio, right?'

Sherwood Klan laughed. 'Wrong. It's not a mere movie I want you for, Thorn.'

'Oh, *television.* Eternal television.' For a moment she was disappointed. Then she registered the state of cinema and the scope of TV. 'A made for TV movie? One of those best-seller blockbuster serials?'

'Not television, Thorn. Nothing so *trashy.*'

'A commercial?'

'A cat house, Thorn.' The man laughed. 'Sherwood wants you for his brothel.'

'I don't believe it.' She sat down quickly.

'*Now before you hang up*! – Gemini – that's the name of my

establishment, Thorn – is the most expensive, exclusive, discreet house of its kind in America. We are conoisseurs, specialists, dealers in divine beauty. Our girls are perfect facsimiles of everyone's own favourite goddess. Who's *your* favourite actress, by the way?'

Thorn laughed. 'Is this a joke? It's very clever.'

'No joke. Choose.'

'Lauren Bacall.'

'Oh, Thorn! You're a sharp girl. You've cut me to the quick, hit me in my Achilles ache. I can't find a Lauren. I got a Lana, and an Ava, and a Liz. I got hair stylists, wardrobes packed with ravishing replicas of everything Garbo ever took for an airing on the silver screen, I got maquillage masters, a doctor, a *lady* doctor for all you shy Southern gals, I got brilliant security, better than the Chase Manhattan. There's no trouble, no abuse, no fist fights. I don't serve hard hooch. Don't worry about the police. And the clientele! We get, we get senior executives from the film industry, guys on the boards of multinational corporations, one guy who owns the major slice of a huge recording label, doctors, dentists, professors, everything! It takes all sorts! It's a big, happy world!'

'Goodbye, Mr Klan.'

'Listen! Listen to me before you ruin your life.'

'I'm listening.'

'The chick that played Marilyn in that TV show in the *Private Lives* season. You know the chick I mean?'

'Yes.'

'Well, prior to that great break she did a six-month stint with none other than your old fan Sherwood! So don't shoot me, Toots, not until you hear me out. You there?'

'Yes.'

'Nothing low or illegal, ok? Most of your fans are fifty plus or fags or both if you don't mind me saying so, Greta. They just want to see you lying on a couch coughing prettily in your Camille clothes. Maybe they just want to pull your dress up and take a peek or something. Is that too much to ask?'

Thorn laughed. 'It's the least I can do!'

'Of course, if you *should* find the guy attractive, you'll also find an extra zero on your salary cheque. *It's completely your decision*. But if you dig the creep, why not? That's the way I look at it.'

Thorn took a deep breath. 'Mr Klan, you are the original

Ugly American. Begone.' She hung up and laughed, deflated and delighted.

Jap Goddard stood at the foot of the stairs, staring at her without expression.

'Let me cheer you up, Jap!' Thorn cried, clapping her hands. 'That was a Mr Klan, proprietor of a Bel Air brothel that caters to myopic millionaires. Hopeful whores are strictly vetted. Passport; a film star's face. Understand?'

'He wanted you to put out while playing Garbo,' Goddard said flatly.

'Right! Isn't it a riot? When you're famous even lechers are a kick! They can't touch me now!' She rushed laughing to his side. He winced away from her.

'What's up *now*, Jap?'

He glared at her, his eyes swimming with Gordon's gin and vicious suspicion. 'You'd love to do it!' he declaimed. 'Wouldn't you? *Wouldn't you*? Why don't you admit it?'

Thorn stared at him, thinking about Elle and discovering that she wasn't just a perfect face.

'Ah, I don't care,' Goddard slurred wearily. 'You're all the same. *Every model in the world wants nothing more than for every last man in the world to look at her*. Exhibitionists, the lot of you. I don't care.' He took a long pull on his drink and threw his last shot over his shoulder as he weaved back to the bar. 'I'm sure you'd break all set records with your turnover.'

She went upstairs to her mirrors and lock and thought she had a career. He stayed downstairs with his photographs and his gin and thought he had Thorn Sayre.

# thirteen

She'd awoken that morning to find him crouched over her taking photographs of her naked sleeping face. It was an invasion of her person and it infuriated her. He'd lowered his Nikon sheepishly to groin level. 'Just a couple of shots. I couldn't pass up a chance like that, Thorn. You look so beautiful when you're dead to the world.'

'You'd like me best if I was stuffed and mounted!' She sat

up straight and was pleased at his disappointment in her high-necked, long-sleeved white Victorian lawn nightdress.

'That's not true,' he whined.

'How the hell did you get into my room, anyway?'

'The door was unlocked.'

She stared at him coldly. He was probably lying and had a spare key stashed away somewhere, but she couldn't be sure she'd locked her door, come to think of it. Last night had been strange, what with Sherwood Klan's call to think about and all. 'You're a fat, useless lush, you know, Jap. And that camera is getting a grip on you. You should have it removed, like a cyst.'

'You *owe* me this much. You don't give me any rent. You *owe* me,' he sniffed with offended hospitality.

'I owe you *nothing*! I gave you your career back, let alone *rent*!' She snatched the camera swiftly and disembowelled it before his befuddled hungover motor reactions could register the theft.

He wailed.

'Is this the only film?'

'Yes! And you've ruined it. Happy?'

'Very.' She threw the camera and ticker-tape film at his feet. 'Now get out.'

Goddard shambled to the door. 'You know, you're nothing new, no surprises,' he muttered maliciously. 'Elle was just the same. No make-up, no pictures. Why don't you girls sleep in your make-up? It's perverse.'

'Jap?'

'What?'

'That party tonight.'

'What about it?'

'We *are* going to it, Jap.'

'You know I don't like parties. I can't take pictures with a roomful of sweaty cretins breathing all over my light meter.'

'And I can't breathe with one sweaty cretin drooling all over my shoes. If you don't accompany me, I'll go alone. It's up to you. I'm sick of sitting around every night with you pointing that camera at me every time I draw a breath.'

'I'll take you there,' he sighed.

'Don't you trust me, Jap?'

'I trusted Elle. I trusted Elle every minute of every day. Look what she did to me.'

'She took a raincheck on being resident human sacrifice to the all-seeing eye about the house,' spat Thorn. 'What a treacherous Jezabel. We leave for the party at nine, ok? And don't bring Nikon. I'm sick of playing gooseberry.'

'I'll be bored to tears there. What will I do?'

'Grin and bear it, gin and tonic,' she prescribed. 'You'll manage somehow.'

The party swung in spite of itself. It was contained within a vast open plan office three floors above the drab pleasure-seekers snapping up bad porn and sad prostitutes down in the Soho backstreets. The room was lit by nothing but the neon stutters of pseudo sex signs. Everyone said it was like living in a B movie. They said it again and again and again, just to prove they appreciated the trash aesthetic. The wine flowed like red vinegar.

But the music was Kid Creole and The Coconuts, Thorn wore a black lace cheongsam and a deep red carnation behind her left ear and the people at least were *young*. By the tawdry illumination that briefly interpreted the party Thorn could see five eager young faces for every old, grim one. The oldest, grimmest face sneered smugly at her side.

This was the attempted launch of a magazine calling itself *The Painted Mirror*, a fashion fanzine created by a dozen slight young things who had been rejected by their true love's cruel guardian – the uncaring world.

Jap Goddard watched it kid itself, and took a contented hit on his pint mug of table red. 'Our hosts are the people with hysteria in their eyes and a bailiff on their back. It's the new look, darling.'

'Who are they?'

Goddard shrugged. 'Designers who graduated – got spewed out by, more like – from the Royal College of Art and made clothes that no one was stupid enough to buy. And a gaggle of marijuana-minded *alternative* journalists that no one is alternative enough to employ. All of them are lower middle class except for one, who has an inheritance. Never take an inheritance anywhere near the media. It's a better investment to put it on a bobtail nag, as you say in Alabama.'

'Virginia. How long do you think *The Painted Mirror* will last?'

'In the Sixties, if you were young you were fashionable. In

the Eighties if you're young you're unemployed.' He drained his glass. 'The rag will last until about thirty seconds after the drink runs out. So I'd better get a refill, fast.' He waddled off in search of refreshment. He was dressed head to toe in denim, the pig. The Latin music slipped Thorn into the sway of the fray and she snaked across to the other side of the room, smiling to herself. Goddard wouldn't be able to find her again without the help of Alcoholics Anon and one of those dogs with a crate of brandy for a necklace. She felt a little like she had when she'd left the Sayres. She was delirious to be with *people* again, to look into a pair of eyes rather than a circle of ground glass. She was a pampered prisoner, she was going to cut loose.

I am *someone*, she thought. What's the point in being someone if you don't go out to be stared at? She took from her clutch bag a slim gold cigarette case that had arrived that very morning as a package forwarded from the office of *Caesar's Things*. Engraved inside it, the legend The Last Beauty Of The Twentieth Century and a Bel Air address. It was obviously a sweetener from Sherwood. She stared hard at the address. Wishful thinking.

Yes, she'd keep it. She didn't like the taste of cigarettes but she loved the way they looked. Warning – this fashion accessory can seriously damage your health. She laughed and a bland man of around thirty who had been standing nearby, staring, took it as his cue. So did a similarly smitten young lanky art student. They approached her smartly, but their smiles disappeared when they took in the confident competition. Then they both blared grins at her.

'Phil. You're the most beautiful girl I've seen since breakfast.'

'I'm Stephen. And you're the last beauty of the twentieth century. *Loved* the spread, Thorn.'

The fair man glared. 'Thorn. Of course. Thorn, let my Maserati and I take you away from all this tack. We could be on the Champs Elysee in one hour.'

'Why should she want to be taken away from all this? What's there to get away from? Apart from the embarrassing attentions of arthritic swingers, that is.'

'It's a bore. This party is a crushing bore.'

'No it isn't. It's my friend's party. If you can't enjoy it you are not anti-fashion and you shouldn't be here. Didn't you read the invitation?'

'Boring party, boring people,' Phil insisted.

Stephen was amazed. 'Who's boring?'

'You are, for a start.'

'I'm not boring.'

'You will be.'

Thorn sipped a glass of sour red wine that someone had thoughtfully abandoned on a nearby desk. She said nothing, and she laughed at their bungled *bons mots*. Let them fight over her – the winner takes nothing. Let Jap see other people panting after her – the alked-out wretch. Who needed him? Certainly not the last beauty . . .

She saw Roche across the room and she smiled broadly with shocked glee. The quarrelsome pair stared after her soulfully, but by the time they came to blows she had erased their existence from her mind for ever.

Roche stood waiting for her without a smile. He looked so familiar yet she hadn't thought of him once since meeting him. Roche was aware of what he was, a good Samaritan superfluous after the favour. His good heart was unscathed by a life of crime, his clear mind was uncracked by the tools of his trade. He wasn't alone. Thorn was just a few feet away from him when she saw his date. A skinny blond boy stood close to Roche, staring up at him, the expression on his face midway between faithful pup and thwarted policeman. His silky hair was cut into a fringe and petulance had all but driven prettiness from his face. He wore dark, run down, well cut clothes and around his head he sported a striped tie.

'Hello, Roche,' Thorn said jauntily, her head swimming from the sour grape.

'Hello, Thorn. Meet David Waymouth.'

The boy's eyes flicked disinterestedly over her before clamping on to Roche once more. 'How do you do.'

'Very well, thank you. What's that you've got on your head?'

'This? My pa's old school tie. It's my tourniquet. You're an American. Do you know Green?'

'Green who? I mean, who Green?'

'It's a *drug*. Don't you take drugs?' David Waymouth swanked like a child showing off his first pair of long trousers.

'Sure I do. But I don't feel the need to advertise the fact

everytime I open my yap. Drugs are for taking, not talking about.'

'Talk's all I get from Roche.' The boy pouted and then wrang his hands, literally. 'Please, Roche. Don't be cruel to me. I'm only little.'

Roche spoke, in a patient, weary voice. 'David, isn't Clemency here? Why don't you go and find her? I'm sure that she and Miss Sayre would have a lot to talk about. Where *is* your sister?'

'Somewhere around,' Waymouth shrugged. 'I'm not bothered. The only flesh and blood I'm interested in is my upper arm. They say blood's thicker than water, Roche. I wonder if you can jack it up.'

'Spare us the gory details. Won't you go and find Clemency?'

'Won't you sell me some of that lovely H of yours?'

'I'll have it for you around dusk tomorrow.'

'Scout's honour?'

'Yes.'

'Great. I'll go and get Clem.'

They watched him scurry off.

'Why would I want to meet his sister, Roche?'

'She's a model. She's just a decoy, actually. I thought we could give him the slip.'

'A leech would be less trouble.'

'A leech wouldn't pay good money for a bad drug.'

'Do many people pester you?'

'Only the people I don't want to be pestered by.' He looked at her with sad adoration.

'Why are you so down, Roche old sport?'

'I was watching you. You're drinking and drinking seems to make you like too many people. You should stick with speed.'

'What's this? A hard sell?'

'Call it a special offer.'

'I'm suddenly on the wagon. I'm very pleased to see you, Roche. But what are you doing here? Rough and ready rag trade tea parties are barely your beat.'

'I'm looking for you,' he whispered. 'That's what I'm doing here.'

'Trying to tempt me into a chemicals binge? I'm a big shot now, I can pay instead of ponce.'

'That's it, Thorn. I'm after your money.'

They laughed and then Thorn stared at him seriously. 'What

makes you think you've got a chance with me, Roche?'

He smiled. 'Johny's gone to America, Jap's gone to pieces.'

'Sounds like a sinister nursery rhyme.'

'I'm not afraid of the word *no*, anyway.' He looked at her with shy regard. It was easier to take that look from him than from Johnny. Johnny had wanted to get too close up to her, it had been life or death with Johnny. Exhausting. 'But I feel very strongly about you and I'd like to take you home and go to bed with you for as many nights as you're agreeable to. I've got more drugs than you ever knew existed back at home. And I don't want your money. I got my own. Masses of it.'

She smiled, touched and impressed. 'You really know the right things to say to a girl, Roche.' She removed the red carnation from her hair and slipped it through his top buttonhole. 'Go get a car – a *good* car – and we'll escape.'

As Roche did her bidding Jap Goddard grabbed her arm. 'Remember me? I'm the creep who created you.'

'You're hurting my arm.' She stared at him disdainfully.

'So?'

'So let go or I'll kick you where your balls used to be and shout things that will make you cringe.'

He released her. 'What are you going with him for? Cocaine or cock?'

'What are you offering? Hot lights and hangovers?'

'Ah, go! Your kind are ten a penny.'

'But I know I'll never find another you, Jap.'

She watched him swagger away belligerently, she saw him accost some old Sixties cronies and heard him railing about her perfidy, punctuating the poignant monologue with a finger jabbed in her direction. Roche returned and she weighed the two men up in one long sweeping stare, the lure of low life adventure against the blankness and money in the bank of the empty camera eye.

'Mercedes,' said Roche.

'*Merci.*'

Jap Goddard watched them exit, and tried to write Thorn Sayre and her future off in a loud, pained bellow. 'Lines on the mirror, lines on her face! I made her something special, now the drugs will make mincemeat of her!' He snatched up a half full bottle of wine and drained it in one gulp, but his sorrows were expert swimmers.

*

They all said that the black French kid was going all the way. He soared up through the rankings like a greased comet and everyone agreed that he was the only one young enough, hot enough and good enough to take over from Bjorn Borg at the top of the mountain. The Swede and the French kid even played the same game – endlessly patient potentates waiting at the back of the court with double-handed groundstrokes that served as guillotine for every big game American hot head on the circuit. That's what they all said.

When Johnny Sangster met the French kid at the York University Tennis Centre at the end of the summer and when Johnny wiped the court with the French kid in brief straight sets that made the boy look totally bewildered and out of his depth they knew that everything they had been saying was horribly wrong.

'Usually I'd rather pay a fine than talk to you people,' Johnny told the post-match press conference. 'Today I wanted to see your faces. Answer your questions. Rub your noses in it – you know, the *truth*. You remember the truth.' He felt a restraining hand rest momentarily on his arm and he turned to look at Dave Pepper.

The coach looked nervous. 'Easy, John. You proved you're the best young pro on the circuit. You're up to five on the world rankings. Why do you want to make enemies? Do you want people to hate you?'

'I want *justice*,' Johnny hissed. 'These creeps – and the no neck crowds, remember those stinking rednecks down in Dallas? – these creeps have done me dirt for years because I wouldn't tickle their butts with my tennis racquet. Because I stick up for myself.'

'The Oliver Twist of the tournaments.'

'Let's get this show going, Fagin.'

Dave Pepper looked at the assembled representatives of radio, TV and press. 'First question. Ok, you at the front.'

'Johnny, why was it over so quickly today?'

'It wasn't a match. It was a mercy killing. I can't be expected to choreograph my game so that it doesn't mess up the network schedules.'

'Why did Albou lose so badly?'

'Because you boys built him up into believing he's better than he is. You didn't do him any favours there. You did it out of spite. Put the crowds behind him and on my back. Give him a white hat and send him off into the sunset with orders to bring back the Son of Superbrat – and that's really infantile, you must admit – dead or alive.'

'Why should we want that?'

'Because you want my scalp. We all know how you hacks – country club weekend players to a man, I bet – hate to see a big-mouthed public park brat come along and commit the unforgivable crime – being *best*.'

'So you hate Albou, Johnny? Is that it? Because you imagine that we, the media, are grooming him to take over from you? Is that it? Have I got it right?'

'No. I don't hate him, don't be more stupid than you can help. I respect Albou. I *like* him. He'll always be in the Top Fifty on the world rankings. But he's nowhere near the level you conned him into thinking he was. He wasn't beaten by me alone – he was beaten by himself, too. He came face to face with his own mediocrity and he caved in.'

'Most of us were covering the Circuit when you were still wetting your pants in Massachusetts,' a loudmouth put in gratuitously.

'Big deal,' Johnny shouted. 'You still wouldn't know the truth if it came up and bit you on your freebie Cordon Bleu bellies.'

'Sangster, why do you hate the tennis establishment so much? What's your beef?'

'Listen.' Johnny leaned forward. 'Goading the French kid on was the last morsel of mud you are ever going to sling at me. For ten years now the media and the tennis authorities have treated me like a kid and now you're telling me I'm an old man.' He stood up. 'Out there today I showed you how wrong you were. I showed you I won't stand for it. I told you you'd better keep your lip buttoned about Johnny Sangster if you can't tell the truth about him. I'm going to be around for a long, long time.'

He stalked off, Dave Pepper trailing close behind him. At the door a reporter grabbed Johnny Sangster's arm. 'I heard it wasn't us that made you merry as a skylark. I heard it was a broad.'

'You can't believe all you read,' Dave Pepper responded automatically. 'Come on, John.'

'Is that right?' Johnny marvelled sarcastically.

The reporter nodded, pushing a microphone close to

Johnny's mouth. 'How do you find playing with a broken heart?'

'Where you from? Some down market *National Enquirer*? How would you find doing your interviewing with a microphone up your ass?'

Dave Pepper hauled him through the door. The car's engine was running and the airline had held up the flight for five minutes, all for Johnny Sangster. Dave Pepper thanked the stewardess and Johnny dropped into his seat, grunting for a strawberry daiquiri as the plane taxied down the runway.

'Why are you sniffing, John?'

'A cold.'

'A cold.'

'You got it, Mom.'

'I know it's not a cold, sonny boy. I know what they were passing around at that club last night.'

'Cold germs.'

'It's not funny. You've got bags as big as barrage balloons under your eyes.'

'I may have *bags* under my *eyes*, Dave, but I also have the *cheque* and the trophy you get when you win the Canadian Open, *Dave*.'

'I'm just giving you my opinion, John.'

'If you want to give me something, Dave, give me my prescription.'

Dave Pepper handed him just what the doctor re-ordered. 'There's practice tonight, John.'

'Well, I hope you and Tom Dougherty have a real good time, Dave. Because there's no practice for Johnny tonight. Johnny doesn't need practice. He's having dinner with some friends instead.'

'Fine. If your game is that good – fine.'

They seethed in resentful silence all the way to Kennedy. Johnny jumped into his white Dino and took off for Manhattan in a bonfire of rubber. Dave Pepper waited with his bags for a taxi, and reflected that he'd preferred his boy when he'd been with that damn girl.

Johnny Sangster dined at a frantically coveted address. Every apartment in the block was protected from the felonious city shadows *out there* by such home comforts as hermetically sealed bullet-proof windows, armed guards on discreet tap around the clock, the latest in electronic photo-cell alarm systems and enough freelance firearms to start or suppress a violent revolution in the sun-scorched, dollar-backed banana republic of your choice.

The pampered paranoias had come from every corner of the world to be imprisoned at their convenience here. But whatever their colour or creed under the skin they were all members of the brotherhood of Mammon.

There were Iranians who'd hustled their ill-gotten gold to Switzerland and their well-fed carcasses to the States before they got what was coming to them from the forces of Allah. There were widows of rock stars who had come into millions and a state of mourning after an overdose or an assassin had taken away the breadwinner to that great jam session in the sky. There were restless, useless, beautifully groomed women of forty or so who had hauled themselves out of the wreck of a marriage to some portly potentate Greek shipping baron or Arab oil sheik, men with lawyers who informed the ex-wife heading west that she could live out all her days in the lap of lazuli and luxury if only she would take her inside story to the grave and not to the papers.

And there was the doctor with the massively successful practice out on Long Island that pandered exclusively to well-heeled hypochondriacs, and there was the doctor's sleek, plain wife, sole heir to the munitions fortune that had been in her family for three generations, thriving from Government contracts to supply Uncle Sam's stooges with hardware from the Somme to Saigon. The doctor had a passion for opiates injected intravenously and the doctor's wife stalked sex conquests like an alley cat with a private income. A few years back the happy couple had hung around Johnny Sangster out at Flushing Meadow until the seventeen-year-old tennis pro had accepted an invitation to dinner.

Since then he had spent the night at their apartment maybe ten times. There were always new people and endless claret and clams and coke, there was always a bed for the night. It was a lush last resort when he was lonely in Manhattan.

Waiters in white jackets stooped to clear the table. The doctor dipped a small silver spoon into an elaborately engraved snuff box, sent a spoonful of white powder up each nostril and passed the snuff box on. His eyes were pinpoints, scanning the faces of his guests with amused speculation.

His wife was getting shrill as she berated a weary young actor about the meteorically climbing crime rate while the young man set fire to the tip of a Havana. 'Just because technology's given us emergency buttons on the floor of every jacuzzi, don't kid yourself that the old laws no longer apply!'

The actor smiled laconically, swirling his cognac. 'I assume you mean the gospel according to John Wayne.'

'Go ahead and sneer! The frontier laws are as valid today as they ever were. The right to bear arms and shoot to kill – once it was a constitutional right, these days it's a patriotic duty.'

'Ah, the American way . . . the star-spangled six-shooter . . .'

'Go ahead and work on your ad libs. Maybe when some murderous scum out there comes bursting into your life one dark night you can keep them busy with wisecracks till the cops arrive.'

'What do I need a gun for? What's wrong with the good old NYPD? They've got enough guns for all of us.'

'What's wrong with the NYPD is that they just can't cope! Murder's a growth industry *and* a leisure activity – if they can't kill you for profit then they'll kill you for kicks. You've got to take care of *yourself*.' She looked to Johnny for support. 'What do you say, Johnny?'

Johnny reached for the decanter and cleared his throat. 'I don't hold no truck with guns.' His voice sounded slurred and far away. 'But it's different for me. I move around too much for any goon to get me in his sights.'

The pale Oriental girl smiled across the table for him. Johnny looked at her over the rim of his glass and told himself that he should have forgotten Thorn Sayre by now.

'The problem with guns,' said the Oriental girl, 'is that they tend to get used.'

A young copper-coloured beauty in a powder blue suit shook his head, looking pained. 'The tools of Satan. No good can come of them.'

The doctor's wife regarded him with lecherous contempt. 'Sonny Babe, you are contender for the middleweight championship of the world. You've grown rich and famous by beating your opponents to a brain-addled mush. So where do *you* get off lecturing *me* about the evils of violence?'

'If Allah wanted me to be on welfare he would have given my gift to someone else. I'm spreading his word.'

'Oh, really? I thought you were making a mint and making

every young fox that comes sniffing by the work-out room. Why does every black kid who can string a couple of punches together think he's Ali?'

'They don't. That's the trouble.'

'You don't expect me to believe you don't have any bodyguards with bulges under their jackets?'

'No bodyguards, no guns.'

'What about all those crazy crackers who want to spill your beautiful brown guts? What's there to stop them blowing you away?'

'Allah. I'll die when he says so. Until then nothing can touch me.'

'No offence to Allah, but I'd rather pack a rod,' the doctor's wife sniggered.

'Me too,' said a fair-haired girl with a nasal honk and a horse's head, typical Boston blonde. 'But I know I never could. The very thought of carrying a gun terrifies me. I'd be afraid of it going off before I was ready!'

'A firearm has no mind of its own,' sighed the doctor's wife.

'How very like the people who carry them,' the actor chuckled.

'Very funny.'

'What about the Guardian Angels?' Boston Blonde demanded. 'They fight crime without firearms.'

'How would you know? When did you ever ride the subway?'

'I read about it.'

'Well, ok, those guys protect the poor pretty good. But what happens when the lead starts flying? Are the Guardian Angels going to make like Superman and catch the slugs between their teeth? When the going gets threatening the threatened get armed, it's a fact of life. When it's a matter of life and death you have to take *care* of yourself. You have to get yourself one of *these*.' The doctor's wife reached down into her handbag and whipped out a snub nosed revolver. It had a dull black gleam and the fragrance of fresh oil and dozens of laughter lines on its butt. She brandished it proudly above her head like a crazed majorette.

The doctor had his little black bag on the table in front of him and one of his shirt sleeves rolled up as high as it would go. A napkin with a frilly lace trim was tied tightly around his upper arm. He emptied a syringe full of morphine solution into a bulging blue-black vein and shuddered convulsively. 'Did you know that the first junkies in this land and England were doctors?' he asked his dinner guests with conversational peacock pride. 'It's true! We . . . were . . . the . . .first . . .' He smiled serenely at his wife and her ugly black handgun and then he fell forward, lost in a deep narcotic sleep before his head hit the table.

The party hardly noticed. They were watching his wife and her weapon.

'Put that thing away, woman,' Sonny Babe growled.

'Button your lip, my man. Or I'll ventilate your forehead. It's pacifists like you people who've nourished crime and set it loose upon your betters. Turn the other cheek and all you get is a baseball bat across your teeth.'

'Is that thing loaded?' Boston Blonde asked.

'What you think it is? A *toy*? Sure it's loaded!'

'Then I'm frightened!'

The doctor's wife stroked her hand. 'Hush, now. I'm just trying to give you a little education. Listen, I went to Radcliffe and what I learned there was *nothing* compared to what this great guy taught me at Gun School! How to blast a hole in the intruder's chest from lying, crawling, running, standing and falling positions! Blow his balls off, drill a cavity between his eyes!'

'After a hard day at the office what better way to relax?' Johnny muttered, helping himself to the claret.

The actor raised his hands with sardonic finality. 'Ok, sweetness. We've all got a shock from your splendid penis substitute. Now please put it away.'

The Oriental girl laughed and winked at Johnny Sangster. 'What? You're not subjecting us to stupid Freud! I'm sorry, I can't go along with the concept of the universe as revolving around Sigmund's shrivelled old member.'

'It's a fact, Nancy! We've all been flashed! I bet she sleeps with it! You sleep with the gun, right?'

The doctor's wife gaped. 'What if I do?'

'I *thought* so.'

'It makes me feel safe. It's like a cross between the President and Seconal.'

'It gets you to sleep? You mean it gets you off!'

'What's going on in your sperm-ridden bleeding heart, sicko?'

'You people with your damn guns are all the same. They're not protection – they're sex aids.'

'I told you two years ago you shouldn't have come out of analysis.' The doctor's wife threw a glass of claret at the actor. He poured a jug of cream down her decolletage. She cursed him and flounced fuming to her bedroom.

'You shouldn't have . . .' said Boston Blonde.

'Ah, it was karma,' said Sonny Babe, 'waving that wicked little mother around like a magic wand . . .'

'I'm just glad she took her finger off the trigger,' said Johnny Sangster, looking at the gun where it lay by their hostess's wineglass like a place mark. 'I don't know about the rest of you, but I'm priceless.'

'You should go in there and say sorry,' Boston Blonde told the actor.

'You should go in there and settle the argument,' the doctor murmured without lifting his head or opening his eyes. 'You should go in there and fuck her at gunpoint. See who's right and who's a liar . . .' He went back to sleep.

The actor stood up and stared at him, vague disgust and an uncertain smile flickering over his face. '*These* are the people we place our healthy minds and bodies in the trust of?' He picked up the gun and went into the bedroom. The guests heard voices raised in anger, soon subsiding to nervous laughter and fading away to silence.

Conversation and conspicuous consumption were resumed at the table. Johnny scooped out the snuff box and sprinkled the debris into the decanter. The doctor began to snore. The Boston blonde was fixing her face, pretending not to pine for the actor. Sonny Babe looked for more seafood. The Oriental girl smiled at Johnny Sangster and he smiled back.

'You're a sweet boy, Johnny. So I won't waste no more time on you.'

'What are you talking about?'

'I can see you're not quite spontaneously combusting every time you look at me . . .'

'Is that what's expected of me?'

'I expect and accept nothing less. I can see you're in love with a certain girl so I'll wish you luck, cut my losses and sink my pick in elsewhere.' She passed the last of the clams to Sonny Babe and began to discuss the Koran with him.

Johnny glowered into his glass. Who said anything about

*love*? Chinese takeaway. There was a lot of noise coming from the bedroom. You needed earplugs here, not napkins. The bed banged under a steady body rock rhythm punctuated with soft moans, yelps of teasing pain and low voices now suddenly urgent.

*Almost there*, Johnny thought bitterly.

Then there was the shot, come and gone in one black moment, followed instantly by the scream, which seemed to last for ever.

Johnny kicked the door down.

The actor was bent double at the side of the bed, howling with incoherent hysteria, trying to *explain*. There was vomit on the carpet. The gun lay alone in the middle of the room, even uglier with the thin belch of blue-grey smoke snaking from the barrel.

The doctor's wife sprawled on the bed. Her clothes were scattered across the floor. It looked like a James Bond film, except for the top of the doctor's wife's head, which was spread over a shockingly wide area of the walls and ceiling.

Johnny slumped against the door jamb, too weak to move.

Someone must have put in a 911 call because soon he could hear the sirens ringing through the city streets as they raced towards the latest mess Manhattan expected them to clear up. Then the police were all over the apartment with dogs, photographers and forensic people. A plain clothes man grabbed Johnny and began firing questions at him. Johnny muttered something about calling his lawyer, knowing his rights. Then he saw the cop's soft brown eyes cloud over with a righteous wrath ready to break bones and Johnny Sangster felt afraid and ashamed.

The doctor stirred from his comatose bliss and blinked at the chaos all around. 'Where's everyone going?' he asked plaintively. 'Is the party over?'

What remained of his drugs were taken in for analysis and what remained of his dinner party was taken in for questioning.

Just after midnight Johnny Sangster was taken to a stark white room suffused with a grubby yellow glare. It was furnished with a flimsy table and three metal chairs. On the windowless walls were HAVE YOU SEEN THIS CHILD? notices, most of them faded and curling. Every sound outside the room was a sad metallic echo and the atmosphere inside the room was one of harried despair. Johnny felt lousy. The French wine and Peruvian cocaine that he had gorged and snorted with abandon only a short while ago were now making him suffer.

Two impassively tough detectives came to the room with coffee and Camel filters and two pens and a stack of notepaper. They introduced themselves and got started. All night long they grilled Johnny with the same set of questions repeated again and again and again.

Johnny told them all he knew, he told it to them endlessly until finally he had had enough. 'I *told* you that, you fucking goons!' He smashed his fists down on the table. 'What do you want from me? A confession? Inconsistencies?'

'All we want is what you saw. All we want is all of us to be real sure of what you saw,' one of the detectives said calmly.

'Yeah? Well, I hope we're real sure soon because I got better things to do with my time than. . .'

His words strangulated in his throat as the other detective hauled him from the chair and slammed him against the wall. 'A young woman gets her brains blown out tonight and all it means to you is an interruption of your beauty sleep – people like you make me sick, *germ*. Don't you think that law enforcement officers are slightly more qualified than *ball-hitters* when it comes to calling the shots in pursuit of justice?'

Johnny nodded passionately, ashamed and afraid for the second time that night. The detective sent him back to his chair. He sat down and repeated a subdued recital of all he knew. Just when he had begun to think that the night would never end a black policeman walked in and showed the weary, determined detectives two charge sheets. The doctor had been arrested for illegal possession of controlled medicines. The actor had been charged with homicide.

'No problems with the actor?' one of the detectives wanted to know.

The policeman shook his head. 'Once he came out from sedation he couldn't get it off his chest fast enough.'

The detective yawned, nodding with job satisfaction. He told Johnny that the DA's office would be in contact with him if his evidence was needed in court, and he told him to go away.

Dave Pepper was waiting, his track suit pulled on over his pyjamas and his face pale with worry. He touched Johnny's arm lightly. 'You ok, John?'

Johnny nodded, rubbing his eyes. Outside the dawn was a cold grey limbo.

'Brace yourself. The circus is waiting and guess who's the main attraction?'

The story broke already?'

'Every rag on the planet is running it on the front page. You've got to admit there's a lot of raw material there – sex and drugs and games with handguns, a socialite killed mid-orgasm, Johnny Sangster and Sonny Babe sitting on the touch-line . . .'

'It had nothing to do with me. Nor with Sonny, either. We just happened to be eating there.'

'They don't want to hear about the menu.'

'Well, I'll tell them.'

'Tell them later. Now you make like a mute. Come on.'

'There he is! Hey, Johnny!'

As they descended the few steps to the sidewalk the photographers' flashbulbs went off like the fourth of July. A massed crush of bodies and microphones pressed in on them. White hot TV lights bathed the uproar in a phosphorescent glow. A camera crew front man grabbed the sleeve of Johnny's jacket, urging him with urbane sycophancy to reject all others and pledge his troth to the network. Johnny shook him off and followed Dave Pepper to the purring car.

'Is it right the corpse was a BLONDE?'

'Can you substantiate the rumours of ANGEL DUST and GROUP SEX?'

'Do you always carry a GUN, Mr Sangster?'

'Hey, SANGSTER – how does it feel to have blood stains all over your public image?'

Dave Pepper bundled him brusquely into the back of the limo and the driver pushed his foot to the floor before they had the doors shut.

Johnny swooned into the impossibly soft seats. 'Those goons make me homesick for all my old sportswriter pals.'

Dave Pepper was looking back through the window. 'Good. They're not following. They're going to wait for Sonny Babe.'

Johnny felt momentarily resentful. 'Who sent the car, Dave?'

'Harald sent the car.'

'That was real thoughtful of the slob. I'm going to go home and sleep for ever.'

'No, you're not,' Dave Pepper said. 'Harald sent the car to retrieve you.'

'Harald won't be at the office at this hour. He'll still be dreaming dirty dreams.'

'Harald is awake and waiting for you at the office. Nobody slept last night, John.'

Harald O. Holden sat at his desk stiff with affronted dignity, flanked by Global Management Enterprises' second best lawyer and an unidentified lackey. They were standing and their faces were grave, respectfully mimicking the countenance of their pint-sized master.

When Johnny Sangster strolled in Holden made no attempt to smile, stand up or shake hands. Instead he nodded curtly to Dave Pepper and watched Johnny Sangster slump into a chair. He regarded the shop-soiled young man with stern disdain.

'Why so suicidal, Harald?' Johnny smiled. 'Lost a dime or something?'

'You're in the news, Johnny,' Holden said. He tossed a pile of newspapers across the desk. They all boasted seedy Sangster-associated headlines and most of them carried photographs of him snarling and scowling in tennis shorts.

Holden nodded to the lackey. He hit a button and Johnny's smiling face appeared on the huge TV screen facing Holden's desk. Some shrill sow gloatingly escorted the viewing hordes through a drip by drip guided tour of the instantly notorious dinner party. Holden nodded again and the lackey turned the radio on. It was a news station and they were carrying a report on the day's big human interest story.

Holden nodded impatiently and the lackey silenced the radio. 'You're in the news, Johnny. And all the news is bad. It's got to stop.'

Johnny shrugged. 'Don't worry. They'll have forgotten everything they're being fed with by tomorrow.'

Holden made a church with his hands. 'Johnny, you are a bad ambassador.'

'Before you burn me at the stake, Harald, I think it's worth mentioning that I was an innocent bystander – bysitter, rather. I was in the next room when New York notched up another accident statistic – that don't reserve me a place in the Inferno.'

'At Global we have to consider the reputation of *all* our clients, Johnny.'

'Since when have you been handling the Moral Majority, Harald?'

'Johnny, you are getting Global a bad name. I don't give a flying fuck about anybody's morals until they start costing me. Then I care a great deal. Then I can't sleep nights. You can have a hot time or you can have big fat endorsement contracts – you can't have both. No company with a product to sell is going to want it endorsed by a superstar who has a dirty word for a name. That's a *fact*. And I have to remind you that your contract with Global *does* contain a morality clause.'

'And I have to remind *you*, Harald, that I'm not in a cell on Death Row. *I haven't committed any crime*! Ask the police!'

'That's a technicality. If your name is linked with a lot of dirt and scandal then the image will *stick*. Oh, Johnny, Johnny! You know me! I love a good time as much as the next guy. That party last night sounds like a beaut.' Holden winked horribly. 'Wish I could have been a fly on the wall! But we're in direct competition with Mark McCormack's International Management Group – he's got Borg, Ali, Pele, he's got clients so big that they're known by one name *the world over* where everybody else needs two. That's our competition.'

'I get it. You want megabuck geldings who don't scratch their ass without first considering if it's in the best interests of the company.'

'I knew you'd understand. You've been letting the side down a lot, lately, Johnny. Last night was the last straw.'

'Listen to me, you leech. I come up out of nowhere and now I'm number five out of everyone in the world. You take fifty per cent – *fifty fucking per cent*! – of every dollar I earn. I'm not letting the *side* down, mister, because I don't *play* team games, sucker! I'm the only one. I could walk out of this cheap dump right now and I'm telling you McCormack would have a red carpet waiting for me over at IMG! Watch me!'

'Johnny, don't say these things! I only suggested this fatherly chat because I care so deeply about you and your endorsements!'

Johnny stood up. 'Don't you worry about keeping companies with endorsable crap sweet, Harald. You just concentrate on keeping Johnny Sangster sweet. Unless you and your Global want to earn fifty per cent of nothing. Let's get out of here, Dave.'

'Johnny!' Holden called. 'Please think, Johnny!'

'Please kiss my famous white ass, Harald!'

A herd of reporters were kicking their heels outside

Johnny's block; Dave Pepper told the driver to keep going and offered Johnny a guest room at his place.

'Just like back in the scuffling days,' Dave grinned proudly.

Johnny smiled and nodded. He knew that stuff meant a lot to Dave.

Dave Pepper owned a restored colonial farmhouse out on Oyster Bay. It was magnificently apt that the address Dave Pepper called home was in a holiday resort. He didn't *live* there – he lived on the Circuit. Oyster Bay was the place he reluctantly returned to during the odd moments of the year when Johnny Sangster was between tournaments.

Two years ago after seeing his boy upset the strawberry cart at Wimbledon – Johnny had made a mockery of the seeding by barnstorming through to the quarter-finals – Dave Pepper had gone back to Oyster Bay in high spirits to find that old home town wasn't looking quite the same. Renata – his long-legged, jet-haired ex-show-girl with aspirations to a gossip column – *writing* one, not being in one – Renata, his wife – had packed her bags, kissed her children and left. She wrote a note that told him that she was sick of being kept in storage like some expensive, rarely used racquet.

Dave Pepper ached with regret for one maudlin moment and then began to get accustomed to her face not being around. He didn't blame her. It was for the best. If he had known he was going to run across a once in a lifetime talent like Johnny Sangster he would have stayed single anyhow. Nothing could come before this special boy. Being his coach made Dave Pepper feel like he was taking part in history.

The two teenage Peppers knew that Johnny came first. They didn't care. They had the run of the Pepper home for most of the year and enjoyed autonomy in a private world, the freedom of being grown up with none of the bills. They had the luxury of being teenagers with none of the noise levels, curfews or regulated mealtimes that their High School classmates complained of.

The most requested 45 on the juke box by the swiming pool was Eddie Cochran's 'Teenage Heaven'.

'They can't believe their luck,' Johnny said as they turned off the Southern State Parkway on the road to Oyster Bay. 'They think it's all going to be snatched back from them one day.'

'It's good for them to feel like that. It's the only thing between that little wooden shack and anarchy with acne.'

Sure enough, when the Pepper progeny saw that their father had brought his work home with him they killed the music, cleared up the mess and began to shoo their friends off the premises.

Johnny curled up in the room that always waited for him and slept round the clock. He awoke with a huge appetite for breakfast and practice. He could hear two pairs of feet coming up the stairs. A knock on the door preceded Owen Pepper, fifteen, carrying a tray of bacon and eggs and orange juice and coffee followed by Lake Pepper, fourteen, carrying tennis whites and the flame red tracksuit with SANGSTER – USA emblazoned across its back. He thanked them warmly. They bowed and exited smirking.

Johnny demolished his breakfast and got down to the court at the back of the farmhouse where Dave Pepper was adjusting the net. Every smash Sangster hit was given extra bite by picturing Harald O. Holden's greedy munchkin face where there was just a tennis ball. Dave Pepper was overwhelmed. Johnny always beat him, but never before with such emphatic mastery.

They shook hands at the net.

'Either you're ready to take those final four or I'm ready for an old folks home.'

'You'll be happier living among people your own age.'

They strolled off the court, laughing. Life was very good because the very top was in sight.

Then they saw the small panting pack of men and women running towards them chased by Lake and Owen Pepper. The intruders struggled under the weight of tape recorders and related technology, hobbling for the court as fast as their Gucci loafers would carry them. The pair in hot pursuit shouted apologies and excuses.

'They pretended they knew you!'

'They tried to bribe us!'

'Then they just sort of charged!'

'It's ok, kids, I'll take care of it,' Dave Pepper shouted understandingly.

He looked at the reporters with loathing. 'You are all trespassing, every lousy last one of you.'

A woman with a stick microphone pushed him aside and strode right up to Johnny. She barked into her stick mike. 'Johnny Sangster, how do you feel about the fact that Global

Management Enterprises have terminated your contract at this moment in time?'

Johnny stared at her, his face full of incomprehension. Then he stared at Dave. Pepper grabbed him and hustled his boy back into the house before he had the chance to start swearing for posterity and burying them alive in libel suits.

'It it true?' Johnny demanded when all the doors and windows were locked. 'They can't do this to me . . . can they?'

Owen and Lake looked up from the TV, staring at Johnny Sangster wide-eyed as Johnny stared at his TV face. The channel had chosen a photograph taken at full reach for a shot so he looked suitably desperate. The picture cut to city streets and vox pop quotes from Johnny Sangster's public.

'Ah, there's lotsa young kids who look up at him, so, you know, he should set an example.'

'Success has spoiled him. He was a real fine boy and now he's nothing but an arrogant person.'

'Well, I think the guy is a great tennis player – but what a lousy human bean!'

The report cut to Harald O. Holden, personal representative, sitting importantly behind his high-powered executive desk in the offices of Global Management Enterprises. The smug little bloodsucker oozed cloying regret and banal sincerity, giving his self-esteem a hard-on as he related the moral fable of how Global's fiscal acumen always had to be balanced with the company's social conscience.

'A corporate agent's gotta do what a corporate agent's gotta do,' muttered Johnny feverishly.

'You made Harald lose face. They made an example of you so their other clients wouldn't get bolshie. Same old Holden, equal parts shrewdness and stupidity. Your trouble, John, is that you were never *grateful* to them. The nothing little bastards!'

'Very sad, very sad,' Holden was droning. Unfortunately we had no choice. An unacceptable number of sponsors have telexed us to terminate John Fitzgerald Sangster's contracts to endorse their company products.'

Johnny and Dave looked at each other.

'Sadly, we at Global Management Enterprises had no choice but to end our association with Johnny – who I might add is a very dear and great personal friend of mine.'

Johnny winced.

'What exactly do you mean by an unacceptable number of sponsors, Mr Holden?' The interviewer had a rich, earnest, English voice of tender years.

'Two,' Holden announced. 'Two so far. I must say we appreciated their attitude. We felt the same way. You see, Johnny failed to honour a clause in his contract.'

'Which clause is that, Mr Holden.'

'The morality clause.' Holden looked pious. 'Let he who is without sin throw a stone through the glasshouse – cast the first brick, rather.'

'How do these sponsors justify their decision that Johnny Sangster is immoral?'

Johnny turned to Dave Pepper. 'Who's the interviewer? She's good.'

'What?' Dave stared at him incredulously. 'Who cares? Some English fox, a touch of class and all that. Shut up and listen.'

Holden had asked the reporter to repeat the question. Now he gasped with surprise and said 'This is B.U.S. young lady. *Business* doesn't have to justify *anything*.'

'Thank you, Mr Holden.' The girl appeared, announced her name – Susie Blond – and her channel and disappeared. She was small and breakable and very dark – an archetype of what used to be *his type*. Looking at her and feeling nothing he realized that his ideal had been intercepted and irretrievably changed. Blond. Thorn. If she could see him now she'd wipe her feet on him.

'I like Susie Blond. I reckon she's a fan of mine, telling Harald O. Halfwit I'm not immoral.'

Dave Pepper looked grey and grim. 'She'll be your *only* fan if you keep on babbling like an idiot and playing footsie with corpses.' He got up and went to make some phone calls.

Owen Pepper turned down the TV. 'Is it very bad, Johnny? What's a corporate agent?'

Lake Pepper looked scornful. 'Don't you know *nothing*, stupid?'

'I make the money and they make it last and grow and they go round the world looking for places where I can make some more. They get – *got* – half of everything I earned.'

Lake frowned. 'That isn't fair.'

'That's right. Now they've thrown me out and they get nothing. I can easy get another corporate agent, though.

Really it's just someone to hold your wallet. You can always get someone to hold your wallet.'

Dave Pepper returned. 'The situation is this. The two sponsors who have decided you're a commercial leper are Eisen-Kinder Leisure Activities and Tora Sports and Games. Eighty thousand dollars gone. Havington, Bandolero-Matchplay and Metalon-Fabey left. Maybe they won't panic, not catering to the kiddies. Who knows?'

'What do we do now, Dave?'

'Come on, Lake,' said Owen Pepper, pulling his sister discreetly and forcibly from the room.

'Global held all the contracts. When we've got you with a new corporate agent they'll have to work out some kind of settlement with Global and the companies that still want you. These corporate agents are all run by lawyers so I'm sure they'll be wise enough to keep the negotiations well away from the courts.'

'Well, it all sounds quite painless.'

'Another thing – Global held all your insurance policies. They'll be automatically cancelled now.'

'Yeah, I remember those policies. They cover everything from a sprained ankle to insanity.'

'Actually they only covered everything from a short lay off to the permanent lay off – illness, injury, disability and death – cover for every possibility, the kind of cover you need. We'll go see my broker first thing in the morning and arrange adequate cover while we're talking with prospective corporate agents. You'll have to have a medical, of course, but it's just a formality.'

'Not tomorrow, Dave. Tomorrow's Acapulco.'

'My God! I forgot all about that!' He'd forgotten that his boy was due to play an exhibition in a different Central and South American city every night for the next two weeks. 'Of course you must go. You've given your word.'

'Of course I must go. They're giving me a small fortune.'

'But maybe I should stay behind and take care of business at this end.'

Johnny shook his head. 'I want you with me.'

'*Someone* has to look out for your finances, get you insurance, start talking contracts.'

'Some clerk can take care of the paper work when we get home. That's what corporate agents are for. That's what my personal representative gets paid to do.'

'John, you don't *have* a personal representative anymore.'

'I'll *get* one. They'll be clawing each others' eyes out to get a percentage of Johnny Sangster's career.'

'What about insurance? You should be covered.'

'Dave, when was the last time I had an injury so bad that I had to scratch from a tournament?'

'It was before I knew you. You pulled a stomach muscle. I think you were thirteen.'

'Exactly. My only unlucky year. Nothing bad can happen to me again. I can feel it.' Johnny yawned and stretched, scratched his rogue curls and grinned sleepily. 'I'm going to turn in. It's all ahead of us now, Dave, you and me, and I want to look my best.'

# fourteen

Thorn did not expect to rescue her wardrobe without one last drunken scene. But spite got the better of Jap Goddard and when Roche turned the car into the mews she saw all she owned sitting on the doorstep. A neat pile of suitcases, dresses dressed in plastic and the mechanic's toolbox containing her make up. On top of it all was a cracked mirror with KEEP IT scrawled in white lipstick bought long ago for the mouth of Elle. Thorn stood it against Jap Goddard's lone empty milk bottle. 'I see he's awarded himself custody of the photographs he took of me,' she observed. 'There's no movement of net curtains so I deduce that he's in his natural habitat – locked in the lavatory, playing with his Nikon.'

She watched Roche load her personal effects into the back of the car. He held the door for her and when she smiled his face lit up with the poleaxed joy of the only man on earth who had *everything.* They drove home to a cozy little nook in the corridors of power. You could hear the Division Bell from the tiny Westminster flat – it was cramped and cost the earth but they were right there at the source, hanging on to the very heart of the city by the fingernails. The neighbourhood was ideal for Roche's small business. It was central – getting anywhere in town was a cakewalk. It was respectable – a clean cut young man in a dark business suit did not warrant a sideways glance. And it was nocturnal – politicians skittering to and from their *pied à terres* when there was an all-night sitting at the House, travelling businessmen reeling back to a company-let property after a tax deductable night on the tiles – keeping the hours of a night owl was almost expected.

Thorn Sayre considered it a very desirable residence.

At home bacchanalia held hands with a thriving business. The refrigerator was full of fruit juice and cellophane bags. The orders mounted up on the answering machine as teenage rakes with titles and household names with records on the chart all left a message for Roche.

How unlike the mythical satanic dealer who forced his evil wares into innocent veins thought Thorn.

Roche never went looking for business, it always came to him. He was conscientious and kind, a mad gleam in his eye and a mind as sharp as a restless razor. He relished living peacefully outside the law, surviving on his wits while the masses had the full itinerary from cradle to grave all mapped out. It gave Roche a kick. He knew it was childish. As penance he was generous with the few clients who treated him like a human being *at all times.*

Too many of those who came to him were sickeningly ingratiating before pocketing the deal. Then, in the grips of post-coital triste, they treated him like a gatecrasher – until the good stuff ran out and then the charade would start again. It hurt him, at first. He made a note of names because nobody should mistake diffidence for a doormat. Those who did so abused his good nature at peril of future supplies. David Waymouth had owed him money for years. Roche had had enough of David Waymouth. One of the reasons Roche rarely dealed in hard drugs was because he did not like the way the smell of opiates lured every last neurotic out of the woodwork. When Waymouth had been on the verge of running home to Mummy and Daddy telling tall tales, Roche had obtained some heroin fast and sold it to him at twice the going price, just to dissuade him. But the David Waymouths of this world never thanked you for such favours – instead they marked you out as a Jack of all trades and just kept on begging.

Roche had the BBC six o'clock news turned down low as he watched Thorn sleeping in the next room on the top bunk bed next to the *Last Beauty Of The Twentieth Century* spread from *Caesar's Things*. He'd torn it from the magazine and pinned it on the wall when she was just a beauty he had talked to for a few minutes at some party. When she saw her face on his wall she was touched by it. He blushed and it made her smile.

He never dreamed she would stay. He was desperate for her to be happy. He would give her everything she wanted.

Roche went out into the kitchen to sort out what was coming out of the refrigerator and going out on the town. Thorn slept on.

She always slept the day away. She was up all night every night bingeing on all the new chemicals at all the right soirees. It took it out of her. She needed all day to rest up and recover from the night before so she would be refreshed for the next.

She told herself that every drug she took she took for a purpose, every drug she took was in a good cause.

Cocaine was for a languid, soft focus surf around the calling list of private parties. Cannabis was for sex in a rapacious, tactile sleepwalk. Amphetamine – there would always, always be amphetamine in her life – was for astute exhilaration, exalting herself at the mirror for hours as she plotted revenge and paths to glory. Seconal, Valium and Irish Cream were taken in search of some sweet amnesiac slumber.

In the nights it was easy to believe that her career was in the glittering ascendant. Roche and his gorgeous consort were in demand at every hot party where only winners were allowed – no, *welcomed* in – to rub shoulders with all the young, scandalizingly rich aristocrats and beat stars, all the other success stories. They all said that Jap's studies of her were perfectly slick. They all turned to Roche and said, 'Have you got It?'

In the nights she felt young, numb and ecstatic, she felt like what was happening, the new noise in town. In the nights success was a narcotic. That Roche had the divine right of dealers never crossed her intoxicated mind.

In the days she was not so sure. She couldn't get the taste of poison out from under her tongue. She was terrified to look too closely at her upper thighs, because she thought she'd glimpsed the seeds of cellulite there, bitter harvest of all the toxics building up a dam of bile in her precious body. When she lay at the top of the bunks too weary to stay awake yet stoked up beyond sleep, then she would stare at her face, so beautiful, so proud and eternal in the glossy images on the wall and she could have wept.

*Is that all I get?*

In the days she remembered the snatches of acid in party corners. She calls herself a model? So does every sow in Soho . . . She heard the juicy parts of the post-mortem. They said to her face that her accent was perfectly slick but she heard the casual hate they had for Americans. They said she should have been a roaring success – English models, though so beautiful, were too smart and got sick of people picking faults with their face, assuming they were dumb or available or deaf. But everyone knew that American models were so thick-skinned, none of that stuff came near to touching them! – yet Thorn Sayre threw it all away.

Oh, they agreed she still turned the head of every living creature when she walked by. She still made bones and eyes read like a manifesto or magic rite, she still walked like there were lights. She was still perfect but she was now trouble, impossible to work with. She had had her chance. She had failed to turn up for two crucial advertising assignments she'd come by without trying – and then there were all the stories Jap Goddard told about her. You could hardly blame the poor old piss artist for kicking her out. Yes, they still stared, but then they surveyed the spectacular ghost town of Thorn Sayre's career, and they shrugged, and they talked about someone's *success* instead.

The last exhibition was in Rio.

Outside the temperature in the shade was as high as the inflation rate. Inside the stadium was another world. The arena was palatial and the air conditioning was turned up as high as it could go. The crowd came in Cadillacs and Calvin Kleins to watch players who got twenty thousand dollars just for turning up.

When Johnny Sangster rushed the net for the finish the audience cried out with frenzied awe, leaping to their feet as one as if to salute the sudden appearance of the Stars and Stripes. Ray Velez hit Johnny with his best shot and it wasn't good enough. Johnny anticipated the pass and drove the ball back between his opponent's feet with a staggering easy brilliance. The winner. Johnny went to the net with his hand out. Velez shambled up and Johnny saw that a light had gone out in his eyes.

They had been rivals for so long and now Johnny had left

him behind. Johnny was not in competition with Velez – or Falconi, or Tom Dougherty, all the good old gang, heh heh – any more. Johnny was in the big playground. If he was going to go any higher he had to do it at the expense of Lendl, Connors, McEnroe, Borg. That was the opposition now. Velez would never get there. They both knew it.

They shook hands and it was like saying goodbye.

'Well played, Ray.'

'Ok, Johnny ok.'

Johnny Sangster walked off court to a standing ovation. The pale, portly organizers laughed like grateful madmen as they plied him with a six-figure cheque and a huge silver cup. They begged him to return next year. Dave Pepper waited in the wings with a dozen moustachioed giants in uniform, who carved the way through a fawning crowd. Pepper got Johnny inside the locker room and quickly secured the door.

'What time's the flight to Kennedy, Dave?' He tore off his whites hurriedly.

'Eight. I know it's early but the next one's not until noon. And there's a million papers for you to sign tomorrow.' He watched Johnny head for the showers. 'I'll have the driver bring the car round to the door. We'll be back at the hotel in ten minutes.'

'*Aw,*' Johnny hooted from out of the steaming hiss, 'not even *you* can want me matchfit for signing my name a few dozen times in some Manhattan office! Not even you, Dave!'

'I want us to catch that early flight, John.'

'*Sure*, Dave. It makes sense! But don't expect to get an early night after two weeks of exhibitions just to sign some *autographs* tomorrow.'

'Where are you going? Out for something to eat? I'm pretty hungry myself.'

'There's a party. Avenida Atlantica. Some friends of the organizers. Coming?'

'No, No,' Dave Pepper said. 'I'll take a raincheck, John. But you go ahead, I'll see you down in the lobby at seven. That's *seven.*'

'I'll be there. Pleasant dreams, Dave.'

When Johnny came out of the locker room a uniformed chauffeur saluted him, took his bags and escorted him to a Silver Cloud. An old man in a white suit and a young girl in a red dress that Johnny recognized as a Halston through bitter experience (Sherry Ward) were sitting in the back seat.

The man was tall, heavy, bald, his reptilian features coppered and corrugated by clime and time. He rested his unsteady hand on the gold head of a black walking cane. He smiled at Johnny with ravenous bonhomie. 'Welcome, Mr Sangster! Welcome!'

The girl studied Johnny with impassive golden eyes. She was pale and slender with rich brown hair, a serious faced beauty even taller than the old man.

'I am Castello Ferrocio. This is my little Carmen. You're coming to our party, Mr Sangster. It's a great honour, isn't it, Carmencita?'

'Yes, it is.'

Johnny shook hands with the old man, smiled politely at his daughter and got into the car. The man rapped his cane on the floor and the Silver Cloud slunk off.

The stadium had emptied and an endless stream of sleek opulence poured out of the parking lot. Cars by Mercedes and Maserati, Porsche and Ferrari, Rolls Royce and Volvo. Both the old man and the girl were watching Johnny. His face was without expression.

'How do you like Rio?' Ferrocio asked him.

'Rio's fine. You folks sure know how to throw a dandy tournament.'

'In Rio we have the best that money can import,' said Ferrocio, puffing up with pride. 'Isn't that right, Carmen?'

'Yes, it is.'

The route from the stadium to the centre of Rio afforded the passengers of the Silver Cloud spectacular views of the waves breaking up where the mountains met the sea. Then the road was flat and the lights of the city rose up in the distance. They drove into a sprawling, filthy slum containing thousands of ricketty hovels that spilt garbage and barefoot children into the road. The driver of the Silver Cloud pressed the horn furiously.

Johnny had never seen such poverty. He looked at the Ferrocios. They stared at the scene without interest or alarm.

'What is this place?'

'Shanty town,' said Carmen Ferrocio.

'These peasants come in from the country to find work and lack even the intelligence to go back to the country when they find *this*,' said her father. He sighed and spread his shaking hands. 'They are diseased, illiterate and dishonest. They have no water and no work. What can you do with such people, Mr Sangster?'

Johnny stared out at Shanty Town. 'I don't understand,' he said. 'What keeps them down?'

'Oh, our police do their best,' said the old man.

'In Brazil we have the biggest gap between rich and poor in world. Even bigger than America,' said Carmen. 'It has been so for many years.' She nodded at the slum. 'They know it. At least they sense it. Yet they do nothing. If they were wanting to rise up . . . they would have done so by now.'

Ferrocio laughed and patted Carmen's knee affectionately. 'My little girl is the expert on shanty town, Mr Sangster!'

They were leaving it behind now. A huge-eyed brown child in ragged shorts looked up from the skinny chicken she was playing with and choked on their dust. 'Is that right?' Johnny was saying.

'Yes, it is,' said Carmen.

'Usually sports bore her. Tonight she was very impressed by you, Mr Sangster!'

The apartment in Avenida Atlantica was dark, cool and crowded. The blinds were down, the guests huddled into small groups and the air conditioning roared. Against one wall a huge black and silver sound system imported from West Germany towered over the room, booming old fashioned disco rhythms. On the opposite wall a complex of Japanese video equipment was flickering with images of Nazi pornography. Johnny looked once and didn't look again.

Instead he looked at the women. Whether girls like Carmen or women in their twenties they were all tall, pale and slender. They sipped Scotch with four hundred per cent import tax and willed themselves to enjoy it – after all, it had cost one hundred American dollars a bottle. They trailed around after squat old reptilians who wore too much jewellery. Johnny began to suspect that Carmen and Ferrocio were not related, not even by marriage.

Castello Ferrocio excused himself to Johnny and hobbled away with some clonish cronies. Carmen disappeared into the darkness for drinks.

Young men in a whisky sweat with cocaine eyes brushed past Johnny raising their voices at each other. Somewhere out in the party blackness there were punches landing. Johnny heard laughter and dancing. A glass broke into flesh. An infuriated old man screamed something in Portugese and a girl began to sob bitterly.

Carmen appeared. She gave Johnny a strawberry daiquiri. They clinked glasses.

'Why is it so dark in here?' Johnny said. 'I can hardly see a thing.'

'In Brazil escaping the sun is a luxury. Pale skin is a sign of wealth. Only peasants are brown.' Carmen traced the outline of his cock with a long fingernail. 'Don't you like it in the darkness, Johnny? Isn't it exciting?'

Johnny took a pull on his daiquiri and felt her tug down his zip and slip her hand inside. He grabbed her wrist. 'I already put on one show tonight. And I don't think your old man would be such an appreciative audience this time out.'

'It's what he wants.'

'He wants *this*? You and me?'

'Me and anyone he . . . likes. You and me right now. He always wanted it like this. Ever since he met me at the Carnival when I was sixteen. I was poor and came to dance. He was of course rich and came to watch. Always this way.' Sinking to her knees she pulled his cock out in her fist and smothered it with her mouth. He pushed her away with a curse. Her sharp teeth scraped against him, he felt her lips linger. He looked around.

'No one saw,' said Carmen, getting to her feet. She wiped her mouth with the back of her hand and smiled at him with mild contempt.

'Somewhere else. My hotel.'

'No. My place. It's nearer.'

Ferrocio was standing by the door as they left. He winked at Johnny. Carmen didn't look at her protector.

'Don't look like that,' she told Johnny. 'Not so frightened! He doesn't mind, I tell you, he *likes* it. It's what he *wants*. But . . .'

Johnny had been expecting this. 'But what?'

'Please make it interesting. I'll have to give him a blow by blow account later. And it had better be good.'

Johnny was relieved. 'Oh, is *that* all.'

They went down to Avenida Atlantica where the Silver Cloud was waiting. Carmen gave the driver the usual amount and Johnny got in behind the wheel.

*

David Waymouth hung shivering in the shadows of Westminster. Somewhere the Division Bell was tolling. David Waymouth held his head in his hands and made a personal appeal to God. It had been a very bad day for the usually privileged Waymouth family.

The Right Honourable James Waymouth MP had been all over the nation's breakfast tables and in every commuter carriage. James Waymouth had hired a team of high grade PR people years ago, to keep his name *out* of the papers. But this time there was nothing they could do. It was all over the wire services before the boys had a chance to even reach for the plug.

James Waymouth's Arab mistress had opened her ripe red mouth to assure the waiting world that her pregnancy and divorce proceedings were both progressing extremely well. She was still playing coy about the identity of the father and co-respondent. The Right Honourable Member gritted his teeth on every front page except *The Times* and *The Morning Star*, afraid he could not comment. His wife Imogen was also present and photographed, stiff-upper-lipped and standing by her Honourable Member. *Poor* Imogen, everyone said. She looked every inch the English Rose who had gagged on too much manure yet still struggled on trying to bloom bravely.

If the paternity gossip wasn't enough, James and Imogen's teenage daughter Clemency had enlivened the morning's Dempster with revelations of an elopement to Notting Hill with a dissolute young guitarist from the Gorbals. And now the Right Honourable Member's son and heir was falling to pieces on the street where Roche lived. He stared up at the dark window, a big aching sob of self pity welling up inside him, waiting for the light to come on. He couldn't go up till then. Because, David Waymouth grimaced to himself, Roche is in *love*.

It's not the bloody money I mind, Waymouth thought. It's not the constipation or the incontinence or the nausea or the impotence or the bad needles or the air bubbles or shaking like a jellyfish having a fit as I jack up in some disgusting public lavatory.

It's the waiting, all the bloody *waiting*.

The light came on and Waymouth trotted across the street without giving traffic a passing thought. He took the stairs two at a time until he stumbled and fell, taking the skin off the palms of both hands. He hauled himself up. He didn't care. He was going to see Roche. Waymouth hammered on the door. Roche checked him through the peephole and opened the door, seething.

'David, for Christ's sake, *quiet!*'

Waymouth gave him what was intended to be a friendly smile. It emerged as a grotesquely twisted leer. 'Roche, please . . .'

'There is nothing *here* for you, David.'

'Just let me in for one second, Roche. Just let me in for one second . . . there's filth out there.'

'I take it you mean the police. Get in, quick.' Roche bolted the door behind David Waymouth. Waymouth peered into the flat with rabid interest, perhaps hoping to actually see some DRUGS on display. He saw through into the bedroom where Thorn Sayre lay on the top bunk wearing red lipstick and a black sleep mask. Roche closed the door testily, though he knew that things of the flesh were beyond Waymouth's realms of possibility.

'One more time, David – I have no opiates for you. Not ever again.'

'Why the fuck not?'

'Go find a mirror.'

'But you know *where* I can get some!'

'No, I don't.'

'You got me H before! You got me coke! Roche, you lying cocksucker! I come into a shitload of money soon! I'll pay you twice, thrice the price! One more time, Roche?' He attempted to throw a frail arm around Roche.

Roche shook him off. 'The more I help you the more you think I owe you. I'm not going to have smack around Miss Sayre. I'm not going to have it in the house. I'm not going to sell or give or lend smack to you. Now you are jamming up my answering machine, David. Please go elsewhere.'

'I've got nowhere else to go!'

'Look, keep the money you owe me. It's a gift, ok? But I'm not Father Christmas. This thing doesn't work like that. Go and get a tab somewhere even softer.'

'Don't be an absolute shit, Roche. At least let me have some coke.'

'Sorry, David.'

'*Please.*'

'Not a chance.'

'Do you want me to beg, Roche? I'll beg if you want me to . . .'

'David, your begging would do nothing at all for me, I'm afraid. All I want is for you to get out.'

'A pinch of your cocaine . . . a pinch . . .'

'You don't even *like* coke!'

'*I like jacking it up.*'

'And I don't like talking about it. That needle's a sex thing with you, David,' Roche opened the door and shoved Waymouth. 'Go. Now. Please don't ever come back.'

The door was locked and bolted and suddenly Waymouth *knew* as certainly as he knew his favourite needle that Roche and his moll had a big chunk of chinese rock in there that they just didn't want to *share* with him. Selfish bastards!

He'd show them. There was life in the old junkie *yet* . . .

Waymouth scrambled down to the street with a ten pence coin in his pocket and a score to settle. The call to Scotland Yard was long enough to convince them that he knew what he was talking about – they took one earful of his frightfully correct accent and his imaginative insider's slang and brand names and they had no doubts – but not long enough for them to get a trace on the call.

David Waymouth nursed a cup of very sweet tea in an all night café and he saw the police cars come without their lights and sirens and take away the contents of a refrigerator as well as Roche and Thorn Sayre. As the police gunned off with their catch they let Westminster, Whitehall and the workers savour the taste of the rampant Met – flashing lights, burnt rubber, the victory song of the valkyrie. It pulled quite a crowd on the pavement and gave David Waymouth a chance to slip out of the café without paying for his tea.

The sun was just coming up over the top of the mountains when Johnny Sangster got out of her bed and began to dress. Carmen stirred in her sleep, moaning peacefully. She curled up, the sheet pulled up under her chin. If she was Thorn Sayre he would have tucked her in. If she was Thorn Sayre he could have fucked her again.

He went to the bathroom and doused his head with cold water until it started to clear. He went back to the bedroom and picked up the car keys from the dresser. Carmen had suggested he use the Silver Cloud to get back to the hotel in time to make his flight. She would send someone to collect the car later. Johnny had jumped at the chance. He checked himself in the mirror, glanced at the sleeping girl and silently let himself out of the apartment. By the time Carmen began to wake, dreamily reaching out for Johnny Sangster, he could see the coastal road twisting steep and narrow below him.

A light mist was blowing off the still clear ocean. He could see the foot of the hill and the road in both directions. It was empty and inviting. He drove fast with the windows wound down and the radio on. The engine raced with a lyrical purr. Johnny put his foot down. The road was a ribbon winding down to the sea. The Silver Cloud hummed with soothing velvet monotony. The sun edged above the mountains and blazed into his eyes, already hot. Johnny squinted, touching the brakes. The Silver Cloud responded immediately. Johnny laughed softly. Beautiful car, he thought. A noise like a lullaby, a seat as soft as a bed of feathers. Johnny swallowed.

Then he was down too low for the sun and he blinked his eyes, surprised how close he was to the foot of the hill. He could hear the waves breaking up on the rocks. He eased off the speed and brought the car down into the mist at the bottom. It was thicker than he had anticipated, swirling treacherously in the well of the hill.

Johnny eased the Silver Cloud through the fog. He reached the junction and turned right on to the Rio road. The mist was thinning, the sun carving through it with a sharp yellow light that dappled the road ahead of him. He stepped on the accelerator and the Silver Cloud responded, shooting out of the last of the fog and directly into the path of a flame red Chevrolet that was turning at reckless speed left off the road from Rio into the mist. The Chevrolet and the Silver Cloud sprung on each other at point blank range.

Johnny swerved hard with a sickening screech of rubber, clipped the Chevrolet's tail and went into a careering skid. The Silver Cloud bounced off the safety barrier like a ton of pinballs and hurtled into a murderous spin with the road and the sky and the ocean and the mountains sucking each other out of position with a mad poisonous logic. Up ahead was a sharp bend in the road with a sheer rockface on one side and beyond the steel safety barrier a straight drop to the sea. Johnny fought for control of the wheel and lost.

The Silver Cloud ploughed into the rockface and Johnny Sangster's face burst through the windscreen in an explosion of blood and broken glass. Then he lay very still.

The patrol car came upon the Chevrolet first. It had skidded to a halt at the foot of the hill, spun sideways as if attempting a roadblock. The Chevrolet had its bumper ripped off and the paintwork down one side completely scraped off. A swarthy gangling youth in a cream-coloured light cotton suit stood in the middle of the road bawling like a baby and pawing at his bloody nose. His right arm was black and blue. But he was otherwise unharmed.

The two patrolmen looked at each other and breathed with relief. Twice during the night they had stopped the boy for drunken driving but let him go because his father was their Chief.

Then they saw the Silver Cloud crumpled against the rockface like a cigarette pack crushed under a boot heel. They ran towards the wreckage. No one could survive that. They looked inside for the corpse. His jacket was ripped to shreds and his right arm was pinned behind his back by the mangled steering wheel. His head jutted through the windscreen surrounded by stained shards of glass. The right side of his face was a pulp, hanging off in raw red ribbons. One of the patrolmen gasped and covered his mouth with his hands. The other crossed himself and vomited.

Johnny Sangster was still conscious.

He saw the patrolmen's distress and suddenly he was very afraid. Then the pain overwhelmed him. He cried out an agonized, useless denial. Then the belligerent, merciful blackness pulled him out of the horror and there was only bad dreams.

From the Rio de Janeiro AP ticker September 13 1983, 06.59 am.

Rio de Janeiro, Brazil (AP)

Wimbledon semi-finalist Johnny Sangster was seriously injured in a car collision just after dawn this morning when the Silver Ghost Rolls Royce he was driving hit a Chevrolet driven by 19 year old Paulo Mendoza on a road in Bueno Cabana, a pleasure resort on the outskirts of Rio de Janeiro. Mendoza, son of popular Rio police chief Raul Mendoza, escaped with a broken nose and minor bruising. The Chevrolet sustained only minimal damage. However the Rolls Royce was a write off and Sangster's injuries

are described by doctors as extensive and his condition is said to be critical. The tennis pro, currently ranked fifth on the ATP computer, has suffered a broken jaw, broken teeth and broken thumb, cracked ribs, concussion and what doctors describe as massive lacerations to the right side of his face. Doctors are endeavouring to stop Sangster's massive loss of blood and are operating to remove fragments of broken teeth from Sangster's throat, which it is feared he could choke on. Doctors describe Johnny Sangster's chances of survival as hopeful. Doctors refuse to comment at this time as to Sangster's chances of resuming his career in pro tennis. Ends.
O6:59 am. Sep 13 7908B AP.

The black cab swept Thorn up to the entrance of the Dorchester. She stepped out of the taxi in black shoes and stockings, a black raincoat, black gloves and a black pillbox hat with a black lace veil. The doorman saluted her.

In reception she was told to wait while they checked if Mrs Dave Brown was in her suite. The next thing Thorn knew Sal and Henry were hovering around her shoulders with itchy fingers.

'It's me,' Thorn assured them. 'Maxine's not still fretting about a crank with a cause, now *is* she?'

'Worse than ever. Come on up and see her.'

'Maxine said *no one*,' Henry reminded his partner in brawn. 'No offence meant.'

'None taken,' smiled Thorn.

'Thorn Sayre is not *no one*,' Sal said tersely. 'She is Maxine's oldest and dearest friend.'

Henry shrugged, absolving responsibility. They took her up to the suite and Maxine flinched at the sight of her dear old friend.

'I said fucking *no one*!'

'It's *me*, Maxine. It's *me*, honey.'

'Thorn, Jeez! What are you dressed up like *that* for? Is this some kind of sick joke? You look like you're going to a funeral. *My* funeral.'

'I've just come from court. They've turned down Roche's application for bail.'

'Yeah? That's too bad. I heard about Roche. I was hoping to do some business sometime. What will he get?'

'I don't know. It could be anything from three to fifteen years what with the selection box he had on the premises.'

'That's *obscene*!' bellowed Maxine. 'Why don't those faggot judges do something about *real* crime, *violent* crime? My God, this place is getting to be just like America. A real home from home! I'm glad I'm getting out.'

'You're leaving again? But what about the BBC show? What about *Resting*?'

'Guess,' smirked Maxine. 'Right now I look pretty good, don't I? Pretty much like I used to look, right? I mean – thanks to my clinic script – I lost all that brown blubber.'

'You look beautiful, Maxine.'

'Unfortunately I also lost my nerve. The death threats have started again over *here*. A harmless little sitcom, right? A wacky bunch of multi-coloured kids and their merry moments at the bottom of the thespian ladder. Oh, they're some wonderful human beings, my fans out there. If I spent my life in sackcloth and ashes, walled up in a nunnery with only woad for make-up – they'd still find a million little demeanings and deaths for me to suffer, just to let me know they care.'

'So you're still taking it seriously.'

'It's all right for you, *Thorn*. You don't know what it's like.'

'Ok. So I'm not coloured, but—'

'Coloured?' screeched Maxine. 'Who said anything about being coloured? Baby, I'm talking about being a *star*. Anyway – enough about me, what are *you* going to do now? I can't see you waiting around outside the prison gates for the rest of the century.'

'Well. I thought maybe I could move back in with you,' suggested Thorn confidently. 'Team up like in the old days. Help each other. With our work.'

'Well,' Maxine mused, 'like I told you, I'm quitting *Resting* and I'm quitting the country. I've got plenty of money. I can afford to live in the mobile fortress to which I've become accustomed.'

'Where are you going, Maxine?'

'Switzerland. If you're rich there, nothing happens to you. You're welcome to come along, Thorn. I'll see you have work.'

'You've got modelling contacts, Maxine? Jeez, I guess you have, working in TV. Or do you think I should try acting?'

Maxine looked astonished. Then she laughed patronizingly. 'Thorn, Thorn, it's not the old days anymore. It's not all room mates created equal anymore. The *work* I had in mind for you was something along the lines of personal assistant . . . Girl Friday . . . that kind of thing.'

'Goodbye, Maxine.'

'Where are *you* going? I thought you wanted a *job.*'

'I think my sights are set a little higher than cultivating neurosis among the gnomes, clocks and hills, Maxine.'

'Mountains!' Maxine yelled. 'Go ahead – walk out! You walked out once before and came crawling back. You'll do it again! You'll never work in this town again!'

Thorn was shaking hands with Sal and Henry. At the door she looked back over her shoulder and smiled. 'I wanted to say goodbye to the boys, Maxine. When we meet again I doubt very much you'll be able to afford them.'

'The public *wants* me!' Maxine shouted proudly.

'Yeah, but what *for*?'

'They want me for myself,' said Maxine. 'Ah, what they want me for doesn't come into it. There's a collective hard on out there waiting for me. That's why I'm in Park Lane and you no doubt are in . . . the Ball's Pond Road or something.'

'Kensington. But thanks for the advice. I'll try to go one better than you, Maxine, and find me a collective hard on that doesn't fire real bullets. Happy insanity, honey.'

Thorn waved and went.

From the Rio de Janeiro AP ticker September 22 1983, 10:56 am.

Rio de Janeiro, Brazil (AP)
Doctors in Rio have confirmed that Johnny Sangster is off the danger list. The number five tennis player of the world is still in strict isolation, seen only by doctors and by his coach Dave Pepper who still believes that Sangster can make a full comeback to professional tennis. Doctors confirmed that the right side of the player's face is paralysed. They added that scar tissue on the face was healing well and that both the doctors and patient have every confidence in the modern developments in cosmetic surgery. Doctors refused to speculate on Sangster's future in professional tennis but said it was hoped that Sangster would be out of his wheelchair in a few months. Ends.
10:56 a.m. September 22 9068D AP

Thorn Sayre displayed a tactical genius during her re-entry into the rarified atmosphere of London fashion. The entrance had to be perfect. No comeback was ever built on a snivelling penance. She would have to be a bold, predatory last beauty, she would have to be unrepentant. She knew that Jap Goddard would be at *The Painted Mirror*'s closing down party. He had predicted the magazine's failure at the moment of its happy birth. If there was one thing he liked almost as much as drinking and taking snaps it was gloating. And even if Jap Goddard chose not to pick up his option there were plenty more photographers where he came from. The important thing was to get back where she belonged – in the viewfinder of a camera.

She walked into the party dressed as Mata Hari at the height of her temple dancing days, head-dress and paste jewels and yards of pagan flesh on display, a phantom femme fatale in a hard bright light. She was flesh and dream fused, a scandalous power with a soft Southern drawl.

The party instantly forgot drug gossip and *The Painted Mirror*, Jap Goddard forgot all about being disobeyed and deserted. She made them take turns at eating out of her hand and then she went home with Jap Goddard.

'Don't come to my room. Just take my picture.'

Jap Goddard was once more left in the room next door with his photographs of Thorn Sayre. Looking closely at them he realized that he had captured her as perfect as she would ever be. In Jap Goddard desire slept and would never wake up. In its place he cultivated sedition.

He went downstairs and into the lavatory and stared at the pictures of Elle. Pale brown hair, white skin, thin features – all a backdrop for vast violet eyes, the eyes that had made her so elusive and compulsive. Elle was never captured, not really. *She* turned her back, *she* never doped herself, *she* never came back. Eternal unimpeachable Elle. *She never came back to him.*

He thought coldly of Thorn Sayre. Once and for all he would kiss off her career and keep her for ever. Sure, she can stick around, he mused. She's decorative and she'll let me take all the pictures I want now . . . But there would be no more insurrection, no more *Caesar's Things* or amphetamines. No more solitary *jogs*, even. God knows what she picked up out there alone.

He would keep her away from drugs by never letting her out of his sight. He would keep her away from the prying eyes of perfect strangers by keeping her out of the magazines.

Jap Goddard took all the pictures he wanted of Thorn Sayre and told her that she was not what the magazines were looking for right now. There was a new young American called Lisa who looked like a junior Sherry Ward . . . she was what the magazines wanted right now. But in reality, the fifty plus rolls of film that Jap Goddard filled with Thorn Sayre each day never left the house in the mews. Jap Goddard showed them to no one. He kept them for himself, and even as her career atrophied, Thorn Sayre could never have guessed.

Dave Pepper had started taking calls at the hospital in Rio. The nurse brought him the telephone. It wasn't another choked, frightened rich fan who needed soothing. This was Metalon-Fabey on the line, this was business.

Metalon-Fabey were cancelling Johnny Sangster's contract to endorse their range of male toiletries '*Caesar* – The Smell Of Success.' It was all over now.

Metalon-Fabey were at pains to point out that their decision had nothing to do with what had happened to Johnny Sangster's face. That was the *last* thing on their minds.

Dave Pepper hung up the telephone and began to cry bitter tears. For the first time in his life he was crying for someone else and not himself.

# fifteen

Jap Goddard had drinking and shaving days. Today was a drinking day. He sat watching *Blow Up* for the fifth time that week. Every time David Hemings walked on the video screen, Jap Goddard's right index finger twitched.

Thorn sprawled in a chemise, her hair straggling and her face bare of make-up. She ate a bar of chocolate as she turned the pages of the new *Caesar's Things*. A svelte creature with hair the exact shade of hers eyed Thorn disdainfully from the security status of a dead animal skin. Thorn rubbed the gooey end of the chocolate all over the paper face until the mannequin looked like a lady mud wrestler.

'Doorbell,' Jap was droning, 'doorbell.'

'Big deal. Big deal.'

'Get it.'

'Fuck it.'

He heaved himself out of his chair and clicked off the VCR. When he ambled down the hall and opened the door she heard a man's deep voice, a man's deep laughter. She made a gesture towards pulling down her chemise to cover her thighs but it wasn't made to stretch – besides, why bother? The voice and laugh only belonged to Keith Callaghan, Jap's fat old stooge and sidekick from the Sixties.

In those days he had competed with Jap just for etiquette's sake; now he felt free to confess that being Number Two made him happy as a sandboy. He worked six days a week, shooting glossy adverts and prestigious supplement spreads; he grew richer and richer as his name slipped further and further back into ancient history Sixties obscurity. He had never pined for the Sixties; why should he, he hadn't earned as much then, nor been married to his gorgeous Guyanan wife, nor had as many children. *These* were the days of plenty.

Keith Callaghan's face was soft and round, its squashiness inviting hands to use it as silly putty, his fists dissuading them. He looked like a baby who overnight had shot up to six foot and become a weightlifter. Today he wore Italian clothes so casual that they looked as though they just couldn't care less whether they stayed in the wardrobe or were taken for an airing. He carried just one camera, he was that good.

He smiled at Thorn. 'Hello, Camille. Who's the pictures for? *Crotch Chronicle*?' He wheezed, fell heavily into Jap's chair and turned on the VCR. 'What's this old tat?'

'The Roaring Sixties. *Blow Up*. Ogling that guy is as close as your friend gets to taking pictures these days.' Thorn parted her legs a little and slouched lower on her spine, eyeing Callaghan. Just because he had a cock? . . . or was it a camera? She laughed. She felt like a slob. Fat lot of good either of them had done her. 'Why don't you take a picture of me sometime?' At the door she could hear Jap talking to himself; advanced senility.

'Get an agency to find you an ad and I will. I don't take pictures for pleasure any more, love.' He jumped up. 'Reminds me.'

He left the room and she heard the front door close. When he appeared again he held the wrist of a bonfire of expensively tattered flame satin. On further inspection it proved to be a girl, a perfectly round face topped by pale lacklustre curls, two blue fried eggs of eyes staring solemnly at Thorn and one lop-sided mouth grimacing a smile of greeting. Her body was thin and jarred with her head, but her legs, sheathed in darkest brown nylon beneath the red satin tatters on her thighs, dwarfed everything. Absurdly gorgeous caricatures of molls legs, a cartoon of the perfect Copa showgirl. Thorn felt both flabby and scrawny; she tucked her legs beneath her and smiled coldly.

Jap appeared and walked over to Keith. 'May I sit there?'

'Of course, you old tart!' He stood up and caught the girl's arm. 'Get the legs, Jap! When did you last see legs like that?'

'On Verushka, I think.'

'Verushka! Old Sixties stuff! Anna's *seventeen* – she was in her pram when Verushka was in her prime! And look at Thorn here – she can't be more than twenty-three.'

'I'm twenty,' she hissed.

'You've obviously never worked with the Countess, Keith.' Jap hung the familiar SHUT sign on his face and retreated back into the screen.

'Thank God! Her and her kind – STAR models, for fuck's sake! Star statues! I don't know why you don't buy a second-hand time machine off a crafty Maltese dealer and piss off back to 1965, you and Bailey and Uncle Twiggy Cobley and all. Snotty models taking LSD and nightclasses in Cockney, locking themselves in the lav smoking funny fags and wasting hours of studio time, tarts getting white lipstick all over your Hush Puppies—' He fell down beside Thorn and gestured expansively to include Anna. 'Give me girls like these two anytime, girls who don't have any illusions about their worth. I'll tell you, Jap, that day in the Seventies when models became overnight anonymities should be a photographers public holiday. I don't remember the last time a model was late for a job; because they *know* now that none of them, not a one of them, is special, a star, a symbol, a someone, whatever. They know they're just tools.'

'For your information, Keith.' Thorn tried to keep her voice away from hysteria. 'For your information, *Caesar's Things* called me the last beauty of the twentieth century. That's hardly a ten a penny title, is it?'

'They called you that *again*?' He pulled Anna down beside him.

'No . . . what do you mean? You know, the pictures Jap took . . . the spread.'

'Oh, *that*! Yonks ago, love, that was *yonks* ago. Besides, they were just impressed that Jap, the old bender, fancied you. He hasn't been associated with any model since young Jill.'

'Elle.'

'Elle's a figment of your imagination.' He patted Anna's knee cheerfully. 'Not like these legs!'

'Jap rang Elle the other day and recorded her saying hello and who's there on a cassette. He never said anything, just waited till she hung up. He did it again last night. He'll have a whole LP's worth soon.' Thorn laughed. 'Don't you think that's a weird way to act, Keith? I mean, would you do a thing like that?'

'I'm not an artiste, love. Creative temperament and all.'

'Thorn, you're an embarrassment,' Jap said, his eyes never leaving the Sixties romp through streets and studio he and Elle had talked in, walked in, been young in. 'Excuse us, Keith. Thorn is American and therefore inclined to make every social occasion a cross between an analyst's couch and a bull session. Share it, Thorn. Let's hear about your Octopus complexes or compulsive cocaine taking traumas. Don't stop exposing yourself yet, wait till you've bored us to death – at the moment it's only to tears.'

'Sarky swine.' Keith Callaghan winced, worried. He poked the Allan Jones coffee table – a waxwork young woman on all fours dressed in standard bondage kit with a glass oval on her back – with his toe. 'Not sold yours yet? I sold mine yonks ago. Got a million for it.'

'The first time I saw it I thought it was the cleaning lady and she'd dropped a contact lens,' said Thorn.

Keith Callaghan roared.

'The cleaning lady doesn't wear contact lenses,' Goddard said with bad-tempered stupidity. 'She has glasses.'

Callaghan pointed an incredulous finger at Goddard. 'Can you believe this geezer? A laugh a minute, ain't he?' He panicked, mad to change the subject. 'Anna's a leg model, Thorn – ever done any specialized modelling?'

'No.'

'Best legs in Western Europe, Anna's got. We sat her in a red sports outside the Mum of Parliament, feet on the wheel, and these three old lechers done up as MP's dropping their

'Ansards in awe. Tricky business, though – manoeuvring so as not to get the ugly mug in the shot.' Keith Callaghan nudged Anna enthusiastically; she sprawled on the carpet and then jumped brightly to her feet, holding up her huge parachute silk tote bag.

'Want to change out of the gladrags, do you? Thorn, show her a bedroom, there's a good girl.'

'Next floor. Either room.'

'She only speaks Swede. You'll have to show her.' He laughed to Jap. 'God, it's great to work with a model who can't talk. They should all have their tongues cut out.'

Thorn took Anna to Elle-Jill's room. 'Thank you,' said Anna.

'You can't talk English.'

'I talk it better than you.' Anna laughed nervously.

'Well! . . . what's the point in pretending you don't?' Thorn sat on the bed; deception was always interesting.

'So men like Keith don't expect me to do the jokes and smut, you see.' Anna pulled on a hideous chunky sweater, then a pair of pink stretch denims. Thorn gazed at her clothes in fascinated horror.

'How long have you been in this country?'

'Five months.'

'Would you like me to take you shopping? You seem to be terribly behind the times in Sweden.'

'No thank you. Swedish clothes suit me well. I save my money for a legal training later in life. I'm very clever and should do best.' She smiled proudly, then looked at Thorn. 'Besides, begging a pardon, you're not the best groomed person on earth. To tell a truth, I was amazed and disappointed when I saw you'd retired and stopped bothering to be beautiful. The magazine pictures, when I saw them I said to myself, 'This must be most beautiful girl alive.' I sent to my mother, best Garbo fan, and mother say same thing. And now you're not you any more.'

'You don't know what you're saying. I never retired. I'm a *model*. I've been called the last beauty of . . .' Thorn shook her head. 'You're very rude. It must be because you can't speak English properly.'

'Forgive me. Beauty yes, model no. If you don't work you're no model. I'm plain faced but I get lots of work. Because I take career, even silly career, *seriously*. Very bad for woman to doss about the house all day. Please stop dossing.'

Thorn laughed. Then she burst into tears.

'See you're hysterical. All doss and no work makes a girl a moron, fit for nothing but the booby hatch.' Anna picked up her bag and touched Thorn's shoulder. 'Put on make-up, then you'll be too perfect to cry. And take one of these.' She closed Thorn's limp hand around several familiar small shapes. 'Happy pills. I take to keep weight off. Won't hurt you.'

'I know.' Thorn stared at the pills.

'Bye bye then. Big luck.' Anna closed the door quietly.

After a minute Thorn got up and locked the door. She pulled on black tights and twisted her hair into a plait. She knelt on Elle-Jill's bed and turned her clutch bag out, shaking out her make-up. She looked at the pills, swallowed two and tried to think of a place to keep the other two. The slim gold cigarette case. She put the pills away and read the engraving; that swank address beneath her title. She put her make-up on meticulously, and when after half an hour it was finished, the new face, the speed and the remembrance of that extravagant standing invitation slowly but surely pulled her right out of the big sleep. A standing invitation to lie down for a living! A *big* living . . . acting experience, *being* someone else twenty-four hours a day. Yes, modelling was definitely a mug's game, a stopgap, a goal for those with nothing behind the bland façade and their ears. Jerry Hall was in films and the gossip columns, Amanda Lear sang and was an icon in Italy, even the chunky Swede was bent on being Perry Mason. Sherry Ward and Cheryl Tiegs were multi-millionairesses – but only guillible America accorded them any *respect*. Grace Jones didn't earn one half of their salary yet everyone knew her name. She had brains, she'd hated being a model. Why should *she*, brilliant Thorn, tolerate it?

Much better to be an actress. It wasn't a real brothel, Mr Klan had said as much. Sex wasn't compulsory. More of a drama school. Some Hollywood big shot will drop in, thought Thorn, and he'll just be so impressed when I tell him that I never sleep with my admirers. He'll employ me, he'll make me massive.

She looked at herself in Elle-Jill's long mirror. She had to be perfect before she was free again. I'll fast for two days, she planned, and then live on grilled steak and lemon juice. I'll exercise all day tomorrow, till I literally drop, and from then on regularly. I'll get a manicure, a pedicure and a facial and I'll cut off half my hair.

Six days later Thorn Sayre took two amphetamine pills and walked out Jap Goddard's front door, twice as terminally perfect as she had entered it and abandoned all hope.

The banks of bright TV lights were switched on as the private plane hired by the ATP touched down at Kennedy airport. The cameras panned in as Johnny Sangster left the plane with a nurse and his coach. The police held back the masses and the media.

'There hasn't been this much interest in a *tragic* car accident for many years,' drooled a hardened talking head. 'Montgomery Clift, Niki Lauda, Johnny Sangster – young men who survived *tragic* car crashes, spared their lives but not their looks. James Dean, Jayne Mansfield, Eddie Cochran – they were the lucky ones. They died.'

He had suffered a broken jaw, teeth and bones, concussion and severe lacerations on the right side of his face. Doctors had operated on him more times than he remembered. And the operations had only just begun. In the wheelchair, his legs covered by a blanket, Johnny Sangster looked very small.

The crowds pressed in. Adults stared, grim faced, grim ghouls, making comments about the salvage and state of his face with smug sympathy or turning to their friends, gawping and chattering. Children shrieked and pointed. Photographers pushed cameras into his ruined face. Johnny bowed his head. The nurse pushing the wheelchair stared straight ahead. Dave Pepper aimed punches at camera eyes. The police ushered the three of them through – some cops sneaking a look, some staring pointedly away, most so busy keeping the mob at bay that they didn't have a chance to do either.

Once upon a time there was a mean old umpire at Flushing Meadow – seventy, silver-haired, myopic, vengeful – who Johnny Sangster had had removed for incompetence. The old umpire was there. He wanted to see and savour but there was no joy on his face. He stared blankly. A disgusting loud pair of pantomine heterosexuals elbowed a black policeman aside to scream vicious eleation in Johnny's face. He couldn't answer; too much wire in his jaw.

'Don't talk so loud now, do ya, Sangster? Hot shot! Look at the hot shot!'

'The money, the girls, the drugs . . . *it all goes, Sangster!*'

The police pulled Dave Pepper off them. The woman was screaming and had dropped her popcorn.

They made it to the waiting limousine. Global won't be sending any more limos, Dave Pepper thought, no one will. He'd hired it himself. He helped the nurse lift Johnny into the back seat. In the corner sat Johnny's small and sympathetic reporter, Susie Blond, the only media Johnny had agreed to talk with.

He grimaced a greeting.

She gasped. 'Oh my God.'

Dave Pepper instinctively reached across Johnny and pushed her out of the car. 'Out. Out or I'll kill you.'

Outside, Susie Blond tapped on the window frantically. 'Forgive me. I didn't mean it. Forgive me. My boss'll kill me.'

Johnny stared straight – or as straight as his unsymmetrical face would allow – in front of him.

She'll never make a talking head, thought Dave Pepper. She *apologizes* when she acts like a pig. He watched Susie Blond get smaller and small as the driver put space between them and the mob.

'They'll soon forget about you, John, don't worry,' comforted Dave Pepper. He wished he was brave or stupid enough to bite his tongue off. Johnny stared at him. The right side of his face was petrified, only his right eye showing any sign of life. It gleamed mad and bright, giving his face the look of pure mania. He crooked a finger at Dave. The coach bent his head.

Johnny spoke with difficulty. The nurse protested the fact that he spoke at all. 'I'll be back. They'll never forget me. I'll be back and if you don't believe me tell the driver to pull over. I want you out this car.' The right side of his mouth drooled. He couldn't feel the saliva as it trickled down his chin.

'I believe you, John. Of course I do. I just meant all this will blow over when you've recovered. Of course they'll never forget you.'

The nurse held John's chin and wiped the spit away.

He closed his eyes, sick and weary. 'I'll be back,' he whispered. Then he slept.

# sixteen

There was no sign above the door of the place called Gemini. Inside there was too much red velvet and not enough light. The wine was old – no spirits were sold at Gemini (spirits were famous for causing violence and ego-dwindling impotence, both total strangers to Gemini) and the clients were too awed and grateful to ever complain – and the visitors were even older.

Sherwood Klan was the kind of capitalist that had for the most part ceased to exist in America – he made his money ingeniously, gracefully and with a degree of honesty. The people who worked for him admired him and he didn't despise them. He was a mystery, living through his business; his only known Achilles ache was for the late Marilyn Monroe. He thrived on his business; he was matinee hunky and large, booming health. He had a wife – or was she a sister? they shared the same glossy bottle black hair and staged suntans and even featured, ever-smiling faces – called Kirsten Klan, who ran an establishment, strictly for men's men, across at Malibu. It was called, cutely, Gemini Rising.

Sherwood Klan sat expounding his business philosophy, his secret of success, with the new Marilyn. The girl was a little too short, her cosmetic surgery a little too cheap to pull off Norma Jean's dream with total conviction. But the lighting was peach, and no lighting flattered better.

'I've seen other Marilyns get spreads in *Oui* with less than you've got, Marilyn!'

'Thank you!'

Thorn Sayre came down the stairs. Sherwood crossed the room and brought her to his table. Their relationship was pure business – Klan only had eyes and hands for the Marilyns.

'Hi Norman. And how is Mrs Mailer tonight?'

'Huh?' said the new Marilyn.

Sherwood frowned. 'You know the rules about stepping out of role, Greta.'

Thorn lit a cigarette and stared at the TV, set discreetly into the wall. A wheelchair was arriving at Kennedy carrying precious prime time cargo. It was chaos. The media were covering the event with their usual wholesome hysteria. The crowd were whipping themselves into the ugly elation of a well-fed, law-abiding mob. The cops were doing their best and it wasn't good enough.

The camera zoomed in for an intimate close up as the person in the wheelchair looked into its blank eye. Thorn flinched. She saw his face and heard his name leap out of the running commentary like an invitation to a wake that would never end.

The American Dream as accident statistic. His career – which meant his *life* as far as he, and she, was concerned – was in ruins and they were still using his name to sell tickets to the show. She was numb with rage. Why couldn't the sick bastards leave him alone? Get off his case, thought Thorn, wishing that she could. She didn't want to think about Johnny Sangster. She could not stop thinking about him.

On the cruel screen he was almost at the car. Thorn felt tears sting her eyes. She blinked them away, fearful for her self-control and kohl. But she felt for Johnny Sangster.

She remembered last spring when they had London and Paris, when they shared the chemmy shoe and dexedrine, cologne and fame. They were good times. They had been young together. There was no getting back there, and it made the remaining life a tragic travesty.

It was over for Johnny and there was nothing she could do to change that. All she could do for him now was become a winner. A winner like he used to be.

She watched them load him into a big black car and drive him away. Her throat buckled with sorrow and she closed her eyes. She coughed quietly, once. Then it was gone.

'A Marilyn is a must at Gemini,' Sherwood was saying. 'All our guests are goddesses from the Golden Age – Ava, Rita, Lana, Greta here and of course yourself. When superstars weren't ashamed for sex and beauty to walk hand in hand, Marilyn. All beautiful faces from the past.'

'Why just the *past*, Sherwood?' the new Marilyn asked before practising her baby goldfish pout.

'Well, who the fuck wants to sleep with Barbra Streisand or Meryl Streep?'

A man with a face like corrugated liver spots approached their table. Sherwood shook his hand, introduced him to Marilyn – on a first name basis, to keep things friendly – and watched the happy couple go upstairs to consummate the charade.

'What's the matter with *you*?' Sherwood wanted to know.

'Nothing,' Thorn said.

'Was that guy on the news the tennis pro who was in the car smash?'

'That's right.'

'I didn't know you liked tennis.'

'I don't.'

'Oh, I see.' He gave her a strange look.

'When am I off the job next, Sherwood?'

'Oh, *Greta*. You're hardly an oppressed twelve-year-old junkie working for a homicidal PR in one room off Times Square. That extra zero makes you sleep with the clientele, not me. It'll be *quiet* around the weekend – you know that most of our visitors like to spend every minute with their grand-children. Going anywhere special?'

'I doubt it.'

A middle-aged man, jumpy as a pre-pubescent on his first date, approached them. Discreet Sherwood table-hopped over to the contemptuous, chain-smoking Joan Crawford, her mouth a red slash slick in the low light. She looked tired. Ever since the brood of adopted Crawford children had revealed in tome and tabloid that Joan tended towards sadism, her business had doubled. Sherwood loved her – platonically. Thorn glanced at herself in the ornate mirror across the room. Perfect – Do Not Touch, she reflected.

'Would – may I order wine?' the fan said, staring and sweating.

She shook her head curtly. Being fucked was bad enough – being hungover in the morning would be hell. She stood. He looked up at her, swooning at her height.

'I vant to be alone,' droned Thorn. She walked to the door, then looked, long and languorous as her stature, back at him.

Ironically, he wouldn't let her alone all night.

Johnny felt sick as the sweat started to flow. Dave Pepper hit a long hard approach shot and the shell of Johnny Sangster chased it, the right side of his body one searing burn. He pounced on the ball and drove it back at his opponent. But it didn't feel *right*. He could weep with despair. It would never feel right. He was in pain and under par.

He still had his strokes but now he had to think about them.

He still had his power and pace, his style and guile and dancer's grace. But it all took one second longer.

It's not enough, Johnny thought. He sprinted painfully to the net for a soft Dave Pepper return and he knew it wasn't enough.

It should have been an easy volley to put away. Johnny Sangster would have punished it with contemptuous ease. Thank you and goodnight. Johnny put the ball into the net.

'Come on you fucking *faggot*!' he screamed, lashing at the bobbing ball with barbarian frustration. Then he put his foot on the neck of his Tora Matchplay tennis racquet – which he was no longer being paid to use – and smashed it to useless varnished splinters.

He hurled the jigsaw of his Tora Matchplay tennis racquet into the empty stands. Then he looked brazenly at Dave Pepper.

'My God, John!' Dave Pepper bawled, banging his own racquet hard on the ground. 'Stop acting like a weak-gutted feather-brained spoilt little brat fucking up at the country club!'

Dave had been shouting at him a lot lately.

'My God, Dave! Stop thinking you're bullying me for my own *good*!'

Dave Pepper subsided into an uneasy compassion. 'It's a bad day,' he said.

'Yeah. It's going to be a bad day forever.'

'You never were a practice player, John. You were a match player. *Always.* It'll come right when you get your hands on a match.'

'I can hardly wait,' Johnny said, blinking hard. 'Might as well get it over with.'

'Oh, *John*.'

In the club locker room waited all his old rivals. Velez, Falconi, Tom Dougherty, even the kid Billy Lennox. Funny, but the kid's game was coming on by leaps and bounds these days. Funny.

They were all pretending not to stare. They felt sorry for a former pro and pleased for what this would do for their computer ranking. I'm a loser, Johnny Sangster thought. The truth hurt him like hell. Losing was what had happened to the other person in the old days.

But the old days were not enough for Johnny Sangster. The old days would never be enough.

Even though they were all he had left.

Thorn Sayre walked along a windy beach down at Topanga. The greyness of the spitting sky did more to keep the hoards away than any fence or guard dogs sign. Beside her walked a young man huddled into a red windcheater. From a distance he was a perfect James Dean facsimile; on closer inspection he really didn't have the cheekbones for it, though every move and expression he tried on disputed the cruel truth.

He called himself Byron and he worked for Kirsten Klan. They often met, Greta and James, to walk and relieve cabin fever. Thorn was glad to step beyond the bounds of her role. Byron never wanted to.

'How many of the characters working for Sherwood fake it, Thorn?'

'How many pretend to come? How should I know? It's not exactly a coffee klatsch up there. And I'm not exactly the most popular co-ed on campus.'

'No no *no*. I'm not talking about *sex*. I mean how many of them believe in their *roles*.'

'Oh, only you – and all the Marilyns, of course.'

Byron squinted, hunched his shoulders and scratched the back of his head. 'That's bad. Then they're – not *you*, of course – but the others, they're just hookers in star drag.'

'Are you kidding? What's your job description – valet?'

'I'm an *actor*.' He skimmed a stone glibly across the surface of the sea. 'Just because I blow, bend and bugger don't mean I'm not an actor. Something stirring in the crotch is the sincerest form of audience appreciation. It can't be faked. Clapping hands is for nurds.'

'Oh, the world is your stage and your stage is a whorehouse.'

'You call yourself a model.'

She flnched and pulled her arm away from his.

'Hey, don't get sore.'

'I'm not. Just irritated. It's so dumb. Why the hell does your world revolve around some bratty old fruit who's been dead since before your mammy met your daddy?'

'He – *Jimmy* – gave me a chance to *be* somebody.'

'But not yourself.'

'If you're a boring nobody what's the point in being yourself? Jimmy was just the last word in men. Today they're either rich queens or poor pigs. Why not follow the only formula that ever got it right?'

'But you'll never *feel* like him.'

He looked at her, pained and pathetic. 'I'm doing my best.'

'What did he ever do for you?'

'I owe it all to Jimmy.'

'You mean that part you had in *Happy Days*?'

'Jimmy is everything I ever wanted to be. I wouldn't be in showbusiness, in *Hollywood*, if not for Jimmy. I'd be working at my father's *garage*. There, he's done that for me.'

'You're not in showbusiness, Byron – that's just more make believe.'

'It's not make believe.'

'Make believe with semen stains.'

'You don't know. What are you, the all-seeing eye? My clients don't want just any *cowboy* off the street. They love Jimmy; a few of them knew him well, were his *friends*. And now they love *me – us*.'

'You really believe they were his *friends*?'

'What I do may not mean much to you, Thorn, but it's the nearest I'll get now to being Jimmy, being somebody, anybody. I am an actor. Movies and TV don't want to know the first-rate, or even a first-rate *copy* of the real thing, makes them nervous, shows up other *actors* for the bland shit they are. Oh, it's ok to *steal* from Jimmy and pretend it's all your own work – Pacino, de Niro, any skinny old ethnic actor – but an honest, first-rate homage they don't want to know.'

'What about that little fat guy, the one built like a postbox?'

'Thorn,' Bryon said with patient disgust, 'Martin Sheen may *dream* he's the spitting image of the godhead but the most cursory glance will reveal that he's a wagonload closer to Jimmy Durante than he is to James *Dean*.'

'There's no future in all this, Byron. Will you still be slouching around mumbling and screwing up your face—'

'—I am a *Method* actor—'

'—sorry, when you're an old guy, thirty-two or something? You'll just look *ridiculous*.'

'Oh, I guess I know it. When Jimmy was my age he'd made *three* films. Jimmy *died* when he was my age. When I'm twenty-five it will all be over and you'll be proved right, Thorn – I'm *not* him. What do you do when the bottom drops out of your world?'

'I'm the last person who'd know. When's your birthday?'

'The day after tomorrow.'

'You'll have to do something special.'

'Yaah. Hey – the bottom will have dropped out of my world before my bottom drops! I'll make a good-looking corpse some day.'

'It won't be so bad, your birthday. When you get *him* out of the way you can get to work on building a better character. Or – hey, talk to Mrs Klan. Maybe she's got an opening for a Martin Sheen!'

'Funny girl.' Byron punched her playfully. 'As Kirsten herself would say – who the fuck wants to fuck Martin Sheen?'

Once upon a happier time Johnny Sangster's game had had a whipcord gleam about it. He had been sprinter, dancer, fighter, poker player, he had been what Chekhov called grace – *the ability to complete one definite action while making the least possible number of distinct movements* – incarnate. He made everything seem effortless and heroic back then. But those days were long gone now.

It was his first match since the car crash, the comeback that became a swansong.

The massed spectators aimed loaded cameras and the photographers crowded on one side of the court. They didn't want a keepsake of the game, they wanted a warped memory of Johnny Sangster's poor petrified face. Johnny missed his shots by one split second. That's all. But it was the one split second that his short blazing vainglorious career was built upon.

In the stands those who loved him agonized and wept over this hollow shell. But most of the crowd were gloating – glad to see a success story relegated to their wonderful world of bitter mediocrity.

Billy Lennox pounced on a short return and with a fast easy movement whipped a deep stinging skimming ball back at his opponent's desperately inert feet.

It was all over. Billy Lennox had destroyed Johnny Sangster's game in straight sets. All over at last.

Johnny shook hands with the kid at the net. He could see it was the happiest day of the kid's life. Back in the locker room Billy Lennox' coach was waiting to celebrate. Dave Pepper put his arm around Johnny's shoulders and glared at the happy couple with green-eyed vitriol 'They better make the most of it,' he said. 'Oh, they just *better*. That kid is nowhere – except off the ATP rankings altogether.'

Johnny flopped down on to a wooden bench. 'I just made him look as though he's going somewhere big.'

'Ah, we tried to bring you back too *fast*. We put you in the ring before you were yourself again.'

'I'm as near to me as I'll ever be.'

'A shorter practice tomorrow, John. No more than two hours. Or you think you should have a rest day tomorrow? Great thinking!' Dave stared at his boy with last-ditch desperation. 'That wasn't John Sangster out there today,' he finished quietly.

'That was what's left of him.'

They stared at each other.

And they both knew that Johnny Sangster had quit pro tennis.

Thorn didn't walk along the beach with Byron anymore.

On the eve of his birthday he took out his flaming red Chevrolet and drove it into a wall.

The more frustrated thespians that made up the Gemini/Gemini Rising cast list reacted to Byron's death with mawkish hysteria – Marilyn made a cautious suicide bid with a bottle of aspirin, Liz drank heavily for a while. Marlon smashed some coffee tables. Even sorrow was a sideshow to them.

Thorn lost her appetite and slept late daily. She even forsook sex money for a few weeks. But she couldn't cry; Byron's life ended not with a tragic suicide but with a triumphant punch-line.

The thing that saddened Thorn was that the likeable fool's budget hadn't stretched to the silver Porsche Snyder of his dreams.

# seventeen

Johnny Sangster was in retirement, in retreat, lost in a black static depression while the world and the Circuit kept right on turning, *unbelievably* kept right on turning without him.

The Circuit still moved around the globe, a combination of big business, show business and endurance test. What was once the pivot of his world was now another world he could never be part of. Except as some kind of grotesque sideshow, the mobile booby prize. The press kept calling, people still stared, photographers peered through the windows of the apartment across the way. They camped outside downstairs, waiting to pounce.

*Vultures.*

At first he went out in the daylight, like a *normal*, and it was a horrible mistake. The ghoulish hysteria which erupted almost anywhere he walked was unbearable. So when the sun was up he stayed in, locked inside his big bright box of a home, the curtains drawn and the mirrors gone. The lights were on and inside his twelve-foot high trophy sideboard his silver and gold cups, medals, shields, plates and bowls glinted dully in the artificial light.

Johnny only went out at night. At night it was better. Let my people see. The rich and famous could forgive his face, were hidebound and parasitic enough to respect him for his gone glory and extant fortune.

They were cool.

All Johnny Sangster wanted was respect. He could only get it from his own kind. the Circuit didn't count, couldn't count. They weren't his kind any more. Johnny's people were the people who spent their pointless, aimless lives throwing and going to parties. It wasn't The Circuit but it was all he had now.

There was nothing like the Circuit. With all his money, all his invitations, losing the Circuit had left a gap in his life that would prove impossible to fill. Ah, there was nothing like The Circuit, nothing in the world. Tennis was the only sport that never closed, the only place to be. It seemed unnatural not to be living like a nomad on a Spartan schedule with thrills and fat cheques in every port.

Johnny Sangster grew up on the fun, money and glory that pro tennis promised and delivered. Then he drove a certain road and it was impossible ever to be happy again. So he went to parties while his name dropped off the ATP computer rankings like a dead friend's number from a telephone book.

In the New Year the Circuit came to town for the Masters in Madison Square Garden and Johnny had to run. The entire population of New York City seemed to be comprised of tennis players, tennis coaches, tennis promoters and tennis fans, everywhere tennis fans. Johnny could not face any of them. He could not even face the temptation of turning on the TV to the channel that screened the tournament. He had never smashed a TV set before and he didn't want to start at his age. Johnny Sangster was twenty-one. He escaped to London.

London because its people were reserved and unpushy. London because – after the initial tantrums of early success – they liked him. London because England had no tennis stars of its own and therefore only a minute amount of tennis was shown or reported on. It was getting bigger slowly, but it was still a largely tennis-unconscious place outside of The Fortnight. Most of all Johnny flew to London because that was where his name and Thorn Sayre's had been linked.

It was bizarre, being in London in January. He still thought of people and places in terms of the Circuit. London was stormy blue spring skies, staying at the Grosvenor, eating at Alexander's and nightclubbing at Simone's. All that had changed now, of course. But Simone was glad to see him. Never mind that Simone was always glad to see anyone for the first few seconds.

'Johnny darling! *Mechante* Johnny! You've been lured to my lair out of season!'

'Yeah,' said Johnny, sheepish in the opulent darkness of the club. 'Me and that Circuit parted company. It cramped my style. How are you, Simone?'

'Well, I'm sublime, my pet! And yourself? Oh, tell me all your *fofoca*! Let me look at you! As beautiful as ever!' Simone did not flinch at his face; indeed, she kissed it with an elaborate mmm sound, as if he was extra delicious, and then she led him off to the dance. 'There's a million people you *must* meet. Oh, wasn't it awful about Regine's place? I almost *died*.'

There were only two tiers in Simone's caste system. For a start, conveniently, the un-rich did not exist for her. The top tier were friends of Simone's who were famous, millionaires or famous millionaires. The rest were acolytes of Simone who were lazy, loud and empty, lavish in their praise for the glitterati who were richer and more famous than they, popular – which meant tolerated *in extremis* – for knowing all the dirt – or *fofoca* as Simone would have it – a season before Dempster did. Simone's caste system contained no Untouchables. No one was untouchable here, not if the toucher was a rung up from the touched. Simone was neither witty or pretty. The nights spent in her club were not espcially riotous. The rich came to Simone's for that most unlikely of experiences, *security*.

In the Sixties when the jet set were young and not censured by the all-round affluent society for their extravagant ways, the rave places to be seen changed literally every week. In the Eighties times were more austere and less tolerant, there was more violence and less money – if you were one of the self-styled golden ones you could never be sure if the brown-shoes man in the street would greet you with an autograph book or a bullet. The jet set froze and stopped experimenting, leisure and pleasure began to come in crumbs to be grabbed with both hands and hoarded in Polaroids, leisure and pleasure were no longer theirs by divine right of king pins.

In this new world capitals mostly boasted only two or three clubs where the very rich felt secure enough to enjoy a quiet high life. In the Sixties the very rich had been bright young things. Now the leading lights were older, wealthier maybe but definitely a dying breed despite the occasional young wife or protegée in tow. Their children clamoured for invitations to wilder, poorer parties thrown by musicians and the occasional rag trader, leaving the staid old jet set to brood over the youth they could not command and the youth they could not buy back. They sat and sweated it out in the safety of their rare clubs, their jewellery safe in some subterranean vault protecting them from the ravages of alimony and school fees, from the price of Krug and krugerands.

And they flocked to Simone for the balm of her special gift – the ability to infect all around her with the belief that something was always *just about to happen*, the great gift of at all times encouraging and cultivating the anticipation of revelry.

Simone's London and Paris clubs were havens, their atmospheres a hybrid of a waiting room and a wake. Simone's desire for a constant party sprung not from Reginesque poverty but from marrying a millionaire. Back in the Fifties when Simone was a plain teenage vendeuse in an avenue Montaigne sock shop she had been chosen by the jaded American playboy as the perfect companion, likely to estrange both his friends and his family – the first because she was drab, the second because his family were sufficiently *nouveau* to their *riches* to be chronic snobs about such things. They settled down in a renovated farmhouse in the village of La Basoche in the lush countryside south of Paris. Their neighbours were Rothschilds and Grazias in renovated farmhouses of their own. Simone's groom consummated the marriage and started work on his heart's desire – the Great Un-American Novel.

'Un-American,' Jack explained, 'because there are no American playboys. There's no such thing as an American playboy. They're all workmen.'

She wanted to scream; she needed *fun*. They had married at cross purposes. Jack spent years trying to write his atrocious novel. Simone spent the same years too frightened of being catapulted back into poverty to protest, terrified as she read the obituaries of the world's great playboys – Rubirosa was the biggest blow, he who Jack had been so friendly with that Portfiro would do intimate things like skipping off with Jack's girl of the evening while Jack was in the men's room. Why couldn't *he* have chosen her? She would have been happy to die in his car, after all the good times he would have shown her.

Simone felt pure terror at the way the world's party was winding down before she'd even set foot in the door, terror that ate away at her various other interests and ambitions and made her a secret obsessive.

Jack was kind; he never stopped trying to write and never stopped ignoring her, but he would have given her anything money could buy, bar fun. When he died in the late Sixties she could feel no sorrow and no guilt at her lack of sorrow, her obsession was so all-consuming. She rushed to rake the embers of the Big Party and had dedicated her life to keeping it alive ever since.

To Simone, Johnny Sangster seemed a multi-faceted delicacy – a sports hero, a youngster and a *freak*. It was hard to find a presentable famous freak these days. The combination would be sure to attract a wagonload of *fun* people her way. Simone had to have Johnny Sangster. Johnny Sangster went to Simone's nightly. He was flattered by her attentions. He didn't think much of the clientele – but as a tennis pro he'd never really stayed in a foreign country long enough to become aquainted with the nation's real, *young* nightlife. So he didn't really feel he was missing anything, yeah, it felt fine being feted by twice-survived-suicide starlets and their financier or football manager sugar-Svengalis. At least there wasn't a single strawberry or ball boy there to remind him.

The weeks passed. The Masters passed through New York.

But Johnny didn't want to go home. He remained in London with Simone and her set. He half-hoped he would one night see Thorn Sayre across a crowded club. But he would have stayed anyway. There was nothing to go back to.

Simone sensed it and one night she took him into her office. 'Take a seat, Johnny. Strawberry daiquiri, isn't it?'

'You remembered.'

'A *noctambule* never forgets,' said Simone crossing from her bar to her desk.

'A *noctambule*?' Johnny queried. He almost glanced towards where Harald O. Holden should have been, for an explanation. 'What's a one of them?'

'A night person, my pet. A *noctambule* is a night person, like me. Like you now.' She handed him his pink poison. 'To all the *noctambules*.'

Johnny smiled and sipped. 'You didn't ask me in here for a French lesson, Simone.'

'You're right, my pet. You need a new career, Johnny. Night work, not under the bright sun, the bright sun that makes you think of your past and of your imperfections . . .'

'What is this? An employment office?'

'Sort of. I want you, Johnny. You will be my chief *noctambule*.'

'Well, I sort of am, already. I mean I'm here every night.'

'No, no. A *chief noctambule* – a night person on the payroll, Johnny. We can pay you very well. And we can call you anything you wish – you chose, from "host" or "front-man" or even "co-director".'

Johnny stared at her, hard. 'I see. You want me to be a *greeter*, Simone. That's what they call it in the States. A *greeter*.'

'I'm sure you'll agree, Johnny, that Americans – despite their many virtues, such as . . . well, there are *many* – are not feted for their delicacy.'

'A greeter,' Johnny sneered. 'Some famous, faded face at the door of the dive to *greet* all the suckers. Which means to *kiss ass*. Some broken down wreck for the suckers to shake hands with, stare at and *laugh* at over fucking cocktails. Poor Joe Louis, *Joe Louis* for God's sake, wound up in Las Vegas being dumped on to the very same job description. The poor bastard.'

'If it's good enough for the Brown Bomber, Johnny . . .'

'It wasn't good enough for him, and he was a punchy boxer of seventy-one. For a tennis pro of twenty-one it's even less of a deal.'

'Ex-tennis pro, Johnny. Come, come, my pet. It's free money. Don't be so defensive. It's *fun*. You *live* here, practically, anyway – why not get paid for relaxing?'

'I'll tell you why not, Simone. I've seen these greeters and it's glum, it is *no fun*. Smile sweet while sucking ass. that's the general idea, isn't it? Always, always battered sportsmen, damn good ones in their day, hired to be hospitable to stinking nobodies who want to gawp at the wear and tear of fame, who want to be reassured that their anonymous little sub-lives are the lives that see you all right in the end.'

'You don't understand, Johnny.' Simone stood up, smiling calmly. 'I'm offering you the post of chief *noctambule* at my London club.'

'I understand fine, sure I do.'

'No, you don't, my pet. I'm doing you a favour. You should be grateful, Johnny.'

'*Grandma*,' Johnny hissed, incredulous and incensed. 'I don't think you understand. I'm not exactly on Skid Row, Grandma.'

'I do not doubt that you tip your taxi drivers handsomely, Johnny. But you are not rich. New money . . . it goes so quickly, yes? Loot needs roots. You were not big enough for long enough. We all have our needs.'

'Yeah, you need to keep your fat yap closed and I need some fresh air.'

'I have offended you. I apologize.'

'Take your apology and shove it where the sun don't shine.'

'The sun doesn't shine any place I go.'

On the pavement he stood fuming. A carload of young rich, searching for Swinging London on a later shift than their parents, pulled up in front of him.

'Johnny Sangster! Hey, Johnny! Want to come to a party?'

You could have knocked them down with a feather boa when he climbed into the car.

Percy Street lived way out and his finest – or least mediocre – moment was long past, so his party had been postponed for hours, a total lack of guests holding up play. His home was a bank clerk's idea of a pop star's Surrey stately home, mortgaged to the hilt of the suit of armour's sword. His career was up the creek without a recording contract.

Invitations to his comeback ('I've never been away!') party had gone out to everyone with power – journalists, DJs, radio programmers, producers and musicians – especially those he had put on his hate list and refused to communicate with in the heady days of his hit record. They were all conspicuous by their contemptuous absence.

'My friends are important,' he consoled himself.

He so wanted them to hear the tapes of his new triple album. He so wanted a contract. He so wanted a friend in high places. Or a picture in the papers.

Like salt in the wound, a band of thugs, stooges and sycophants who had known Percy Street since the happiest days of his life – this collection celebrated as the Lewisham Mafia in happier days in happier songs – frolicked around his rococo palace. Percy smiled back and gave them the thumbs up, but he sneered inside. They loved him. They could do nothing for him.

Stella Sloan sighed at the scene as she came down the stairs in her Janice Wainwright party dress and red Charles Jourdan shoes. Her scent was Imprevu, her underthings were Janet Reger, her mascara was Mary Quant, she wore a crystal flower on a fine gold chain from Jones around her neck and kept a current passport in a Gucci case in her Fendi bag. Stella Sloan was the last friend to the stars in captivity, and these things were important. A friend to the stars can live by labels alone. Stella surveyed the ghastly solitary scene and wondered what was going on, going *wrong*. You never saw a root on her head. She was a pretty blonde. When a paramour scorned she had never stolen credit cards, talked to tabloids or destroyed the contents of wardrobes. She had only been unable to cope with drink or drugs when spiked. You couldn't even really brand her as a *groupie*. She wasn't that tatty; she was a *music-lover* who sometimes fell in *love* with musicians. But . . .

But she was sleeping her way to the bottom. Each succeeding lover was lesser, each succeeding liaison was shorter. What was she short of? Stella Sloan often wondered in her coded diary. She was into Tarot and worried about her future. The groupies of the Sixties, really hard-bitten old battle-axes, Stella thought, were now mistresses of assorted mansions and mothers of million-dollar divorce-tickets. Today's new pop stars, who seemed to have been *born* with wives and children – a girl couldn't get a look in – puzzled her and made her desperate to make a good deal soon.

Even *she* wasn't so desperate that she'd settle for Percy Street, though. She looked around, hand on the stair-rail. She'd thrown out his teak and leather-look plastic and furnished the house with choice Albrizzi and Zarach and cane and chrome. She'd put Badedas in the bathroom and Willie Fielding's sexy drawings on the wall. There was one of two apes making love. The male's tongue was hanging out. She'd thought it a lark at the time but now it reminded her too much of Percy taking his pleasure.

Stella shuddered to herself and smiled at Percy. 'I'd love a citron pressé.'

He stumped off bad-temperedly to get her a drink, the boor.

She was sick of Surrey, for a start. The last guy she'd had a thing with had had a nice London place in Cadogan Lane. He'd had a Corniche (white; such a good frame for a tan) and taken her to Mombasa twice. He'd taught her to play backgammon and bought her a Shih-Tzu, who was presently lodging with her mother in Great Bookham.

God, Great Bookham! They way things were going she'd be back there soon. Anything was better than Percy the Plod. She hadn't had to run back to Mummy's since 1977 . . . but how much longer could she tolerate the antics of the Lewisham Mafia, especially when they gave each other bunk-ups to peep through the glass panel in the bathroom door, or even worse did lewd things with the Rigaud candles at dinner?

Percy just laughed, the pig.

Percy trolled up to her clutching her citron pressé in his grubby paw. She'd stopped him wallowing in lager and taught him to appreciate tequila, but it put him in a lousy humour. She took the drink delicately. Everything he touched turned to *merde*.

He looked at the neckline of her new Janice Wainwright critically. 'Not enough tit,' he pontificated.

He really was the most ungracious yob. Ungrateful too. She'd taught him everything about everything. There was only one thing she couldn't teach him and that was how to stop being a yob. He would always be one. If she slipped any further down the social scale she'd be an organ grinder's monkey, Stella Sloan reflected, sipping her citron pressé.

There was a banging on the oak doors and some types stumbled drunkenly in. They were mid-bracket slobs, probably DJs, judging by that unmistakable blow-dried, bulging-bellied look. At least they were *guests.*

Stella had never been so pleased to see a non-face in her life. There were rich kids from Kent chasing last season's trend and the inevitable DJs, all of whom lived nearby on small, tweely fashionable farms. They'd been tempted out to Percy's by stories that he took out a second mortgage to pay for the catering. It was displayed impressively on a long buffet table covered with mirrors.

Within a half hour Percy had a sour taste in his mouth. The party was a breeze – for everyone except the host and hawker. The guests took his drugs but didn't take him seriously. A DJ even had the nerve to turn off the tape of his triple album – 'What's this old tat, Perce? One of your proteges?' – and thumb through his record collection for some old Tamla Motown records.

'Listen, JoJo. Howzabout you doing a Percy Street Special featuring my life and work sometime? About an hour long. Like the Smokey Robinson thingummy.'

'Ring me in the week, would you, Perce?' said JoJo the DJ.

You stopped returning my calls nine months ago, Percy thought bitterly. He pulled on a pair of headphones and sat cross-legged on the floor, determined that someone would hear his tapes. Through the smog of his surliness he saw Stella Sloan laughing at something JoJo the DJ was saying to her. Everyone wanted to listen to *her*; you'd think she was *his* life-line, not the other way around.

Percy Street picked up his Stowaway. He ambled up to Stella and JoJo and scowled at his lovely consort.

'That dress needs cleaning,' he leered at Stella Sloan.

'No, it doesn't, Percy.' She eyeballed him disapprovingly.

'Yes, it does, cheeky.' Percy threw his Tequila Sunrise at her torso.

Stella gasped and ran up the stairs.

JoJo giggled and faded away.

Stella changed into a Missoni and retraced her steps. She was ready to forgive the smallest love of her lifetime – you always blame the one you sleep with – in his hour of need. Until she saw the boy. Percy Street was embracing him with overbearing mawkish affection. The boy was tanned and athletic, his rough good looks ruined by half-paralysis. She recognized him instantly – she read all the magazines *and* all the papers. He was Johnny Sangster, *yes*, Johnny Sangster . . .

'I've written a song about you, Johnny, me son,' Percy was drooling into the famous, half-dead face. 'All about your heartache. Anyone ever written a song about you before?'

'Actually, yes.'

Stella Sloan caught Johnny Sangster's eye and smiled at him, a stunningly friendly and fresh smile. He smiled back, surprised and pleased. Percy didn't notice.

'Not like *my* song,' Percy slurred. 'It's going to be my hit. My *latest* hit, I mean.'

With great abandon, Percy Street gripped Johnny in a bear hug, fully expecting a camera to click to attention. None did. Johnny sipped his tequila (Stella thought sweet fruity drinks such as daiquiris tacky), relieved, and smiled at Stella again, this time more glibly.

But Percy Street looked around, squirming with embarrassment. He felt that he had failed his friend. '*Sorry* about this, Johnny. One can never find a bleeding photographer when one wants one. Oi, Stella! Get over here, girl!'

Stella shimmered across the room.

Percy Street began babbling instructions without so much as an introduction. 'Stella, I want you to go upstairs and fetch me Pentax. You can take some pictures of me and me mate Johnny here and I'll mail 'em to the scandal sheets meself.'

Stella felt sick. God, what kind of man *was* he? She didn't know she'd sunk *this* far. She felt herself pale beneath her Guerlain Teint Dore.

'I don't know where it is.'

'Yes you do, you silly cow,' Percy Street smiled nicely. 'Don't you remember those snaps I took of you last night? Oh, forget it. I'll get the bloody thing myself. If you want to get anything done in this world you have to do it yourself, as my old probation officer used to say.' Street shambled off in search of his camera.

Stella Sloan looked at Johnny Sangster with combative lust. 'Pretty soon now he's going to make a comeback.'

'That's what they all say.' Johnny nodded at crowds of revellers heading for the door. 'Where's everybody going?'

'Home. The drugs must have run out. Did you get a sniff?'

'No.'

'I don't indulge either.'

'What's your name?'

'Stella Sloan.'

'I'm Johnny Sangster.'

'Absolutely.'

JoJo the DJ weaved over to her, tipsy and talkative. 'Hey, Stella, you hear what the Lewisham Mafia are up to? They're peeing in the jacuzzi and cutting dollies out of Percy's stage clothes.'

'They've been bitter about the lack of bitter all evening,' Stella said, never taking her eyes from Johnny's. 'But this! Well, that's what happens when people discover that their meal-ticket turned out to be a forgery.'

'Yeah . . . and Percy . . . Percy had a big crying confrontation with them . . . and they said he was sold out and washed up and he went off to swallow the medicine chest . . . can I give you a lift somewhere?'

'Thanks but no thanks, JoJo.'

'Suit yourself.'

'Our host may be sometime with that camera,' smiled Stella.

Johnny drained his tequila. 'Can I get you something?'

She nodded, pressing a buffed fingernail against his hard flat abdomen. 'Johnny, you can get me out.'

She ran up the stairs and threw her passport, her hairdryer, her roll-on lip gloss, her coded diary and her Fiorucci jeans into a Vuitton bag. In the cab back to London she reached for his cock and scrambled to her knees.

Johnny closed his eyes. 'Don't you have any more luggage?'

'None worth burdening myself with. Percy had atrocious taste. I'm sure your taste is great.' She sucked him hungrily.

Johnny Sangster's career in the tennis world may have been over, but Stella Sloan's had just begun.

# eighteen

The telephone purred and Johnny picked it up. 'Hello?'

'Mr Sangster?'

'Yeah.'

'Mr Sangster, I have a long distance call from Los Angeles for you. Please hold the line. I'm putting you through.' There were a few seconds of silence punctuated by metallic clicks and then a young woman's voice came across six thousand miles of wire as clear as a bell.

'Mr Sangster? Johnny Sangster? This is Canis Communications of Los Angeles. I have Mr Jesse Wolfe on the line for you.'

A rich beige voice came on to the line. It was full of status, sunshine and self, a voice that was overwhelmingly friendly without – amazingly – being forced. 'Johnny? Jesse Wolfe! Good to *talk* to you, Johnny! We've *heard* of each other, of course!'

'Sure,' said Johnny. Sure he had heard of Jesse Wolfe. 'You run that magazine. That magazine *Moi*.'

'*Moi*, that's me,' Jesse Wolfe chuckled. 'Owner, publisher, editor, creator – no partners, no shareholders, just me. You're familiar with *Moi*, Johnny.'

'I've seen a few copies when I was waiting around for planes.'

*Moi* magazine was a heady blend of All-American airbrushed blondes and notes on Narcissism. It eschewed *Playboy*'s fringe politics in favour of features on diet, sport and exercise. It was closer to a pre-Pill housewives magazine than it would ever admit.

'Johnny, let me tell you something,' said Jesse Wolfe with a wonderful approximation of earnestness. 'I believe in *Moi*, Johnny. I really do. I believe in a world where experiences and relationships are consumer durables. I believe we all have the moral and spiritual responsibility – *responsibility*, Johnny – to live creatively within the concept of permanent orgasm. I believe, Johnny, that you and me can do business.'

'What you want me to do? Take out a subscription?'

'Heh-heh-heh! A sense of humour. I like that in a person, Johnny. What I'm calling about is a position I need to fill. I just spoke to a man out on Oyster Bay. Dave Pepper.'

'You spoke to Dave? What about?'

'You, Johnny,' said Jesse Wolfe. 'I need a tennis coach.'

'A *coach* job? And you thought of good old Johnny Sangster?' Memories of Simone flashed through his mind. 'What am I? A fucking registered charity? Why don't you—'

'You're gonna hear me out,' Jesse Wolfe said with affable

firmness. 'Listen, Johnny – I know you don't need the bread. I also know that you and pro tennis have terminated your association. That doesn't matter – Johnny Sangster will always be number one pro to me.'

'Sure, sure.'

'Another thing I know, Johnny, is that hedonism palls damn quick when you've got nothing to do between parties. What I'm offering you, in return for a couple hours coaching a day, is a suite of your own, a sunny clime and ten thousand a week.'

Johnny thought. He remembered his college days, he remembered earning money. The combined appeal of roots and dollars was almost irresistible. 'But I've never coached anyone in my life.' he said. He thought of Dave Pepper. 'I don't *know* coaching.'

'You know tennis,' said Jesse Wolfe. 'And that's what *I* need to know. I'm not expecting a snap decision. Think it over and get back to me. My personal assistant will give you my personal number.'

'Ok, I promise I'll think about it.'

'Oh, one other thing. My friends call me Jesse, Johnny. Often. Please call me Jesse.'

'Ok,' Johnny laughed. 'Jesse.'

'Thanks,' Jesse Wolfe glowed. 'Later, Johnny.'

'Later, Jesse.'

Johnny stared out the window of his hotel room. It was nearly April but the cold dark winter still had London in its icy grip. He wondered if he should take up Jesse Wolfe's offer. And if he did, he wondered if he should take Stella Sloan along. He considered the month he had spent with Stella with detached amusement.

Stella had shown him a younger, looser London. Simone's neurotic round of revelry – all that old money blown on new diversions too desperately too late – could make a young man feel thirty before his time. Now nights were spent at The Venue and Dingwall's. The people were younger and relaxed but he sometimes felt a little uncomfortable when droves of musicians that Stella had once slept with stopped by the table to wink their respects. It would've been ok if they'd been musicians he liked, but he'd grown up thinking they were *dead*.

Still, those were just a couple of Stella's old music business haunts. She knew her way around other places, too. She was fun to talk with, to dance with, to eat with, to enter with. She made him take her to Morton's, the Brasserie and Tramp. She put Badedas by the hotel bath. She gave him Vitamin E and tried to give him a bracelet. She made a long lingering job of his cock at least three times a day and never acted as though she was doing him a *favour*. (Shades of Thorn Sayre? Forget Thorn Sayre.) She bought him Guerlain's Vetiver and used it herself. She wanted him to take her to Lyford Cay. She wanted him to get a little place off Berkeley Square (so convenient). She hinted that she'd enjoy being beaten with his steel tennis racquet – he drew the line at that (he certainly wasn't ready to hold a racquet again so soon). She washed her hair every morning and barely ate a thing when they weren't in company. He only saw her angry once – when her hairdryer fused.

He sat, weighing up the pros and cons of Stella Sloan when she walked out of the bedroom in white boiler suit and Maud Frizon black boots. She wrinkled her nose at him cutely and smiled apologetically. 'Sorry things were a bit of a bummer last night, Johnny. Dingwall's just hasn't been the same since '76. The punks spoiled everything with their weird girls and hostile drugs. Killjoys, that's all they were. You should have been at the Speak . . .'

He cut her off mid-maudlin reminiscence. 'Where are you going?'

'The Dance Centre. The solarium.' The solarium was a must at least once a week for the horizontally working girl. It made a huge hole in his American Express card but it was a matter of pride to an ex-poor boy that he could pay for her trichologist, her manicurist, her Schumi hair, her Dance Centre sessions.

Johnny crossed the room and caught her by her thin wrist. He smelt the mint of her mouth and the Caleche of her cleevage. 'Don't go.'

'But you like me brown!'

'I do. That's why we're going to Los Angeles.'

'Oh!' Stella sat down fast. 'All *right*! The times I've had . . . the Roxy, the Rainbow . . . you know the Coast well, Johnny?'

Johnny thought back and remembered a dazzling blur of poinsettia, success and oranges. 'I nearly grew up in California.'

# nineteen

Stella Sloan coasted across the shimmering surface of Jesse Wolfe's obligatory swimming pool, listening to the traffic on California 1 mingle with the roar of the surf. She sucked greedily at the straws that fed her orange juice and stretched on the raft, basking in heavy-lidded contentment. Stella Sloan wore shades that aped Lolita's, a white bikini and a platinum ankle bracelet, a token of Johnny Sangster's affection. Her tan was turning to copper, going very well indeed. The buzz of the power mower and the sound of one-way tennis fused into a soothing drone.

My boyfriend's rich and I am good-looking, she thought. So hush, little Stella . . .

She pulled down her white slivers of shoulder straps and reflected that life with the Malibu Colony was easy, so very *easy*. She almost dozed . . .

On a palm-shaded tennis court Johnny Sangster was feeding Jesse Wolfe ball after ball and endless advice. Wolfe was learning how to volley. Johnny was learning how to handle a client.

It was a new, though quite painless experience for him. Just be yourself and remember everything Dave taught you, Johnny thought, remember the things he taught you back in the days when you could do them without thinking . . .

'Be at the net when the ball arrives! *Anticipate*, Jesse! *Punch* the ball! Don't try to be polite to your opponent! *Punch* the ball at your man! And *bend your knees*!'

Jesse Wolfe was tall, thin and tanned with thinning fair hair. He struggled after Johnny's softest shots. He grunted and puffed as he did his best. He wanted to be a good student, he wanted Johnny Sangster to like him.

Jesse Wolfe was making Johnny's job a cakewalk. Any opponent who didn't make his *living* out of the game still gave Johnny Sangster a feeling of effortless supremacy. And as a lodger at Wolfe's mellow mansion he was treated more like a prized guest than a hired hand.

Johnny tried to teach Jesse Wolfe everything he knew. Wolfe knocked himself out, and in his best moments, with Johnny's conscientious assistance, he managed to grasp the tip of the iceberg.

'That's the one, Jesse! Don't try to hit it over the net! Forget the net! *Hit it into the court*! That's *it*! You got it!'

Jesse Wolfe grinned shyly, fighting for breath. He walked back to the baseline and they wound up the session with a three set match. Jesse Wolfe managed to salvage one service game and he was delighted.

This was the way to handle a client, Johnny had decided – beat them without humiliating them, win without making them lose face.

They walked off court, Johnny glowing and breathing easy, Jesse Wolfe grinning and sweating as though he was undergoing a particularly rigourous sauna. Wolfe was a fit man but he wasn't so fit that he could exist comfortably in the same zone as a pro athlete.

Ex-pro athlete, Johnny reminded himself. Remind me to laugh on my day off.

'What you want to do this afternoon, Johnny?' Jesse Wolfe gasped, slapping his coach on the back. 'Go sailing in San Diego? Surfing at Point Duma? Horseback riding at Sequoia? Snorkelling at La Jolla? The snorkelling sucks around Malibu. But we have the best scuba diving on the Coast. Anything you want, Johnny.'

'I never was much of a one for outdoor sports,' he quipped bitterly.

Jesse Wolfe laughed. 'That's fine. We cater to all tastes.'

An inflated blonde got up from a poolside couch. She looked like Sherry Ward after a course of silicone injections. She was *Moi*'s Reflection Of The Month and she knew just what drinks Jesse and his friends would want at any given time of the day. She disappeared into the house and returned carrying a strawberry daiquiri and a long glass of iced Perrier with lemon on a silver tray.

Johnny Sangster and Jesse Wolfe sat down at the side of the pool. Stella swam over, hauled herself out of the water and snuggled up to Johnny. Wolfe waved her away, almost as a reflex, and she retreated to lick and warm her wounds a few feet from the pair. Smug *Moi* girls and men with briefcases hovered nearby, knowing better. Just one of them tried to catch his master's eye.

'Not now, Maurice,' Jesse Wolfe sighed. He eyed Johnny Sangster appreciatively. 'Tell me, Johnny – how'm I coming along?'

'Well, maybe you ain't ready for Ivan Lendl yet. But you could take Hugh Hefner in straight sets, I'm sure.'

Wolfe stared seriously at still blue water. 'Please, Johnny. Please don't confuse what I and *Moi* are doing with *Hefner* and his Halston hippie tribe. *Moi* is post-politics and post-sex, practically. My readers – I should say my *followers* – would rather look in the mirror than get stoned, they would rather diet than vote. They would rather suck a vitamin cocktail than a cock. Ok?'

'Ok.' What was he supposed to do? Johnny wondered. Take notes?

'Ok.' Jesse Wolfe touched Johnny's arm and smiled. 'I knew you'd understand me, Johnny. Would you like to eat?'

'I could stand a cheeseburger.'

'I'll put the kitchen to work straight away.' Wolfe snapped his fingers and watched *Moi's* Reflection Of The Month do his bidding. 'I myself need never chew another mouthful of food in my life. A rich man can exist quite adequately on mousse and caviare. Hey – you going to Tom's wedding, Johnny?'

'Tom who?'

'Why, Tom Dougherty, of course! You didn't know? Tom is getting hitched on Saturday. To that girl. What's her name? You know – Miss Universe.'

'Francesca.'

'Right! You're going, of course?'

Johnny shook his head. 'I don't know nothing about it,' he confessed, feeling stupid.

'Oh, your invitation must have gone astray. In London, maybe. Tom is a great friend of mine, as I'm sure he is of yours.'

'Yeah, the Circuit is like one big happy family,' Johnny said bitterly. 'The Circuit never forgets.'

The sarcasm was lost on Jesse Wolfe. 'You know Francesca too?'

'We met.'

'You must come, Johnny. All your best buddies will be there.'

'I don't know.'

Stella sat up quickly, pricking her ears and pulling off her Lolita shades. 'Oh, we *must* go, Johnny!' she called insistently.

The *Moi* disciples stared at her curiously, mildly shocked by the desperation in her voice.

Stella shrugged, and laughed nervously. 'I mean,' she said, 'it sounds like fun.'

It was a Circuit wedding and the young pros wished them well.

They also wished that Johnny Sangster was elsewhere.

Johnny Sangster was living proof of how one bad break could take it all away. Johnny Sangster was a jinx, a bad luck charm, a voodoo dolly.

Stella Sloan saw her beau through these new eyes and was shocked at his lack of status here. Her own eyes were everywhere; she had recently cancelled her subscription to *Rolling Stone* and taken up with *World Tennis.* She said 'I must do something about this face, Johnny. Don't go away,' and got away from him.

Maria Salewicz accosted him and announced that she was now twice as American as he, Johnny; she'd forsaken cocaine for celibacy, *Cosmo* for *Moi*, and she said, 'Oh my *Gard*! That car crash was *the pits*! What a bummer! Hey, lemme take a picture!'

Johnny smiled for her. The camera clicked mercilessly.

His eyes were blindfolded by a pair of slim, suntanned though slightly withered hands. He turned round and Sherry Ward smiled at him. 'The Smell Of Success was a flop, due to you. But I love you anyway.'

'Sherry. What are you doing out here?'

'I met this great guy, this analyst. But he won't come East. So I come out here. I must tell you what he says about my exhibitionism . . .'

'Hello, John.' Dave Pepper shook his hand like a stranger. It was the first time a handshake had hurt Johnny. Sherry Ward melted away like a gregarious meringue to tell someone else what the mad analyst made of her exhibitionism. 'Glad you could make it.'

'God, Dave, I'm glad to see you.'

Dave Pepper just looked at him, guest to guest. 'Tom's a fine boy. He'll be pleased to see you, John.'

Johnny stared at him non-comprehendingly. He'd never thought of Tom Dougherty being anything but a simpleton with a weak second serve. 'I wouldn't have missed it for the world.'

'She's a lovely girl.'

'I beg your pardon?'

'Miss Universe.'

'He should have married the runner up.'

'Did Jesse Wolfe call you?'

'Yes, Dave, I'm really in demand. Just fancy. I'm hanging out at the dude's ranch right now. He's here somewhere.'

'That's great, John – and how's your game?'

Johnny stared at him. He isn't kidding. *What* game? 'Not quite what it was, Dave.'

'Well, at least you're still in with the crowd. See many matches these days, John? There's some great kids coming through, huh? I like that boy from Texas, Sammy Giammalva, and how about Thierry Tulasne? He has Borg's forehand and Guillermo's backhand, huh?'

'I don't follow tennis anymore, Dave. I don't know what he's got.'

Tom Dougherty and Francesca Universe were emerging from the house. The tennis pros cheered them before lining up and forming a corny arch with tennis racquets. Johnny looked on in fascinated repulsion. There was one empty place, one racquet idle. Surely it wasn't waiting for . . .

'Hey, where's Ray?'

'What happened to Ray?'

'Velez, get your black ass out here!'

'It's no use, I can't find him.'

'I think I saw him leave with his chick.'

'Ok, ok.'

'Hey!' Maria Salewicz pulled Johnny into line next to her and shoved the racquet at him. 'You'll do, dollface!' She smiled broadly at him; no one else even looked.

A cheer went up and rice and confetti rained down. Tom was now Mr Universe. Tom Dougherty Snr hissed through his proud grin at the photographer he'd brought from Boston; 'If you don't keep that face full of *jerky* out of my boy's big day I'll make sure you never photograph another Dougherty wedding – another *Boston* wedding again. Dodge Sangster's mug, I'm telling you, or stay here in Disneyworld and dupe tourists for dollars.'

The wedding party passed by. Johnny brushed off his jacket and looked around for Stella Sloan. He wished she'd up and have her picture taken with Nastase – or whatever, *whoever* the reason was that she wanted to come here in the first place – so they could clear out fast.

But Stella Sloan was already gone. Dumping people felt *good*, it had *dignity*, it sure beat being a dumpee, she decided as she hung the DO NOT DISTURB sign on the door of Ray Velez' Beverly Wilshire suite. She smiled up and down the cool deserted corridor. She was upwardly mobile once more.

Johnny romped home pulling punches and sometimes missing punches altogether. At the net he shook Wolfe's sweaty, blistering hand and nodded encouragement to his employer.

'Did you zero in on the handshake, Mitch?' Wolfe shouted to the man with the camera at the side of the court.

Mitch the camera man nodded. Yes, he had recorded his master's noble failure for private posterity. Mitch packed away his equipment and hurried off to the cutting room with a *Moi* moll. They went to the poolside for the obligatory relaxation session. Jesse Wolfe was tired of big blondes and had recently acquired a personal secretary/nursemaid who he called Kitty, a stunning hunk of Mexicana who had the longest legs and the sharpest shorthand in Southern California. She handed them their drinks and held Wolfe's hand.

A smattering of young women dressed for the beach and old men dressed for the boardroom hovered nearby. They longed to be close to Wolfe. He waved them over and made them take the telephones away. Then he lay back and grinned at Johnny. 'Old Mitch is from your neck of the woods, y'know.'

'Yeah?'

'Ol' Vermont.'

'I'm from Massachusetts.'

'Yeah? Anyhow, he's a Californian now.'

Johnny laughed.

'It's true,' Wolfe worried, 'all real Californians come from somewhere else. But I'm a *real* Californian.'

'Yeah? Which part of California you come from?'

'Boise, Idaho.'

Kitty laughed.

Johnny grinned wearily.

Jesse Wolfe leaned close to him. 'Where's Stella? Doing a little light shopping?'

'Probably.'

'Up on Rodeo?' said Kitty.

'I guess.'

'Did she make her appointments?'

'I don't know.'

'*You* don't sound like a man who's picking up the tab,' Wolfe suggested suggestively.

'I'm not.'

Jesse Wolfe looked delighted. He nudged Kitty. Then he leaned closer to Johnny and gestured expansively at the bikini'd clones on the other side of the pool. 'Take your pick.'

'You don't have my size.'

Kitty roared with laughter. Wolfe giggled. 'You're putting me on! I like that! Money, a big dick and a sense of humour – what every man needs, and every woman wants! What do you want, Johnny? You want Kitty to get you a girl that looks like Stella?'

'Better he should have the real thing,' said Kitty softly.

Wolfe looked at her quizzically, then lovingly. 'You mean . . .'

'You know . . .'

'You got it!'

'I'll get it.' Kitty got up and ran into the house, returning with a large buff-coloured envelope. She handed it to Johnny. Johnny thumbed through many glossy colour photographs of a younger, dumber, unclothed Stella Sloan.

Wolfe leered lustlessly over his shoulder. 'Cute, eh? We considered Stella for a spread around five years ago. We were sorely tempted – her eyes hadn't seen so much, she was twice as wholesome and attractive as the broad you ditched yesterday.' Jesse sighed regretfully, then brightened. 'But we decided not to stray off the All-American straight and narrow girl. Take them. Keep them. She'll never make it . . .'

'Ray Velez, Jeez . . .' Kitty whistled dismissively and shook her head.

'. . . I'll never need to run them. Keep them. With my blessing.'

Johnny returned the photographs to their envelope and dropped them into Wolfe's lap. 'Thanks, but I don't want them. I'm not at all hot for Stella. Not tepid even.'

'Somebody else?' Wolfe pried.

'Just restless.'

'I know what you boys need. You need a little escapism,' grinned Kitty.

'Thanks, but I never could sit through movies. I twitch.'

'Oh, this is a different kind of drive-in.'

Wolfe smiled admiringly at her, relish ravaging his features. He murmured in Johnny's ear; 'Up in the Hills there's a guy called Sherwood Klan. Eever hear of him?'

'No. Why? What's his business?'

'Oh, he just sort of specializes in your wildest dreams . . .'

The black butler dusted the immaculate rosewood table with a soft yellow cotton cloth and smiled kindly at her. 'Resting, Greta?'

Thorn Sayre nodded. 'The Marilyns and that new Judy Garland never even have the time to use a bidet. Garbo wasn't a lovable mess, she never spilled her guts for public consumption – I think that's the trouble. Being your own person is like putting bromide in a john's hock.'

He laughed and she stared at her face in the ornate Lalique mirror across the room. Perfection. It would be even better if I didn't have to wear this theatrical guck, she reflected. If it's not my make-up it's not *me*.

The butler looked past her. 'I think you've got a fan.'

'Gimme a whiskee, babee, and don't be stingee,' chanted Thorn, holding up her empty glass. The butler recharged it with white wine. Just because the spirits were missing, no need to lose the dialogue. She glanced back arrogantly into the mirror to inspect her intended, feeling the naif's breath heavy down her neck.

Even the peach lighting could not throw a kindly veil over Johnny Sangster's features. He stood there behind her, a mad eye smiling grimly out of his frozen face.

They stared into the mirror for a long awful moment. He didn't know what he wanted to do – get her out of there or get even. Of course, he knew he had the authority to do neither. His knuckles were white and his eyes were wet.

Thorn turned and smiled at him. 'Hey, ain't you that Johnny Sangster?'

'I'm what's left of him.'

'Poor you.'

'Yeah, poor me. A face like a bullfight.'

'You never *were* an exquisite.'

'But these days I cross the street rather than run into a mirror.' He pulled up a chair and sat across from her, his back to the looking-glass. 'I'd rather have a rabid mutt in every room than a mirror. How about you? Still get a kick out of looking at yourself?'

'Oh no, I always put my eyes out before I look in the mirror. Such a drag when all you want to do is pluck your eyebrows. *Sure* I like looking at myself, Johnny. What would you like?'

'What would you like?' asked the butler.

'Well, for a start, I'd like *you* to stop lurking and leave us alone, pal.'

Thorn drained her glass. 'Another Chablis for me. He'll have my head on a platter and some rosé to wash it down with. He'll have the Chablis too, I'm sorry. It's not *his* fault, Johnny.'

'Then name names.' A sly bitter look came across his face and a taunt came into his voice. 'Say, does everyone get the small talk or am I buying the de luxe experience?'

'Everybody gets it. Look, Johnny, what do you want from me? Sex or a written confession or what?'

'I want to know how the hell you got into this, that's what I want to know!'

'Isn't that a little predictable?'

'How can you talk like that? *How could you do this to me*?'

'Oh, Johnny! The nerve! *We slept together and then we split up*. Do you remember? Did you take a vow of chastity – you been making like a monk, Johnny?'

'Guess,' he leered smugly.

'You're a hypocrite, Johnny.'

'You're a—'

'We don't like those words here in the drawing room. In bed maybe. But act like a sick hick in the salon and two sadistic giants – we call them chaperons, Johnny – will stroll in, take you for a ride up past the Hollywood Sign and make such a mess of—'

'Someone beat them to it.'

'I wasn't thinking. I'm sorry.'

'Stow it. I don't believe you've been thinking at all lately. To end up *here*.'

'It's not the end of anything. Neither is it any of your business.'

'I could have helped—'

'I'm not in need of help. Our lives are not entwined, Johnny. You don't have exclusive rights to me – you don't even have first option.'

'Who does?'

'*Me.* And to maintain the property I sub-let it when it suits me.'

He crushed the glass in his hand. She reached across the table to clear the splinters off his bloody, wine-soaked hand.

'Don't touch me.' He looked at her with naked loathing and love.

'Look, feel free to crack up, make yourself at home. But if you stay you have to take a room upstairs and you have to pay by the hour. Now you don't want that. Go home, Johnny.'

The butler materialized. 'What happened, Greta? What's your problem, *sir*?'

'We – there was an accident. It was nothing.'

'Greta.' Johnny Sangster's face twisted into an approximation of a smile. 'Ok, Greta, you'll do.' He pulled out a thick bank roll. He was acting drunker than he was. 'See?'

Thorn took it and counted it to herself. About five thousand. She handed back less than half and gave the butler a shockingly philanthropic gratuity, which he accepted serenely and silently.

Thorn and Johnny went up stairs.

Thorn locked the door and turned around to watch Johnny tearing off his clothes.

'How do you want me? I mean, do you want me to get undressed or should I—'

'Just keep your mouth shut. I'll let you know how I want you.'

He grabbed the top of her dress and threw her back on to the bed. There was the rip of renting material. A strap hung torn and a nipple pouted out.

'That'll cost you extra, Johnny.'

He fumbled with his belt. 'I can afford you.' He tore away the top of her dress and sucked her with a hard vicious greed.

'You're hurting me,' she said. He ignored her. 'I said *you're hurting me*.' She clawed bloody trails across the backs of his hands.

He laughed, spitting out a nipple and hiking her dress up around her flat hard stomach. He tore off her underthings and spread her legs. She watched his eyes.

'Don't look at me,' he said. 'Don't look at my face. Turn your head.'

'Anyway you want it.' She turned her head into the pillow. 'You're picking up the tab.'

'Thanks for reminding me.'

His hardness parted her and he pumped her with slow hard strokes until he had the satisfaction of hearing her scream.

He looked into her turned away face and saw she was smiling. He couldn't hold it back after that; she was still special, he was still as helpless as the first time. He bit her neck and crammed himself in to the hilt. The warm rush poured deep into her, making him arch his back and cry out. He lay in her arms, expended and breathing heavy until he felt her histronic hand gently toying with the hair at the nape of his neck. It was so out of character – it had to be a lie.

He pulled out of her abruptly, staring at her with hateful love. 'Thanks, Thorn,' he said bitterly. 'That was one of the worst fucks I ever had. I suppose I'm not allowed a refund.' He got off of the bed and began to dress.

'I never promised you *The Perfumed Garden*. You got the standard transaction. No one else has ever complained. Three thousand satisfied Garbo fans can't be wrong.' She pulled down her dress and smoothed her hair with long calm fingers.

'People *pay* you for *that*? I've had better fucks for the price of a banana daiquiri.'

'Yes, Johnny, good for you, but you're not in the Little League now. You're talking to a professional.'

He grabbed her shoulders, his trousers half on. 'I'm talking to a *hack*. Who exactly do you service here – film buffs or necrophiliacs? *I* felt like a fucking actor, too – male lead in a snuff film, taking advantage of a poor defenceless corpse. Why won't you ever kiss me on the mouth? Scared you'll catch my ugliness? No doubt I've caught something ugly off *you*.'

'It's better to give than to receive.'

'Do you kiss your customers if their features have been put on properly?'

'No. If you want to play the consumer then I'm entitled to play dead. But I do a good summary of the earth moving for a small additional fee. Sorry. Should have publicized it. Next time I'll draw up a menu.'

'Next time! When was the last time one of your johns came back for a second chance to commune with the dead?'

'Since you ask, I have around a dozen visitors who call every week. Bet that beats the notches on your racquet.'

'How many will you get through after I've gone?'

'You're entitled to all of the night doing nothing fancy.'

'You think I'm going to spend the *night* with you? Jeez! How many?'

'Is this market research or do you want me to talk dirty? Talk is far from cheap around here, by the way. Look, Johnny, I'm not ever going to apologize for my ability to make a lot of money by simply switching off – but I really *am* sorry to see you so mixed up and sad.'

'*Sad*? Me? What have I got to be sad about? You're nothing to me. You're *nothing*, full stop! You think you earn a lot of cash with your convincing corpse impersonations? Sherry Ward *tips* what you earn in an evening. *She* calls all the shots when she decides to sleep with a guy! Nobody even knows your name, *Thorn*, except me! Sherry Ward could *destroy* any man who called her by the wrong name!'

'Keep talking, Johnny – you sound just like a naive young trick extolling the virtues of a prize ponce. You know, you're not so secure. When the bottom falls out of the travesty of past glories market you should get in touch with a gal named Kirsten Klan. She runs a little joint identical to this establishment across at Malibu, except the hirelings are men, or *excuses* for men.'

He finished dressing and slammed murderously out of the room. She grabbed her kimono and ran out on to the landing. Looking down the stairwell she called to him, softly yet clearly; 'There's always an opening for a convincing Frankenstein's monster.'

Through the tears she had tortured out of him Johnny saw Jesse Wolfe's driver leaning against the car, gorging. 'Want some, Mr Sangster? Nuts! Plenty of protein.'

'Just take me back to Malibu.'

'I can't do that, Mr Sangster.'

'Why not?'

'The chief is still attending to business.'

'Come back for him.'

'We couldn't do that, Mr Sangster. Where the chief goes his car goes. Employees can't suddenly start joyriding alone and leaving the old chief to *walk* home. To hitch hike.' The driver grinned broadly at the very thought and tossed a nut into his mouth. 'He may treat you like a pal when you've got a bat in your hand, but let's face it – you're on the payroll with the rest of us.'

Johnny got into the car and waited two hours until Wolfe

emerged, exhilarated and exhausted. He was helped into the car, laughing and incoherently reciting snatches of Tennessee Williams' screenplays, by three muscley, pouting boys dressed in Levis and torn T shirts. Johnny didn't know who they were meant to be playing at; probably exclusive little delicacies concocted to order by the clever Klan for the jaded Wolfe.

Kitty was waiting up for them. She wore a prim white nightgown and her dark hair down to her waist. She looked so dark and warm and wise, she made Johnny feel so lonely. No girl would ever look at him again and want him. Once upon a time it happened all the time.

They worked together to put the smirking, comatose Wolfe to bed. Kitty tucked him in and smiled at Johnny in relief. 'Let's leave him now. He likes to be alone with his memories.'

Johnny walked her to her bedroom door. He was curious. 'What exactly is he into?' he asked.

Kitty laughed. 'What have you got?'

'Ah. A man of many orifices.'

'And every one of them yawning. I guess Jesse's a pretty hard guy to relate to. But you can easily tell if he really, really digs you.'

'How's that?'

'He'll turn on your vibrator himself.' She kissed his cheek and closed her door.

Johnny packed his bags. He was going home. He was sick of Thorn Sayre, sick of Jesse Wolfe, sick of being in love and working for a living. If that was all he had to do with what was left of the rest of his life he'd rather do nothing. He could certainly afford to.

He wanted to be back in Manhattan. I want to be alone, he thought bitterly. The cab got him to LAX with five minutes to spare and he flew back East on the red eye flight.

Jesse Wolfe's calls clogged the answering machine for a week and then stopped. There was nothing more to say. Wolfe found a new coach somewhere – some ex-collegiate hotshot with a bad back who needed ready cash, lots of it, for an operation on his spine. Nights Jesse Wolfe took him to Gemini, or, as a special treat, Gemini Rising. The new coach was working his way through Graumann's roll-call, losing his operation money faster than he was finding it.

Johnny stayed in, his face captive behind closed curtains as he watched endless video of his perfect self. He always seemed to be winning back then. He drank too much and cried too often. Desperately devoted sycophants who came to visit found his drunken temper tantrums tough to handle and eventually stayed away altogether. Invitations to parties poured in and remained unanswered on the answering machine. Johnny was glad he had the answering machine. It was his best friend. It saved ripping the telephone out of the wall.

Eventually the invitations dried up. The word was that Johnny Sangster was an abusive recluse, bad news. He did not want to go out and soon no one wanted him to go out.

Soon the press and photographers stopped camping out on the street where he lived. Johnny Sangster just wasn't a story anymore. It seemed the world had forgotten him. Johnny liked it like that.

Then early one morning the doorbell rang. And rang. He tried to go back to sleep with the sheets pulled up over his head, he tried yelling at whatever sucker it was to go away, he tried waiting it out. Nothing worked.

Muttering bitter oaths, Johnny pulled on his robe and stumbled across his garbage tip of an apartment to the door. He opened it, surly and unshaven.

Two men in dark suits stood there, clean-shaven and courteous.

'Yeah?'

'Mr Sangster? Mr John Fitzgerald Kennedy Sangster?'

Johnny glared balefully at their attache cases. 'Sorry, I don't need insurance. That's like trying to sell Paul Getty III a pair of earrings.'

He tried to shut the door. It would not shut. Johnny looked down and saw a shiny black shoe obstructing him. He looked at the loafer and then at its urbane owner. Johnny jabbed a warning finger at the man. 'I'll tell you just one time, buster. There's nothing that you or your pal here can sell me, got it? Who the fuck let you up here anyhow? Who the fuck do you think you are?'

'The Internal Revenue Service, Mr Sangster.'

'May we come in, Mr Sangster?'

They brushed past him easily, not waiting for an answer, murmuring their thanks. Johnny stared at them dumbly for a moment and then followed them into his apartment. He sneered at it through their cool eyes. They had already pulled up chairs. They smiled at him, opened their attache cases and got right down to business.

# twenty

A showcase, an education, a back door to the big screen – Gemini was none of these and less.

Producers passed through, as did masseurs and merchant bankers. The clientele wanted her to do many things. Signing contracts certainly wasn't one of them.

She'd kidded herself that Gemini was her big chance when it was just the easy option. She had pretended it was a red carpet stepping stone when it was just a plush red crushed velvet dead end. All it had got her was away from Geek Goddard. She could have had that just by putting one heel in front of the other. Byron was dead and Johnny was against her, but these things hadn't turned her against Gemini. Her ego was her catalyst and conscience. She sat on her king-size four-poster bed and resented the boredom and frustration that had been her constant companions since she buried herself under a mistaken identity. She especially resented losing her own name and make-up. It didn't seem to worry the others; they saw this as the one chance they would have to see awe and appreciation in the eye of the paying customer, and they grabbed it, wallowed in it. Thorn Sayre sat at her dressing table, getting ready for the night's business, layering on the theatrical Thirties black eyeliner and matte red lipstick that she had come to hate. She got up and snagged her gauzy evening gown on the stool. She cursed; wearing these clothes – her work clothes! – was akin to walking with one's thighs strapped together.

On the landing Liz touched the creation's arm. 'Ya got any Murine, Greta? These contacts are moidoir.'

'Send out for drops. It's not my fault you've got brown eyes. I've noticed another discrepancy; you have one chin too many. The real thing is bountiful, but you're *gross.* And I've never seen anything as tattily fake as those rocks since – why, since

Marilyn got lazy about her roots last month.' She walked on by.

'What's the matter with *her*?' Liz asked a passing Marilyn.

'You know these Northern Europeans,' Marilyn breathed. 'A *cold* race.'

In the salon two teenagers, a dazzling Rita Hayworth and a sultry Veronica Lake, glanced at her, almost audibly dismissed her and carried on their conversation. Thorn was shaken at the smallness of the stir she created in these younger girls. They were the all-important inviolate *teenage*, with all the time in the world; they didn't look at her and see an enviable beauty, they looked at her from their teenage bubble and thought '*I* won't be here when I'm her age. I'll be *someone*.' She'd felt that way about Liz when she first arrived. How horrible it felt to be part of the furniture. It seemed as though her whole life had been a series of flights from the fate of furniture.

She found a fan and lay upon her bed. He was younger than usual, firmer than most. Someone who got into old movies in a camp kind of way at college, no doubt, and now takes it seriously and sexually. He was intent upon his foreplay, oiling her body, not missing a pore while singing her praises. Nice work if you can get it, Thorn thought lazily . . .

'How lovely you are, Greta. You are the very, very best, my lonely, my lovely Greta . . .'

Something snapped and Thorn smiled. 'You're very sweet. So let's drop the aliases, huh? The lady you're thinking of may well be an enigma and a legend etcetera, but what you're touching is *mine*, *mine* not hers, and my name is Thorn. My name is THORN SAYRE.'

He jumped up, staring at her with such shocked horror that for a moment Thorn thought he had misheard; maybe he thought she'd confessed to being a sex change triumph or whatever. The oil seeped and spread from the bottle onto the bed.

'Hey, I said, my name is *Thorn*. You seem thunderstruck. What's up? You didn't really believe I was a Greta . . . surely?'

But he had dressed in record time and disappeared.

Enter Sherwood Klan, fuming.

Thorn sat up and grabbed her kimono. 'Don't you knock before entering a lady's room, Sherwood?'

'Don't you find out who a guy is before you open your fat

yap, Greta? The gentleman who just ran screaming out of here was a most valued visitor. He comes from CITY HALL and he didn't come! Do you know what that could mean for us? No doubt I'll smooth it over like I smooth everything over – at a high price – but you really did a stupid thing, Greta, you really did. Do you know what he accused me of? Luring him up here under false pretences! I've *never* been called a liar before, *not once in my life*. He said I set him up as one half of a sordid cliche. He said he saw his goddess dismantled in an instant by her alter ego – a modern, anonymous tramp. That's *you*, miss!'

Her cheekbones burned scarlet. 'Shut up.'

'*You* and you alone.'

'This is madness, Sherwood! I only told him my *name*!'

'He told me that you brazenly flaunted the fact that your name isn't Greta. He claims that you bludgeoned his fantasy to death with your own banal, intrusive identity crisis.'

She couldn't help smiling. 'His speech patterns are *trés* purple, aren't they, Sherwood!'

'Shut up. He says I promised him the fulfillment of his most epic fantasy and gave him a nightmare farce.'

'But I only said my *name*! It's not my fault that certain jerks can't tell fact from fiction. I can dress up as someone, sure, but I can't re-write history. I can't *stop* being me. I'm a person, not a vessel.'

'You're a conceited, unimaginative shrew who won't be happy till she gets a silver paper star put on her door. I know for a fact that you persecute Marilyn, forever finding fault with this and that detail of her grooming. You're not here to rock the boat and frighten away the money, Greta. You're here to make life easier for everyone.'

'Call me by my name and I'll think about it.'

'For fuck's sake! If you want to hustle under your real name, *Thorn*, you go right ahead! Get some spade pimp to keep you on bad smack and a tight leash, breaking your nose once a week just to keep you from even *considering* getting ideas above your station. Those dudes are bad enough with black babes from the North – you'd be their El Dorado!'

'Don't sweat it, Sherwood. This job always was a temporary thing. I never planned to spend a lifetime perfecting phoney orgasms. I'm too good to waste time practising and pretending.'

'Oh, you never let us forget how special you are, Thorn, don't worry. You've always looked down on Marilyn and the others, haven't you, treating them as though all their brains and ambition were between their legs whereas you, oh, you're classy Scarlett O'Hara with a career! Well, listen, miss, you are *nothing* without my marketing, my *brilliant* marketing. How many men, women and children of the twentieth century have made themselves come while thinking about *Thorn Sayre*? Not damn many. Apart from *yourself*, of course, of course. It's my *marketing* that sells you so many times a week and nothing else. If you're so damn special why are you still hanging around after all this time? What's been holding the maverick nova back?'

Thorn snatched up a Kleenex like it was a gauntlet. She dragged it across her mouth, leaving a crimson smear across her cheek, and she said 'Lousy make-up.'

'Mr Sangster, I have your balance sheets from Global Management right here – they make for rivetting reading, I must say, intensely rivetting – and your personal finances are . . . what's the word? I think a catastrophe says it best. Yes, a catastrophe. Your personal finances, Mr Sangster, are a catastrophe,' said the man from the IRS.

Johnny Sangster had had heavy overheads hanging over his head for years.

Since he turned pro at seventeen, his corporate agent Global Management had taken half of every dollar he earned. When he was off the Circuit his highish life – his East Sixties apartment, his Italian shoes, his Italian car – had taken a large chunk from what Global left him of his massive yearly income. When he was on the Circuit he had to pay for all those countless first class aeroplane tickets out of his own Gucci wallet. Outsiders probably thought he got it *gratis* because he was *Johnny Sangster*.

Ha! The suckers knew nothing.

The men from the IRS, on the other hand, seemed to know everything. They certainly knew much more about Johnny Sangster than he did. He watched them interpret the balance sheets of the best days of his life. They marvelled at them in a detached sort of way, they discussed them as if he wasn't there.

'A staggeringly low figure of the net income was left to accumulate capital.'

'Staggering. I see here that Global invested his assets heavily in gold and silver when the market was at the peak of the boom.'

'Most unfortunate – when the market crashed so did his assets.'

'What the hell is all this about?' Johnny asked, his stomach tight with nervous nausea.

They told him, and for the first time in his life Johnny Sangster felt unemployed.

At the end of his last fiscal year as a pro he owed the Internal Revenue Service upwards of two hundred thousand dollars.

No one at Global had been particularly concerned about this at the time. It was a minor hiccough in the profit and loss margins of an immensely fiscally talented young man who still had a good ten years in the megabuck league. In the coming years he would clear up this minor back taxes debt in a matter of matches. Two hundred thousand dollars was loose change to Number Five. So confident were Global that Johnny would clear up the debt with supreme ease that they never even mentioned it to him. And now the glamourosi was unemployed and owed the IRS over two hundred thousand dollars in back taxes. Johnny walked to the window and stared down at Central Park.

His advisers never dreamed that his career could run short on time or money. They could not foresee Rio, they had no way of knowing that a fortune, a career, a life would be buried in the wreckage of a Silver Cloud.

Johnny turned to face the IRS. He forced a little laugh, feeling a little sick. 'My future ain't what it was,' he said. 'I wish one of those advisers of mine up at Global had had a crystal ball instead of a college education.'

The IRS did not crack a smile. The duo looked at him, saying nothing, their facts and faces without pity, and he knew how bad it really was. They were not here to collect weak jokes or sob stories. They were here to collect two hundred thousand dollars. *Their* two hundred thousand dollars.

'I don't have that kind of money,' Johnny said. 'Not any more.'

'Then get it,' they murmured in perfect unison.

He flew back to the West Coast. The last time had been for pin money and a pleasant way to kill time. This time was for survival.

His problems were physical as well as fiscal. For three weeks he trained mercilessly, seeking out precocious talent on the numerous public tennis courts (they only cost a couple of dollars an hour, even up in Beverly Hills at the Municipal Park, which was kind of neat as a couple of dollars an hour was all he could afford), taking them on two at a time until they were exhausted and ready to be replaced. Every night he returned to the shabby, spartan room he rented on Sunset Boulevard and dropped on to the single bed that covered two thirds of the hatch, sleeping immediately, oblivious to the debilitating street deals and stammering splashes of neon that poured through the tiny window.

At the end of the regime he was as lean as he ever was before the crash, as sharp as he ever could be after the crash. He stocked up on painkillers to deaden the inevitable pain of injustice and injuries that would never fully heal and would now have to get used to being pushed past the limit.

Then he walked down to the pay phone on Hollywood and Vine and called Jesse Wolfe to announce his comeback.

Applause.

A huge barbecue and its followers spilled over new mown lawns and into the pool. Guests chewing steaks and dressed for swimming turned to clap the four men dressed in tennis whites emerging from the house. The throng crowded eagerly around the court for this party was in honour of the match.

Jesse Wolfe and Johnny Sangster stood on one side of the net. The *Moi* man had been delighted to welcome the prodigal coach back on to the payroll. The boy with the bad back had been shipped off to hospital, all bills paid. Jesse even tried to give Johnny a raise. Johnny had a raise of his own in mind.

They whacked balls across the net at their opponents, tall, dark and tanned, good-looking in a banal sort of way – the Palladino brothers. They were the sons of a hard-drinking Hollywood crooner and a hard-drinking Las Vegas showgirl, both deceased.

The Palladino brothers were only a little better off than their parents. Both of them languished in the lower regions of the ATP computer rankings. They'd grown up in Beverly Hills coached by club pros to that level of superlative mediocrity that only money can buy. They had been good enough to turn pro in haste and bad enough to repent their decision at leisure.

They had already been introduced to Johnny Sangster. In fact he had ritually humiliated the Palladino brothers on the courts of five continents for years. They knew he had slipped, they knew Jesse Wolfe was just an enthusiastic amateur. They felt full of knowledge and sure of winning.

The Palladinos were glad there was a big crowd, crammed with big names. They felt set to exact a crushing, casual revenge. It was Johnny to serve to open the match. He wound up, glaring across at the Palladinos.

The brothers glanced at each other, smiling with amused contempt. Johnny Sangster's face looked Vulcanized, a deep frozen death mask melting in the warm California sun. It looked weird, it looked *funny* – you only had to look at Sangster, and *everyone was looking at Sangster*, to see he was nothing now – *it gave them a smile.*

Johnny wiped it off.

Wolfe stayed on the baseline playing a game of patience and topspin, following Johnny's instructions with painstaking zeal. Johnny poached at the net with anticipation and ferocity, volleying into the whites of bewildered brown Palladino eyes. Pretty eyes, he sneered to himself.

The Palladinos seemed to be playing two separate games – leaving balls for each other, going for the same ball, staying back for Johnny to take the point with a deft drop shot, both rushing the net for Johnny to scoop a lob over their puzzled heads.

After winning three match points, Johnny sent Wolfe to the net. Wolfe hit the winning shot. The party roared. Wolfe gasped with emotion, shouted to Mitch to check the camera, kissed Kitty, and threw his arms around Johnny Sangster.

'Johnny Sangster! He taught me everything! Everything!'

Johnny grinned modestly and winced inwardly. I'll never know what Borg felt like, but at least I can identify with Bergelin. He looked at his winning boy, a balding bearded man almost twice his age, and gave his best approximation of admiration. Guests were peering at him with curious awe. Kitty was explaining him to would-be athletic household names 'Yes, yes, Johnny Sangster, you remember he was Number Five on the computer . . .'

The Palladinos sloped off to binge on bile and blondes. Jesse Wolfe, wet-eyed, ran off to the house to find Mitch before he cut anything. He felt like a myth, a hero, not a soft-bellied soft-porn baron. He felt young again.

On returning he looked for Johnny. He scouted around until he found him in a cabana, one hand holding a hot dog and the other hand holding Kitty's. A crowd were clamouring elegantly around him.

'How much do you ask?' asked a man from a record label.

'If you ask that you can't afford me.'

Everyone laughed. They liked to hear that kind of talk, it made them feel as though they had *arrived* and were too *there* to ever be toppled.

Jesse Wolfe accepted their congratulations, sidled up to Johnny and whispered in his ear. 'Getting over, Johnny?'

'Just a few initial inquiries, Jesse.'

Jesse Wolfe put an arm around Johnny and an arm around Kitty and steered them out of the cabana, smiling and nodding to his crowd. 'You planned all this, didn't you? Winning the match in front of a crowd comprised solely of California's richest swingers – or didn't you recognize them?'

Kitty laughed. 'Don't forget that death blow of yours. He planned that too. Especially.'

'Well spotted, Kitty. Right, Sangster? All that was purely an advertisement for yourself.'

Johnny smiled. 'What should I have done? Confined myself to the Want Ads?'

'You should've told me like it was. *I* would have helped you. You don't think I expected to have a monopoly on Johnny Sangster? Do you? Why didn't you tell me? Why didn't you come to me, partner?'

'I'm not cut out for partnerships or helpmates, Jesse. Nothing good can come out of team games.'

Wolfe patted his back understandingly – wasn't *he* a magnate? Hadn't he clawed his way up from the bowels of Boise, Idaho? – and Kitty smiled, but Johnny felt stupid, still.

That old line had been fine coming from a winner. From a face that fairly regularly looked upon its own failure it didn't really wash.

But it was still the manifesto that had seen him through this far. And it was still the only rule that he could find to believe in or stick to.

# twenty-one

Here in the place that the lazy-minded choose to call Paradise, they rented his skill by the hour. They wanted him for many reasons – to learn tennis, to talk to, as a fashion accessory, to stare at. Most mixed and matched.

Gyms buzzed with the latest truths about him. The massive gambling debts back East, the plastic surgery that will cost a small fortune, the girl who will not marry him unless he is very rich. How did all these rumours start? Maybe because he could never remember the reason he gave to the last person who asked.

His face inspired revulsion, arousal, conversation, fascination, the odd nightmare. A terrible tragedy – you must see it. *Meet* him, I mean.

The guy's done wonders for my wife's technique, so she tells me. Na, I go out for a round of golf. I tell her, just have it out the house by the time I get home.

His new career masked the old obsession, but being so near it couldn't block it out. He tried to bury her memory under the bulk of work, but he saw her on every street and he saw her in his sleep.

'Cock the wrist and swing from the hips. Follow the arc through to head height. You got it.' He stood behind her, adjusting her grip on the racquet handle.

Rose Snyder, cool and pearly in her I. Magnin's tennis whites, turned and looked into his face. She was an auburn-haired matronly English beauty, over-ripe but a good few decades from rotting. She was in an advanced stage of her career as the wife of successful men and she knew she was missing something. She wondered what it was, or if Johnny Sangster had it. She was searching his face for a clue.

He saw her stare and scowled. 'End of freakshow,' he mumbled, backing off.

'What? I mean—'

There was a bellow and a snarl and a fat man stumbled shouting from what the architect had fondly imagined was a Spanish-style ranch. Brod Snyder liked his Spanish-style ranch, he said it made him feel more like the matador he was at heart. The matador and the doormat, he liked to call himself and his

Rose when he was drunk in front of a small circle of friends . . . Which was often. He was the only male in Bel Air over the age of twelve who didn't use an underarm deodorant. He had the arms of a middle weight and the hands of a clerk, with which he wrote bloodthirsty, best-selling novels. They were less best-selling than they had been at the time of his first marriage and he tended to blame successive wives for less successful sales.

Johnny saw him stumping down the steps and on to the court, stocky, grizzled and sweaty, a full glass of brown liquid in one hand and a sheet of screwed up foolscap in the other. He had created a few scenes in his time, and now he sensed one just looking for somewhere to happen.

Snyder cradled his glass tenderly against his big belly and grinned at his wife. The smile dripped slime. 'Rose, why are you wearing a doily on your ass?'

Rose coughed. 'It's a tennis skirt, Brod. You signed the check yourself.'

'Jeez, do I remember! The money I paid out, I thought you was buying a *limo*, not a *loincloth.*' He drank greedily and dribbled half of it down his chin. 'I wouldn't mind being skinned if you looked any good in the duds. Remember Cindy, that steno I had last year? She useta play that game when I had to take her out to Bermuda on that trip. *She* didn't look like you. Why don't you look like her?'

'Well, Brod, your secretary was nineteen and I'm –' Rose Snyder glanced at Johnny '–forty-one. That could just have something to do with it.'

'So? See what I mean? Don't they make old women's rig-outs? For the fuller figure? Or for the figure that's falling apart?' He cackled and drained his glass. 'Every woman over the age of seventeen should stand in front of a mirror – naked – every morning and say, 'Every day, in every way, I get worse and worse.' Go over to the High School and take a look at the nymphets if you don't believe me. Tell ya what, I go over twice a day, I'll take you with me tomorrow as a treat! I'm telling ya, Rose, as soon as you women are *legal* it's all downhill for you. And *you*, sweets, have been screeching down that hill with busted brakes for more than half your life now. For Chrissakes go and cover your legs up.'

Brod Synder turned to go into the house. Rose turned to follow him.

Johnny narrowed his eyes and cleared his throat. 'Sir, it's impossible for me to raise the standard of your wife's game if her legs are tangled up in some kind of toga. Tennis wear *must* be as brief as possible.' He hacked impatiently at the court with his racquet. 'As anyone who has half a liver knows.'

Snyder turned back and leered at Johnny with combative interest. 'Ah, the fairy speaks. I've been watching my wretched wife trying to attract you, kid. Why don't you tell her she's wasting her time? No *man* plays pat ball. That's why so many of the *males* in this sewer go in for it.' He peered and began to waddle up to Johnny. 'What's wrong with your face?'

'For God's sake, Brod.'

'It's ok, Mrs Snyder. I was in a car crash. One side of my face is paralysed.'

Brod Snyder grinned broadly. 'Hey, you that Johnny Sangster! The car crash! The rags to ruin boy! Yeah, I know about you!' He pulled up his polo shirt and pointed to two small scars on his flabby torso. 'See that one? A bull in Spain. See that big mother? A Commie in Korea.' He slipped an arm around Johnny's shoulders. 'I like you, kid. We both fought our way out. And when we get there, what's there? This big desert full of dykes and fairies. On a clear day you can see Long Beach. Huh!' He marched him into the house and pointed up at at the heads of many beautiful animals. 'My trophies. Hunting. My wife's protected wild life, in case you're wondering. Not that she's worth poaching anymore. Lemme pour you a drink.'

'Strawberry daiquiri.'

Snyder stared at him, threw back his head and laughed. 'Kid, you drink Scotch when you're with me. Scotch or nothing.'

'Nothing.' Johnny tried to brush past him. The dismembered animals made him feel queasy.

'Hey, listen.' Brod Snyder grabbed him by the scruff of his tennis shirt and forced him to his knees almost casually, like shaking hands. 'You're girl enough to drink *fruit drinks*, you're girl enough to suck my cock. Suck it.'

'Suck it yourself.' Johnny swung at him and shoved him against the wall, moving fast.

'You coy little cocksucker.' Snyder brushed himself off and tried to look manly.

'You wish.'

Snyder poured himself a strong one and stared up at the remains of dead animals he had known.

Rose was on the porch looking worried. 'Gosh, I'm sorry. Did he try to fight you? It's nothing personal. He's always like this when he has one of his blocks.'

He smiled at her. He felt suave and on top of things. 'A writing block? Or what kind of block?'

'A you-name-it block.' Snyder bellowed her name and she went into the Spanish-style ranch.

On the tacky tennis court of a Marina del Ray singles apartment block, Johnny coached a boy who looked like a cat. An English boy who called himself Nile Paul Martin. He dressed well and played badly, but he struggled gamely with Johnny for thirty minutes before running to the net.

'Can we sit down now? I'm very parched. I'll run and get us some Evian.'

'Sure.' Johnny felt quite relieved to find proof of youth in California, even if it was foreign youth.

Nile Paul Martin had long grey eyes under a silky black fringe. Those eyes stared out calmly at everything, never showing disgust or delight. But he looked at Johnny happily. He wanted to talk about himself. Other swingers took the court. Johnny watched them idly. No-talent panty-waists.

'I came out here to act, you know. But the casting directors were too ugly to tolerate. No, I tell a lie – I'm actually not a terribly good actor. So now I fuck rich women for a living instead of career women for a career.'

'You're a stud!' Johnny had never met one; he looked anew at Nile with a mixture of respect and contempt.

'I hate that word. It reminds me of the things my father puts in his shirt cuffs, bless him. I don't hang around on street corners and I *rarely* accept money. My friends pay my rent, buy my clothes, little things like that.' Nile laughed. 'You'll be appalled, but *you're* being paid with dirty money.'

Johnny was fascinated. 'You get a lot of work around here?'

'Masses. I have to turn a lot of it away. The spirit is willing etcetera. In London and New York I hear the demand is diminutive unless you're a man's man. But out here there are women who care about their reputations, rich men's wives, divorced women with children, film widows, grass widows. A woman like that can't go out to a bar and pick up a slob and catch a disease. But a dapper little English boy who can play tennis, too – that's safe, and that's style. And they're so *grate-*

*ful.* Their whole lives centre around making some slug of a man happy, and they're amazed when their wish is my command all afternoon.'

Nile was paged. He took the call and returned. 'Sorry about that.'

'Business or pleasure?'

'Pleasure is my business.'

Johnny laughed and shook his head. 'I can't believe you're real. You're sure you're not still an actor and this is some *cinema verité* flick?'

'How old are you, Johnny?'

'Twenty-one.'

'Great! So am I. Are you a Libra?'

'No.'

'Oh. There're some quite good bars over at Marina del Ray harbour. Come with me sometime. We're the same age, Johnny, yet I've never met more of a foreigner than you. I'd like to be friends, though. I haven't had a friend who was a man since I was twelve. *That's* when women realized what I was.' Nile's cool eyes were fixed serenely on invisible vistas, as usual. He didn't look at Johnny as he spoke. 'I'd like to sleep with you.'

Johnny spilt the Evian from his paper cup. He was dumb with horror. Two fags in one day! One married and one in demand!

Nile smiled at him sideways. 'Don't you think I'm pretty, Johnny?'

'No, you scrawny fairy. And if you want your capped teeth knocked down your cute throat, just you make another pass at me.'

'Oh, Johnny! I've offended you. I'm so sorry. I didn't *dream* you'd be upset.'

'Ah, you subscribe to the 1972 Myron Le Poove theory that everyone is bisexual, right?'

'On the contrary. I *loathe* most men. They either run in packs or they're some fat woman's beast of burden. I love *alone-ness*, Johnny – that's why I can fuck rich women so well. They're so self-obsessed and small-minded – I swear, apart from my cock the only thing on their minds is their next helping of those chocolate-covered strawberries they serve up at Beverly Hills – that they've got alone-ness, and it excites me, even in a forty year old. You've got a lot, and I wanted you for it. I'm sorry. I apologize for throwing myself at you.'

'Forget it.'

'You're in love, aren't you?' Nile made a dreamy face. 'Have you got her or are you still waiting?'

'Now why would *I* be *waiting* for a *girl*? We're not all on call, you know.' Johnny looked at Nile's mild harmless eyes and felt like Brod Snyder. 'No. I haven't got her. That aloneness you talk about, God gave her seconds.'

'I see.' Nile jumped up. 'I see my car. I won't change my clothes, I think. Ladies love athletes, don't they? – the smell of the locker room, honest sweat, the comunal bath. All that stuff. You must have been knee deep in girls before—'

'—before I bust my face?'

'No. Before you fell in love. I'd barely noticed your flaws. I'm not interested in anybody's *face* but my own. You *are* touchy–' Nile winked '–but I like you!'

He strolled up to the patient Silver Cloud, said hello to the chauffeur and was whisked away. Johnny stared at the car until it disappeared. Somewhere a rich woman's hand shook with anticipation as she poured herself a gin with tonic.

Billy Sciarra had hard flat shots and endless stamina. He was a gentle man who spoke English as though it was a second language and gave the impression of immense reservoirs of power whether he was in conversation or covering the court. Occasionally he even managed to take the odd game off his coach when Johnny wasn't taking a dive to keep a client sweet.

Now Billy Sciarra tossed up a lob and Johnny leapt for it at full stretch, grunting with effort as he smashed the ball back at his opponent, too fast and furious for Billy Sciarra to come up with an answer.

'Game, set and match again,' Billy grinned. 'Ah, I get you one of these days, Johnny Sangster!'

'I wouldn't bet against you, Billy,' said Johnny, shaking his hand at the net. He had discovered that amateurs loved this old pro courtesy more than anyone. 'What you want me to do now?' Johnny glanced at his Rolex. 'You've got another twenty minutes. You want me to work on that service of yours?'

'Nah, that's enough for today,' Billy said, looking up at the house. 'You want a drink, Johnny? Could you use one of them banana daiquiris?'

'Strawberry.'

'Say which?'

'Strawberry daiquiris.'

'Yeah, yeah.' Billy Sciarra smiled at him with sad brown eyes.

'Sure,' Johnny said. He knew he wasn't really here because Billy Sciarra wanted tennis lessons. He was here because Billy Sciarra wanted someone to talk to.

They carried their racquets up to the house. It's my last booking of the day, Johnny thought. I deserve a drink. At least this guy won't jump on me.

Billy Sciarra had too much on his mind for any of that stuff. He had once been the best stunt man on the Coast. He had given up paid danger a year or so ago to look after his wife. All Johnny knew about her was that she was a famous beauty with famous problems. So what else was new?

Up at the house roving photo-electric cells and armed security guards in green uniforms were everywhere. But they went to the bar and Billy fixed drinks. In every dream home a carbine. Johnny found a chair for his racquets and saw something stir in the shadows. He looked up at a pale drawn woman in shades, a towelling robe and a state of panic. Their eyes met for a moment and Johnny was shocked to see Mrs Sciarra visibly flinch. She ran down the hall and disappeared into a room. Johnny heard desperate locks rattling home.

Billy cleared his throat and handed Johnny his strawberry daiquiri. 'You must wonder what troubles my wife.'

Johnny shrugged and sipped his drink. 'Not really. I sort of understand people who don't like people.'

Billy laughed softly. 'You're very kind, Johnny. But you must wonder . . .'

'Honestly, Billy, it's none of my business.' But you're going to tell me anyway, he thought. Ah, what are you bitching about, Sangster? That's what you're here for. Dr J. F. K. Sangster and his invisible analyst's couch.

'Somebody once said that the price of love is having somebody else hate your guts,' Billy said.

'Yeah, I heard that one.'

'Well, a lot of people love my wife. From a distance, Johnny. She has many fans. But there are also a lot of people who hate her guts.'

'Professional jealousy,' Johnny diagnosed. 'It happens all

the time. She's very successful, I understand. She must expect other actors to get greeen-eyed . . .'

'No, it's not other actors, Johnny. It's her public. She seems to have the gift of inspiring mass psychosis. The death threats aren't so bad. It's the obscenities, the threats of torture. They never stop. Oh, everybody in the public eye gets them, sure . . . but not so many, not so mad . . .'

'Why doesn't she quit?' Johnny said, knowing it was a dumb question.

'Oh, she would dearly love to escape TV and the . . . *lynch mobs*, the lynch mobs who track her down through it. But her paranoia needs protection, Johnny, and her protection costs plenty. More than the West Coast's best-paid stunt man ever dreamed of, even, much more. She has to be self-sufficient, she has to keep working.' Billy drained his glass. 'I just do what I can.'

'Your wife . . . I mean, does she have any idea why she attracts these people out of the woodwork so?'

'Well.' Billy Sciarra looked at his hands. 'My wife is a very good woman, from a very good family – poor, but very respectable, you know what I mean? But she's very beautiful, and exotic, and the only type of acting roles she is offered are those of . . . home-wreckers, I would say.'

'I see.' Her face is only good for one thing. She's one up on me, at least.

'So I do what I can. I got a secretary who burns the mash mail. The murder mail goes to the police. I got a secretary who screens all the incoming calls and transfers all the threats and obsecenities through to this young drama student from UCLA who I took on to pretend she's my wife. If they deliver their messages they're less likely to call again. Unfortunately there's always another one.'

'Your wife never goes out?'

'Frequently. But only in the limo to the studios and back again. Only to earn money. You *must* have seen her, Johnny.'

He shook his head. 'Sorry, I don't watch much TV. And I can't recall an actress named Sciarra. I'm bad on names.'

'Of course. She acts under her family name. Capra. Maxine Capra.' Billy Sciarra picked up a photograph from the baby grand and handed it to Johnny. It showed two young women at a window. 'That's Maxine, my wife, the beautiful one.'

Johnny stared at the other one, the fair one, the one looking at the camera. 'Who's that with her?'

'Her room-mate. Her name was, ah—'

'Thorn Sayre.'

'That's right! You know her?'

'I dated her. Does Mrs Sciarra keep in touch with her, Billy?'

'Maxine keeps in touch with no one.' Billy Sciarra picked up the piano's other photograph and handed it to Johnny. It showed Billy Sciarra grinning in the pilot's seat of an old biplane. 'Look, here's me—'

'Could I talk to your wife, Billy? About Thorn Sayre? It wouldn't take more than a minute. It's very important to me.'

Billy looked doubtful. 'I don't think so, Johnny. I'll ask, though.'

He left the room, clutching both photographs to his chest. He returned a few minutes later lugging only the unwanted biplane portrait and replacing it on the piano. 'No, Johnny, I'm sorry. Maxine says they are strangers now. Different people. Know nothing of each other. No use to you.'

'You didn't bring the photo back,' Johnny pointed out dumbly.

'Maxine wants to look at it. She gets so homesick.'

'For New York?' He could understand that.

'No, for the past.'

# twenty-two

'This town has more so-called models than Southern California has Med-flies,' sneered Thorn. 'It's ridiculous – so many models after so little modelling.'

'More models than Med-flies,' the new agent cackled appreciatively. 'Maybe if I slipped the Governor a couple of G he'd arrange to have all your rivals sprayed.'

'If you did it would be the first thing this agency has done for me since you called me the most beautiful girl in the State and asked me to sign on the dotted line.'

'*Thorn*, we're doing our very best.'

'Modelling assignments are more elusive than speed here. I'm not enjoying unemployment, you know.'

'And we're not enjoying fifteen per cent of zilch,' the new agent said, staring at Thorn with mesmeric glee in eyes like huge blue headlamps. The new agent always looked like that. Thorn had seen so many poor rich women like that out here, women who had had one face lift too many. Cosmetic surgery waits for no one, Thorn reminded herself.

She fixed the agent with a cool gaze. Thorn had been living off old immoral earning in a small sub-suite in Brentwood for months. The agency had got her nothing. Something had to give. 'Listen, Coral, I wouldn't whine if I was missing out on jobs because some high-grade mannequin was beating me to the punch. But it's just plain dumb bitches for whom a walk-on in some sub-mediocre soap or sit-com with them as the punch-line is the apex of their dumb sub-mediocre career, for God's sake.'

'I know, honey, I know,' Coral the new agent soothed.

'Time and time again this agency has sent me to audition for TV commercials, and the competition is a cast of thousands of failed actresses. *Not* models.'

'I know, I know,' Coral said. 'But you must understand this, Thorn – this is California and those girls are what we out here on the edge of the world deem models.'

'They're not models,' Thorn bitched. 'They'll never be models.'

'They'll be models for as long as it suits them,' Coral said. 'They'll be models until something better comes along. Look, when some young hopeful finally lands the soap of her dreams it sounds so much better to say that one was previously a *model*, rather than a no-count actress permanently between parts.'

'You mean every actress who says she used to be a model really only did commercials?'

'What's wrong with *that*, honey? What's wrong with *commercials*, baby? It's not as though they're selling used cars or peanut butter or something they don't really believe in. Of course the only product they're advertising is *me, me, ME*!'

'You?'

'One. You're so sweet, Thorn, so quaint . . .'

'Thanks a bunch, Coral.'

'And *you* could be *one*, Thorn, if only you'd get a tan on your body, a smile on your face and the South out of your voice.'

'There's too many girls like that already,' said Thorn. 'Every day thirty new ones file into Schwab's pretending they've never even *heard* the legend of Lana. If they're lucky they get to turn a trick and earn the plane fare back to... Albequerque.'

'Oh, and you want to keep your integrity.'

'No. I want to keep my *selling* points. Because one day they'll get me everything I want. If I try to change I'll lose something very special. Better a first-rate Thorn Sayre than a fifth-rate Sherry Ward.'

'That's debatable. What are you getting out of life that a fifth-rate Sherry Ward isn't?'

'Well, for a start I'm getting to go to a lot of parties that super-scrubbed health bores wouldn't dare to risk their piss-ant daisy-fresh complexions on.'

Coral laughed. 'That will get you a long way.'

'It will,' maintained Thorn. 'Some of the most important men in TV go to these parties.'

'To slum. *Not* to spot talent. To cross off the list, not to note. Thorn, this is sponsor country. Have you met many TV moguls at these parties?'

'Yes. What's wrong? Should I stop going to them?'

'Do what you like now. It doesn't matter anymore.'

The new agent's eyes stared right through Thorn Sayre.

Johnny drove Nile to the Spanish-style ranch. 'I'm looking forward to this,' Nile enthused, shaking clenched fists like an excited tot.

Johnny laughed, putting his foot down to overtake a dawdling coach with TOUR OF THE HOME OF THE STARS emblazoned along it's side. 'So is Rose. I think it's what both of you need. Your games are equally good.'

'Equally bad, you mean,' Nile grinned, blowing his fringe out of his eyes.

'That too. But beating hell out of someone as good as you is the best way I know of improving.'

'Is that what you did, Johnny?'

'Nah, I stuck to beating hell out of my betters.' He drove up the Snyder driveway. 'Ok, gorgeous, here we are.'

Rose was waiting. Johnny made the introductions, watching Nile and Rose eye each other with appreciative warmth as they shook hands.

'I've heard so much about you!' smiled Rose.

Nile's plucked eyebrows arched feyly. 'From Johnny?'

Rose shook her head teasingly. 'From women!'

Nile smiled too. 'All good, I hope.'

Rose still had hold of his hand. 'All unbelievable, I fear.'

'Girls!' Johnny shouted. 'Can we ditch the dirt and dish it later?'

They spun one of Nile's racquets for choice of ends or service. Johnny hammed it up as umpire and watched Rose win a mediocre match. When it was mercifully all over the three of them sat on the terrace while one of the Snyder staff served a tray of Perrier and champagne. Johnny drank and sat mute with boredom while Rose and Nile swapped mutual acquaintances and related marital and mental problems, moving over to merry olde England and moving back again.

He finished the champagne just to be polite. Then he made his excuses and said goodbye, leaving the two aliens alone on the terrace.

All around its bored centre of attention the party droned on with a desperation that had had too much to drink.

Hood Bailey was the soiree's famous focus and if there was one thing Hood Bailey loathed it was this wretched sun-kissed Coast. He was only here for the earthquake. Someone had once told him that sitting out an earthquake was the ultimate rush, something akin to kissing God. Another someone at a New York party a few days back had told him that the San Andreas fault was about to tear the roof off the sucker, so Hood Bailey went West to score. An earthquake! Now that would be a kick worth writing home about, it would put the wind up his mum no end! That would *really* be living on the Edge!

But the earthquake never happened. Hood Bailey seemed doomed to sit this life out at some party, numb with narcotics and fondling some random flesh, yawning with excruciating self-pity.

Hood Bailey was the leader of The Cobras, a rock band conceived in the Sixties who came out of England – the Home Counties, actually – screaming sexual anarchy and violent revolution. The Cobras preached the virtues of throwing hand grenades with a hard-on and butchering thy neighbour and it made them a mint. Twenty years later they were still trying to hold up the flagging façade of erotic insurrection for the sake of their public. In private, however, The Cobras' sole socio-political interest was wrestling that extra one thin dime out of the tax man.

In Britain the sharp youth had seen through the sham band years ago but in the States Hood Bailey and his boys were still idolized as the wildest men of rock. The rich twosome who were hosting the open evening smiled at each other for the first time in three years. They were ecstatic to have someone *dangerous* on their premises, someone *dangerous* but not so dangerous that he might come at them with a knife. A careerist criminal! Oh, it felt so *baaad*!

Hood sat on the circular bed. He tore the silk sheet with his boot heel and poked his toe through moodily, wiggling at the hole to make it bigger. He was pale and shaded, dissolute and detached, he was looking into the ornate hand mirror he had picked up from the dressing table and now held in his grubby skeletal paw. Meanwhile the rich and famous and the merely hopeful made a massive effort to drift *casually* into the master bedroom, to *coolly* lay out another line, roll a spliff, place a sweaty hand on Hood Bailey's legendary crotch.

One senior celebrity even got up the nerve to offer Hood the joint in his hand.

King Cobra emasculated him with one weary eyebrow.

The senior celebrity sloped off into the night, his shoulders slumped in defeat. Those who remained glared after him with bitter contempt. Dumb old-timer. It was *understood* that Hood Bailey was post-everything. He's done it all, he shuns it all – it was understood.

Hood Bailey lounged, cloaked in the mystique of tedium, and the pilgrims and lemmings gazed at him, waiting for something to happen. Some people were under the sheets. They lay perfectly still, waiting to catch Hood's eye, to do Hood's bidding. They thought he looked so cool, so coiled, so ready to oversee anything with that mirror in his hand.

All Hood Bailey was was bored. There was nothing left to do, nothing else he wanted. Well, just that one thing – to turn back time. It wasn't *that* much to ask for. After all, he *was* Hood Bailey. He wished he could go back, meet the love of his life again, feel the new nausea of the heroin novice again, he wished . . .

He was aware of the figure in the doorway.

The figure was conspicuous because it was not being casual. It stood in the doorway, peering tentatively into the inner sanctum, and Hood Bailey saw its moist lips part in the midst of its stunning face. He got to his feet and the room really gasped.

The figure in the doorway thought quickly. It was beautiful. It was going nowhere. Hood Bailey! It had taken a rock star to change Jerry Hall's career from standard fee to phenomenal success. He was coming over to her. Hood Bailey.

Thorn Sayre hated his music but she loved the sound of his household name.

'What the fuck happened to you?'

Rose Snyder looked at Johnny through two fading black eyes. 'I don't want to discuss it, Johnny.' She brushed past him but he grabbed her by the wrist. She was wearing her whites and carrying a wagonload of racquets, all ready to learn. She looked so small, so sad, so hurt standing there looking at him with her poor swollen eyes that he couldn't stand it.

'Did he do this to you, Rose? Your loving husband?'

'I said I don't want to talk about it.'

Johnny heard a drunken whoop and turned to see Brod Snyder stumbling on to the court carrying a bottle of brown liquid and a baseball bat. He came up to them. Johnny let go of Rose.

'Holding hands?' Brod Snyder sneered. 'How touching. It must make a change from—'

'Did you do this?'

'No. She was born that ugly. What's your excuse?'

'I asked you a question.'

'Let me answer you as best I can, sweetie.' Snyder emptied what was left of the Jack Daniels down his throat and threw the bottle over his shoulder. It shattered on the baseline. Then he punched Rose Snyder full in the face. He smiled as she screamed and stumbled backwards holding her mouth. Snyder advanced on Johnny, a belligerent sneer twisting his bloated features. 'Guess,' he said.

Johnny waded into him. Brod Snyder made no attempt to fight back. Johnny wondered what was wrong with him and decided that he didn't really care. But he stopped hitting him.

Brod Snyder ran into the house, grabbed a bottle like a baby and drove off.

Johnny turned to Rose, breathless and bewildered. 'God only *knows* what you're doing with him. Where will he go?'

Rose looked at her feet. 'Oh, he'll find one of his cronies eventually. They'll hit the bars, pay a couple of girls to be abused, get some catatonic sleep and start all over again when the bars open.'

'How long will that go on for?'

'Until he collapses or until the police find him.'

'Yeah, yeah. Will you be ok now?'

She smiled shyly. 'Yes, Johnny. So will you.'

Rose took a while to get started, but once she was – well, Johnny had never known a woman so rapacious. He was slightly shocked that a woman of that age could like it so much. But he reckoned she must have been in cold storage a long time, and that explained it. Brod Snyder was certainly no sixty-minute man, what with his penis substitute bats and bottles and brawls. Johnny dropped into an exhausted sleep, Rose still murmuring sweet nothings to his groin.

The phone awoke him just before dawn. The police had found Brod Snyder this time. He went into the back of a truck and it sliced the roof off his car, killing him and two others instantly. An additional young woman was on the critical list at a hospital downtown.

Johnny woke Rose. She showed no shock. He went with her to the city morgue. The official showed no shock that the widow had a young man in tow. Everyone knew about Brod Snyder and had sympathized with his nearest and dearest while he was living. His death brought no condolences.

She didn't speak as he drove her home. As the car turned into the drive Johnny said, 'Rose, are you ok?'

She smiled at him quickly and patted his hand on the wheel. 'His head looked like one of his terrible trophies,' she said, almost dreamily.

At the Spanish-style ranch they took all the trophies down.

Within the weekend, Thorn had been initiated into heroin's grim gauzy bubble and hijacked to Berkshire, England. Hood Bailey led her lyrically into his stately home. The house was a wonderful white elephant, a divine disaster area. For a start it was impossible to heat – guests staying the weekend, even those bolstered with the best drugs Hood could buy, frequently did moonlight flits in the early hours of Saturday morning due to fear of frostbite.

But all that would come later. Now Thorn stood transfixed, lost in the portrait of the beautiful girl that blared from the wall of the banquet hall above the huge blazing open fire. Daredevil dark blonde hair, chiselled cheekbones, eyes shining with scorn and sedition and a red malleable slash of a mouth . . . it's . . .

'Juanita,' said Hood softly, following her eyes.

'Oh, yes. Yes, of course.'

'It was painted to celebrate our first gold record. Fifteen years ago. Before your time.'

'But I've heard. Of course, I've heard.'

If Hood Bailey was feted by the tame as the wildest man in rock, his consort Juanita Franz was feared as the weirdest woman ever to wield the power behind the plectrum. Two myths are better than one; Hood/Juanita, a two-headed monster that has dabbled in and been drained by junk, Satanism and sadism. Thorn thought back to late Sixties grade school gossip. The Cobras had worshipped and lived vicariously through Juanita until that New York night in 1969 when she approached a beautiful black girl at a party. 'I hate Negroes,' she muttered in her guttural Bavarian husk. She drained and smashed her bottle of Southern Comfort; she punctuated her statement by screwing a full stop into the girl's face.

The girl turned out to be the wife of an estimable Black Panther so Juanita and Hood fled New York and didn't return until the mid-Seventies when every Panther had been Born Again or killed resisting arrest. With their son and heir Little Elvis, the Hood/Franz household roamed from England to Cannes to Manhattan like millionaire gypsies leaving a trail of newly converted junkies in their wake. When they were feeling especially energetic Juanita changed her underwear and Hood had his blood changed.

'Welcome home, darling!' rasped a thrilling voice behind Thorn. 'And oh! you've brought me back the clone you promised me!'

Thorn turned, expecting to see a preview of her future beauty. Instead she saw a grotesque. It was a woman, tall and blonde and inflated like a conjurer's arrangement of balloons. Its legs resembled young saplings. Its face was a circus of circles. Its hair was thin, combed and cajoled across its scalp. It was Juanita Franz.

One of its huge hands stroked Thorn's face. 'You look confused. Forgive me. You're the poor little drug fiend that Hood told me he was bringing here to kick the habit. A bad man made you take drugs against your will, isn't that right? And now you're hooked.'

Thorn stared at Hood uncertainly.

'Don't let her phase you, kid. She loves her little games.'

Thorn tossed her hair. 'Well, tell her to toy with someone her own size.'

'Well, what a little bore you are. Why did you bring this little bore into our happy home, Hood?'

Hood Bailey slumped into his favourite armchair in a bad grace and picked up a copy of the *Star*. 'Stop bitching, the pair of you,' he commanded. 'Can't a man get a bit of peace in his own castle anymore? My Dad's word was law – and *he* wasn't Hood Bailey. Shake hands and shoot up and shut up, you chicks. Really.'

Juanita prepared the needle for Thorn, loathing the girl, loving the gift.

Rose looked lovely in black. Everything she had looked great in black – her face, her body, her bank balance and bonds. Johnny Sangster, feeling ugly in black, stood by her side as the funeral service droned duplicitly on.

Assorted offspring of Snyder's from various marriages and liaisons glared at him, already hating his intractable face. The coffin rolled into the flames.

Back at Rose's he said hello to her business manager and goodbye to his back taxes. Then he said goodbye to the business manager too.

Rose touched his arm. 'That's the least of what I owe you. You've been a true friend.'

He mentally crossed his fingers and told an off-white lie. 'I want more than that, Rose. I want to marry you. At least, I want us to try. Let me move in. You won't regret it.'

She sighed, and she poured them drinks – her a gin with tonic, him a strawberry daiquiri. She had stocked up on a rainbow of daiquiris since Snyder snuffed it.' Don't let's be silly about this, Johnny. I like you very much. Well, you know just how much I feel for you. But I've lived in the shadow of some man for more than half my life. I want to please myself for a while, maybe for ever. I'll see how I like my own company. And if I get lonely – well, I want to choose a companion in my own time and on my own conditions.'

'Cash or credit?' Johnny was shocked to be rebuffed by an old woman. His pride hit back feebly. 'You make a relationship sound like a shopping spree. What am I? Bargain Basement, right? If you're looking for something you can hire by the hour, then forget a *man* – give a *gigolo* a call. In fact why don't you call Nile Martin this minute? I'm sure he'd give you a discount on account of you being English.'

'Ok, Johnny. Enough. Out.' Rose pointed towards the door. 'Don't try to act the big man with me. I've been bullied and belittled by real bigshots. Go and berate a ball-boy. Better still go out and find yourself a nice girl, a girl of your own age. All this revolving around your rich old clients, it isn't healthy.'

'I'm not healthy, haven't you heard? Isn't that why you hired me? I'm a wreck.' He walked away.

'Johnny, don't be—'

He slammed the door of his car and drove for a long time. After a while his scheme seemed salvagable. Give it time, give it just a little time. She's English, she doesn't want to shock people. She wants to wait a while. Just a while.

They only burnt the old bastard an hour ago, after all.

He waited three weeks for her call but it didn't come. Finally he rang her. She sounded tolerant and offhand.

'What's gone wrong between us, Rose?' He tried to put on a bedroom voice, a souvenir of what had passed between them. 'We were so good together.'

'Well, Johnny. When we met you wanted to take care of me. Later on you wanted to take care of my money, I think, and take me for a ride. Maybe I shouldn't have picked up your IRS tab. If you'd valued me less you might have appreciated me more.'

'All I want is for us to be together . . .'

'Yes, that would be very convenient for you. Unfortunately it's nowhere near good enough for me.'

'Why is it always *you* who calls the shots?'

'You know very well. You've been here. Now it's my turn.'

'Oh, Rose, Rose. I understand, baby. Let me come by tomorrow. Rose? You there?'

'Yes, Johnny. Just checking. Yes, I think you'd better come over tomorrow. Don't bring your racquet. I'm through with tennis.'

Nile Paul Martin was waiting for him outside the Spanish-style ranch. Johnny somehow felt defeat immediately in his stomach. When Nile opened the car door and slid into the passenger seat Johnny laughed nervously. 'Too many rich women make you blind? I'm not one of your chauffeurs. What are you doing here? Rose is expecting me.'

Nile looked thinner and prettier than ever. There were pale grey shadows beneath his pale grey eyes. He stared at Johnny from beneath his fringe. 'Rose is a busy person these days. She delegated the responsibility to me.'

'I don't think you understand, kid. This is between me and Rose. Where do you come into it?'

'Start driving, Johnny. Thanks. Well – I come into it as the third point on that boring old eternal triangle, I suppose. Johnny, Rose asked me to tell you . . . that we're going to be married.'

Johnny gasped. 'You lying, cowardly little bastard.'

'Why do you say that? That's not fair.'

'*I* introduced you to her, for God's sake!'

'But you don't *own* her, Johnny. She wasn't promised to you at birth or anything. I feel very badly about winning Rose at your expense – but I didn't *take* her. She chose me, and I can't help but accept her offer. You've got talent and a career. I want a rich, quiet life and a good marriage would seem to be the ideal avenue to it. I'm no good for acting. I can't be a hireling for ever. I'd rather be happy as a husband than bored with a career. Why work for it when I can make a few promises and thereafter maintain certain standards I've had since I was twelve?'

'You're a gold-digger,' Johnny said pettishly. 'I'll tell Rose.'

'Don't be dim, Johnny.' Nile studied his unpainted pink fingernails. 'Rose knows I'm not marrying her for love. She wouldn't marry me if I said I was. She knows I'll enjoy spending all that money. But she's happy with her side of the deal too. Fair exchange etcetera.'

Johnny pulled over. 'Have you fucked her?'

'Yes.'

'When?'

'Last night.'

'When did she ask you to marry her?'

'This morning.'

Johnny felt pathetic. 'Well, I guess that's why she wants to get it in writing. You must be a real live wire in the sack.'

'I try.'

'Yeah, so did I. Did *she* tell you I wanted to marry her?'

'Rose said you'd asked. She didn't say you *wanted* to. *I* don't think you want to either. You'd never be happy as a mannikin. An organ grinder's monkey.' Nile smiled happily at the thought of it.

'Is that how you see yourself?'

'I *am* rather a doll . . . but it's my duty to be beautiful. It suits me. Drive, will you? I look good and I fuck good; this marriage was made in heaven. You couldn't stand to be an older woman's pet, Johnny.'

'Couldn't I?' Johnny laughed bitterly, heading back to the Snyder house. 'If I closed my eyes and thought of all that money I might be able to swing it.'

'You see? Self-loathing colonizes your voice when you talk about living off a woman. Kept men always suffer from ingrown ego – booze, screw around, play the big boss man. Messy slobs. Well, I must be some kind of evolution because there's none of that destruction in me. I'll love the life. I can't wait to become Mr Rose Snyder . . . Nile Snyder . . . no, dammit, I don't like it. Let *her* change! Have you actually ever *seen* Rose's full name? It takes her about half an hour to write it down. Rose Marie Odette Calderan Russell Villiers Snyder! I'm telling you, Johnny, she'll be glad to settle for Rose Martin.'

'You're already forgetting who pulls the purse strings, kid.' Johnny stopped the car. 'Here we are. I won't embarrass you young folk by poking my fright mask in where it isn't wanted.'

'Oh, Johnny.' Nile got out of the car and leaned against it. 'There's one main reason why Rose chose me. Apart from the unalterable fact that I'm English and she's homesick. She chose me because I've never been worshipped; not by more than three people at a time and not outside of the bedroom, anyway. But *you* – the adoration you've had! You're not going to be happy carrying parcels up and down Rodeo all day. You'd live off her until you felt confident enough . . . then you'd go back out into the world and search for . . . I don't know. The girl, the glory. Rose has endured three rich pigs to get where she is today; she deserves to *cruise* for a while. I want to cruise, too. I'll never rock the boat that feeds me etcetera. But you're still moving, Johnny, and I don't know if you'll ever stop. Can't you see how wrong it would be to disturb Rose?'

'Yeah, you're right.' Johnny started the car. Nile jumped back. 'I wish you and the bride a big sleep and many of them. May you never know a rude awakening.'

'Bye, Johneee!' Nile sang, waving him off the property, out of Bel Air. Beware of the scarecrow. Johnny drove fast until he was squeezed into the seedy embrace of bad jokes that had once been unimpeachable legends – Hollywood and Vine, Sunset Boulevard. He felt at home here, as at home as he ever would feel on this coast. Go west, young zombie.

Hollywood and V was lousy with used car lots and used bodies. Impossible to believe that Harlow's, Garbo's, Monroe's feet had hurried their owners to work along those sidewalks. Impossible to believe that anything epic or worthwhile would ever happen here again.

Johnny drove his car into the next used car lot he saw.

# twenty-three

It was the eve of Hood Bailey's fortieth birthday. What had once been an insurrection was now an institution but Hood approached the menopause with his head determinedly buried in the sandpit of extended adolescence.

The party was in its eighth hour. Bottles and bodies were everywhere – smashed, drunk, being passed from hand to hand. Unsteady white lines snaked across mirrored tables and disappeared up Cobra noses.

Juanita, bent on a makeshift black mass, had gathered together a collection of nubile-ish young daredevils and taken them out into the woods. Out there they chanted and danced naked, feeling stupid and scared to offend. Juanita, well wrapped in her black wool cloak, cackled happily.

Inside Hood held court and Thorn hovered.

'Why do your birthday parties start a day early, Hood?'

'Because every one might be the last, babe. I just want to squeeze out every last drop.'

'Of what, Hood?'

Hood Bailey looked blank before grinning smugly. 'Juice, babe, juice.' Smelling amyl nitrate he stumbled off across the room.

A wonderfully pale, thin, dark teenager girl sipped a glass of gin and addressed Thorn in a South London accent. Thorn paid attention; the girl was obviously Someone, her face famous and maddeningly, elusively familiar. Thorn flicked through the index of importance in her mind. 'He's said that every year since he was nineteen and kept his first gold record under the mattress. Now he's got grey hairs – count them! – and he's still playing the doomed troubadour singing all the way to an early grave. Pathetic!'

Thorn looked at her disapprovingly.

'Mutton dressed like lamb. Hardened arteries dressed like greasy hoodlum. When he started out he wanted to be Elvis Presley – now he'd be happy as Peter Pan. The Queen gave The Beatles the MBE, do you remember? If he sticks around much longer she'll be sending him a telegram.'

'You don't like Hood very much, do you?'

The girl shrugged. 'He makes himself a laughing stock. With you, for instance.'

Thorn sneered at her.

'He's not even sowing his wild oats quota – he's looking for the elixir of youth. He won't dump you when he sees you getting older – he'll dump you when he sees you're not helping him get any younger.'

'Then why does he stay with Juanita?'

'Well, she is the mother of his son and heir. You must have met him! Little Elvis, dark and curly, about three feet tall. He's got the hottest heroin habit this side of Harlem. You smile, but you shouldn't underestimate the kudos these old hippies place on sons. But excuse me. My Siamese will be worried.'

'I think you're jealous,' drawled Thorn. 'Because Hood leads an exciting life and you don't. I think you'd love to be me, or even Juanita – to be *close* to him—'

The girl laughed in Thorn's face. 'You can think what you like – but I really think I know my own father a little better than you do. Now *move*.' The girl pushed past her grinning, a young healthy Hood with real teeth behind red lipstick.

Thorn scanned the soiree for him. She spotted him and began to sidle.

Hood was busy haranguing the only rock journalist tame enough to be allowed in. 'These kids coming up today, what do they know about rock and roll? When they've been wrecking hotel rooms as long as I have – twenty-five years, man and boy, man! – maybe then they'll be able to, uh, talk! I could give them a few swearing lessons . . .'

'I agree absolutely, Hood.'

'These kids hanging themselves and getting all the credit – it amounts to queue jumping, it does! Dying young is just a publicity gimmick with them – they don't really *believe* in it.'

'You're right – you're so, so, *right*, Hood.'

'But actors, painters, writers, they ain't obliged to die young. Why does the rock musician carry the can? Why are we expected to die before we get old?'

Because you promised, thought Thorn. She leaned her head on Hood's shoulder and he grabbed her ass. All the better to melt the media into sheer molten awe, she thought.

The reporter grinned inanely at her and shrugged submissively for Hood. 'Hood, I totally, totally—'

Hood Bailey shook his head disbelievingly and exploded. 'Strewth! These pop paper people don't even give you a chance to *speak*! Talk about ego problems! Search him! Take his drugs! Now throw him out! . . . there he goes! The press are out to destroy me.'

Hood swayed perilously.

Thorn eased him on to a couch around which the remainder of The Cobras were grouped, staring each other down and ignoring the revellers.

'Get the box of tricks, babe,' Hood stage whispered to Thorn.

The Cobras looked even more bored, in an anticipatory sort of way. She skipped off for the First Aid box, thinking about Hood Bailey's track record. He made Roche look like a two-time user. Every few years Hood Bailey got busted, and the ensuing furore reaffirmed his fans' faith. The leader of The Cobras would be crucified, metaphorically, at some European airport for a small cache of chemicals. The possibility of Hood Bailey caged was always a frisson – noble savage behind bars. The three free Cobras always hurried to compose and rush-release an anthem of freedom. (The most efficient Cobra had recently begun to stockpile several original freedom anthems – there would be no rush next time Hood disgraced himself, and no shared royalties.) Within the month Bailey would be released – drugs cut very weak, legal advisors made very rich – with the most token of reprimands. Juanita was fluent in French, Italian, German, Spanish and Swedish; Hood made sure he was persecuted in countries that could talk her language. You didn't need a team of translators around you when you were bribing some local berk bigwig. Thank God he'd never been busted in Japan, like McCartney. A bowl of rice and all those little yellow bleeders running around – Hood would have felt as though he was going cold turkey on the *Bridge Over The River Kwai*.

Thorn retrieved the box and carried it to the couch. Juanita was back from the woods. She leered at Thorn's thin arm, around which Hood tied his silk scarf. *She* used to look like that. She muscled in to get a closer look.

Hood elbowed her irritably and glared her way. He was impatient with Juanita when he and his fellow Cobras – and now this tender young convert, a fitting consort in crime – were jacking up. All other Cobra eyes evaded Juanita; the puffy, bloated wreck – the ex-goddess who every one of them had loved and begged at different times in the late Sixties – reminded the musicians of their own middle-age and mortality. They preferred to use Thorn as their mirror.

Juanita's habit waited patiently at the end of the queue. She didn't care. She could wait. And seeing Thorn Sayre indulging so heavily gave her a rosy glow.

Thorn didn't really go looking to incur Hood Bailey's wrath. She just spoke her mind of the moment. 'This stuff isn't very good, is it, Hood? What do they cut it with, do you know? You have to take a massive amount to get any effect. Your coke too, I've noticed.' She thought of Roche again, this time with fondness. 'I used to go with this boy, a young, really unknown London boy, and his coke used to put me straight into orbit, so to speak.'

Hood Bailey put his hands on his hips and bitched at her belligerently. 'Listen, babe! I *have* to take massive doses, killer doses, because I have what is probably *the highest tolerance level in the world*, that's all! Do you seriously believe that a dealer man doesn't get out his best stuff when he sees Hood Bailey of The Cobras coming?'

'No, Hood. They give you their *worst*. That's been proved time and time again when you've been busted and the laboratories have analysed the stuff.' Inside her semi-detached smack buble, Thorn giggled. 'How much heroin was in that last lot they caught you with? Five per cent? Seventy per cent talc and twenty-five per cent vermin exterminator.' Thorn smiled at Juanita. 'God only knows what rat killer does to a girl's looks.'

'Listen, man.' Hood Bailey pointed rudely at Thorn. She found it hard to believe that he was addressing *her*. 'Hood Bailey has the best guitars, the best drugs, the best women . . .'

'One minute to midnight!' Juanita bellowed.

The party howled 'Happy Birthday, Dear Hood'. Hood howled his menopausal pain like a trapped beast. He was at that difficult age. He took up his crossbow and ran about the mansion, shooting every last clock. The party watched, awed. 'Chuck yer Timexes out of the window, you ponces! Let's see a bit of audience participation!'

Only The Cobras demurred. They stared coldly at the rampaging Hood and at the lemmings who were dropping their wristwatches on to the tarmac two floors down. Grand gestures didn't come cheap these days, and their Cartiers came from the sweat of their plectrums. No way were they going to have their expensive timepieces mashed up just to illustrate some mangy metaphor of King Cobra's.

The church bells chimed. Everyone cheered. Hood cranked up the stereo and The Cobras' latest long playing offering corralled the crowd until ears bled. Hood tried to throw Juanita over his shoulder. He collapsed; she picked him up and led him into the master bedroom. As the door closed everyone cheered again. The clocks were shot, the watches smashed, the bells were silent but time marched on. Just listening to The Cobras' latest try made Thorn realize just how late it was.

She sat shivering from the heroin, trying to plan. It was so easy to scheme awhile ago. One thing was sure; somewhere there was a party where the people were her age and on the threshold of righteous, record-breaking triumph. She should be there. Yet she was sitting shivering on a floor somewhere in the wilds, the scratched Cobra song taunting her to snap out of her stupor. *I'm not on the side that's winning. I'm on the losing side.* They were the worst words she had ever spoken to herself.

Johnny had gone underground. In her bunker Simone showed

no surprise. 'Ah, Johnny – I was wondering when your lovely face would come home. Do you want a dance or a position?'

In the private rooms that Simone alone killed time in there was no fatted calf – all she gave Johnny to eat were his words.

'I heard about your tax troubles.'

'That's ancient history.'

'Any other debts?'

'None.'

'You're a volunteer, Johnny! The last volunteer of the world!'

She handed him a glass of absinthe and turned the spotlight on to his face. He sat like a desperate statue while she stroked the broken side of his image. 'Beautiful. So exotic. *Mechante* Johnny. But I always liked you. And you know what Simone say – what's sauce for the goose is good for the box office.'

Johnny smiled like a stewardess.

Hood Bailey watched the groundsman rake the leaves from the courts.

Hood Bailey had reached the age of forty due to regular check-ups and a fear of Hell. Whenever hedonism brought the abyss into spitting distance he would be pulled back kicking and screaming via remedies as diverse as methadone, acupuncture and hypnotism.

His doctor prescribed simple solutions to be administered by the patient himself – dieting, pills without thrills, abstinence. Hood, who hated rules and regulations with a zombie's zeal, felt like Che when he disobeyed.

'Lose fifteen pounds,' the doctor said. 'It's all the cake you eat. If you want to keep your sweet tooth without acquiring a cardiac – exercise.'

But the nearest Hood got to exercising was watching the groundsman rake the leaves from the courts.

Still, even this tempted Hood Bailey's athletic-aesthetic palate a little. He found a bottle of Jack Daniels and a few grams of toilet cleaner posing as cocaine and he sat down in front of the VCR, flicking through his tennis tapes.

He'd swopped drugs and models with quite a few of those Circuit dudes in dark New York City discotheques . . . a bit misty about their names . . . but so what? They were all great! Fierce young turks, drooled Hood to himself, both ends burning, on the road all year long, forever looking behind them for that maverick nova that's going to stab them between the shoulder blades – and in the death everyone goes ahh, then forgets. He found himself quite excited, he fumbled around for a pen to write some lyrics down with but there wasn't one, he didn't need a hassle and he hit on his Jack Daniels.

Hood's line of work had once enjoyed a similar short-fuse turnover, Hood reflected, but Hood's generation had changed all that. Why move over if you didn't have to, why let middle-aged spread get in the way of your piece of the rock?

He could go on for ever.

He watched the tanned celluloid boys cover the court, duelling with a skill and savagery that took his breath away, took it away nearly as good as a steaming seven-minute Hood Bailey axe solo. Too bad me and the guys don't get to see much of each other, Hood moped, but that damn Circuit, it never stops. If The Cobras were on the road that long, thought Hood, I'd be a babbling old wreck.

Thorn Sayre walked into the room. He pretended to ignore her but he checked her out in the corner of his eye – greasy and washed out in some kind of grey sweater. Typical junkie. He sighed and wished she'd move house. She couldn't make him feel young again, have fun again – maybe those boys on the Circuit could, but she wasn't them. She was just a soppy girl. And the junkie joy of converting an innocent to the hopeless cause had passed. Hood concentrated on the latest Lendl –McEnroe high noon.

Thorn stared at him unhappily. What happens now? she thought. Juanita, holding a sleepy Little Elvis by the hand, scurried in after her. She hissed at Thorn; 'Nothing left? Nowhere to go? Try *Hell.*' She hovered in the doorway, smiling. 'Hood, do you know what Tiger told me?'

'Of course I do.' Hood Bailey's eyes never left the gladiators. 'I'm an effing mind-reader.'

'Tiger told me, Hood, that Miss Thorn Sayre used to be quite a little sideshow within – what do you call the damn thing? – the Circus.'

'The Circuit?' Hood Bailey almost looked at Thorn with interest. 'What's all this then?'

'I'm sure that the Bearded Lady here knows more about the circus than I do.'

'No abusing my Juanita in front of Little Elvis,' said Hood sternly. 'Have you no respect for people's mothers? No, Thorn,

I mean, is that right? Who, I mean, how many? Which ones?'

'Just one holiday romance.'

'Who?'

'Oh – Johnny Sangster.'

'Johnny *Sangster*! He's the one—'

'Yeah, he's that one.'

'And you never told me! You kept Johnny Sangster all to yourself! You naughty girl! I ought to – let's have him over tonight!' Hood was really excited.

'Well . . . he must be in the States . . .'

'No, no, he's scarecrow at Simone's. Simone'll ship him out, she's been sniffing around rebel music for years. Get the old ratbag on the phone, Juan. And tell the pilot to dust off the copter.'

Thorn headed for her room, horrified.

Juanita scurried after her, dragging Little Elvis by the hand.

'Hey, Thorn!'

Thorn turned to look at her.

Juanita grinned. 'What's it like fucking somebody with a deformed face?'

Thorn smiled, stroking Little Elvis' heap of woolly curls. 'Hey, Juanita. Why don't you ask Hood?'

The end of the night.

The hard core at the heart of the revelry was revealed in all its glory. Only the mega-*noctambules* remained, some by choice, some on the payroll, all sharing *le confidences d'alcove*.

'Christina had a tunnel built, you know. To stop paparazzi. To connect 88 avenue Foch with . . .'

'Well, Fahzia is Iranian, and they're all reduced now, even Farah, poor theeng. Fahzia sprinkles golden caviare on top; you 'ave to get there early or – yuk! you get the ordinary black bilge underneath.'

Laughter.

'You know the last estimate of Jackie O? One hundred million dollars – just from investing gold! Just pocket money!'

'Oh, Jackie O remind me of Mrs Samuel Newhouse Junior, so throwaway chic. Mrs Samuel Newhouse Junior ask her husband to get her *Vogue*. So he did, and now Samuel Newhouse Junior is chairperson of Conde Nast.'

The gossip was just meagre, middle-aged reminiscence, but the talkers were scared to go home because they knew that their peers would talk about them the minute the cab pulled off from the kerb. They spun out the eternal line, the eternal drink, laughing big gasps about absent friends. Going home to sleep until dusk was close at hand, but right now it seemed like a white flag.

Simone cared nothing for their qualms, and cared only to talk about herself. Her friends were too boring. She stood up and announced; 'I have only three phobias. I hate to go to bed, I hate to get up and I hate to be alone.'

She sat down. Her friends didn't know whether to laugh or look sad. This annoyed her. She looked at Johnny and called for another bottle.

He fetched it. All eyes were on him. His job was an aberration of fame. His looks were damaged goods with drawing power. Girls with no flesh on their bones and boys with no hair on their bodies still leaned towards him, but less so.

Their flesh was willing but Simone's spirit wanted a submission of body and soul. For second best she would settle for seeing him broken.

She felt the bottle. 'Tepid. Change it.'

He picked up the bottle.

She smiled warmly, kissing him on his bad cheek. 'Mmm.'

Johnny took the bottle back to the bar and exchanged it for a bottle in a bucket of ice. Simone was taking a call at the table, her eyes flicking over the assembled *noctambules*. If she had a tail she would have wagged it.

Johnny remembered the days when he had been an honoured *noctambule*. He didn't enjoy being fawned over but it was better than now. Now he was one of the people who were at every party but had no means of support, visible function, vocation or invitation.

Simone hung up, ecstatic with relief. The party had a new lease of life. She wouldn't have to face being nowhere just yet. Simone gathered up her choice *noctambules*, and Johnny, and swept out into the grey dawning streets. Beyond the peach lighting Simone and her crack force of party people revealed their imperfections as though in a confessional.

Like vampires heading for a crypt they hurried for the heliport, desperate to reach Hood Bailey's sanctuary by daybreak.

The scared forced revelry of Simone's people mingled with the studied decadence of Hood's molls. Cocaine was the common ground. Very soon it was hard to tell the two tribes apart.

Johnny was privileged – for him there was a seat reserved at Hood Bailey's right nostril.

Simone was delighted, even deferential to Johnny. Suddenly he seemed like her passport to the elusive rock and roll wild party where, she'd been hearing since the Sixties, It All Happens.

Hood Bailey put his arm around a befuddled Johnny. 'Let's have a picture here.' Johnny was surprised that so many photographers snapped to attention. 'Move over just a little, Sim.'

Simone also was surprised. 'But I'll be out of the pic— oh! of course, Hood!'

'Grisly old mongoose,' Hood whispered in Johnny's ear. The shutter clicked. Hood steered him into a corner. 'Take a powder?'

'Ok.'

A line was easily manoeuvred. Johnny sniffed it. Immediately he was underwater, unable to breathe. He was sick and unable to speak.

'That wasn't coke,' he gasped eventually.

'Smack!' Hood celebrated. 'Nothing but the best, Johnny! Say, you always honk up *that* side of your face or you able to – hey, where ya going?'

Johnny lurched to his feet, slamming into the ceramic pseudo-coffee table, toppling glasses. He stumbled unsteadily through the party and out on to the balcony. He sank to his knees. He heard a familiar voice.

'Johnny?'

He half-turned and looked up at her. She looked frail, she looked plainer.

He felt more love.

His mind was moving in slow motion.

She knelt beside him. 'What's wrong? Speak to me.'

'Heroin.'

'Oh, *hell*. Straighten up, now, breathe as deep as you can. Come on, Johnny. That's it. Breathe deep. Do it.'

He watched her amazed as she put on a great show of sucking in lungful after lungful of air. He began to imitate her, staring with mute bewilderment.

She smiled reluctantly. 'It's weak stuff, Johnny. It'll soon wear off. It's got less kick than a flea bite – probably the crap it's cut with is making you sick.'

'It's Thorn. It's really you, Thorn.'

'That's right.'

'Old Thorn Sayre.'

'You got it.'

'Hey, Johnny! Come out and play with me!' Hood Bailey's voice blundered up at them. He stood on the tennis court, floodlights glinting on the steel racquets he held in each hand. 'I got you a bat, Johnny. Come on down.' Yellow balls spat out of the ball machine. Hood stumbled and fell, the bottle of Old Grandad he carried in his back pocket dropping on to the court and smashing.

'Johnny, Johnny.'

'God, it's like the lovers' balcony scene from *West Side Story*.' Thorn stared down at Bailey, her features restored to their former beauty by contempt. 'Ignore him, Johnny.'

Suddenly there were people on the balcony with them, all hating them.

'You were not brought here to look pretty, Johnny Sangster.' said Juanita.

'Why were you brought here, Juanita?' asked Thorn. 'To scare away the crows?'

'He should play. Hood wants it. So.'

Simone prodded Johnny. 'Go and play, fool. What's wrong with you? Go and play with Hood.'

'Can't you see he's sick? Leave him alone.'

Simone stared at Thorn. 'Who the hell are you?'

Juanita giggled. 'She's his wet nurse. She's nobody.'

'I ought to push your face in, Juanita.'

'But you won't.'

'What would be the point? Nobody would be able to tell the difference.' Thorn smiled for Johnny and took his arm. 'Come on. You lie down.'

Simone grabbed his other arm.

'He's *sick*. Can't you understand?'

'I don't pay him to be sick, nobody. Johnny! Play or I sack you! You're fired! You're finished!'

Thorn took him to her room and sat him on the bed. 'How you feeling?'

'Much better.' He smiled weakly. 'I can't believe you're here.'

'You'll have to take my word for it.'

'You got out of that – place?'

'The back lot? Sure, it was dragging me down.'

'What you doing here? Moving it as a model?'

Thorn winced.

Others laughed.

Thorn and Johnny turned to see Juanita and Simone flanking Hood.

The entire party pressed close behind them, watching and smiling.

'She's in service, Johnny,' said Juanita.

'Like your lovely self, Johnny,' said Simone.

'I'll play you for her,' suggested Hood. 'If you win you get a night with her. If you lose you get a week with her.'

Johnny got to his feet and went for his throat. He felt his fingers tearing into Hood Bailey's skin, he felt hands like hams roughly dragging him back. One of Bailey's bodyguards bent Johnny double with a blow in the abdomen. Another kicked him just below the ear and sent him sprawling. Gravel cut his hands. The side of his head was screaming. He lifted his head as much as he could and saw them moving closer, all around him.

Johnny let his head fall and listened to the sound of fear in his breathing.

'Not here,' said Hood Bailey.

'Do it down there. On the tennis court,' said Juanita.

They lifted Johnny Sangster as if he was weightless and carried him down to the floodlight court where they beat him until he was half-conscious and coughing up blood, until he couldn't cry any more.

Hood Bailey, Juanita and Simone watched it all from the balcony like royalty at a Command Performance. Thorn sat it out on the bed in her cell. When it was over and the goon squad were carrying Johnny to the car, the people on the balcony applauded. The goons bundled Johnny Sangster into the back seat and drove him thoughtfully to the hospital. They dumped his broken body on the pavement and got back into the car.

Two nurses came out as the car sped away. They crouched over him.

'My God! Look at that face!'

'Let's get him inside. Quick!'

'Don't you recognize him? Can't you see?'

'What? Who is it?'

'He used to be Johnny Sangster!'

*

When he woke up she was sitting by his bed.

'Well, here we are again,' he said cheerfully.

'They were telling the truth.'

'Well, I don't believe them.'

'What are you trying to save my honour for?'

'For later. You never know when you might need it.'

'It's like a crusade with you.' She stood up, smiling sadly.

He touched the lumps on his face, wincing. 'Stay awhile. Don't go back to the Happy House yet.'

'I don't live there anymore.'

He became tired and emotional. 'It was always you, Thorn. I need you, kid. Stay with me.'

'I need to get back to New York.'

'Sure, sure. We're hardly king and queen of the heap here.'

Thorn closed her eyes and sat on the bed. He thought of them as a pair, two losers who had to cling to each other against the slings and arrows of outrageous failure. This couldn't be the right route. Two suckers don't make a success.

'We'll be fine in New York,' he was saying happily. 'I count for something there. Ok, Thorn? It's a date. As soon as my face heals.'

It never will, she thought. 'Ok, Johnny,' she said. 'We'll do it your way.'

# twenty-four

Johnny sat at the window watching the clock across the way, waiting.

The money he had hoarded from scarecrowing at Simone's had rented this apartment in Little Italy – they had found it by scouring the obituary columns for the names of people who would no longer be needing their accomodation. The money had bought new clothes for Thorn – mostly cheap Kamali's and Armani's from the Unique Clothing Warehouse. The money had stolen a little time. But not enough. Behind him the prizes in his twelve-feet-high trophy sideboard glittered in the sunlight of a blazing fall. He turned to look at it. It wouldn't be around much longer, collecting dust. He didn't feel a thing.

Stuff like that wasn't what was important to him now.

The clock chimed the hour and he heard the key in the door. He ran to greet her. 'How'd the casting call go?'

Thorn sank on to the sofa and yanked off her shoes. She examined them moodily. 'Manhattan in the grip of an Indian summer is all I need,' she said. 'The asphalt melts just enough for stilettos to sink into the sidewalk. *Great.*' She tossed her shoes in the general direction of the quaint old shoe-tree.

'So how'd it go?' Johnny said again. 'Thorn?'

'It went lousy.' She lit a Gauloise. 'The same old problem. Do I have to draw you a diagram?'

'I don't get it,' Johnny said. 'How can it be the same old problem? I thought Sherry Ward wasn't Queen Bee anymore.'

'She's *not*,' said Thorn with bitter relish. She closed her eyes and sighed. 'But they replaced her with more of the same. Her name is Lisa Ford. She's a junior clone. Surprise, surprise.' Thorn opened her eyes and stared at him. 'She's a year younger than me. For God's sake. Lisa Ford. More of the same old stuff, more of the same old problem.'

'I don't know why in hell they didn't hire you,' Johnny said. 'There's no competition. You're the best looking girl I ever saw.'

'I don't *care*. They want Aryan Barbie dolls and nothing but. They want girls who look like Lisa Ford. Who in turn is identical to Sherry Ward. You remember Sherry, don't you, Johnny? Back in the days when you were in work, wasn't it?'

He said nothing, just stared at the floor, hurt and ashamed.

When he looked up she was putting on some new red heels.

'Where are you going?'

'Out,' she said. 'I've got a job. A small job. A very fucking small job. But at least it's work.' She shot him a poison look and headed for the door.

'When will you be back?' he asked desperately.

'When I'm finished,' she said. 'Don't bother waiting up.'

She slammed out.

Johnny waited until he heard her footsteps fading down the hall and then he went to the telephone and called an Oyster Bay number. Dave Pepper had something for him. A situation vacant that would never reach the Classifieds.

Johnny thanked him politely and hung up. He called the number Dave Pepper had donated and within the hour he was on a train passing through upstate New York.

The only other passenger in his carriage stared at him. It wasn't his fame that acted as a magnet for their blank curiosity. He knew what it was. It was his face.

Johnny didn't give a damn. Thorn Sayre wasn't repulsed by his paralysed face and that was all that mattered. Because he had written himself off. Because from now on everything he did would be for Thorn Sayre. Starting here, Johnny Sangster sang to himself, starting *now*.

'Ok, Sea Nymphs, could we have you crawling on the rocks? Move it, Sea Nymphs, we don't have all day. Bare your teeth, baby, you're not meant to be a damp squid. Good girls. Ok, turn those hoses on.'

Thorn gasped as the icy water hit her. She was one of half a dozen soaked sea nymphs perched on rocks on grey foam rubber. This was the first half-day of work she'd had this month. On her back was a swimsuit from a new range called Siren. It was scant, scaly and expensive; Thorn would have wiped her ass on it if she wasn't being paid. It looked like Martian eczema, she decided.

The photographer bullied and cajoled his way through ten rolls of film. It was quite a step down from being Jap Goddard's epic love icon. This one was just an anonymous greasy bore. Thorn wondered where those great photographers had gone that Cuba had talked about in Paris; the little fruits who used to shriek, weep and lend you their kohl? They probably danced into a disco in the late Seventies and danced out with a place in The Village People. A shame; they sounded amusing, a vast improvement on the militantly manly lensmen of today.

The hoses were turned off and the sea nymphs stumbled down sneezing and coughing from the foam rubber rocks. This is the high point of my month, Thorn thought incredulously. My glamorous career! I've had more fun changing a tampon.

The photographer leered at her. 'Was I good for you, honey?'

She kept the tone light, trying not to offend. 'If once a month is the best you can manage you're not much good for anyone, darling.'

He watched her walk into the dressing-room and turned wild-eyed to his grinning assistant. 'Lying bitch – she loved it, didn't she? Didn't she love it?'

*

'Why do you want the position of resident coach, Mr Sangster?'

'I want a job and playing tennis is what I excel at.'

'Of course, we are very pleased to be approached by a player who until *very* recently was in the ATP top three . . .'

'I was never in the top three.'

'You must have come very close.'

'But that doesn't count, does it, sir?'

'You are aware of our terms. Forty thousand per annum.'

'I'm aware that if you want me you'll have to double your money.'

'Ah.' The country club chairman laughed softly. 'Well, to be perfectly frank, Mr Sangster, some of our board have expressed concern over your physical well-being. They have their doubts.'

'My injuries are well under control. Don't think I've got a body to match my face.'

'Well . . .'

'Who's the best player in the club?'

'I am.'

'Ok.' Johnny stood up. 'Try me.'

The pain caught up with him on the train back to Little Italy, but by then it didn't matter. Johnny had a job.

The agent was new but the news was old, and all bad.

'I've had more agents than jobs,' Thorn stated flatly. 'I respect bag ladies more than I respect agents. Something for nothing, that's all agents want.'

'A bad workman always blames his agent, Thorn. Have you quite finished?'

'No. Why do you people take me on, take my time if you can't give me a career?'

'Well, Thorn, I can't speak for your previous whipping boys, but the reason that *this* agency signed you is because you're an exceptionally beautiful girl. There. Better?'

'Then where's the *work*?'

'Who said that the powers out there were looking for an exceptionally beautiful girl?'

'Ok, you don't have to brief me about the Lisa Ford look. I know it better than anyone. But if that's the competition it's only a matter of time before I take over. I don't believe that people will settle for a lifetime of mediocrity.'

'How little you know of human nature.'

Thorn leaned across the desk. 'I know what I've *got*. Apart from this face, I'm five feet ten inches and one hundred and eighteen pounds. For a *model*, which is what I want to be when I grow up, that's *perfection*. Tell me it's not.'

'It's just wonderful.' The agent smiled. 'And it's tragic. Five feet ten, one hundred and eighteen, that face – you're so perfect, and so wrong for America. So easy to look at, so hard to employ. You may be perfect to Thorn Sayre and her special friends – but the public see a different story. Your skin is too pale. Your make-up is too sultry, your smile is too rare. You look tough and beautiful – you *should* look soft and pretty. Too much spirit and not enough sun-worship. You take the wrong pills for all the wrong reasons. You should be wearing clothes to jog in, *not* solicit.'

'Oh, Jesus, I can't believe the way they're still dressing over here . . . all that baggy crumpled Klein. Those guys pretend they invented the track suit, for God's sake. And the geeks who buy that stuff – if their designer labels came off in the wash they'd have an identity crisis. They'd have to be wheeled off to Bellevue.'

'Those guys know what sells.'

'Yeah, so do I. They loved me in Europe.'

'You're in the land of the free now, Thorn, and we do things *our* way. If you want to make it on your own terms I suggest you return to London or Paris.'

'This corny old country will soon acquire the taste. Believe me, I speak from experience.'

'I'm not talking about Thorn Sayre in bed, bars or the street, dear. I'm sure you're just wonderful in all those places but they have nothing at all to do with real life. You haven't grasped that yet. *Model* – something to be copied, worthy of imitation. There's too much unhealthiness, shadiness . . .ah, *sex* about you for the American man to want you for a wife or sister or mother or daughter. We're not talking about Maxwell's Plum and how well you could score there – we're talking about American modelling, which ultimately means TV commercials. And people just wouldn't want you intruding into their homes every night.'

'Europeans would laugh at the importance you place on paltry little adverts. The fashion industry would label you a learner.'

'Money doesn't hurt easy, Thorn. It's the American way, for better or blander. Take my advice – make a good marriage. A good-looking son of a rich man. Someone crazy about you. You could find one easily. Do it. You deserve it for looking that good.'

'I've got a boyfriend.' She thought of him. 'And anyway I want *more.*'

'Goodbye, Thorn.'

'Good riddance. But you'll see me around, count on it – and it won't be coming down an aisle.'

She let herself into the apartment and stared at the red roses. Everywhere they weren't there was Krug on ice instead. She didn't know which made her more nauseous.

Johnny smiled at her with lopsided joy, plucking a bottle out of a bucket and struggling with the cork.

'What's all this ham in aid of?'

His face fell. The cork popped. 'I've got a job. Resident pro up at Deerwood Hills.'

'Coaching?'

'Yes.'

'I thought you hated coaching.' She tried to imagine herself as the head of a modelling agency; the thought made her feel physically sick.

He poured two glasses of Krug. 'Yeah, but, see—'

'None for me, thanks.' She went into the kitchenette and returned pouring Tab into a glass.

'Why are you drinking that, Thorn?'

'Because, Johnny, it has less than one calorie.'

'But I bought a crate of this stuff.'

'I hope you and the plants enjoy it. What's the money like at this tennis school?'

'Country club. Forty a year. Double if you're Johnny Sangster.'

Thorn smiled, shocked. She sat down. 'You did real good, Johnny. Real good.'

He sat beside her quickly and took her hand. 'So if you don't want to try for any more modelling jobs—'

She stood up. 'And if you want me to walk out you'd better say that again.'

'It was just a suggestion.'

'A lousy one.'

'Why don't we stay in tonight?'

'Because the nights are for socializing. Staying home is a waste of life.'

'Parties aren't?'

'We don't go for stupid *fun*. We go to make contacts. Contacts have a way of leading to contracts.'

'They've never led you to any.'

'Well, shut your mouth.' She put her hands on her hips and narrowed her eyes at him. It frightened him. She was capable of walking out anywhere, anytime. 'If you don't like to party, stay home and give yourself a facial. I'll go alone.'

Johnny sipped his sad celebration drink and shrugged. 'I'll come.'

Every night he was bored at a party, a party on the fringe – but never at the root – of fashion, the media or showbusiness. On the rare nights they had no party things were even worse; they would sit by the telephone until the early hours, just staring at each other.

But Johnny was happy. Things were better between them since he got the Deerwood job. The job had bought her time. He had always told her he loved her and now she had sweated proof.

He had said it with cash.

'Come up to Deerwood with me this weekend,' he enthused. 'I'd love you to come with me.'

'To watch you coach some rich brats?' She laughed and kissed his face to take the sting out. 'I'm sure you do it brilliantly, Johnny, but I'm sure you'd do it even better without me sitting bored stiff on the sideline. You know what a sulky bitch I am when I'm bored.'

'But I won't be coaching this weekend, Thorn. There's a barbecue. I've got to go. These things are very important on the country club circuit.' He smiled painfully. 'They care more about their little social functions than they do about improving their game.'

'Do you *have* to go? There's some important people – some important *parties* in town this weekend.'

'And are we invited?'

'No. But we will be, believe me.'

'I've got to go up to Deerwood, Thorn. It's part of the job. I'm asking you to come with me and help me through it.'

'No, Johnny. No, no. I don't think so. They're not my kind of people.'

'They're rich.'

She stared at him coolly. 'Yeah, but not beautiful. I'll see you when you get back. And Johnny?'

'Yeah?'

She laughed. 'I love you, Johnny.'

'You do?'

'Yeah.'

'You – you never said . . .'

'I only just realized.'

Johnny Sangster smiled.

He rode the train to Deerwood Hills alone. He was happier than he had ever been in his life. He was happier than he would be again.

Something was wrong.

He had attended socials at Deerwood before. But none had been like this.

No one was talking to him. Everyone was staring at him when they thought his eyes were elsewhere. The paid-up members of Deerwood Hills country club stood on the grass in their tennis clothes – you could always tell a weekend player, a pro wouldn't be seen dead in his whites and track suit if he was off duty – they stood there, ignoring him, scrutinizing and avoiding him. Even the ones he coached – rich kids, so rich – even the ones he coached treated him like a leper, averting their eyes when he waved to them. Some of the parents glared at him as if he had just committed an act of cannibalism upon the new mown lawns. Something was very wrong.

Johnny stood bewildered on the edge of the party, munching on a gristly charcoal steak. Then the chairman touched him lightly on the arm. 'Johnny . . . can I talk to you?'

'Go right ahead.'

'Not here. Not here, Johnny.'

'Hey, what is this? Can't *you* look me in the eye either?'

'In my office, Johnny. In my office.'

Johnny followed the chairman towards the administration block. The hostile revellers parted silently in imitation of the Red Sea to speed their passage.

Or maybe it's to avoid touching me, Johnny thought. Tennis never was a contact sport.

In the chairman's office the elected representative of Deerwood Hills country club hurried to the bar. 'Can I get you something, Johnny?'

'You can get to the point. But you pour yourself a stiff one. You look as though you need it.'

The chairman bolted down a large measure of bourbon and turned to face Johnny Sangster. 'I'm afraid I have some bad news, Johnny.' Johny felt a familiar sickness in the pit of his stomach. I should have guessed, he thought, I should have fucking guessed.

'Unfortunately,' the chairman was saying, 'we are going to have to relieve you of your coaching responsibilities here at Deerwood Hills.'

Johnny's mouth tightened. 'You mean you're firing me?'

'If you want to put it like that.'

'How the hell do you *expect* me to put it? What's the matter? Isn't my coaching up to scratch?'

'It's not that, Johnny. Your coaching has been impeccable. Absolutely impeccable. Please.'

'But your board figures I'm not worth the money you're paying me.'

'No, no,' the chairman flustered. 'You're worth every cent. Twice as much. All of us here at Deerwood really truly believe you've got an excellent future in coaching and that you've given excellent value for money. Johnny, we really do. I mean that most sincerely.'

'Then *what is it*?'

'I – we – everyone here knew about your accident, of course . . .'

'Yeah, it's written all over my face.'

'We – everyone knew about your injuries, of course. But not the *extent* of your injuries.'

'My face doesn't fit,' Johnny said. 'My ugly smashed-up face doesn't fit. I might as well be black to you guys. *What happened*? Who exactly is it who finds my fucking face so offensive? Some important little member of the board? Or one of their fucking brats?'

'I don't wish to go into details, Johnny.'

'Oh, I bet you don't! What's the matter? Aren't I human any more, you bastards? What's—' He choked and he shook his head bitterly. 'Ah, what's the point?'

'This isn't easy for me, Johnny. Please don't make it worse.'

'Why the fuck shouldn't I? It's a hell of a lot harder for me. If you want to have a trauma you'll have to get in line.'

'Please try to understand, Johnny. One of the mothers complained. A very big mother. She complained that her ten-year-old son is prone to nightmares. I have her letter right here . . .'

'I can guess what it says. *Lord knows how many nights Junior'll keep me awake with this one,*' Johnny mimicked. 'Which mother? Come on!'

The chairman quickly put the letter into his desk drawer. 'It's not just the one mother, Johnny. It's all the mothers. And all the fathers. And a large number of the children . . .'

'What about the board, chairman? Is it all the board?'

'It was a majority decision. It's out of my hands, Johnny. *Please* try to understand.'

'I understand fine. My looks make too many people with too much money too uncomfortable. They don't like looking at the American Dream when it's been put through a mangle.' Johnny stood up. 'I understand perfectly.'

'I wish things could have turned out differently, Johnny. You're the best resident pro we'll ever have here at Deerwood.'

'I know.'

'But it's out of my hands.' He held one of them out for Johnny Sangster to shake.

Johnny stared at it with theatrical contempt. The chairman took it back. 'Out of your hands,' Johnny sneered. 'Sure it is. I'll see you around, Pontius.'

Johnny Sangster walked out of the office. He walked through the silent barbecue staring straight ahead, walked through the gates of the Deerwood Hills country club and hailed a cab to the station.

A country club, he thought. Country club! It had been madness to even try to cut it in a stifling, snobbish little country club. He would dig ditches before he set foot in another country club.

He had been more than all of them. Once. It was better than never. They could rot. If not for the money he was kissing goodbye he would have been exhilarated.

As it was he cried on the way back to the city.

I let her down, he thought, I let her down, and he wept.

# twenty-five

'The wrong face, Thorn,' Johnny apologized above the roar of the party. 'What can you do when you've got the wrong face?'

Everything was gone bar pocket money and the parties. Trying to make 'contacts' and dreaming of contracts was just a cruel joke now. Eager to please outsiders meant only one thing to the bored and brutal rich – floorshow.

The fashion fringe's hags and fags were dressed to kill. They'd spent years trying to hold on to the last vestige of pace-making, of bright young empire building. And now here were two young vulnerable toys from the generation who put fashion out of business. The party licked its lips. The couple were fair party game.

'The lovely ventriloquist and her dummy,' someone cackled.

Thorn smiled sweetly and saw someone she knew. He sat there and watched.

'How does it feel to lose the only thing that matters, Donny?'

'How do you fill that gap, Ronnie?'

'Is it true you give a sick bag to anyone who stands under the mistletoe with you, Sonny?'

'Is one side of your *tongue* paralysed, honey?'

'Does this have any advantages, Mommy?'

They shrieked like hyenas. Johnny pretended not to hear. He couldn't hit back. He didn't know who they were. One of them might be Someone. He couldn't risk damaging Thorn's career opportunities. He had nothing to look forward to but her success.

He looked across the room to where she stood talking to a photographer's assistant. She wore a black bodystocking, dancer's tights and high shiny black heels. The photographer's assistant was taking a slow guided tour of every curve and crevice of her body.

Thorn felt Johnny's eyes and smiled back at him before devoting her undivided attention to the gopher.

A *gopher*, for fuck's sake! She had to make up to *gophers* these days!

Johnny lifted his glass to his lips but it was empty.

When she awoke the next afternoon with a mouth like a bidet in a brothel Johnny was standing by the bed. He tossed a roll of bills on to the bed and dropped two overnight bags on to the floor.

'I sold my trophies,' he said. He didn't look sorry for himself, not in the least. She was quite surprised. He even looked sort of proud.

'Your tennis trophies? All those cups and bowls and shields you won when you were a tennis player? Since you were a kid? A little kid?'

'Yeah, those trophies.'

'Well, what a sacrifice!' She picked up the money. 'How much d'you get? Hmm, ok. It'll do for mugging money and cab tips. Till next weekend, at least.'

He put his bags away in a cupboard. She couldn't see his face. But he said, 'I never expected a bigshot like you to say thank you, Thorn. Why, a girl like you's used to having men shower her with sacrifices. Why you're holed up with little old loser me I can't imagine.'

'Twisted words from a twisted face.'

He stood up and looked at her, disgustedly, defeatedly, adoringly.

'I'm sorry.'

'That's ok.'

'I really am.'

'Forget it.'

She looked at him sadly. 'Hurry up and change your clothes.'

He shook out his best shoes to check for roaches. Only two.

Pretty good. His luck must be changing.

They got ready for the last party.

Johnny was drinking a lot. Thorn was drinking too much. Thorn had smoked a lot of someone's dope. Johnny had taken a little of someone's speed. He felt clear-headed and tense, ready and waiting.

'I'm wondering,' Thorn announced aloud. She had left the tights at home tonight. Her legs were bare and beautiful. Johnny was the only person in the room not looking at them.

'What are you wondering?' he asked her patiently.

'I'm wondering what I'm doing with you.'

'No, the booze is wondering what you're doing with me.'

'Why do you stand so close to me?'

'Because I want to be with you.'

'Yeah? Are you sure it's not so you can make sure I don't run away?'

'Yeah. Yeah, I'm sure.'

'Don't worry, Johnny. Nobody's going to steal me. I carry your brand. It's stamped all over me. Look close, look *real* close, Johnny. Can't you see it?'

'No.'

'Look *real* close, Johnny. See it? It says F-A-I-L-U-R-E.'

'Very fucking funny.'

'Isn't it a scream? But Johnny's not laughing, is he? He's all hurt. Ah, c'mere, Johnny and let Thorn give you a big kiss on your lovely face.' She threw an arm around his shoulder and pushed her face close. 'Let Thorn kiss it better . . .'

Johnny pushed her away. 'You've passed through the belligerent drunk phase. Can I take a raincheck on the mawkish drunk phase?' He took her glass.

'That's not empty yet.'

Johnny poured it on the weeping fig. 'It is now.'

'Fuck you,' Thorn said. 'Who are *you* to tell me what I can't do? Do you think you own me, Johnny?'

'I think you owe it to yourself to sober up, Thorn.'

'Yeah? Well, I think you're becoming a real bore, Johnny Sangster.' She pushed him hard in the chest. 'A real bore, boy.'

'Don't do that. Don't you dare.'

'I'll do what I like, *boy*, and don't you ever forget it. Now go get me a drink.'

'No.'

She pushed him again. 'Go-get-me-a-drink-or-go-home.'

He weakened. 'Ok.' He relented. 'What do you want?'

'I want you to come back with something clear – white wine, gin, vodka, anything that won't spoil my lipgloss. In fact I'll have one of each,' she leered. 'And I want you to come back with a real good excuse for your deplorable behaviour. I've never been so insulted.'

Johnny smiled sadly. People were staring. Thorn looked slurred, smug and triumphant. She was hideously drunk.

He went to get the drink.

When he started back across the room with the long glass of white wine he saw her with another man. Some smarmy photographer she'd done a bit of work for. He was biting her neck, sucking it hard. She was laughing. She saw him watching. She closed her eyes and moaned with pleasure.

She looks like that when she's with me. He stood transfixed. It was what she wanted. He couldn't stand it. He started across the room.

He felt a restraining hand on his shoulder. One of the photographers friends? Johnny would take them all on!

But the small neat old man wasn't anyone's friend. This wasn't personal. This was business.

He smiled. 'Mr Sangster?'

'You know I am.'

'I'm Sammy Carr. I'm pleased to meet you. I produce a TV favourite. Name of *Winners And Losers*. I'm sure you've viewed. I'd like to discuss the possibility of a star guest spot with you.'

'What kind of money are we talking about, Sammy?'

'I can see we're going to get on just fine, Johnny.'

Later he went looking for her. But Thorn Sayre was nowhere.

Thorn Sayre awoke with a head fit to split.

She hoped it had been a bad dream, but the proof of the pudding was in the photographer, lying beside her sated and snoring. Now she was sober she saw him as the unsavoury creep he was. Last night all she had seen was the green sign marked EXIT.

She went into the smelly bathroom and tried to wash the photographer off of her. Then she dressed and left. Sleeping Beauty didn't stir.

In the taxi she wondered what she could say to Johnny and couldn't think of a thing. Poor Johnny.

She met him at the door of the apartment. His bags were packed.

'Where are you going?' she whispered. 'You're leaving me, aren't you?' Regret and hope fused in her voice.

He looked at her with red loving eyes and shuffled his feet self-consciously. 'Only for a little while. I would never leave you, Thorn. You know that?

'Oh, Johnny,' she said. 'Last night—'

'I don't want to hear about last night. I don't want to think about it. It's ok. I've got it all worked out.' He smiled. 'Here.' He pushed a thick roll of bills into her hand.

'Where did you get *this*?' she said. 'There must be two thousand here.'

'That's just the start. That's just part of my advance. I'm going to collect the rest. That's where I'm going right now.'

He looked so proud, so brave, so very young and lost.

'I don't understand. Where does this money come from, Johnny?'

'A man named Sammy Carr gives it to people whose faces he likes. He's the producer of a TV show called *Winners And Losers*. I got a place in the show. Sammy loves me,' he said. 'See, Thorn, I figure if I can break this scene we're in, break the stranglehold that poverty's got on us, that and the fucking party circuit, then it'll be enough to make things *right* with us.'

'Johnny.' She leaned against the wall. '*Winners And Losers*?'

'Yeah, a residency of six weeks. They pay for the motel, too.'

'*Winner And Losers*, Johnny – don't you know what that thing *is*?'

'Sure,' He smiled.

'They humiliate people who used to be famous. They chop them up and feed them to the mindless masses. That's what they do.'

'I know. But at least they'll be paying me, Thorn.'

A horn blared down on the street.

'My car,' Johnny said.

They stared at each other awkwardly. Johnny held out his right hand. Thorn shook it and took him in her arms and held him tight.

'I wish you wouldn't, Johnny.'

'Did you mean it?'

'What?'

He looked at her wide-eyed. 'Did you mean it when you said you loved me?'

'Yes.'

But she wasn't sure anymore.

'Then I don't care. Nothing can hurt me.'

The taxi driver leaned on his horn.

'I got to go.' Johnny said. He picked up his bags. 'I'll see you soon, Thorn.'

'Yes. Goodbye, Johnny.'

She went into the apartment and bolted the door.

He lost his tennis job because of his face. He won the TV job because of his face.

She went into the bathroom and examined herself in the mirror. The wrong face, she reflected, what can you do when you've got the wrong face?

# twenty-six

Ritualized humiliation for all the family had made *Winners And Losers* top of the ratings. It made such a refreshing change from all those jiggling girls and violent cop shows.

The host wore more make-up than any of the women in the audience and he babbled inanely. The canned laughter was too loud and the studio lights turned the studio into a parched plastic desert. It was hard to concentrate. The producers meant it to be that way.

They wanted the watchers from Portland, Maine to Portland, Oregon to tune in again next week, same time, same channel. Oh, the producers knew better than anyone how hard it was to concentrate when you were appearing on *Winners And Losers.*

Johnny sat sweating with two other losers who used to be winners, a singer and an ex-screen siren. It was his turn and it was hard to concentrate.

Johnny got the answer wrong.

The host happily read his fate from a cue card, raising his hand slightly, asking the canned laughter to control itself just a little.

Johnny Sangster got to play pat ball against a five-year-old boy.

Johnny Sangster got to play with a paper bag over his head.

The laughter roared from coast to coast as Johnny lost.

The producers smirked at each other when it was time for a commercial break and a word from the sponsor. They called it a *message. Winners And Losers* was top of the ratings still . .

In Massachusetts Mrs Sangster cried tears of real joy. Her Johnny, on her favourite show! Mr Sangster crowed inside, triumphant.

Bel Air sent a telegram – APPALLED AND AMAZED AT YOUR PRESENT OCCUPATION STOP LET US LOAN YOU WHATEVER YOU NEED – signed Nile and Rose Martin. Johnny laughed later as he tore it up – fuck Lady Bountiful. And Rose, too.

Billy Sciarra turned it off.

His wife glared at him, turning it back on. 'I was *watching* that, for your information!' said Maxine. 'It helps a little to know there's some poor sucker worse off than I am!'

Jesse Wolfe got Kitty to video it, holding her hand tight and shaking his head and saying, '*Really.*'

Thorn put down the ashtray; she couldn't afford to smash the TV. It would have only meant Johnny had to earn *more*.

The wrong face got the job. She went into the bathroom and stared into the mirror. She'd been doing that more than ever lately. Who can do anything about their face?

Through the doorway she saw a Lisa Ford commercial flickering across the screen. It was for placenta shampoo – Thorn wanted to retch – and Lisa Ford was saying, 'The most important thing in life is health. And the best health is natural. And what could be more natural than . . .'

All this talk about nature. It was unnatural. Thorn stared at the small image of Lisa Ford and to Thorn the blonde void of a face held the full horror only hinted at in Johnny's.

A *girl*. A girl with bones and eyes can do something about the wrong face.

'And now – back to *Winners And Losers*!'

She began to take off her make-up.

No one is more intimate with the secrets of the victor than the vanquished. Her dark blonde hair became light and bright. Her skin toasted itself a golden brown beneath an infrared lamp. She fasted for a weekend at a spa just outside New York where she paid 120 dollars to drink apple juice, sleep on Japanese mats and have her feet tickled to improve her digestion. Back home she went on a serious diet of cherry stalk infusions and when that was completed she overhauled her regular diet completely. No more slipping round to Mimi's Stand for thick juicy hedonistic slices of pizza. Now she ate Japanese raw fish, nibbled handfuls of walnuts and dried apricots as snacks and forsook her gin and vermouth for nightcaps of a whole lemon liquidized with water and a little honey. She cleaned her teeth four times a day and brushed them once a week with baking soda. She drank eight glasses of water a day and slept eight hours a night. She started buying *Self* magazine and haunted Macy's Self Center. She took to jogging around the Central Park track every morning. In the street she tried to ignore the potholes and the metal falling off Manhattan's rusted bridges and the sober but unwashed people sleeping near the steam valves and eating out of the garbage cans, even here in Little Italy.

There were about 36,000 of these unfortunates inhabiting the streets of New York every night, the papers said, and one million New Yorkers had left the beloved city in the past decade. She wasn't going to follow either route.

She had to stay here and conquer this city, for herself, for the way the sky was forget-me-not blue even in winter, for the way the sun rose a clear ruby red above the giant Pepsi sign on 1st Avenue.

So she changed. She thought positive. Her make-up took hours to apply and, when completed, was imperceptible to the naked eye. It was almost impossible to sneer or sulk or look smart with a non-face like this. She sat in advanced asanas like the locust and lotus and she sat and waited and she substituted vitamins and vegetables for drugs. And she vegetated and bloomed.

She hated it, but it was healthy. Doing what made her happy had never got her anywhere. It was time fore a little post-hedonism.

Johnny spoke to her on the phone and couldn't understand what was happening to her voice.

It was losing the South – *a distinguishing feature.*

She didn't tell him about the elocution.

Johnny sent her cheques. He would have been amazed at the casual, baggy chic she spent them on.

All she told him was that she went for a TV commercial.

And she got it.

Seeing Johnny on *Winners And Losers* made her change. Seeing what not being a success did to you, what it let people get away with doing to you.

She never felt more for him than when she watched him *losing* to a five-year-old child. She felt anger, sympathy, loyalty, empathy and genuine affection. For a moment she wavered on the brink of love. But there was surviving to be done, the market place wouldn't wait.

She changed. It was the only option. Sometimes she thought she changed to save Johnny Sangster and sometimes she thought she changed to save herself. After a while she couldn't remember a time when she'd been someone else.

The word caught and spread like sweat in the saunas she took twice a day. Offers poured in. Fashion was the number one big bucks bronco in New York City and beauty was its deputy; she could have a body in one camp and a face in the other and all that money in her hand. Offers to sign contracts, offers to share a king-size bed after an evening of conspicuous consumption at the Peppermint Lounge. She only had eyes for work.

She would smile and shake her head. 'I find that the earlier I go to bed and the earlier I get up, the better I feel. I'm so sorry. Forgive me.' They did, of course, they understood. They liked sleeping best themselves. They only asked her because she was the new girl in town and they had heterosexual reputations to protect.

Johnny called. His six weeks were up. He told her how much money he had earned. He was very pleased. It seemed like a modest amount to her.

But it was better to give than to receive. She looked forward to his gratitude.

She was wearing green silk running shorts and hanging from her Kim Lee box when he let himself in.

For one horrible moment he flashed back to his twentieth birthday, when he walked through her empty apartment, too late. Now she was gone, escaped him, and this blonde had moved in.

She jumped down and smiled and he saw it was her. Appalled, incredulous, cheated again.

'Thorn?'

'Not any more.' She walked right up and shook his hand. 'Hi, John. Great to have you back. By the way, I'm called Paula Revere now.'

'Paula . . .'

'You bet. Business. Kitschy but classy. Besides, Johnny—' She hugged him close and smiled numbly up into his numb face. 'When all else fails, try patriotism.'

# twenty-seven

He walked through the apartment, a different apartment now, on the East Side. In the lobby there were chandeliers and doormen in tails. In the apartment there was a cat who had cost 900 dollars and had no name. He liked the cat.

He hated the apartment. It was a duplex, duplicity decorated in earth shades with flashes of green courtesy of Thorn's florist. He hated her bed and most of all he hated her gym, so large and well-ventilated and full of monstrous black machines, each devoted to toning a different muscle of the human body. A shrine to health. A wealthy whine.

He hated it even more when she deserted the gym and went out to the Health and Racquet to work out. He hated it when she went out for her saunas twice a day; one for work, one for play. He hated her to play, or to work. God knows what she got up to, who she got without him around.

He walked through and watched her watching herself on television. She was saying, 'I'm personally acquainted with every bone in my body' and she was lapping it up.

The bubble floated up, up, up; he felt disorientated, bewildered, as though some awful soul-destroying joke had been played on him. She smiled up at him athletically, somewhat eagerly. She wasn't used to it either. 'How do I look, Johnny?'

'Like a blonde.'

'Well.' She stood up. 'The *public* thinks I'm something special. The business certainly thinks so.'

'Lisa Ford was blander than Sherry Ward, and Paula Revere – *you* are blander than Lisa. I'll grant you that maybe you've taken being a blank as far as it can go.'

'You wish I still looked different? That old trash? Do you miss being broke?'

'I miss you.'

'This is me.'

'No. You were beautiful. My Thorn was beautiful. And smart. She would have told the public to stick their fan mail up their ass. She would have told the business to fold its money the Rothschild way and stick it where the sun don't shine. Everyone was scared of my Thorn, she was so beautiful.'

'And now I'm ugly?' She smiled.

'Do *you* think you're beautiful?'

'Number One is always beautiful.' She crossed the room and sat at the table. 'Come on, John. Let's eat.'

Johnny found that avocado was all the rage in their new dream home. He wished for Little Italy and spaghetti, London and spaghetti, days of spaghetti and Thorn Sayre. He hated avocado. Paula Revere put it into her mouth and on to her skin and into her hair.

'They contain B and C,' she exalted, 'plus potassium for fluid regulation.'

She even put avocado on their table – half an avocado with lemon juice for lunch, the other half in the evening with a salad.

Johnny pushed his plate away. 'If I eat one more of these green little bastards I swear I'll retch.'

'The calorie count for a medium-size avocado is around three hundred,' she said. 'Which is not bad for such a yummy food.'

'Sorry, I can't eat this stuff, Thorn. Or should I call you Paula?'

'Call me what you like, John. You always have in the past. Why try to kick the habit now?'

'I could demolish a couple of cheeseburgers, though. How about you?'

'John. I will not put junk in my body.'

'I'm not *talking* about jacking up morphine – I'm talking about eating a couple of Big Macs.'

'So am I . . .' she said.

Johnny sighed and lifted the coffee pot. He poured himself a cup and looked around. 'Where's the sugar?'

Thorn nudged a bowl full of sachets at him. 'Here.'

'What's that crap?'

'Sweet 'n' Low,' she said.

'Crap,' Johnny said. 'Diet crap. Where's the fucking sugar?'

'I threw it away,' she said. 'Try some Sweet 'n' Low. You've never had the calorie conscience you should have had, Johnny.'

'Calorie conscience? You make it sound like a social conscience! Very Un-American!' He laughed at the very thought.

'Oh, a calorie conscience is *much* the better. You can actually *change* things with a calorie conscience.'

'Such as yourself.'

'What else?'

Johnny reached for the Spumante. 'How about some wine?'

'No. The worst enemies of a woman are drugs and alcohol.'

He pushed the bottle away. 'I give up.'

'Johnny, you gave up *years* ago.'

'I hate you.'

She got up to go.

'I didn't mean it,' he said.

'Don't sweat it,' she said. 'I'm eating at Un Deux Trois with . . . anyhow.' She headed for the door.

'With *who*? You didn't say with *who*?'

'Forget it,' Paula Revere called over her shoulder. He heard the door close behind her. He sat alone at the table. He didn't eat any more and he didn't go after her. But after a while he went down on to the street and hung about the block for a while. He was waiting to see his girl.

There was no sign of her. He got into the big car that the big blonde bought him, and he drove.

Johnny looked at the boy.

He had been a teenager for seven days and a contender for a while longer. Dave Pepper had dug him up and now devoted all his time to him. He resigned his position with the Davis Cup team just for the kid, something he did before ten years ago.

The men on the Circuit were already looking over their shoulders for the boy, knowing that he was coming through the ranks like a scalpel through butter and that in a few years time there would be no avoiding the whites of his eyes.

He was on court now with Dave Pepper. He had a vast battery of shots, the ability to choose his weapon without thinking about it and the guile to prepare the shot without advertising it. His behaviour was impeccable. Johnny marvelled at him. He didn't throw tantrums or racquets, he didn't argue, spit or curse. When he got a bad call he smiled faintly, and occasionally crossed his eyes. Despite his fantastic youth he had never been called a brat, and never would be.

Dave Pepper crossed the court to Johnny. He seemed pleased to see him. Dave admired Johnny's new car. Johnny admired Dave's contender.

'Come for a drink, Dave. Let's talk about old times, huh?'

'I'd really like to, John. But we've got a lot of work to do.'

'Sure. I understand.'

'Come round for dinner some time.'

'I'll do that. See you around, Dave.'

'Bye, John.'

Johnny walked away.

'Dave, was that Johnny Sangster?'

'That's right. You like his work?'

'Sure. My dad says he was pretty damn good.' The kid contender swung his racquet. 'What now?'

'Living at the net,' Dave Pepper said.

The bad feeling increased as the fights lessened. There just wasn't the time. She worked all day, she played all night, they slept apart.

He hated the people she kept around her – her therapist, her English secretary, her florist, her interior designer, her dermatologist, her body conditioner, her business manager. He especially loathed her business manager and the gimmicks he employed to keep Thorn/Paula.

For instance, he carried her contracts in a bionic briefcase. It was bulletproof and had a burglar alarm siren and a transmitter to help the owner be tracked down if kidnapped.

Johnny knew big business. He knew bigger money than Paula/Thorn would ever know. He knew the briefcase wasn't necessary or even excusable.

He saw her say on TV, 'My marine-based facial is like being Born Again' and he couldn't blame his Thorn. He knew she was out at the Windows On The World and he couldn't name the felon.

But they both asked the same thing of each other; 'We've got the money now. Change your face.' He wanted her original, triumph *her* way. She wanted a nice cosmetic surgeon for him. They both refused angrily, for some reason.

She began to dole out money to him, via a monthly allowance.

She was successful enough now to fall in love, at the Roxy or the Ritz. But not with him. He wasn't sufficiently involved in her life-career.

Her picture was in W. Posed or coming out of the Soho Charcuterie? Are you kidding? The ones coming out of the Soho Charcuterie were the best posed of all.

He didn't know who she loved. He didn't ask and she didn't bring it home. He rarely went anywhere with her now – sometimes he ventured out with her to a party and when they arrived he would frantically scan the strangers' faces as though loking for someone.

Everyone assumed he was looking for her lover. They were wrong.

He didn't feel betrayed that she had fallen in love. He hoped she'd be happy. It just made him more lonely for *his* girl.

# twenty-eight

Paula Revere smooched with an unmarked brown boxer for the designer jeans commercial camera.

Her inner circle were on the set, attending to the most important things in life – make-up, public image, career opportunities, fiscal health. Visagist, camera man, corporate agent, business manager – who did she love?

Those who knew her said the business manager. Those who knew nothing said the boxer.

Everyone agreed, though, that she must be just *seething* at getting this half a million dollar job.

Paula must have heard of – *everyone's* talking about – the fourteen-year-old convent girl who played Eve in a twelve-hour interpretation of the *whole* Old Testament screened last Independence Day. From the moment she appeared, face perfectly serious, fig leaves maddeningly stationary, every merchant in America wanted nothing more than *that girl* pledging her troth to his product.

Lolita meets the Mona Lisa; on the one hand her tragic classic face and darkest blonde hair like a distant European matinee legend, on the other her homework and the mother who chaperoned her everywhere.

Suddenly everyone realized what America had been missing; mystery, in a word. No wonder the turnover in lean clean blondes had been so rapid! Conveyor belt cuties, easily obtained and disposed of. But now America had, after all these years, run up against *star* quality – this elusive young enigma! and it breathed a sigh of relief that it could still produce something so earth-moving. America had a sweetheart once more.

The young love object and her mother waded patiently through Mammon's offers. Somewhere the right commodity waited for them, but they meant to start as they would go on. They ignored most bids; but the love object saw fit to reply to a certain designer jeans offer;

'No thank you, sir. I never work for less than a million dollars and I never wear blue jeans.'

The quote had rocked and shocked America. The love object had worked steadily ever since. She got her million every time, and to each commercial she brought a glamour, a sincerity and a superiority that never faded or became familiar.

Everyone who knew about these things agreed that her future would make *everyone* else's life look like an unqualified failure.

Johnny heard. His heart ached for Paula Revere, who was worth only half a million dollars. He wished the kid could have held back a little longer, given his room-mate a little longer at the top, untroubled. Still – Paula Revere, she believed in the public getting what they wanted.

Johnny crossed the set. Eyes watched him. Paula Revere's business manager was a little scared he'd start a scene – you hear the stories all the time – but he wasn't even looking at her.

The director called for a break. Someone draped a robe of white towelling over her shoulders and her retinue oozed her towards her dressing room.

Johnny didn't like to go with those people. He walked off the set, oblivious to the stares of the crew. He went out to the corridor; you could go ghost-hunting here, where the daily drudge of advertising beckoned its selected and spurned its rejected.

Look there – a cattle call, being broken up.

Perfect timing, he thought, I could have missed her.

He gave out his card to the girls whose eyes or hair hinted at *her*. He did this all the time. They knew him. Johnny Sangster, dirty old kept man. They smiled to his face and laughed behind his back. But they knew who kept him and they put his card in a very safe place.

He'll never sleep with any of them. They all call. But that's not the way it should be. Johnny was waiting for the one who didn't call him, the proud one who rips up his number.

When that happens, as one day he knows it must, Johnny Sangster will leave behind for ever the life he is living now, and he will go looking for her.